KILLING MAINE

MIKE BOND

ALSO BY
MIKE BOND

Saving Paradise

Tibetan Cross

Holy War

House of Jaguar

The Last Savanna

CRITICS' PRAISE FOR MIKE BOND

Saving Paradise

"Bond is easily one of the 21st Century's most exciting authors ...An action-packed, must read novel...taking readers behind the alluring façade of Hawaii's pristine beaches and tourist traps into a festering underworld of murder, intrigue and corruption...Spellbinding readers with a writing style that pits hard-boiled, force of nature-like characters against politically adept, staccato-paced plots, *Saving Paradise* is a powerful editorial against the cancerous trends of crony capitalism and corrupt governance." – *Washington Times*

"A complex, entertaining...lusciously convoluted story." – *Kirkus*

"*Saving Paradise* will change you...It will call into question what little you really know, what people want you to believe you know and then hit you with a deep wave of dangerous truths...*Saving Paradise* is a thrill ride to read and pulls you in and out of plots until you don't know who to trust or what to do any more than the character...Mike Bond is not only an acclaimed novelist...His intellect and creativity dance together on the pages, braiding fiction into deeper truths about ourselves, our nature, our government, our history and our future." – *Where Truth Meets Fiction*

"Mike Bond is...one of the best thriller writers, in the same league as Gerald Seymour and Frederick Forsyth." – *NetGalley Reviews*

"*Saving Paradise* is an absolutely fabulous book...a wonderful book." – *Art Zuckerman, WVOX*

"*Saving Paradise* is a rousing crime thriller – but it is so much more...a highly atmospheric thriller focusing on a side of Hawaiian life that tourists seldom see." – *Book Chase*

"An absolute page-turner" – *Ecotopia Radio*

"He's a tough guy, a cynic who describes the problems of the world as a bottomless pit, but can't stop trying to solve them. He's Pono Hawkins, the hero of Mike Bond's new Hawaii-based thriller, *Saving Paradise*...an intersection of fiction and real life." – *Hawaii Public Radio*

"A very well written, fast-paced and exciting thriller." – *Mystery Maven Reviews*

"A fast pace thrill ride...The descriptions of Hawaii are beautiful and detailed." – *Romancebookworm's Reviews*

"Mike Bond's *Saving Paradise* is a complex murder mystery about political and corporate greed and corruption...Bond's vivid descriptions of Hawaii bring *Saving Paradise* vibrantly to life. The plot is unique and the environmental aspect of the storyline is thought-provoking and informative. The story's twists and turns will keep you guessing the killer's identity right up until the very end." – *Book Reviews and More*

"From start to finish, I never put it down." – *Bucket List Publications*

"*Saving Paradise* is one heck of a crime novel/thriller and highly recommended!" – *Crystal Book Reviews*

"A wonderful book that everyone should read." – *Clear Channel Radio*

Tibetan Cross

"A thriller that everyone should go out and buy right away. The writing is wonderful throughout, and Bond never loses the reader's attention. This is less a thriller, at times, than essay, with Bond working that fatalistic margin where life and death are one and the existential reality leaves one caring only to survive." – *Sunday Oregonian*

"A tautly written study of one man's descent into living hell...Strong and forceful, its sharply written prose, combined with a straightforward plot, builds a mood of near claustrophobic intensity." – *Spokane Chronicle*

"Grips the reader from the very first chapter until the climactic ending." *UPI*

"Bond's deft thriller will reinforce your worst fears about the CIA and the Bomb...A taut, tense tale of pursuit through exotic and unsavory locales." – *Publishers Weekly*

"One of the most exciting in recent fiction...an astonishing thriller that speaks profoundly about the venality of governments and the nobility of man." – *San Francisco Examiner*

"It is a thriller...Incredible, but also believable." – *Associated Press*

"Another fantastic thriller from Mike Bond. He is a lyric writer whose prose is beautiful and provocative. His descriptions strike to the heart and evoke strong emotions. I could not put the book down once I started reading... Gripping, enthralling and imaginative...It is not for the faint of heart, but includes a great love story." – *NetGalley Reviews*

"Murderous intensity...A tense and graphically written story." – *Richmond Times-Dispatch*

"Excruciatingly fast-paced…It was impossible to catch my breath. Each time I thought I found a stopping point, my eyes would glance at the next line and drag me deeper into the story. I felt as though I was on a violent roller coaster, gripping the rail and praying that I would not go flying out of my seat. It was painful but awesome." – *Bitten By Books*

"The most jaundiced adventure fan will be held by *Tibetan Cross*… It's a superb volume with enough action for anyone, a well-told story." – *Sacramento Bee*

"Intense and unforgettable from the opening chapter… thought-provoking and very well written." – *Fort Lauderdale News*

"Grips the reader from the opening chapter and never lets go." – *Miami Herald*

A "chilling story of escape and pursuit." – *Tacoma News-Tribune*

"This novel is touted as a thriller – and that is what it is… The settings are exotic, minutely described, filled with colorful characters." – *Pittsburgh Post-Gazette*

"Almost impossible to put down…Relentless. As only reality can have a certain ring to it, so does this book. It is naked and brutal and mind boggling in its scope. It is a living example of not being able to hide, ever…The hardest-toned book I've ever read. And the most frightening glimpse of mankind I've seen. This is a 10 if ever there was one." – *I Love a Mystery*

Holy War

"A fast-paced, beautifully written, heart-breaking thriller… One of the best reads of 2014." – *NetGalley Reviews*

"Mike Bond does it again – A gripping tale of passion, hostage-taking and war, set against a war-ravaged Beirut." – *Evening News (UK)*

"The suspense-laden novel has a never-ending sense of impending doom...An unyielding tension leaves a lasting impression." – *Kirkus*

"Mike Bond is one of America's best thriller writers" – *Culture Buzz*

"*Holy War* by Mike Bond is a rough, vivid window into the brutal reality of modern conflict...If you are looking to get a driver's seat look at the landscape of modern conflict, holy wars, and the Middle East then this is the perfect book." – *Masterful Book Reviews*

"Intense, chilling and unforgettable." – *Suncoast Reader's Reviews*

"Eye-opening, terrifying and realistic, Mike Bond writes from the heart...I promise you, if you read *Holy War*, you will come away changed." – *Tometender Reviews*

"A supercharged thriller... A story to chill and haunt you." – *Peterborough Evening Telegraph (UK)*

"A profound tale of war...Literally impossible to stop reading..." – *British Armed Forces Broadcasting*

"A pacy and convincing thriller with a deeper than usual understanding about his subject and a sure feel for his characters." – *Daily Examiner (UK)*

"A marvelous book – impossible to put down. A sense of being where few people have survived." – *London Broadcasting*

"This is a true saga that concentrates on a religious war where various factions fight for their own beliefs. Included in the thrills are terrorists, hostages, and enemies fighting in a place that simply cannot find peace…and the passion that ignites just as fast as the exploding of a bomb." – *Suspense Magazine*

"A tangled web and an entertaining one. Action-filled thriller." – *Manchester Evening News (UK)*

"A tale of fear, hatred, revenge, and desire, flicking between bloody Beirut and the lesser battles of London and Paris." – *Evening Herald (UK)*

"A novel about the horrors of war… a very authentic look at the situation which was Beirut." – *South Wales Evening Post (UK)*

"A stunning novel of love and loss, good and evil, of real people who live in our hearts after the last page is done… Unusual and profound." – *Greater London Radio*

House of Jaguar

"A riveting thriller of murder, politics, and lies." – *London Broadcasting*

"Tough and tense thriller." – *Manchester Evening News (UK)*

"There are not enough words to describe how outstanding and entertaining this book is. Intriguing, exciting, captivating, sexy…absolutely incredible…a great thriller." – *NetGalley Reviews*

"A thoroughly amazing book…And a terrifying depiction of one man's battle against the CIA and Latin American death squads." – *BBC*

"A high-octane story rife with action, from U.S. streets to Guatemalan jungles…Bond's kinetic novel abounds with intense scenes…The characters are fully limned…Not surprisingly, the novel ends with a shock, one that might have a few readers gasping." – *Kirkus*

"Vicious thriller of drugs and revolution in the wilds of Guatemala, with the adventurer hero, aided by a woman doctor, facing a crooked CIA agent. The climax is among the most horrifying I have ever read." – *Liverpool Daily Post (UK)*

"A riveting story where even the good guys are bad guys, set in the politically corrupt and drug infested world of present-day Central America." – *Middlesborough Evening Gazette (UK)*

"*House of Jaguar* is based upon Bond's own experiences in Guatemala. With detailed descriptions of actual jungle battles and manhunts, vanishing rain forests and the ferocity of guerrilla war, *House of Jaguar* also reveals the CIA's role in both death squads and drug running, twin scourges of Central America." – *Newton Chronicle (UK)*

"Not for the literary vegetarian – it's red meat stuff from the off. All action…convincing." – *Oxford Times (UK)*

"Bond grips the reader from the very first page. An ideal thriller for the beach, but be prepared to be there when the sun goes down." – *Herald Express*

The Last Savanna

"Tragic and beautiful, sentimental and ruthless, *The Last Savanna* is a vast and wonderful book." – *NetGalley Reviews*

"The novel is sheer intensity, depicting the immense, arid land and never-ending scenes of people trekking across it…The villains are are so strongly developed…but it's the volatile nature of nature itself that gives the story its greatest distinction…Will make readers sweat with its relentless pace." – *Kirkus*

"Mike Bond takes readers into a literary safari of Africa's elephant poaching war with *The Last Savanna*, a novel

that expertly captures the ravenous, chaotic and frustrating battles raging across the continent...and paints a vivid picture of life in the savanna...one of the most realistic portrayals of Africa yet...Dynamic, heart-breaking and timely to current events, Bond's latest book is a must-read."
– *Yahoo Reviews*

"An intense and emotional story about the African wilderness...masterfully done...so many characters and themes that come into this, it's amazing... *The Last Savanna* is intense, beautiful and completely captures the powerful emotion in this story... it taught me a lot about the dangers and mysteries of Africa." – *RealityLapse Reviews*

"A manhunt through crocodile-infested jungle, sun-scorched savannah, and impenetrable mountains as a former SAS man tries to save the life of the woman he loves but cannot have." – *Evening Telegraph (UK)*

"A fast-paced action novel set in Kenya, Ethiopia and Somalia...an intense and personal portrayal of the beauty and violence of Africa, from the brutal slaughter of iconic wildlife species, the stunning wildness of the landscape, and the growth of terrorism." – *Out There Monthly*

"A powerful love story set in the savage jungles and deserts of East Africa." – *Daily Examiner (UK)*

"Pulsating with the sights, sounds, and dangers of wild Africa, its varied languages and peoples, the harsh warfare of the northern deserts and the hunger of denied love." – *Newton Chronicle (UK)*

"A gripping thriller from a highly distinctive writer." – *Liverpool Daily Post (UK)*

"Exciting, action-packed...A nightmarish vision of Africa." – *Manchester Evening News (UK)*

"The imagery was so powerful and built emotions so

intense that I had to stop reading a few times to regain my composure." – *African Publishers' Network*

"An unforgettable odyssey into the wilderness, mysteries, and perils of Africa...A book to be cherished and remembered." – *Greater London Radio*

"The central figure is not human; it is the barren, terrifying landscape of Northern Kenya and the deadly creatures who inhabit it." – *Daily Telegraph (UK)*

"An entrancing, terrifying vision of Africa...Impossible to set aside or forget." – *BBC*

"*The Last Savanna* is shot through with images of the natural world at its most fearsome and most merciful. With his weapons, man is a conqueror – without them he is a fugitive in an alien land. Bond touches on the vast and eerie depths that lie under the thin crust of civilization and the base instinct within man to survive – instincts that surpass materialism. A thoroughly enjoyable read that comes highly recommended." – *Nottingham Observer (UK)*

"*The Last Savanna* is wonderful. Mike Bond's books are a national treasure." – *Art Zuckerman, WVOX*

"The opening of the book alone is so beautifully written that it was hard not to fall instantly into the story. It definitely feels like you are right there in Africa...the kind of book where just about anyone can enjoy it because it encompasses so much and is placed in such a beautiful and yet dangerous setting." – *Exploring All Genres*

"*The Last Savanna* is an unflinching look at the beauty and violence of Africa, the horror of the slaughter of the great beasts, the delicate balance of tribal life, the growth of terrorism and the timeless landscape. Its insights into how elephant poaching and drug sales are used to fund Islamic terrorist activities by Al Qaeda offshoots like Al-Shabaab are shockingly relevant and little known." – *Insatiable Readers*

"Bond's intense bond with Africa palpitates throughout *The Last Savanna*. Each of the characters, both man and beast is both the hunter and the hunted, literally and figuratively, and the tension in the novel begins in the first pages and clutches the reader in its grasp until the end…The violence is unsheathed and unforgiving, and the trek across the savanna escalates into a feeling of near-insanity, the characters confusing reality with their inner demons, clarity and madness only a breath apart, hope dancing just out of reach on the horizon. Bond expertly draws in the reader, using the brutal beauty of Africa to show the blurry line between humanity and the animal world, letting the readers question for themselves which is the most savage. Readers will find similarities to the emotional tension and themes in William Golding's *The Lord of the Flies*, and *The Last Savanna* sheds light on the dark corners of Africa — and mankind." – *Angela Amman Reviews*

"*The Last Savanna* is an unflinching look at the beauty and violence of Africa, the horror of the slaughter of the great beasts, the delicate balance of tribal life, the growth of terrorism and the timeless landscape." – *Book Binge Reviews*

"There were many parts that set this book apart from other books about Africa, but most notably the characters and beautiful writing…And while the sentences were beautiful on their own, together they painted a wondrous pictures of Africa and a beautiful wilderness." – *Book Reviews By Me*

"From the opening page maintains an exhilarating pace until the closing line…A highly entertaining and gripping read." – *East African Wild Life Society*

KILLING MAINE

MIKE BOND

MANDEVILLA
PRESS

MANDEVILLA PRESS
Weston, CT 06883

Published in the United States by Mandevilla Press

LIBRARY OF CONGRESS CATALOGING-IN-PUBLICATION DATA

Bond, Mike

Killing Maine: a novel/Mike Bond

p. cm.

ISBN 978-1-62704-030-3

1. Thriller – Fiction. 2. Crime – Fiction. 3. Maine – Fiction. 4. Political Corruption – Fiction. 5. Environment – Fiction. 6. Romance – Fiction. 7. Renewable Energy – Fiction.   I. Title

10 9 8 7 6 5 4 3 2 1

Cover photograph © Samot/Shutterstock.com
Author photo © PF Bentley/PFPix.com
Cover design: Asha Hossain Design, Inc.
Book design: Jude Bond @ BondMultimedia.com
Printed in the United States of America
www.MikeBondBooks.com

to Bob Diforio

il miglior fabbro

"To govern is to steal, everyone knows that."
– Albert Camus

"Politics: the conduct of public affairs for private advantage."
– Ambrose Bierce

"We have the best government that money can buy."
– Mark Twain

Maine rates next to last nationwide
in citizens' trust of their legislators.
– Gallup.com, April 4, 2014

"Maine is ranked 46 out of 50 states and
rated F for political corruption"
– Center for Public Integrity

"The mission of men there seems to be,
like so many busy demons,
to drive the forest all out of the country."
– Thoreau, *The Maine Woods*

"She's like a cat in the dark
and then she is the darkness."
– Fleetwood Mac

Dead of Winter

A COYOTE BARKED downhill. As I stopped to listen a bullet cracked past my ear and smacked into the maple tree beside me. I dove off the trail skidding down the icy slope toward the cliff. *Whack* another bullet smashed into a trunk as I tumbled past, couldn't stop sliding, couldn't pull off my snowshoes, the cliff edge coming up fast as a shot whistled past my eyes, another by my neck.

My head hit a boulder and I spun jamming a snowshoe in brush. Another bullet spat past my ear and splintered a root. I tore loose from both snowshoes and leaped off the cliff down into a cluster of young hemlocks and deep drifts and came up gasping for air, bleeding and alive.

The shooter was above the cliff I'd just fallen off and had no angle of fire till I moved away from the bottom of the cliff. Unless he descended to the clifftop. Then he could shoot straight down on me.

I was going to die. The cliff of snow-dusted raw ice and stone seemed weirdly primeval, as if I'd been here before. Below me descended the bouldery rubble of what had once been part of this cliff, with another cliff below that, and all down the slope tall frozen hardwoods where if you got pinned down you were safe till the shooter got your angle and then there were not enough trees to protect you.

I'd lost my right boot pulling out of its snowshoe. The sock, ragged and soaked, left a smear of blood on the snow.

Was that footsteps near the clifftop, crunching crust? I was breathing so hard I couldn't tell. If I ran and he was already there he'd shoot me easily in the back.

There was a terrible pain in my left hand. I stared at it stupefied. The ring finger was splayed ninety degrees sideways, dislocated. Once I saw it, it began to really hurt.

Trying to catch my breath and listening for the shooter, I pulled the finger straight but it would not drop back into the joint.

A shadow fell high up across a birch trunk: my shooter was above the cliff.

Like a wounded deer I darted downhill, running and dodging between tree trunks, slipping, skidding and tumbling ahead of the shots. The rifle sound so terrifying, the loud *crack* that crushes your ears, the physical *whack* of it, and if that bullet didn't get you the next one will.

He stopped firing, maybe couldn't see me through the trees. I slid, stumbled and ran a half mile further down the slope then circled back uphill above my trail, found a blowdown oak and broke off a hard limb like a baseball bat. I climbed higher and hid above my trail in a hemlock clump where I could see uphill but not be seen. If he followed my trail down the steep slope I had a chance of getting him with my oak limb as he walked past and before he could raise his gun.

My foot was freezing and very painful as was the dislocated finger. The pain was making me lightheaded, likely to make mistakes. I couldn't move till dark, when I'd be harder to see and harder to shoot. Though I didn't think my foot could wait that long without turning to ice.

And I still didn't know where the shooter was.

Then came the snarl of a snowmobile on the ridge. Maybe it was him, leaving.

Or someone else going while he waited in the gathering dusk for me to return for my snowshoes and boot.

I sat cross-legged in the powdery snow watching my upslope trail, clasping my cold sodden foot, trying to set my finger back in its joint, shuddering, teeth clattering. The sun had quit the ridge and a deeper cold was sifting downhill. It was maybe minus twenty-five but going to get much colder. If I stayed out all night the shooter wouldn't need to come back.

When facing death you sometimes get flashes of awareness, tragic epiphanies of what led to this fatal moment. As you gasp for breath and duck side to side running and falling and dashing on, expecting a bullet to smash your chest, you know how easy it would have been to avoid this.

It didn't matter that three days ago I'd been surfing in sunny Hawaii. And now to help a buddy I couldn't stand but to whom I owed my life, I was freezing to death in somebody's gunsights on a snow-deep mountain in the backwoods of Maine.

Black Witch

LIKE MOST TROUBLE, it started with a phone call. I was sitting on my Oahu lanai with my Tanqueray double martini and bag of Maui chips, watching the sun set in a glorious firestorm across the blue-green sea. In the sinking sun you could see our world spinning on its axis, away from light into darkness. And in the sea's vast horizon see the curvature of the earth, and sense the sun's distance and how huge it is compared to our tiny home.

Two hundred yards beyond the beach a mother whale was teaching her baby to jump, leaping from the sea and splashing down with a great *whap*, the little one soaring after her. With the sunset and blue-green ocean and cool breeze smelling of bananas and plumeria, it was one of those moments when the joy and beauty of the universe unite, and all seems at peace.

Highway to Hell, the damn phone rings. 207, the Maine area code, so grudgingly I answer.

"He ain't here," I says.

"Who isn't?" A woman, familiar.

I said nothing, realizing who she was and how much I didn't want to talk to her.

"Is there any way to reach him?" She sounded rushed, worried.

"Not right now."

"Sam? It *is* you! It's Lexie...Bucky's wife...Remember?"

What the hell did she mean by *remember*? Did she think I'd *forget*? But she wouldn't be calling for no reason. "How are you?" I mumbled.

"I'm not well, we both aren't, Bucky and me..."

Some marital squabble, maybe. So why call me?

"So I called because you two have the same experience –"

What – screwing you? I nearly said. "Lots of us guys did Afghanistan together. No news in that."

"Like I said he's in trouble."

This I couldn't imagine. Not straitlaced Bucky, who never met a regulation he didn't love.

"He's in maximum security at Warren." Her voice thinned. "Awaiting trial for murder."

"No," I almost laughed. "Not possible." By now I was pacing the lanai, looked out to sea and didn't see it. "Who says?"

What I didn't explain you is that Bucky's originally from Maine. He and Lexie live on his old family farm making organic milk and eggs and beef and all that kind of stuff. Going back to his ancestral homeland was Bucky's way of dealing with Afghanistan – all of us Special Forces guys, we have our own ways to forget – and his way was this pastoral hard-bitten life far from people and cities but close to animals and the land. And there could be a no more calming existence than to be there with Lexie, a person you can bury yourself in, she's so strong and kind, and you learn to be there for her as she is for you.

I should know.

"It's because of the windmills," she said.

"I ain't fighting them no more. Happy just to write about surfing... So how's Bucky? Be sure give him my best." *You fake you*, I told myself.

Lexie explained how two Maine governors and a bunch of legislators and "environmental" groups that were taking big money from industrial wind companies joined up to pass a bill permitting industrial wind projects to be built all over Maine without valid environmental studies and with no way for local folks to stop them. And one of the two governors then made millions in the wind industry, bought himself a US Senate seat with part of the proceeds, and installed his son at the top of another big welfare wind company.

And now Hawaii's old nemesis WindPower LLC had dynamited and clearcut all the once-beautiful ridges for miles around Bucky's and Lexie's farm and built howling wind turbines fifty-five stories high – the third-tallest structures in New England – all over them. These steel monstrosities screamed night and day, blotted out the starlit skies and Northern Lights with flashing red strobes, slaughtered thousands of bats and entire flocks of birds, banished tourism and wildlife, made people sick and drove them from their now-valueless homes.

But though there was very little wind and the turbines made almost no electricity, they made billions in taxpayer-paid subsidies for energy companies and investment banks, some of which trickled down to their fully-owned politicians and "environmental" groups.

As I'd learned in previous dealings with WindPower LLC, these turbines did absolutely nothing for global warming. Because wind is so erratic, wind projects must have fulltime fossil fuel plants to back them up, and the result is that wind projects often cause *more* coal-burning, not less.

And the saddest thing is that these billions of dollars wasted on industrial wind projects could be spent on rooftop solar, substantially reducing CO_2 generation and fossil fuel use. But the utilities hate rooftop solar, despite what they pretend, because it cuts their income, so they are avidly trying to curtail it.

"The cows stopped giving milk," Lexie said, a catch in her throat. "They got spooky and started fighting. We went from eight hundred twenty gallons a day to five hundred, then two hundred, then thirty." She cleared her throat. "Can you imagine? From eight hundred twenty gallons down to thirty?"

"I can imagine." It was disheartening that this had been happening in Maine while in Hawaii I'd been hunting and being hunted by Sylvia's killers – WindPower LLC and the rest of the Wind Mafia, like I explained you in that other book.

"We sold all the cows at Bangor State Fair," she said. "For almost nothing. At night we took sleeping pills and still couldn't sleep."

"So why the fuck's Bucky in jail –"

"One night he couldn't stand it anymore...we both had screaming headaches...He took a rifle up the hill and shot out three turbines."

"Hell, Lexie, *everyone* should do that."

"When the cops asked him did he do it, well, you know Bucky – he won't lie – he said of course he did, and *here's why*, but they didn't care about the *here's why* and what those damn turbines are doing to everyone –" She tried to laugh, "So WindPower sued us for ten million dollars."

I was getting mad. "For them that's nothing, compared to their pocket money."

"Pocket money?"

"The thirty percent of total project cost they get up front from the Obama administration, before they even do a thing."

"So I put a second mortgage on the farm, for Bucky's bail."

"How much?"

She said nothing, then, "Fifty thousand."

Now I was furious. "Look, Lexie, I'll come back there and shoot out all the other turbines for you. I'll get some of our Special Forces buddies, we'll shoot out every damn turbine in Maine –"

"This farm has been in Bucky's family twelve generations. Since 1781. But the noise and stress from the wind turbines is so bad we have to move. But we can't afford to buy another farm because now this place is worthless – *nobody* can live here."

"This is dreadful…"

"Wait, Pono – it's much worse."

"*Worse?* How worse can it *get?*"

"While Bucky was out on bail, somebody shot a guy, and the cops say it was Bucky."

"What guy?"

"Some environmentalist –"

"Bucky'd never do that."

"After he shot out the turbines he hid the rifle in the woods. But the cops say the bullets from the turbines match the one that killed that guy."

"Oh Jesus," I sat down. "Who's got the rifle?"

"Bucky went back for it but it was gone."

BEYOND MY LANAI the Oahu wind had cooled. Fifteen minutes ago I'd had the perfect life. *Surfer News* was sending me to cover the Tahiti Tsunami, one of surfing's greatest festivals, in six weeks. I was happily in love with three women, Kim a gorgeous married cop who had once put me *Inside* then freed me, Charity a wild New Zealand adventuress, and Angie who loved and hated me lustfully. The three sexiest things about a woman are kindness, honesty and brains, and they all had them in abundance. Plus there were all the other magnificent women a surfer's life will bring you.

After two tours in Afghanistan and one in Iraq, plus two undeserved prison sentences, plus hunting down and nearly being killed by Sylvia's killers, I'd planned to surf, teach foster kids how to do it, help out disabled vets wherever I could, and peacefully contemplate the mysteries of the universe.

A Black Witch moth fluttered down from the gutter and landed on my wrist. Huge and batlike with incandescent red eyes. In Mexico they're called *mariposa de muerte* – butterfly of death. In Hawaii we say when the Black Witch comes it's the soul of a loved one saying goodbye.

Sure I loved Lexie but we'd lost each other. And Bucky I could barely stand.

So who else was going to die?

Max Security

I T WAS AN ICE-CRAGGED RIDGE at night at 10,600 feet in Afghanistan's Hindu Kush, "Death Mountains". Though we didn't yet know it, we Americans were just the latest of a long line of invaders who'd come here to die.

West-facing, very steep with some junipers and goat-gnawed scrub, it rose toward a black peak called Bandakur. We were moving along it in staggered vertical formation toward what on aerial observation had seemed a stone barn with a lot of foot traffic, most of it armed.

21:20, thirty below, pale moonlight on white snow and black rock. The icy wind ate into your lungs like acid but felt good too, galactic and liberating, closer to the frigid core of space. Gave you a heightened awareness – *at any instant a bullet can smash through you* – but it was also the cold heartbeat of the world, this night, this glacial wind, this barren ridge in the Death Mountains.

The stone barn's slanting stone roof was huddled against the north facing slope. My buddies took positions upslope of the barn while I went forward to listen by a window, as I was the only one who understood some of the local mix of Pashto and Tajik.

Unfortunately there was a lookout in a spider hole we hadn't been able to see, and he got off a few rounds at me as I dove among the boulders, his bullets whacking past me and howling off the rocks. Then a horrible thud smashed my head and I had a fleeting sense *my brain's blown away* and was gone.

What I've been told happens next is my buddies waste the spider hole dude but then all these other assholes in the stone barn start laying down a volley of fire.

Amid the deafening bullets I came back to life, instinctively clenching the frozen earth as I tried to understand what I was and what was happening. Then this bearlike beast leaps on me, throws me over his shoulder and sprints uphill through a hail of howling bright splinters and moaning steel and, I remember clearly, tossing me on the frozen earth like a bag of laundry.

My buddies and the Taliban exchanged fire for at least five more minutes – an eternity – as each side maneuvered for position, my buddies soon outflanking the building where the Taliban had retreated to the rear. I'm told the last three Taliban surrendered. The team searched and flex-cuffed them, did a quick recon of the barn and dead Taliban, took the few things of interest and carried me down the ridge for chopper evac.

By then I was half awake and pissed off. Apparently a round had hit my helmet at an angle, bizarrely spun around the back and out the other side. I was later diagnosed to have had a major concussion with significant intracranial bleeding. What I was pissed off about was the roaring pain, the weird noise like sitting next to an F-18 at full blast, the damned dizziness and nausea, the sorrow, and the fact that when the bullets were flying I hadn't been there for my buddies. And most of all that someone had to risk his life to save me.

Of course his name was Bucky Franklin.

Whose testimony three months later in a military court helped give me a twenty-year sentence.

And who then ran off with the woman I loved. Whom I'd told to forget me.

But more about that later.

IT WAS 88 DEGREES that night when I got on the Delta redeye in Honolulu, and minus 17 when I landed next afternoon in Portland. I didn't find this funny.

All they had for rentals was a small oil tanker called an Expedition. With me at the helm we launched from the parking garage, steered left at Stroudwater village and moored by a small cemetery on a pine knoll.

The air cut like a knife. Everything was white but the black road, far gray roofs, dark pines and pitted granite slabs in uneven rows up the knoll under the pines. The snow so cold it squeaked as I followed an aisle of graves, careful not to step on anyone, to a cluster of headstones and sat on an icy root. "Long time no see, folks."

No one answered. Wind whistled through the boughs sifting fogs of tiny crystals down my neck. "I must be nuts," I added, "coming here in February."

More silence.

"You folks were *nuts* to even *live* here," I said. "At least old Elias had the sense to leave Maine for the Big Island. Do you *know* how warm it is in Hawaii right now?"

Not a word.

My ass was freezing so I got up and ran a fingertip along a name chiseled in lichened granite. A memorial to Colonel Jonas Hawkins, born 1664, died in the 1690 war in Canada against the French. James Hawkins, killed at the Battle of Saratoga October 7, 1777. Dennis Hawkins in the War of 1812. Women one after the other dead in childbirth, then Sarah Hawkins, a Stroudwater school teacher from 1813 to 1848. Timothy Hawkins, wounded at Little Round Top – the battle where a bunch of kids from Maine died to save Gettysburg and maybe the Union.

The children lay in dated clumps, having died of diphtheria or some other plague, like the man and wife who lost all seven kids in six weeks in 1872. Hawkins grave after Hawkins grave among the pine roots: they who once owned vast tracts of Maine which over the years they'd drunk and gambled away, till an uncle, Jack Hawkins, had nothing left but a 320-acre Stroudwater farm.

I'd visited Uncle Jack one summer to learn farm work, and fell for a neighbor, beautiful strong-willed Erica Tillson, salutatorian of the local high school, who later became a famous Portland lawyer. She certainly laid down the law, taking me up the Stroudwater River in a green canoe and screwing me half to death in the hayfield that had once belonged to my ancestors.

I was only fourteen at the time and new to this. She was three years older and quite experienced, though I was a fast learner. But in September she went off to Harvard, and when the haying and apple picking were done I flew back to Hawaii.

Now tracing my fingertips across the ancient stones brought a warm recognition, a sense of kinship, of our common lives, that who *we* are goes back to who *they* were. That this side of my family and my Hawaiian seafarer ancestors were one. That it's idiotic to fight. That all living things are one, we and these majestic pines and the crows calling across the River and all other beings, even those we kill and who kill us.

The vision vanished, the headstones just cold granite, the wind bitter down my neck as it wailed through the pines. I climbed the ridge to look down at the River's ribbon of ice, wanting to understand: the girl and boy paddling upriver in the green canoe and everything that had happened since.

Again no answer. I descended the aisle between the stones and Expeditioned through the gray bitter afternoon to Warren, a lovely old village on the St. George River that is now home to the Maine Maximum Security Prison, where former Special Forces Master Sergeant Buckford Franklin was waiting to be tried for first degree.

PRISONS TERRIFY ME. I've been twice *Inside* and don't ever want to go back, not even to visit. The dread that I've been tricked back *Inside* and now will be there forever.

Warren Max Security did nothing to allay such fears. Its white façade and neutral building pods were like a trip to horror in another dimension: the old jails were evil, but these new ones delete whatever's left of your soul.

Of course most folks in jail *should* be there, and if they weren't, most of them would be perpetrating more crimes against the rest of us.

I should know.

But each time a steel door thunders shut behind you and your steps echo down a gritty concrete hall between two concrete and steel walls under a concrete ceiling, you can smell the heartbreak of all the millions jailed for life.

Jailhouse air. Stench of old sweat, filthy feet, sour farts, clogged nostrils, nasty hatreds and vile food overlaid with the smell of the guards' synthetic uniforms, leather, antiperspirant and oiled steel.

A level of Hades. That contains three kinds of people:

> *Those who have harmed others*
> *Those who might harm the state*
> *Those who didn't do it*

Concrete. Concrete and steel. Every living thing excised except the inmates sallow in the death of life. Condemned means *damned together.*

Most of them for good reason. If you've spent any time *Inside* you know. It's sad but inexorable how some people get screwed by horrible parents, home tragedies and beaten fear, by everything going wrong, and end up committing the crimes that put them there.

Imagine how *they* see *us* on the other side of the glass – as we rush in from *Outside,* from the *world,* free to go back at the flick of a switch? It's how the dead might envision the living. With infinite envy and deadly mirth.

"SO, ASSHOLE," I says to Bucky when we finally get hooked up. "How you get into this?"

He scratches his shaved head and gives me that hard stare through the bulletproof glass. "Who the fuck told *you?*"

"Who you think?"

"She should shut up." He looked me over. "When?"

"Yesterday."

"You got here fast." He shook his head. "Won't do no good."

"You do it?"

He snickered. "You have to ask?"

"I don't have to ask."

He studied me through the smears on the glass from too many people trying to touch each other. "Thanks."

I glared back at him, massive and muscular in his orange prison suit. "So how we gonna get you out?"

"We ain't *gonna* get me out."

Seven minutes left. He was on non contact with a max of three visits a week; Lexie'd already used two for this week so it'd be days before I could see him again. What he said quickly was the night the environmental guy, Ronnie Dalt, VP of Lobbying for Maine Environmental Resources, had been killed in Augusta, Bucky had driven over to Jefferson to see his great uncle Silas, an hour away. But when the cops interviewed Uncle Silas he was having one of his goofy spells (he's ninety-seven) and couldn't remember a damn thing.

The odometer on Bucky's truck was broke and he'd last topped up from the 91 octane tank he uses to refuel snowmobilers when they come through. "Since I get it by the tanker full," he said, "it's cheaper than 87 octane at Cumberland Farms." So how could he prove how much gas he'd used, prove it wasn't enough to drive to Augusta to kill Dalt?

"So who did kill him?" I says.

"You tell me."

I nodded. "It ain't right, Bucky."

The buzzer rang. Such a horrible sound when you're *Inside,* a raw snarl up your spine and clattering in your ears that means the person on the other side of the bullet-proof glass is going back into the world while you stay buried in concrete.

Bucky bit his lip. "Go see Lexie."

We were on thin ice here. "Maybe."

"She could use some help."

I walked the grimy sidewalk past the concertina and machine guns into a moonless night, inhaling the frozen air to flush the prison rot out of my lungs, across the icy echoing blacktop to the two-ton juggernaut that would take me away from all this and leave Bucky behind.

"Turn left in two hundred yards," the cheery dashboard lady said as I sailed the Expedition out of the parking lot. I hate guns but if I'd had one I damn well might've shot her right in the computer.

I headed toward Thomaston, Highway 1, Waldoboro and Route 22 north toward Jefferson and beyond to Route 220 between Liberty and Freedom and the turnoff to Bucky's and Lexie's Eagle Mountain farm. It started snowing, big fat flakes swarming in the headlights, the Expedition slithering all over the glacial roads like a hippo on ice.

Overwhelmed as I was by Bucky's fate, it was easy to forget in Afghanistan I'd disliked him, a guy who lived for regulations and was determined to make me live that way too. For what he'd decided was my own good. And what he'd done to me because of it.

But like I explained in that other book, in Special Forces you never leave a buddy behind. No matter the risk or what he did. Especially if he once saved your life.

That goes for our country too.

Down for Life

THOUGH AT OPPOSITE ENDS of our country, Maine and Hawaii are, other than climate, much alike. Places where you say who you are, be who you are, keep your word, and don't cheat or lie or take advantage of each other. Where you protect other folks because they are your tribe.

Both places independent-minded, rugged, yet conscientious of the common good. Both maritime, enriched yet trivialized by tourism, surrounded by natural beauty which they both love and are diligently trying to destroy. And both plagued by two of the most corrupt political systems in the United States.

Not long ago *Money* magazine rated Hawaii the most politically corrupt of the fifty states. Even worse than Russia, it said. Though lately Maine's apparently been catching up.

It didn't use to be this way.

On the Hawaiian side, my ancestors crossed the treacherous Pacific from Polynesia in rickety rafts lashed with vines, rowing for thousands of unknown miles with no compass, using only the stars, the currents, the birds and the winds, yet often able to reach the exact place they sought.

They had a broad sense of family and clan, an open enjoyment of sex, ferocious bravery in battle and kindness toward each other in peace, and reverence for our 'aina, the precious earth, sea and sky that gives us all life.

On my *haole* (European) side, my ancestor Elias Hawkins grew up in the once-bucolic town of Hallowell, Maine in the 1830s. He lived with his hatmaker father, schoolteacher mother, six siblings and the family cow, ducks and chickens in a little saltbox on Water Street that has only recently been torn down, went to school when possible and attended the Old South Congregational Church on Second Street.

Life was tough; it either killed you or made you strong. As a boy Elias worked at many trades, in winter swimming the near-frozen Kennebec River to push ashore logs from timber drives which he then sold for ten cents each.

Hallowell was the tidal head of the Kennebec, the "long land water" where once a famous Abenaki village, Koussinok, had stood. Many boys from town had gone to sea back when half of America's sailing ships had been built in Maine, and many had Maine crews.

Though a small town Hallowell had six newspapers, several churches and schools, and a growing economy based on beaver skins, lumber and fishing. The salmon and sturgeon runs in the River, Elias later wrote, were so massive you could walk across on the backs of these huge fish – all gone now. And the alewives and all the other smaller fish who once filled the river solid with their migrations.

Growing up as a rough, tough kid, Elias also was drawn to seeking out the mysteries of life, the path with heart. In his words, he wanted to understand how to live deeply and well and share that with others.

He attended Bangor Theological Seminary and fell in love with Ellen Howell of Portland. The day after they were married they sailed on the schooner "Gloucester" for the Sandwich Isles, as Hawaii then was called, and where he had been offered a post as the first missionary on the Big Island.

The journey took nine months, including the perilous passage between Antarctica and Tierra del Fuego. Their cabin was a blanket-draped cubicle in the hold with a bed, a small table, and enough room for one person to stand at a time. By the time they reached Hawaii Ellen was eight months pregnant, and soon gave birth to the first of their nine children. Readers of Michener's *Hawaii* will recognize their story, for the missionary character and his wife in that book are based partially on Elias' diary.

Soon after arriving on the Big Island Elias realized that God had called him not to preach religion to the Hawaiians but rather to help them survive this catastrophic white invasion. He built the first girls' school in Hawaii and the second boys' school, brought sugar cane to the Big Island and macadamia nuts to Hawaii – all in the hopes of giving the people a chance to build their lives, and to keep the girls, as he put it, from ending up as prostitutes in Honolulu.

When King Kamehameha granted Elias a large chunk of the Big Island, Elias passed it back to the Hawaiian people at a dollar an acre and used those funds to build more schools. Life was tough, you built things with your hands, and you cared for each other as one family. Once a year a ship arrived from Hallowell with lumber, nails, clothing and other supplies; in its hold, wrapped in straw, were a few chunks of last winter's ice from the Kennebec River that the family used one day a year to make a special feast – ice cream.

To put it mildly Elias is revered by the Hawaiian people, and his schools, home, public library and gardens are now the Elias Hawkins National Historic District in North Kohala. One of his sons, Benjamin, was the first doctor on the Big Island. He kept a horse always saddled in the barn because often in the night someone would come running from faraway, perhaps Hilo even, or the south end of the island, to report a sick or injured person, and Benjamin would ride the many miles through the darkness to reach them.

It is from this mix of Hawaiian tribal love and New England ecumenicism that my own blood has come, and how I try, for better or worse, to live.

FROM HIGHWAY 1 I turned northwest through the forests and farm fields of Knox and Lincoln Counties, a frigid moon rising over fir-dark hills in a veil of blowing snow. Every ravine, crevice and rocky cleft was silvered, the dark sawtooth ridges like waves rolling to the horizon, the backbone of Maine. The backbone that the Wind Mafia were going to drill, blast, herbicide, and cover with thousands of howling, red-flashing towers twice the height of the clouds... It didn't seem possible.

Long before you get to Lexie's and Bucky's farm you see the red-strobed turbines towering like War of the Worlds monsters over the once-beautiful crests of Eagle Mountain. Below in a fold of the hills lies their farm, acres of pasture in deep drifts, tall dark pines, red barns and outbuildings, the old white house with its steep roof and clapboard siding.

It was snowing harder, small hard flakes flying across the headlights. Lexie's gate was open; I drove across the rattling cattle guard and up the long drive with snow squeaking under the tires.

She came out the kitchen door holding her hair back from the wind, gave me a brief hug. "So you came."

We went inside and I pulled the door shut against the wind. "I had a choice?"

She didn't answer, standing in the middle of the kitchen, arms folded, an angry unhappy face. Her blonde hair was tousled, unkempt. She wore an old levi blouse with torn elbows. The light from the overhead bulb made shadows in the hollows of her throat and under her eyes. I ached to take her in my arms and I hungered to walk out of there and never come back.

"I never wanted this," she said.

"This?" Pretending I didn't know what she meant.

"You're going to say I brought it on myself."

I glanced through the snow-clad mullioned panes at the blizzard hurling itself across the barnyard. "No point in regretting our choices."

"I keep telling myself that accepting them makes us strong."

"No one needs that kind of strength, Lexie."

"I do. Now. Because I'm going crazy. The cows are gone, the chickens, the geese... We even had to sell the pigs, they were crying all night... I can't sleep, the cat's disappeared, Bucky's dog keeps running away, comes home asking me to leave..."

"What do you mean, *asking* you?"

"Lobo? She comes back and sits out there in the barnyard whining. It can be forty below and she won't come in. And when I go out she retreats down the road, doing the same thing, and when you get close she does it again. One time she grabbed my sleeve and literally pulled me down the road." She clasped her temples. "These headaches..."

I was beginning to get one too, an irritating buzz like a bad neon light. The whole thing was miserable. I tried to change course. "So what do you regret? Bucky? The farm?"

She brushed the hair from my forehead with a quick maternal caress, sat opposite at the table. "There's too much you won't understand."

We were both thinking how different things could have been. Would have been. "You had to go and shoot that girl," she said.

"I had no choice."

"The other guys..." She waited. "They didn't think so."

"She was dying. In the most horrible pain. She begged me."

She clasped worn fingers across her knees. "And look what it cost you."

And you? I nearly said.

The turbines' weird howl went on and on, a 747 landing that never lands, an unending demonic torture wheel. My head pounded.

"I'll never give Bucky up," she said. "Not now."

"That's not why I'm here."

"Even if he goes down for life."

Here with the comfortable oak fire in the stone fireplace, the old pumpkin pine floorboards two feet wide, the ancient wallpaper, the sense of many generations having lived in this place, their spirits still there, the fear struck me, for the first time really, that we might not save him. That he like Maine might be lost forever. The world's a very cruel place where the good are often destroyed while evil triumphs.

I could see the years ahead of his gray imprisonment, Lexie teaching school somewhere, not enough money, the weekly visits over icy roads to Warren State Prison. When every week nothing had changed for him and maybe everything for her. And every week he looks into her eyes and tries to figure if she's got someone.

"One time Lobo saved our lives," Lexie said. "Right up that valley."

From where she pointed maybe it was below the far pasture, where a thick ridge comes down steeply, the top towered over by windmills. "We came to a little valley and she wouldn't let us go further. She actually knocked Bucky down, made us turn around."

"So?"

"Fifteen minutes later the whole slope came down. Avalanche."

"Where's she now?"

27

"She leaves because the turbines do something to her ears. She's going crazy."

"Aren't we all." The windmills were a metaphor for the soul destruction of today, the withering earth, humans spreading like melanoma, toxic to almost every living thing except what we enslave.

THE TURBINES STOPPED. Lexie and I breathed out, looked into each other's eyes for the first time since I'd come. The worm digging in our brains had gone silent.

How to describe it? Someone jackhammering beside you, the sound is physical, inescapable. Or the 747 landing, on and on and on but never landing. The electric drill howling through steel... And then, below it, undetected, the infrasound coagulating your blood and screaming silently inside your head.

And now the silence... The stunning silence. You realized you hadn't been breathing deeply, hadn't been able to think.

"Why'd they stop?" I says, afraid they'd start again.

"Curtailment. Only time the turbines produce much power is at night, when there's no demand, so the utilities have to curtail it, dump the power."

She'd made the old standby of Maine baked beans and hamburgers and had bought a handle of Tanqueray and some Martini & Rossi Extra Dry in my honor, so we went to work on all that. The martinis loosened things up a bit, and in her drawn weary face I found the shadow of the tempestuous young stripper I'd loved so much.

Another reason she wouldn't leave, she said, was her biology and chemistry students at Eagle Mountain High, as no new teacher would come here because of the turbine noise. "My Grandma taught in a one-room schoolhouse in the Wyoming mining fields... she used to say she'd had far more influence on those kids than most teachers today. For me, it used to be like that here. Now the kids are so whacked out on turbine noise they're unruly, have ADD, don't study at night... You see the new *Gallup* poll?" she said, that way she has of changing subjects.

"Life's too short to watch TV."

"Maine is next to last nationwide in the trust citizens have for their Legislators."

"Next to last?" Despite all the news about corrupt legislators this was a new low. "Who's *last?*"

"Illinois. Six governors jailed for corruption, fifteen hundred elected officials, mostly Democrats, so far indicted. Governor Blagojevich, fourteen years in the pen for trying to buy a US Senate seat... We could've told them you can buy a Senate seat much cheaper in Maine. With no fear of indictments."

A thud of claws at the door and Lexie leaped up. "It's Lobo!"

But when she opened the door it was a huge gray tomcat. "Max!" she cried, "Where've you *been?*"

He stalked in, the size of a small pitbull, just one ear and a single eye with which he examined me balefully. He also had, I was soon to learn, the temperament of a wolverine, but according to Lexie could be a sweetheart and lie purring on your chest for hours. Though if you moved him he might kill you.

"You've been gone for *days!*" she sat on the floor hugging him and scratching under his chin while he rubbed his forehead against her chin and purred like a locomotive. "He hates the turbines," she said, "hardly ever comes home... Oh Max it's so good to *see* you!"

He meowed like a tiger I'd once heard in Honolulu Zoo. "Yes, yes," she said, "I'll get you some." She rummaged in the freezer for a hunk of ground venison and popped it in the microwave. "He doesn't like cat crunchies," she explained as Max came over to check me out, turned round and sprayed my leg.

"Oh my God!" Lexie laughed. "He's never done that!"

I gave him a mild push with one toe and he lashed it whiplike with his claws and ambled to the pail of milk Lexie had put down. "He normally only sprays the TV and Lobo's dinner," Lexie said.

We humans sometimes shared our Paleolithic abodes with cave lions and saber tooth tigers, but I couldn't tell from which of these lineages Max had descended. "It's because he doesn't know you," Lexie added as she topped our glasses with more gin.

When the venison was thawed she put it on a platter and Max dug into that for a while, switching between it and the milk like a gourmet between filet mignon and Margaux, growling and flicking his ropelike tail.

"Why do you feed him?" I said. "He could clearly kill his own deer..."

"He's just a kitten, even afraid of birds. Used to sleep on our bed, before the wind project. Better than a heating pad... I don't know where he stays now...far from the turbines..."

After he'd eaten he popped up on her lap and purred radiantly while she scratched behind his ears. He scanned me with a more benevolent eye, and I decided maybe he was going to let me stay.

A few minutes later comes another thump at the door and in rumbles Lobo, a large black-brown wolf dog with a white belly. Lexie rubbed her down with a towel while she panted happily, shook snow everywhere, licked Lexie's face, sniffed me and licked mine too.

Lexie fed her a tray of hamburger, peas and rice which she gulped down, tail still wagging. She shook snow one more time then scratched at the door and Lexie let her out into the swirling gale.

"Sometimes," Lexie sat down again, "I think, since this all happened, that when people aren't supposed to be together... bad things happen to them."

"Even if you hadn't been with Bucky, he'd still've come back here. These bastards still would've built the turbines."

"No, no, that's not true. He came back here because of me. Otherwise he would've stayed with you guys." Meaning SF.

"So?"

"He came back... Because of you."

I looked at her drawn face, wondered at its paleness. This effervescent, brilliant young woman was rotting away and I didn't know why. "Nonsense."

"He wanted to get me far away. So I'd forget you."

In a moment it had all changed. I reached out for her, not in lust or love but condolence. She brushed my hand away. "I've made my bed." She stood. "And now I'm lying in it."

"You and Bucky..."

She gave me a consoling look, that I should be the last to know. "What started out as fun – I thought I could change him – after a while wasn't fun anymore. And then it became duty. For us both."

She stood arms crossed in the middle of the kitchen on the worn black-and-white chessboard linoleum, and I had a crazy vision of Joan of Arc on the pyre. "So I told myself I'll live like my Mom does," she said. "Forty years, her and my Dad. What started out as love became annoyance then hate and now's a sort of grim compromise till death."

I thought of my own Pa and Mom, the intensity of their caring for each other. "It doesn't have to be like that."

She looked at me fiercely. "It doesn't?" Lips crimped she faced away then back at me, tears like jewels in her eyes. "Oh Sam why'd you have to shoot that woman?" She crossed to the window. "Going to blizzard all night." She looked back at me. "I'll never give Bucky up. Not now."

"Nor will I." I sensed we'd crossed some Rubicon I'd always regret. The absolute impossibility of saving Bucky, of saving Maine, crashed in on me. Not since prison have I felt such presentiment of failure.

I stood behind her massaging her shoulders where the neck joins, all those hard tendons that pull the shoulders and head apart, the raw pain of modern life.

I could feel what she felt, through my palms and the undersides of my fingers. Could touch the pain. Soothe it, release it, soften the muscles, ligaments and tendons and draw the pain away.

I kissed her forehead. We stood for an instant cheek to cheek the way we had so many times, her lithe form matched to mine. She stepped back, looked at me steadily. "I think I married Bucky because it was the closest I could get to you."

I repeated almost what she'd said before: "Look where it got you."

She watched me. "You were in for twenty years. What was I supposed to do?"

"I told you not to wait."

"I didn't."

Not bothering to put on my coat I went out across the barnyard to the bunkhouse, shut the door behind me and flicked on the light. Snow had drifted under the door and around the window sash. The fire in the woodstove was out. Without undressing I climbed under the frigid blankets and tried to sleep.

Already I was tired of winter. But in five weeks I'd be in Tahiti for the Tsunami.

So whatever I did for Bucky had to be done by then.

Flicking on my headlamp I opened *The Maine Woods* from Lexie's bookcase. It relates Thoreau's three 1850s explorations in a birch bark canoe of the great wilds of northern Maine, guided by the Indian Joe Polis, crossing lakes, wandering the primeval forest and running rivers and rapids. One day they put ashore on Moosehead Lake to climb Mount Kineo,

> *The clouds breaking away a little, we had a glorious wild view, as we ascended, of the broad lake with its fluctuating surface and numerous forest-clad islands, extending beyond our sight both north and south, and the boundless forest... and enveloping nameless mountains in succession...*

This "glorious wild view" that was soon to be destroyed by thousands of industrial wind turbines all around Moosehead Lake, the wildest and most beautiful great lake in the eastern US.

Unless we could save it. How?

Claws scratched the plank door. I got up and cracked it open, snow blasting in. A white-clad Lobo looked up at me encouragingly. "Where you been?" I said as she squeezed in, shook snow everywhere and took over the bed. I climbed in and shoved her huge weight aside. "You have to learn to share," I said. "Just like everybody else."

I could swear Lobo snickered. At my naïveté, no doubt.

Alibi

RONNIE DALT HAD BEEN SHOT late one night as he crossed the parking lot of his office at Maine Environmental Resources in Augusta. He was struck by a single bullet from a large caliber rifle fired from a line of trees uphill from the parking lot, at the edge of a small park. The bullet had hit the wallet in Dalt's chest pocket, mushroomed and torn through his chest, pulverizing his heart and one lobe of his left lung.

The angle of fire was such that the bullet exited his body and buried itself in the parking lot, easy to find.

Supposedly Dalt had been dead by the time he hit the ground, but that's unlikely. From what I've seen the brain continues to register till it runs out of oxygen, which can take a minute or two, depending on blood loss. I've seen "dead" men look me in the eye and have watched their consciousness fade till it's as dead as the rest of them.

Shooting an unarmed person is a nauseating and life-destroying act – not just their life but yours too. For just as there are no good people who stay in politics because it sucks the good out of them, there are no good people who have executed others – it takes you halfway down the road to Hell.

Apparently the rifle's muzzle blast had attracted no notice, given the time, with most folks in bed and in an area of

Augusta where trucks and motorcycles gear down to climb the hill. Plus the shooter probably had a suppressor on his barrel which would have minimized the sound.

So Ronnie's half-frozen corpse wasn't found till 06:10 next morning when the snowplow came to clear the new six inches that had fallen during the night. Due to the chilled corpse it had been near-impossible, apparently, to determine time of death, but it had probably been after 22:00.

When the cops dug the mushroomed slug out of Ronnie's parking lot they sent it to the National Integrated Ballistic Information Network lab at Mass State Police in Maynard, where a computer program matched its barrel striations with the slugs taken from the turbines Bucky'd shot out. It identified all three as Barnes 180-grain solid copper slugs, fired from ASYM casings like the one the police found in the snow where the shooter had stood. And since Bucky'd already said he'd shot the three turbines it was an obvious step to charge him with Ronnie's death too.

The .308 is one of the most common high-power cartridges, from which the NATO 7.62x5 mm round was developed, as in the M16 and other military rifles. There are endless variations on bullet size and composition, and I didn't yet know enough about the Barnes bullet dug from the parking lot to determine what it was. Or how sure that the bullet which killed Ronnie had really been from the same gun Bucky used to shoot out his three turbines.

Under normal circumstances there would be endless problems with this scenario. Simple criteria could be established: bullet size, and other "class characteristics" like whether the rifling is left-hand or right-hand, on the distance between grooves, and perhaps markings unique to that barrel.

But any bullet hitting a wallet, traversing a body and burying itself in asphalt was going to be seriously deformed, and thus its striations difficult to analyze. Moreover, how could they prove that a bullet badly mushroomed by smashing into a steel turbine still showed the striations necessary to identify it?

That apparently wasn't a problem in Ronnie's shooting, because the police had found a casing where Ronnie Dalt was shot. Which Bucky never would have done. And it was the same as the ASYM casing they'd found where Bucky'd shot out the turbines, where again he would have, knowing Bucky, picked up his empties.

I checked the closet where Bucky kept his guns and ammo and found two boxes of ASYM .308s. And what was unusual about the Barnes bullets, I soon noticed, were the three rings cut into the bullet's shank, that would make them very easy to identify.

I shut down my computer and went outside to think, came back. "Show me," I said to Lexie, "where Bucky hid the gun."

SNOWSHOEING ACROSS the pasture we took turns breaking trail but the snow was so deep we were soon exhausted. It got even harder climbing the mountain, though Lobo ploughed through the snow as if it were hardly there.

The bare-boughed beech, maple and birch trees threw shadows like prison bars across the snow. With each upward step you slid halfway back. The snowshoes grew heavier when snow piled atop them; you had to whack them against trees to shake it off. They were ancient, bent willow and rawhide, the way the Penobscots had made them. "We should be wearing orange," I said, looking for an excuse to take a breather.

"Nobody hunts this mountain any more." Lexie was out of breath too. "Not since the turbines. Deer've gone. Moose too. Infrasound."

"When we go back," I took a another breath. "We're gonna find you another place to live."

She'd knelt to tighten a snowshoe strap, looked up at me. "No way."

"It's driving you crazy. I've never seen you look so bad. Even the dog and cat..."

She stood, eyes on mine. "I'm not moving. Not till Bucky's free."

"What if he doesn't *get* free?"

"We'll see about that." She turned and pushed up the mountain.

A half hour later the slope eased and the trees thinned. We broke out on a ridge which looked carpet-bombed. For a quarter mile across it had been clearcut, razed, and dynamited, nothing left but herbicided brush and scarred stumps. A eroding, oil-puddled dirt road had been bull-dozed through it. The turbine towers rose so high their tops vanished in the clouds. I pointed at the three closest – so tall you were practically looking vertically at them – and whose blades weren't moving. "Those the ones he shot?"

"A clip in each."

"Damn!" I said, impressed. At over fifty stories they were nearly half the height of the Empire State Building, so it wasn't easy for a shooter to compensate for drift and wind, particularly in a near-vertical trajectory.

"He checked out the manufacturers' specs to see where to aim." She turned to Lobo who sat back in the trees watching us. "It's okay, honey," she called, "you go home."

With a bound Lobo raced downhill. "She won't go any closer to the turbines," Lexie said. "She used to love it up here..."

Beyond Bucky's three dead towers rows of about twenty more were turning steadily, their huge blades flashing. Even from a mile away the sound was a low grinding moan, gnashing of steel and wail of huge blades spinning two hundred miles an hour.

"The wind companies," she said, "call them bird Cuisinarts… They think it's funny."

"They would."

"There he is!" she pointed upward.

I looked up seeing nothing. "Who?"

"The eagle. He's been flying for months over the turbine that killed his mate… that one," she pointed again.

Now I saw him. A dot atop the sky. "He hasn't left?"

"I think he's waiting. Hoping she'll come back."

"The bastards who did this," I said, "should be jailed."

"Jailed?" she laughed. "They have Obama's thirty-year eagle kill permit. To kill as many eagles as they want, bald eagles, golden eagles, as well as all the other raptors, the hawks, owls, ospreys, some of them near extinction but no problem, kill them all… Over there," she added, "that's the turbine that took out a whole flock of Canada geese last fall. On their way south…"

"Show me where Bucky hid the rifle."

She led me down the far side of the mountain along a streambed that had washed out with erosion from the construction above, to a low cliff in the hill. Between the white birch, yellow-barked beech and gnarled gray-brown maples the wind had scattered dead leaves on the snow. At an overhang she brushed aside snow and lifted a plywood sheet. Under it was a waterproof gun box that when she flipped open was empty.

"So why'd Bucky hide it here?"

"It was his Dad's gun, a pre-'64 Winchester. Didn't want the cops to impound it."

"So whoever took the gun killed this guy Dalt?"

She shrugged. "Maybe somebody saw Bucky put it there – no, they couldn't have because it was night… Maybe they stumbled on it, took it home and sold it to the one who killed him. The cops say they've been looking but no .308 around here's been sold."

"Not that they'd know."

"Yeah, not that they'd know."

SO WHAT was I doing? Trying to find an alibi for Bucky. Simple as that.

I wasn't doing it *for* Bucky. Sure, he was SF; I'd do it for that alone. He'd do exactly the same for me. No matter we didn't like each other.

I tend to play loose with regulations but Bucky adored them. He was, to my eyes, a duty freak. One who can't stand to be happy. I wouldn't have been surprised if he saluted Lexie before they made love. Or at least checked regulations for time allowed on target.

So was I doing it for Lexie? Seeing her again made me so hungry for her I would have invented any reason to be there. But it wasn't that.

The real reason was simple: Bucky says he didn't murder this guy Dalt. So someone else did. And they were getting away with it, too. While Bucky faced life.

That Bucky hadn't killed him was so obvious, instinctively, that as I'd told him I didn't need proof. And I also knew if Bucky *had* killed this guy, the guy had it coming, and Bucky would've said so.

So if Bucky didn't kill him, who did?

Bucky'd said he went to see his Uncle Silas in Jefferson the night Dalt was killed in Augusta, over an hour apart. But the problem was when the cops talked to Silas he couldn't remember. "He ain't always in his head," Bucky had said. "But what you expect – he's ninety-seven."

When I called Silas he didn't seem forgetful at all. "Sure, I'm here all afternoon. C'mon down... We can talk story –

isn't that what they say in Hawaii?"

So I Expedition myself through the bucolic splendor of Jefferson to Goose Hill Road and over some lovely sweeping ridges to a hilltop meadow with a gravel road climbing through two aisles of towering oaks to a squarish white saltbox and a rambling white barn. Over the front door an oval plaque said *1767*. Damn, I thought, I can barely remember back then.

"Come in!" he yelled before I knocked.

Burrowed in a rocker by the fireplace, a tattered afghan on his lap, he gave me a beady tobacco-toothed grin. He was ancient and wrinkled, freckle-pated and thin as a rail. A tall coffee cup and a jug of blackberry brandy sat on a table beside him. He offered me a bony hand and pointed at the kitchen. "There's coffee on the stove, cups on the shelf and," he eyed the brandy, "we'll sweeten it up a bit. Unless, of course, you're not a drinking man."

"I usually drink gin but that brandy looks fine."

"I like sin too but brandy's better."

"No," I said louder, "I'm happy with gin."

"Special Forces guys like you, should be able to drink women under the table."

"That's not what I said –"

"But not Bucky as I remember. Said it steals your edge."

"Yeah, Bucky doesn't drink."

"Not lucky?" Silas snorted. "Maybe you're right –"

In the kitchen a pitted blue enamel coffee pot sat on an ancient black woodstove with ornate chrome trim. The stove's front door said *Art Eureka*.

This ain't gonna be easy, I told myself.

"I like your stove," I said, coming back with coffee.

He cocked his head. "*Who* drove?"

"The cookstove. The Art Eureka."

"Why didn't you say so? Made in Boston, 1845. Brought

up here by horse and wagon." Silas poured lots of brandy into my coffee. "Makes the best corn bread in the world."

The coffee was the kind that eats metal off a spoon. I understood the reason for the blackberry brandy. "My father," he said, "was born on that stove."

"*Born* on it?"

"Right out there in that kitchen. January 12, 1889, so cold they couldn't keep the house warm even with three fires. So when his mother – my grandmother – was in labor, they laid her on her straw and feather mattress on that stove, to keep her warm."

"That's amazing."

"Lazy? I think not. We worked night and day."

"That's not what I said –"

"You hard of hearing, son?" Silas fumbled in the afghan and tugged out an old tin oil funnel, the kind you use to pour oil into your engine. "Hold this to your ear – you'll hear better."

So I sat with the galvanized oil spout against my ear, lending it to him on occasion till we finally shared it back and forth, and each understood the other better. "Bucky's having trouble finding a lawyer," I said. "Nobody wants to represent a guy who supposedly shot some environmentalist."

"I don't care what the doctors say. This potion here," he raised his cup, "I been drinking it every day for fifty years. Keeps me going. Used to help me get it up too, but we're past those days now."

"That's a shame," I said consolingly, wanting to get back on track. "Do you know if anybody in the family could help pay Bucky's legal costs?"

"You young guys, don't realize how lucky you are."

I thought about that. Any time you're not in jail or dead or wounded you're lucky. "I do."

"You just seen Bucky?"

"Yesterday."

"How is he?"

"Down. It would help if…"

"He don't think he's getting out." Silas shook his head, an exasperated look.

"He may not."

"Bucky's like a steel spring, never relaxes. Even as a kid he was always watching out. Didn't have a bad childhood, worked the farm nights, weekends and summers, we all did. No sir, no watching television for *us*."

"Bucky was that way in our outfit. Which was a good thing. Saved some lives a few times. Including mine."

"He said you were right to shoot that girl but he wouldn't have." Silas adjusted the afghan. "Said it took guts."

I was going to say *anybody would've done it* but that wasn't true.

"He also said you're a pain in the ass."

"So's he."

"He's a pain in the ass to everybody. Keeps us all at a distance, won't spend time with people –"

"That's just PTSD."

Silas glowered at me. "I fought the Germans from Normandy till we met the Soviets on the Elbe. Never got none of that damn PST. Got so many bullet holes in my jacket and so many friends killed… had so many grenades go off in my ears… You young guys ever hear of the *febelwerfer*? Goddamn thing'll kill a whole division – you know how many of them went off around me?"

"I don't wish that on anyone. I hate war."

"So what did you do with those Talibans? Kiss their asses?"

"No. We didn't do that."

There was no point to tell him I'd killed more than I

wanted. That I had hated Afghanistan till I realized how we had loaded all this misery on them years ago. When we attacked them after 9/11 we said it was because a few Muslim terrorists who lived there had destroyed our towers, but hadn't we been the ones who installed those terrorists there?

And hadn't we been using Afghanistan as a geopolitical tool and military pawn for decades? Hadn't we even started their Nine-Year War with the Soviets? Which destroyed much of their country and killed a million Afghanis, mostly civilians? Then used them like cannon fodder? Hadn't we even given them Osama bin Laden to poison their souls?

Like I mentioned in that other book, the trouble with defending freedom is it ain't always what you think. "So," I says, "Bucky came to see you the night Ronnie Dalt was killed –"

Silas waved his hand. "We'll get to it." He picked at the moth-chewed afghan. "Life passes so fast it could've happened in one night. And when you get old and look back, most of it didn't seem to happen at all."

"You mean like with Bucky?" I was still trying to keep him on track.

He gave me a watery glare. "I worked most of my life as a precision lens maker in New York City. More than forty years." He shook his head in wonderment. "And I don't remember any of it. The only damn times I remember is that war, and before then two years riding the rails – it was the Depression, all the tramps' camps, looking for work all over America."

"So why were those times different?"

"Because I lived every moment. Nothing was familiar. Except fear. Or hunger."

"Yeah," I said. "Except fear."

"But how amazing to be young," he added, off on another side trip. "To look at me now you'd never believe I could run faster than the wind, climb trees and swim across Casco Bay and dance under a foot-high bar – of course the dances back then were all about sex – you were showing the girl what you and she were going to do later…"

"You were talking about the night Bucky was here – last December twenty-ninth."

"Yes, yes. We'll get there." He held up the brandy bottle, glanced into his empty cup. "Young man, you wouldn't get me some more ice, would you?" He held up three fingers. "Just three cubes."

When I came back with the ice he'd tucked that afghan over his knees and half-filled the cup with brandy. I dropped in the three cubes.

"Now," he took a long drink. "Bucky never came here that night. Though I was supposed to say he did."

Oh shit. "Why?"

"He went to see his girlfriend."

Double

BUCKY WAS TOO STRAIGHT to have a girlfriend. "Who is she?" I said to Silas, nonchalantly as I could. He leaned forward, rheumy eyes on mine. "Damned if I know."

"Will she testify?"

"That he was with her that night? Seems not."

"How can she let Bucky do life when she knows he's innocent?"

He chewed an ice cube. "They both get blamed for it?"

This was the loony bin. The whole deal was loony. I stood. "Who *is* she?"

"I'll ask, maybe she'll talk to you."

"Silas!" I almost screamed. "Why didn't you *say* this to the cops? If you *knew* he was with her why didn't you just fucking *say* he was with you?"

He shook his head, clacked his teeth. "Hand of God."

I waited. "The hand of God?"

He nodded as if I'd said something profound. Finally I said, "What's that mean?"

He'd wandered off somewhere, came back. "Comes down, strikes you. When you lie."

"But it's *not* a lie! Not if you *know* he was with her!"

He smiled at me fatuously, as if I'd fallen into a trap. "Just because he *said* it, doesn't mean it was *true*."

I wanted to pick up his chair and dump him outside in the snow, get rid of that sappy grin. "I'm going to the cops."

He looked surprised. "You, a two-time jailbird? Who'd believe *you?*"

"I'm saying you lied."

"I have so much trouble remembering things. Don't forget, I'm ninety-seven…"

He had me there. By now the cops would pay scarce attention to anything he said. But they might get very interested in me. More than I wanted.

It was time to see Bucky again. Lucky for him there'd be a half inch of bulletproof glass between us. Otherwise I'd kill him.

DRIVING BACK TO LEXIE'S got me distracted by the beauty of Maine. Hill upon hill of serrated conifers rising toward far blue ridges and raw granite peaks. Some of the world's loveliest mountains cloaked in forests a thousand shades of winter. Wide blue rivers, flashing streams, clear lakes – the greatest outdoor paradise left in eastern America.

So why did these Wind Mafia guys want to destroy this?

Like Pa says, the people who never have enough money are the poor and the very rich.

It isn't just "guys" who want to destroy it. Take a look at an industrial wind company and often their lawyers are women who will do anything for money, or they have brainless cuties to spout at public meetings about how environmental they are. It's unlikely any of those women ever had a good lay in her life. Or she couldn't be like this. Good sex gives you a deep connection to the world, makes you love beauty. If you had that you couldn't build industrial wind projects.

Speaking of good sex, it was sorely missing from my life. I couldn't have Lexie, and there was no one else. Yet to hold a lovely woman in your arms, to get to know and feel her body and who she is, to give her excitement and pleasure and have hers in return is a wonderful gift. One we could give each other much more often, in my view.

But jail will do that to you – all those days in that little cell and there's never a way afterwards to get enough good sex to make up for the months or years you've lost.

6 WEEKS AFTER THE BULLET hit my helmet in Afghanistan I was back with my unit checking a village in the Kush when hideous screams, a sound of crackling flames and the nauseous smell of burning flesh burst from a side alley. We raced toward the sound, watching for trip wires and ambushes and other nasty shit.

It was a girl about fifteen on fire and terribly burned, her face and half her torso carbonized, while a group of men clustered around her, one holding a gasoline can. "I'm sorry," she begged, "Father please please kill me now please oh God please kill me!"

"What happened?" I yelled at the men in my lousy Pashto. They turned toward me angrily, the woman howling and writhing.

"She looked at a man," a white-bearded guy said. "A man not her husband."

"She *what?*"

"In the market. Raised her eyes to him. A woman's eyes trap men in Hell, the *Koran* says… It is our family's honor –"

Her eyes were gone but maybe she heard my voice, this foreign soldier's voice. "Please kill me," she screamed, voice raucous with pain and fire, "Oh God please kill me!"

One of my buddies grabs my shoulder, 'C'mon, man, let's go, this shit happens all the time here –"

"It is a just punishment," a young Afghani in a dirty headscarf says. "God's will."

"Who did it?" I yelled at the old man.

"That is her husband," nodded at the younger man. "It was his duty."

She was dying. In the most horrible pain. There was no way to save her. I shot her in the head. Her body quivered once, stretched out and lay still.

"Infidel criminal," the younger man screamed. "She needed to suffer!"

I shot him too, full of hatred for them all, for this vicious evil culture, this maniac religion.

And that was the start of all my troubles. Perhaps I should not have shot her. She was dying, I just tried to lessen her pain. For the men to burn her was an honor killing, common in Muslim countries, where a girl can be beaten to death or stoned or burned with fire or acid by her father and brothers just for showing her face.

The Army didn't see it that way. I was shipped back to the States and after a couple of months in Colorado's Fort Carson lockup I got a brief trial and a twenty-year sentence in Leavenworth Army Prison. A civilian massacre, the Army said. Bad for our image.

And Bucky testified at my trial that I should not have shot her because my killing her and her husband intensified hostility against American troops. Maybe so, but everybody there hated us already, and what would you have done?

Lexie came to my trial and that's where Bucky decided he wanted her.

And I'd still be in Leavenworth Army Prison but for the West Point grad and lawyer who went to bat for me and got me out five months later. Just long enough *Inside* to learn what a horrible Hell prison can be. I beg you if you've never been *Inside* don't go there. And if you have, *please* don't go there again.

It's better to be play by the rules, no matter how crooked they are.

Which I usually did, to begin with. It's just that events crept up on me.

THERE WAS STILL GIN in the Tanqueray handle so Lexie and I went through that as well as some home-grown and pretty soon it began to feel like the good old days.

But I couldn't decide if I should tell her about Bucky's girlfriend. "If you had to do this all over," I said, "what then?"

She looked at me speculatively. "You son of a bitch –"

"I'd like to know."

"If I knew you were getting out, all that?"

I shook my head. "Not all that –"

"I'd have waited." A caustic grin. "But not twenty years for a guy I'd known five weeks."

"Like I kept telling you."

She gave me a kind smile, squeezed my hand. "I remember."

"And now we can't. Be together."

She looked at the white empty wall, back to me. "That's up to us."

I poured us more Tanqueray, forgetting the vermouth. "Suppose Bucky's ever had another woman?"

Her eyes widened. "Since he was with me? Never."

I downed my glass. "How you know?"

"*What?*" her voice rose, "you're saying he was *fucking* somebody?"

I shook my head, retreating fast. "Just wondering."

She seemed pissed for a moment then forgot about it. "I'm going up the mountain tomorrow," I said. "See if I can figure where that .308 went."

We fried some home-grown burgers and sliced home-grown potatoes and onions, and she steamed some peas she and Bucky had picked and frozen last August. I felt bad for him being in the slammer and I here with his wife. But I wasn't going to cross the line, and I was only here because of him.

I should explain you that before my final tour in Afghanistan I had spent two months back in Hawaii, surfing all day and hitting bars at night. Wonderful times with beautiful women, sometimes the same one, sometimes two – I was filling myself up with life so when I returned to those deadly mountains I had fewer regrets.

Because I expected to die in the Hindu Kush. You would've too, in my place.

Then I met Lexie with her long cashmere blonde hair and sinuous dancer's body that never quit all night, how she inhaled life at speeds that would kill ten normal people, with her razor tongue and even sharper brain. The lovely way she could skewer you with one sentence. And all the way down inside her bones a deep kindness. A love of people. A love of truth. Of life.

Lexie emanated sex the way a rose does perfume. As the sun does heat. And the sexiest part was she didn't even know it.

So it was intense sex at first sight. But we soon fell in love.

She was doing a masters in vertebrate biology at U of H and working nights as a pole dancer in a Honolulu strip club called Tropical Palms. So all day she was in classes or labs or studying and most nights working till two am. I would wait for her, nursing martinis at Tropical Palms, till hand in hand we walked the seven blocks back to her place through the cool misty Honolulu night.

Suddenly I had only twenty-one days left. We watched each day tick off as if awaiting our mutual execution.

Numbed by the hope it would never come. That we could lose ourselves forever in this loving sexual bliss, this endless intense investigation of each other's feelings, minds and bodies.

When I left for Afghanistan we agreed no ties, just the warm memories of being together and the promise to meet when, and if, I got back. When they arrested me for shooting that girl who'd been burnt alive and I got sent for trial to Fort Carson, Colorado, Lexie came from Honolulu often as she could – an expensive ten-hour trip. And that's when she met Bucky, who had to testify too. And when I got twenty years in Leavenworth Military Prison the last thing I told her in my state of benumbed despair was forget about me, I'll never get out.

So when that wonderful West Point grad and lawyer did get me out five months later I never called Lexie. Because by then she was with Bucky.

Now she was sitting across the patchwork vinyl tablecloth, her fierce green eyes digging into mine. "Things happen like they're 'sposed to."

"Yeah. Right."

She bit her lip, hard. "I tell myself that."

"You know it's a lie."

She poured the last Tanqueray into our glasses and sat astride my lap. As perfect there as always, her slim thighs wrapping mine, her silky hair in my face, her mouth so perfect in the corner of my neck.

To kiss her had always been a joy, a melting into each other, lips to lips, tongue to tongue, the hot sucking sharing taking exploring and caring all wrapped in lustful exciting reaching deep inside each other – to kiss her now was bliss, not only recapturing our every past erotic instant but also devouring her anew, a stranger, another new lover on the star-crossed path of life.

I could no more have stopped it than to stand below Niagara Falls with one hand raised to halt the water. Soaring happiness filled me – this gorgeous person opening up to me and I to her and no matter what the cost I had to have her and she me, stumbling into the bedroom chilly because the door'd been shut to keep heat in the kitchen, Lexie falling back on the bed as I kneel sliding her clothes and mine away, naked in the glorious hot throb of life.

Her lovely sex so familiar in my hand, her slim body all muscle and fire igniting mine, skin to skin. I pushed away. "No."

"Yeah." She patted my arm, gasping. "But God I want you."

"I want you too. But it ain't happening."

"Yeah," she said again, turned across the bed and sat on the edge, her back to me. "Some day in another life I'm going to fuck you blind."

I ran my hand down the knobs of her spine, her sleek skin. "You already did. Many times. A wonder I can see a damn thing."

She turned back, that devilish laugh in her eyes, a beautiful breast aslant, pink-nippled. "You ain't seen nothing yet."

Getting dressed I felt like a man who has been saved at the last moment from a firing squad. Only to be placed in front of another. If we'd made love, Lexie and me, even though it would've been wonderful it would have poisoned the rest of our lives.

Not while Bucky was in prison.

After he got out we'd see.

Though his chances of getting out were nil.

"WHO'S YOUR GIRLFRIEND?" I said in Pashto next morning through the mike in the wall of bulletproof glass.

Bucky gave me an angry glance. "I don't have one," he said in English. "Or you mean Lexie? You already fucking my wife?"

"Your girlfriend?" I said again in Pashto.

He looked down. "It ain't like it seems."

"It never is." I glanced at the mike. Our every word was recorded and listened to. It would take them a while to sort out the Pashto. But in English there was nothing I could ask, nothing he could say.

"You remember Tora Bora?" Bucky said in English.

"Like it was this morning." *Fourteen years ago.*

"We ought to talk more, about Afghanistan. In memory of the guys who died."

"I remember. Every day."

"You should write that book about Bush, how he let Bin Laden get away at Tora Bora –"

"Somebody should write it."

"Remember that source we had in Waziristan? He'd tell us what their plans were, and try to steer their strategy to what we wanted?"

"So we could hit them."

"Karim."

"We thought he was a double."

"You should put it in your book, how one of their guys got killed and they blamed it on Karim and burned him alive?"

"We were told not to go in on that."

"Because he wasn't ours."

"So?"

"So this time, that guy is me."

LEXIE AND I took my Expedition back to Portland, rode home in her ancient Volvo, and she gave me the key to Bucky's '86 Ford 150 pickup that hadn't been driven since he ended up *Inside.*

I went out to the barn to look at it. The wind was howling through the slats and snow had blown in and covered it. A lot of mud had hardened on it, and it had plenty of corrosion from Maine's salted winter roads. Part of the floorboards had rusted out, the tires were a little bald, and the heater didn't work.

But it was a glorious truck. In the entire human history of trucks the Ford 150 four-wheel drive three-quarter ton may be the greatest. It is so perfectly engineered that after many years of loving them I can think of few improvements. The engine is easy to work on, the ride hard but secure, and the bodies will take all manner of abuse from a ton of rocks to cattle to logs and even a mattress with two teenagers on a starry summer night.

Second place in the pickup hall of fame would have to be the '49 Chevy half-ton, but that's another story.

When we got back to Lexie's it was 13:21. Time to go up the mountain and search the area where Bucky'd hid the .308.

USING THE TRAIL Lexie and I had broken the day before, I reached the top in barely an hour, crossed the dead industrial zone and headed down the north side to the overhung cliff where Bucky had hid the .308 after he'd shot the three turbines.

Someone had been there since Lexie and me yesterday. Brand new tracks, no crumple in the side walls, no snowshoes, boots a little smaller than mine, size 10 maybe, with a little imprint on the sole that said *Irish Setter Work*.

He had come across the slope to where Bucky's .308 had been hidden then returned, stepping in his own tracks.

A hunter, maybe, for at one place he'd knelt and rested a rifle butt down in the snow, leaving a little imprint that said *BROWNING*.

But deer season had ended late November, and anyway Lexie'd said no one hunted here any more, the animals had all been chased away by the turbines.

The sun had slid behind dark clouds, the woods shadowed and deep. A mean wind sifted down from the slopes above knocking ice crystals off the frozen boughs. Tree trunks were cracking with cold. His tracks left mine so I followed his up the mountain through steep conifers and beech where I had to dig my snowshoe edges into the crust to keep from skidding downhill.

Fifty feet below me the slope dropped over a granite cliff. Here if my snowshoes slipped I'd skid downhill fast and the only way to stop going over the cliff was grab a tree. But they were icy and far apart and by the time I'd slid that far I'd be going too fast.

The wind in my face was razor cold – just its touch caused pain. I reminded myself why I was here, rubbed my stinging cheeks and pushed on.

That's when the bastard took those shots at me.

Two for One

A FTER THE FIRST SHOT and I'd skidded down the ice slope and over the cliff while more shots hit all around me, and I'd slid and scrambled another half mile down the mountain, found an oak limb and circled back on my trail to wait in hemlock scrub, I sat holding my oak limb in my good hand and cradling my dislocated finger atop my frozen, bloody foot and pretending the pain was happening to someone else.

Once an owl called, faraway. There was a distant hum of traffic on 220, the slow settling of forest into arctic night.

Since the snowmobile had left there'd been no sound of my shooter. But I couldn't risk that the snowmobile had been someone else and that my shooter was still waiting.

Chickadees chattered briefly as they roosted in the hemlock over my head. The boughs creaked with their burden of ice. Wind swept away the broken snow from my back tracks, leaving a darker trench.

Hypothermia makes you forget how cold you are, makes you feel warm and relaxed, almost welcoming it. When this began to sink into my consciousness I knew I had to move.

I traversed sideways up the ridge away from where the shooter had been, then back to find my missing boot and snowshoes, and circled the blasted ridgetop down to Lexie's where Lobo gave me a joyous welcome and Lexie threw me in a hot bath and plied me with whisky. "I should take off my clothes and jump in with you," she said longingly. "Sex is the *best* treatment for hypothermia…"

After five whiskies I diligently took my dislocated finger in my other hand, gave it a hard jerk and passed out from the pain.

Lexie pulled my head out of the water. "Idiot!"

"That's what I've always loved most about you," I coughed, "your empathy." My finger was unfortunately still sideways.

Footsteps clattered up the stairs. A tall rangy woman in a blue parka. She scowls down at me naked in the tub and shakes her head. "No wonder I'm a lesbian."

I was very high from the five whiskies and Lexie's home-grown and from the joy of having survived attempted murder, but there was no way I could interpret this as a compliment. "So who the fuck are you?" I says, friendly as I can.

"This is Jane," Lexie says. "She's a neighbor. And the county midwife."

"I don't think I'm pregnant," I says, looking down to make sure.

Jane inspected my dislocated finger. "Nice."

"Can you fix it?"

"You have to twist it as you pull," she said to Lexie as if I weren't there. And gave it a great yank and turn half pulling me out of the tub.

This was not pleasant but it worked. My finger settled back into its joint, and the lessening of pain was blissfully religious. Jane departed to bring another human into the world – God knows why – and after more whiskies and hamburgers in front of the cook stove I began to warm up, that lovely feeling of survival, being with Lexie, re-gifted the joy of life.

It took only a couple minutes online to identify the "Irish Setter Work" boot print. It was a Red Wing, a very good American-made work boot that lots of people wear.

"I think you're crazy," Lexie said, "not going to the cops."

"Don't want them knowing I'm here."

Now that I was safe my fear had turned to anger. Having been shot at many times I'd been acting as if it was normal. But *this isn't Afghanistan,* I reminded myself. *This isn't Iraq.* No one allegedly has the right to shoot you here.

If the coyote hadn't called and I hadn't stopped to listen I'd be dead now. I couldn't imagine *dead now.* Mysterious and horrendous.

The more I thought the angrier I got.

It was time to call Mitchell.

MITCHELL CAN SOLVE any IT problem, tap into anybody's life as deep as he wants. He can use your phone while you have it and take pictures with it, can record all your conversations and tell where you were at any instant and what you were doing.

If your computer's hooked to the internet he can wander around inside it and copy, destroy or alter anything he wants. Even if it isn't hooked to the internet he can climb inside it using external radio waves, and hang out there, invisible. He's "an independent data researcher", engaged by DOD to patrol the borders of our virtual world, hunting interlopers, hackers, leaks and Muslim terrorists.

The same way he and I once hunted al Qaeda in the nasty mountains of Afghanistan and Islamic *jihadi* in the gritty deathtraps of Falluja. And as I've said elsewhere he'd give anything to be like me, and I'd give anything not to be like him. Because in the northern Afghanistan hills he took the RPG meant for me, and on Oahu three years later I took the heavy time meant for him.

But that's another story.

"HOW'S THE SURF?" Mitchell says, answering as always on the second ring.

"Fantastic. I'm out every day."

Having grown up in South Dakota, Mitchell hates snow. If he hadn't lost his legs in Afghanistan he'd be like me back home, surfing all day and rocking all night. Except he would've stayed in SF, and I never had the chance. But now I was in Maine in January, when the surfing's lousy unless you're dressed like a wet polar bear.

I explained him about this guy in Red Wings shooting at me.

"You fuckhead," Mitchell says encouragingly. "You shoulda seen that coming."

"What I can't figure is how did he know I'd be there? Or was it just chance? But why shoot at *me?*"

"You're digging yourself into deep shit again, Pono –"

"So what *you* recommend? That I head back to Hawaii and leave Bucky in this shit?" I didn't add, *and Lexie too?* "So the wind companies planning to wreck Maine with thousands more turbines will win, and soon Maine will look like New Jersey? Actually," I calmed down, "I'd love to go back to Hawaii and surf, but it's not about to happen."

"Course not," Mitchell said.

"So what you suggest?"

"I'll see what satpix I can find for those coordinates, if there's any real time the last twenty-four hours, if I can identify anything. Depends if we have a fix on that area – even if we do the res won't be good."

"I *need* to find this guy."

"Look, Pono –" Mitchell's voice took on a strained tone, like when you're trying to reason with a determined idiot – "you can't kill him."

I reflected on this. "Not yet. Not till it's clean."

"Pono, you got to start *thinking,* not reacting."

I took this in. "Yeah," I sighed, slowing down. "You're right."

"So what else is going on?"

"Bucky needs a lawyer. But I can't find anyone to defend a guy who shoots out turbines and supposedly killed some environmentalist – Maine's full of what the locals call knee-jerk greenies –"

"What's that?" Mitchell says, a little suspiciously.

"People who support industrial wind power without understanding anything about how useless and destructive it is, who want to be green but want the towers on other people's mountains. Like Connecticut, that has outlawed wind turbines there but is putting up thousands in Maine. Or the Dems in southern Maine, who love wind power as long as it's in northern Maine, ruining other people's lives not theirs."

"So Bucky won't get a fair trial?"

"The whole thing's rigged. Whoever killed Ronnie Dalt did it for two reasons: one, to tag Bucky with it and jail him before he causes more trouble, and two," I was thinking it out as I spoke, "they must've wanted to get rid of Ronnie too."

"If he was still useful to them they'd have kept him around."

"So the people who killed him got two for one."

"And who would those people be?"

"The list has to start with the wind companies, particularly WindPower LLC –"

"Same old same old," Mitchell said. "What else you want?"

"Can you get contribution records?" I said.

"Who?"

"Let's start with Senator Artie Lemon. After he was governor he helped write the Expedited Wind Law, and then made millions developing wind projects. He then used some of the proceeds to buy himself a US Senate seat where he's now pushing taxpayer welfare for industrial wind."

"So he made millions on his own wind project and now getting more money from other wind companies to push the same agenda? So he's getting two for one too."

"Be good to know how much he gets, and how much of it's under the table."

"Under the table's hard to find."

"And Maude Muldower, the US Congresswoman whose husband is financially connected to the wind industry and who owns most Maine newspapers."

"Let me guess: those papers are pro-wind? Who else?"

"And Maine Audubon, nearly half their major contributors are wind industry. Doesn't matter that wind turbines slaughter birds. And other enviro groups with big money from the wind industry. To say nothing of public radio, with their wind commercials in return for tons of money from WindPower LLC –"

Mitchell chuckled. "We nailed those WindPower guys so bad, last time."

"Yeah, and I'm the one who almost got killed."

"Only because I'm in a fucking wheelchair and you're not."

That made me feel guilty. "And I'd be dead how many times without you?"

He chuckled again. "I'm still not going to marry you."

"That's a gross thought. To wake up every morning looking at you."

"You should be so lucky. But if you ever do get married, Pono, though I wouldn't wish that on any girl, your IQ's gonna go way up. And hers'll go way down."

This was insulting so I ignored it. "So I'm trying to figure who wanted Ronnie Dalt dead and Bucky blamed. And how we might track it."

"Tracking it's easy." Mitchell's words made me think of tracking the guy who'd just shot at me. "It's proving that's hard."

"That's what I'm afraid of."

"It would be poetic justice," Mitchell said, "if Bucky ended up *Inside* after helping send you there."

"That's the trouble with doing your duty. Instead of what you know is right."

"Whatever *you* do," Mitchell says, "stay off that mountain."

Nirvana

TWO HOURS BEFORE DAWN I put on Bucky's smelly damp boots, took a .243 Winchester and a white camo jacket from his closet and a couple of plastic sandwich bags from the kitchen and headed up the mountain. It was minus 27 according to the thermometer outside the kitchen window but felt a lot colder.

I didn't want to be here but had no choice. My shooter would be back at daylight, looking for a blood trail on the snow or hoping I'd return.

But by the time he arrived I'd be waiting for him.

Yesterday's cuts and bruises hurt with every step. My right toes were still numb, not a great sign. I had to keep the .243 in my right hand because the splinted finger of the left hurt too much to use. But having had a night to dwell on being shot at, I was pumped.

At the top I stood catching my breath in a spruce thicket watching the snowy denuded ridge as the red strobes of the towers flashed luridly across it. The turbines were silent, unmoving, though there was plenty of wind. *Curtailment,* I remembered it's called.

But I was glad they were silent, because to hunt somebody in all that racket would be doubly dangerous. Not that I knew what I'd do if I found him. Even though he'd tried to kill me, it was technically against the law for me to kill him. So what was I going to do – arrest him at gunpoint?

And hope maybe the cops would listen, this time?

No, I'd decided, find out who he is. And who's paying him to kill me.

Just before dawn is always the coldest, and the wind down the ridge was bitter. The underbellies of the low dark clouds flashed rosily from the turbine strobes, like over a volcano. Through underbrush and granite outcrops I headed toward where I'd heard the snowmobile leave, and soon found the dark cut of its track across the snow. I listened for an engine but heard only wind through boughs and branches and across the snow.

I still couldn't figure how he knew yesterday I'd be coming up the mountain. Was it just chance, or had he been waiting for me? Why?

He'd parked his snowmobile at an overhang and from there hiked straight east across the gully toward where Bucky had hidden the .308. It was clear he wasn't trying to find it; he knew where it was.

Where the .308 had been hidden, my snowshoe tracks lay atop his Red Wing boot prints. So he hadn't been back.

I returned to where he'd parked the snowmobile. Another set of his tracks went to the cliff edge where he'd gone down on his left knee, no doubt to fire at me. Beside the imprint of his knee was that of a rifle butt pad with the same *BROWNING* logo.

It was getting light enough to see, a kind of quasi-daylight as if undersea, the trees black, the snow changing from gray then pink as the strobes flashed across it, the last stars dying in a web of branches. A moment of peace and silence, breathing in and out the frigid air, watching daylight seep into the forest, hearing the first chatter of distant crows, the wind sighing over the snow and through the fir and pine branches and the twittering of chickadees as they flitted in little tribes from tree to tree.

Still listening for a snowmobile I knelt and began feeling in the snow for cartridge casings. When ejected they'd have been hot and sunk through the crust. Any good sniper will pick up his empties but in this deep snow it would have been hard to find them all.

By luck I put my hand right on one. Long, slim and brass, Fiocchi .270, an unusual brand for this neck of the woods. But a perfect match for a Browning bolt action. Not removing my gloves I dropped it into a plastic bag and zipped it into my pocket.

06:50. Sunrise. I moved upslope forty yards and made myself comfortable inside a hemlock thicket. After 07:25 the sun cleared the mountains to the east and the temp went up to maybe minus ten but the wind stayed sharp.

When by noon he hadn't come I took several phone pix of his snowmobile tracks then followed them along the ridge till they crossed the devastated top and took a snowmobile trail downhill past a white farmhouse and three barns and a frozen brook under tall oaks and from there into the trees. There was no need to go down; instead I returned to where a bullet had hit a tree root and dug out what was left of it with my KA-BAR.

It chilled my gut.

A ballistic tip, one of the most evil of bullets that do the most horrible damage to whatever or whomever they hit. A hollow point filled with a hard plastic tip. When it hits the target the plastic drives back into the hollow point and literally explodes it. So you get both the high accuracy of a jacketed bullet and the fragmentation lethality of a hollow point.

I can't imagine what it must feel like to be hit by one.

Uphill I found another slug waist-high in an ash trunk and dug that out too. They easily matched the .270 Fiocchi casing I'd just found.

Circling the mountain I arrived back at Lexie's two hours later, exhausted. I hadn't learned much about my would-be killer, except that he was a very good shot, used a bolt action Browning .270 with Fiocchi bullets, and wore size 10 Red Wing Irish Setter Work boots.

And he didn't know I knew.

Now I needed to find his machine. And him.

"THAT'S JANE'S PLACE," Lexie said when I asked who lived in the white house and barns by the oak trees and brook.

"The one who fixed my finger."

"That's Jane. Half the kids around here she's brought into the world. Her driveway's two roads down, under the fourth to ninth turbines."

"Lucky her."

"She's done health studies on what windmills do to people, particularly kids. The ADD, sleeplessness, mood swings and other stuff I see in my students, but the damage to adults too…"

"I need to know if she saw who snowmobiled down that trail past her house yesterday."

"You should go see her. Just don't try to grab her ass, she'll break your jaw."

I fondled mine uncomfortably. It had already been broken several times – all painfully – and I had no desire that it happen again. "I like women too…" I was going to add how I'm particularly fond of gay women because we share the same interests, but Lexie was getting a little steamed.

"Pono," she snaps, "how can you expect me to *ever* get back together with *you* when you keep wanting to screw other women?"

"We ain't getting back together," I answered. *"Remember?"* And to add insult to injury added, "even when we *were* together we were *both* still screwing other people."

She gave me a look halfway between love and hate. "Go see Jane."

JANE'S was one of those stately white clapboard farmhouses you see on Maine Vacationland postcards, under centuries-old oaks, with three vast barns clustered behind it and a wide stream along one side, all nestled against a beautiful rocky slope of beeches and pines. And atop the ridge – outside the Vacationland postcard of course – were WindPower LLC's fifty-five-story corporate welfare towers.

No wind was blowing but the turbines were howling away. Maybe there's wind on the ridge, I wondered. But when I checked the few trees remaining near the top not a bough was budging. Figuring why was far beyond my physics IQ so I let it go.

"I have *no* idea who came down that ridge yesterday," Jane said. " I was delivering twins in Albion all afternoon and night."

She was tall, back straight, an aggressive jaw and strong pretty face, short-cut dark hair like a medieval helmet down her cheeks. A strong grip, slender strong wrists, small nice biceps, small perfect breasts and a runner's beautiful ass.

She led me through an ancient paneled parlor with floorboards foot-and-a-half wide – old Maine pumpkin pine from back when the trees were forty-five feet around and a whole village could stand on one stump. We sat in wooden rockers by the fireplace drinking some kind of strange green tea while I explained her what had happened.

She had a bright sunny smile and wide white teeth, freckled dimpled cheeks and gorgeous blue eyes that you could look into all day and keep seeing more and more.

Everything about her seemed lanky and alert, powerfully together. The instant you met her you sensed she didn't lie or bullshit, would be exactly who she was.

"It wouldn't be surprising if somebody shot at you," she said. "The wind industry's getting pretty desperate, all these towns passing ordinances against it, the lawsuits, even some of the enviros turning on it –"

"Biting the hand that feeds them?"

"Did you hear the latest?" She took the *Bangor Daily News* down from the mantle. "The Maine Center for Public Interest Reporting just revealed that former state Senate President Justin Alfond, a Democrat from Portland, has been introducing bills in the Senate written entirely by wind industry lawyers, and has worked with the industry to intimidate Senators who opposed them. This was after, the Center said, the wind industry gave lots of money to his Political Action Committees, some of which he paid to other Democrats so they'd vote for him as Senate president."

"This boy will get ahead."

"Thank God Governor LePage vetoed it."

"This guy LePage, Lexie tells me, is a conservative Republican but very protective of Maine's environment, while these Democrats seem intent on destroying it."

She shrugged. "This story wasn't even printed in the southern Maine papers owned by one of those Democrats."

"Maybe freedom of speech means the media owners get to say what *they* want."

"This house which is two hundred twenty-one years old, in which eleven generations of my people have lived, and which is on the National Historic Register, is now worthless." She got up and put two more oak splits in the fire. "And it was worth almost a million five years ago. And now because of the Wind Law I can't even sue the windmill bastards."

This seemed impossible. "Why's that?"

"The Law takes away our right to sue. And, as the governor said, it actually legalizes bribery."

"Those turbines up there," I nodded above our heads. "There's no wind but they're turning?"

She scowls. "You don't *know?*"

"If I did would I be asking?"

"Maine has very poor winds. But the damn things have to keep spinning or they seize up."

So why build them here, I started to ask but caught myself: *Follow the money.* "But they were turning."

She looks at me like a teacher at a student so dumb she fears she'll have him back next year. "You know what the three largest electricity consumers are in Maine?"

That got me thinking, rare as that is. "The Millinocket pulp mill – biggest on the east coast, or one of Maine's huge log mills, or the Bath Iron Works?" The latter was a sure thing, one of the world's major shipyards.

What she said next blew my mind. "Three different wind *farms,*" snickering at the last word. "They have to keep them turning when there's no wind so they don't freeze or corrode inside. And so people think they're working. It's an enormous net loss in electricity."

I sat trying to understand, gave up. "Got any gin?"

"I don't drink that crap. But I've got some monster weed."

Her white wide teeth in her wide succulent mouth were giving me trouble down below. "Well if I *have* to I'll take that."

She had a big jar of it up on the shelf with the basil, oregano, sage and other good things. Just the smell when she opened the jar near knocked me out and I kept wanting to take her in my arms but remembered about getting a broken jaw and all that.

Amazing how weed can weld you together, get you seeing inside each other's heads so there's no way or need to lie or in any way misstate because you're so *connected*. In Afghanistan I remember once a few of us smoking hash before standing at attention in front of some Tampa scrambled eggs, or a Senator buying votes with a forty-five minute trip to the safest base we could find. And I could see right into their minds like reading a bad novel.

"So you can't sell the place?" I repeat after a while.

"Wind Power LLC bought a few neighbors off at ten grand apiece. Now they can't sell their places either."

"Serves them right."

"No, some of them were really suffering. Like Don and Vivian Woodridge, she's ill and he was injured in a logging accident so they had to take the bribes. And now the turbine sound's driving them crazy and they're leaving next week."

"Would you have taken the money?"

"From the Wind Mafia? Hell no." She kills the roach, stretches out her long legs. "So why are you *here?* And not Hawaii?"

Useless to explain her why. I try anyway. About Bucky being a former comrade and me wanting to get him out.

"Bucky's an asshole," she says companionably.

"He's your neighbor. Plus he shot out three of those turbines you hate."

Deep in her armchair she smiles at me. "But he didn't get the ones behind me."

I nod, pissed off. "Who knows, maybe *I* will."

As we sometimes do when pissed off we say things we shouldn't. To the wrong people. Or in the wrong places.

Night Recon

AN OFT-BORING TASK you learn in SF is night reconnaissance. They drop you up in the mountains to lock in on somebody and watch what they do all night. A good way to freeze your ass and lose all faith in humanity.

So after dinner I drove an hour to Hallowell to do a night recon of Ronnie Dalt's widow Abigail. It had been almost a month and a half since he was killed, and I was curious to know how she was taking it.

Her White Pages address turned out to be a three-story Italianate Victorian on the steep hill above the magnificent old town of Hallowell. It had magenta gingerbread, tall peaked windows and a widow's walk atop the gabled roof. As I mentioned earlier, Hallowell is where my ancestor Elias Hawkins grew up before he took the boat in 1838 with his new wife to Hawaii, where despite being a missionary he managed to make life better for many thousand souls. If you visit Hallowell you can see the Old Congregational Church where he preached his first sermons, and the roiling River where he swam out to push logs ashore for ten cents each.

Night recon of Abigail was infinitely easier than watching some freezing village in Afghanistan. There you're lying under white camo at 8,300 feet looking at a clump of stone houses huddled in the arctic wind, waiting without hope or expectation till suddenly at 22:18 a black silhouette slips out a back door and starts climbing the mountain, AK in hand.

You're so concerned about his safety out here in this freezing night that you follow him, keeping to the stunted junipers and outcrops so he doesn't see you one of the many times he checks his back trail.

He descends the far side of the mountain and stops, a black spot on the starlit snow, above a large stone house with five vehicles parked beside it. After fifteen minutes of watching, he goes down to the house and slips inside.

After a few minutes I wander downslope and hang out by a window seeing all these armed-to-the-teeth mother-fuckers sitting in council, a map of the Varduj Valley between them, till it becomes clear they're planning a raid.

Impossible to convey the excitement, terror and freezing discomfort of being there, your ears so cold you keep them covered but then can't hear, your fingers numb, your toes too, and all the time the awareness you have to climb four thousand feet in frigid darkness then descend nearly the same then hike all the way back another seven miles to your outpost of smelly bored SF guys and Marines, where the only talk is pussy and football. Plus Master Sergeant Buckford Franklin, who's waiting to chew your ass for being out there alone and following this motherfucker without calling for backup, and for generally screwing with all kinds of regulations.

As I scope out Abigail's house the question does cross my mind how had she and Ronnie afforded this classy Victorian, he on his enviro pay and she doing some job at the Capitol?

I park Bucky's 150 five blocks away, wheels turned toward the curb so if it decides to ignore the parking brake and first gear it can't roll downhill (everything in Hallowell goes straight downhill and then you're in the Kennebec River).

Few years ago, Lexie told me, a huge fuel tanker truck lost his brakes on this same hill going down to Water Street, Hallowell's main road along the Kennebec. So down he goes like a 747 on turbo, faster and faster taking out parked cars left and right then flies across Water Street miraculously not killing anybody and smashes through the front wall of the best left-wing bookstore in Maine, taking out thousands of rare books, first editions, *and* the cash register, and knocks out the back wall of the building so that the now-leaking tank is spraying fuel all over the surviving books while the truck's cab, with its astonished driver, is projected from the brick wall above the River and hangs there perilously.

Even more miraculously, five minutes before the truck's driver had so unwisely decided to descend this street, the manager had closed the bookstore for a staff meeting in an upstairs room, thus they aren't killed but are knocked off their feet by a great crash that shakes the ancient brick building to an inch of its life, and they get to stare with disbelief at the truck cab sticking ludicrously out from the building beneath them.

Only one of many perils of running a left-wing bookstore in Maine.

Anyway, back at Abigail's it's as usual freezing and I'm trying to read Thoreau's *Maine Woods* by a headlamp that my gloved fingers keep freezing to, so cold the paper breaks when you bend it...

> *Only solemn bear-haunted mountains, with their great wooded slopes, were visible where, as man is not, we suppose some other power to be. My imagination personified the slopes themselves, as if by their very length they would waylay you, and compel you to camp again on them before night.*

At 20:42 a rusty maroon Subaru wagon stops in front of her house and a tall slim woman gets out with a lanky long-haired guy who trudges behind her up the walk and proceeds to feel her up while she gets out the keys and opens the door and they stumble through it kissing and fondling and tripping over each other, from which I deduce this might not be a platonic relationship and that she's dealing quite well with her bereavement.

An upstairs light goes on. There was clearly going to be the usual falling on the bed while tearing off each other's clothes, then all that salacious rutting and grunting, but by this time I've seen more than I want so I drive Bucky's 150 back to Lexie's farm. Such a magnificent starlit night till about twenty miles from Eagle Mountain the flashing red strobes blot out every star in the sky.

I don't give a damn, I told myself. In thirty days I'll be in Tahiti under a big curl and all of this will be a bad memory.

IN LEXIE'S BATHROOM there's a black spider in the toilet, running around the edge of the water but can't climb up the bowl.

So I give it a good lookover, like you might a hand grenade, thinking back to a Special Forces field exercise on which bugs not to eat etc., and for sure it was a black widow, no doubt.

But there was a million acres of forest and ridges outside, so all I had to do was lift her out and dump her in the woods and the problem would belong to the next insect she caught.

Then I thought of her fangs in Lexie's thigh and flushed the john.

NEXT MORNING AT 05:47 I'm back at Abigail's keeping a wintry eye on her nascent whereabouts. Which means two and a half frigid hours in Bucky's 150, scraping my breath off the windows while the bitter dawn wind swirls up through the holes in the floor, till last night's beau stumbles out, nearly breaks a leg on the icy steps, navigates toward his Subaru and leaves in a typhoon of smoke.

I was beginning to like this woman. She hadn't bothered to say goodbye, certainly no kiss in a half-parted bathrobe through the open door. She had apparently just fucked his brains out and left him to his fate.

With that in mind I waited. And yes, at 8:41 she was out the door in a gray wool coat, furry indigo scarf and tall black boots. She hustles round the house to the barn which was itself a Victorian masterpiece, from which she backs a white Saab, the iconic Maine car till it went iconically bankrupt. I grind Bucky's truck carefully into first and off we go in gay pursuit.

Up the hill we rattle where my ancestor Elias used to bring the family cow to graze each morning then across his pasture where the freeway now howls its incessant wrath, past a rocky pine-forested ridge that got dynamited to build the Augusta "Maul", and down a back street past a Sherman tank at the American Legion Hall to a parking lot behind the State Capitol – a 1930's Mussolini-ish gray granite block in which the concept of beauty is entirely absent.

Trying to look nonchalant and legislative I follow her into this monstrous edifice but there's cops and a body scanner that she prances through and picks up her keys and iPhone and I head back out to Bucky's 150. Being numb with cold and wanting a few Country Kitchen doughnuts and coffee I drive to the closest café and try to figure what next.

The café windows were steamy and the linoleum table top was cracked. The walls were stained, the chairs worn, the floor aged and discolored. But it was sort of clean, Clapton on the speakers, and the coffee was strong. And there's no way to beat a Country Kitchen doughnut, except in Paris maybe. And like the French who have pastries and coffee for breakfast, if we all converted to donuts and coffee perhaps like the French we would grow thin, live longer, and have a better sex life.

But this wasn't getting me anywhere to helping Bucky. I had a shock wondering maybe I wasn't doing enough to free him. Because if he went down for the long haul then Lexie and I could pick up where we'd left off. It was a cold thought, and I hated myself for it, for even imagining it might be true.

Not the way you treat the asshole who saved your life.

The only way I could be with Lexie was if we got Bucky out, then we'd all be free to do what we chose. It seemed impossible.

Then I actually had an idea.

I FEAR THE LAW but reminded myself I'd done my time and got freed and both cases dismissed. In reality I wasn't a former jailbird at all. But the law doesn't play by reality.

So I didn't want my ID recorded (they'd notice the Hawaii driver's license). Because the first rule of a strategic life is *be invisible* even when you don't need to be. Though something was telling me I needed to be that now.

I drove back to the Capitol wondering how to elude security, wandered the grounds, sat on a bench, feeling camera eyes on me. Tourist-like I ambled back inside and discovered the basement cafeteria was accessible without going through security. It was warm and smelled of lots of good things so I had another coffee, drowsed a bit, and woke when people started coming in, all chatter and high heels, trays slapping down on the counter rails. It was 11:32, the first wave for lunch.

What were the chances Abigail would come in? What was I going to do if she did?

Then she came in.

Scoundrels

SHE WORE tall black boots and a plaid cashmere skirt that ended above her knees, a yellow silk blouse part unbuttoned and thin enough you could see the pale bra beneath it. She had long auburn hair and an insolent sexy walk that looked unintentional, and she moved from her hips like a dancer. She bought a sandwich on dark bread and a coffee and as she walked past I said "Abigail?" and she slowed and glanced down.

"I've met you somewhere," I said, dumbly.

She looked me over. "I don't think so."

"Here, maybe, some political function –"

"Everything here is a political function. But I remember faces…"

I stood. "Pono Hawkins. I can't remember where but know I've met you. You were working for some Senator…"

She took this in. "I can't place your accent."

"Hawaii. You been there?"

She shook her head.

"So we met here," I persevered. "Somewhere?"

"Why are *you* here?"

"Visiting family." I thought of Bucky. "And friends." I gestured at my table. "Can you sit a moment?"

She paused then put down her tray. "I'll be right back."

She got one of those little Half-n-Half cups from the condiments, sat and looked into my eyes. Hers were violet and unblinking. "I don't remember you."

"I'm even getting your last name... Dale? Dalt?"

Her face hardened. "That's not my name anymore."

I took a chance. "What is it now?"

The light in her eyes dimmed, and for an instant she looked lethal. Then her smile was like sun breaking through low clouds. "So if you knew me by that name, it was a while ago." She glanced down at her tray. "I must join my friends." Her hand darted across the table. "Pleased to meet you, Mr.?"

"Most folks call me Pono."

"Pono?"

"Hawaiian for doing the right thing, in accord with goodness in the world."

"My," she lifted her tray, "you must be very busy."

"I'm trying to remember..."

"I don't forget faces. Or voices. I've never seen you before."

What more could I say? That I knew about her dead husband? About *her*? That would ruin everything. But she was leaving, I had to do something. "Please talk to me again? I'll meet you anywhere you like, anytime –"

Her eyes checked the room. "What's this really about?"

"I'm mystified too. That I can't remember where we met. But I know we did."

She turned to go. "Abigail!" I called. She halted, glanced back. I wrote my name and number on a napkin; she took it and walked away.

ROUTE 202 between Augusta and Lewiston is one of those typical Maine high-speed two-lane highways affording glimpses of stunning landscapes between used car lots, rusty junkyards, hick piles, trailer subdivisions, closed restaurants, strip malls, clearcuts, shuttered gas stations, isolated homes and a general economy that has, in every sense, gone south.

Once a thriving textile manufacturing town on the banks of the Androscoggin River, Lewiston like many Maine mill towns has spent the last fifty years sinking further and further into decay as its industry departed for the southern states then for even cheaper and more toxic locations like Bangladesh, China and Honduras. The vast brick textile mills remain, some nearly a quarter mile long and several stories high, beautiful and empty, prey to pyromaniacs and urban renewal.

In the midst of this, among lovely Victorian homes and second-hand stores is the Bates campus, rolling lawns and simple architecture, one of America's best small colleges with an astonishing list of prominent alumni and an unwavering dedication to the humanities. Not that the humanities are much in vogue any more.

Why was I here? To see a Bates journalism professor named Thurston Donnelly, who'd once had a student named Sylvia Gordon. A few months ago I'd gone out to surf early one morning on Oahu and bumped into Sylvia. She was wearing near-transparent red underwear, face down in the waves, very cold and very dead.

I'd nearly lost my life and risked a life prison sentence to find who killed her and why. She'd been an investigative journalist on the track of a big and very crooked wind power story when she died. Even though I'd never known her alive, I'd fallen in love with her beautiful mind, unflagging determination and magnificent humanity.

I was hoping Thurston Donnelly might give me a few clues to what was happening with wind power in Maine. Given that the Wind Mafia folks who'd killed Sylvia in Hawaii were still alive and well in Maine. In fact they were running the Legislature, and I thought maybe Professor Donnelly could explain me why.

Rotund, with a chubby face, merry small eyes and a smile that was pinched yet kindly, he was hardly who I'd expected. As he spoke he tugged often at his full gray beard, and in his voice was a reflective kindness that reminded me of photos of rabbis in Auschwitz caring for their flock when they knew they were all doomed.

"She was one of my favorite students, Sylvia." His voice skipped a beat, the way folks who've had a stroke sometimes do. "She had this most piercing mind, yet she was so kind and unassuming…" He pushed himself up in his armchair. "She had no idea what a remarkable person she was." He looked out the window at the driving snow. "It's sad to speak of her in the past tense… She came from Hawaii, you know?"

"Yeah."

"Of course." Strangely he reached out and patted my hand.

I didn't feel transgressed upon. But it pained my heart to be digging Sylvia out of the grave with our words. "We got the bastards that did it."

"Did it?"

"Killed her. The scum working for the wind companies."

Again he glanced out the window though the picture was the same. "That won't bring her back."

"That's the worst part." Despite myself I glanced out the window too, wanting to change the subject. "Does it always snow like this?"

"Not usually in summer."

"Why does anyone *live* here? Christ you can't even take a leak for fear your dick'll freeze…"

"It's lovely in spring."

"Yeah, with the black flies."

He glanced at me over folded fingers. "So why are *you* here?"

"Half my family's from here since three hundred years ago when it was a bloody wilderness. I visited my uncle several summers here, a winter once." I sat back. "Can you explain me the situation, how the wind industry got so powerful here?"

"It snuck in through the back door. And now it's taking over the state." He sighed. "It's hard for Mainers to realize they're being screwed. Because Mainers tend to be honest and fair with each other, we assume our elected officials are fair with us too. But they're giving Maine the shaft and walking away with millions. And the environmental groups too, they don't really understand electricity or economics or biology, but they're getting lots of money from the wind companies and they've got lots of fine ideas they never challenge – like do these damn windmills do any good, which of course they don't... And the worst part is they're taking funding from solutions that *would* work, like rooftop solar."

"Somebody in Hawaii once said pro-wind folks are like people who don't believe in evolution: no matter how many facts you give them they won't listen."

"It is a religion, this pro-wind thing. Like Islam. And like Islam it relies on faith, not knowledge." He went to the window, stared at the wailing snow. "And like Islam it's poisoning our world."

THE GIST of what Professor Donnelly explained was the industrial wind companies target states whose lawmakers they can buy cheaply, usually those with rural populations, hopefully impoverished.

He added that the nationwide State Integrity Investigation just ranked Maine 46th in government ethics and gave it an F for corruption. "There are absolutely no rules governing how much money a legislator can take in bribes, and no limits on how much state money they can appropriate for their own use."

So these scoundrels shoved the Wind Law through a sleepy Legislature as an emergency measure. With no way to reduce the resulting catastrophe, and with no environmental analysis or citizen input allowed. Most Legislators, including the committee that drafted it, have since admitted they never read it, that it was totally a product of the industrial wind developers and their "green" allies.

"In essence," he said, "Maine is an oligarchy."

"What's that?" I says, not wanting to miss something.

"When a state or country is governed by very few."

Now, he went on, all the southern New England states whose residents don't want windmills near them – *Heavens No!!!* – are ganging up to dynamite, clearcut and devastate the magnificent wild ridges and peaks of Maine with thousands of howling turbines to send a trickle of power across thousand-mile transmission swaths to their power-greedy homes.

"Ever hear of Aarhus?" He spelled it. "It's a United Nations resolution that you can't build a wind project without local approval and environmental review."

"That's all people here are asking for!"

He smiled. "But the US won't sign it."

"Like we say in Hawaii," I told him. *"Follow the money."*

ON MY WAY to Abigail's Mitchell calls. "It's a black or dark green snowmobile. Probably a Yamaha, can't be sure."

"You *got* satpix?"

"But the cloud cover came in. Your snowmobile went north along the ridge then down a long hairpin trail toward a big old house –"

"Jane's farm."

"What?"

"Never mind. Then what?"

"Before it got to the road it took another snowmobile trail west, then the clouds came in and I lost it."

THAT NIGHT outside Abigail's the white Saab rumbles uphill and swings into the driveway. A black Dodge Ramcharger on high wheels slides in behind her. A tall heavyset bearded guy gets out and they go in the house. The upstairs light flicks on.

Lexie once told me that the size of a guy's truck is often inversely proportional to the size of his privates. "Like they say in Texas," she added, "big hat, no cattle? So it's big truck, little dick." A large truck, she'd said, especially on fat tires, is also related to the tendency to hit women, carry a handgun, watch lots of TV sports, and have the amazingly idiotic idea that men are tougher and more important than women.

But maybe this guy was different. Maybe he was so afraid he *wasn't* a man he wanted the truck to prove he was? In any case I'd seen enough, started Bucky's 150 and headed for Lexie's farm, more reassured than ever that six weeks after her husband's death Abigail was managing to find closure.

Lexie had two loaves of bread rising in clay bowls when I got to the farm. She had corrected a pile of chemistry exams and was now sitting by the kitchen woodstove doing needlepoint while she talked to her sister Emily in Michigan. I don't understand how women can do needlepoint and cook dinner and make bread and talk to their sisters and keep an eye on the fires in three stoves and make sure all the chemistry exams have been corrected and the battery chargers are connected to the two vehicles outside, while all the time they're so laid back and easy, when for me to do any one of those things is a stress and to do two or more

probably impossible. But thank God most religions preach
that men are the superior sex or otherwise I'd worry.

So that night I tell Lexie about Abigail. And that something about her seems out of sync with being a new widow.

Lexie ruminates a while. The fire crackles, throwing out
blasts of heat. Then Lexie slaps her coffee cup on the table,
leaving a little tannish splash on the red and white plastic.

"Pono," she says, "when was the last time you got laid?"

Oh Jesus. It's been days, worse than staggering across
the Sahara with no water. Not since a hot afternoon with
Kim then a long fun night with Charity before I left Hawaii. "Little while," I says primly, then added, to be mean,
"What about you?"

She jabs a finger at me, this beautiful bitch I've loved so
much and who's loved me so much then ditched me for all
the right reasons. And who I'd love to make love with right
now.

"Pono," she says, "you *have* to fuck this girl."

That was back in the good times, before terror replaced
joy, and all hopes for Maine's future and Bucky's vanished
under a well-funded hurricane of public relations, evil lawyers, credulous media, bribes, rich scoundrels and political
connivance.

Too Easy

I T TOOK ALL MORNING to get Bucky's old green
Kawasaki snowmobile running. Even then it spit black
smoke and orange flames and ran ragged as a clogged
lawnmower. The barn was so cold I hated to take my gloves
off but otherwise couldn't clean and set the plugs and points.
I washed the oil filter with gasoline and drove the truck to
Cumberland Farms for a gallon of SAE 5-20 and changed
the Kawasaki's oil.

It finally stopped refusing to start, and after it idled a
few minutes I drove it to Cumberland Farms and filled it
up. It was a nasty big blathering machine fit to deafen you
forever and remove all the cartilage between your vertebrae.

Back at Lexie's I grabbed the .243 and drove the Kawasaki two miles along the roadside past Jane's farm and up
the snowmobile trail a half mile to where my shooter's recent
track came down the mountain and swung west through a
willow copse and across a frozen swamp. Keeping the .243
on safety I followed my shooter's track.

We crossed the swamp and over a low knoll and through
the young conifers of a regrowing clearcut. The Kawasaki's
noise was so all-encompassing I could hear nothing else,
could not tell who was coming. So every few hundred feet
I shut it off and listened, hearing only the wind in the coni-

fers, the *tick tick* of the cooling engine and the hiss where it touched the snow.

A mile ahead another track joined in, also going west. Then another, then two more, all more recent than my shooter's. Often his was erased, then would appear a brief moment between the other tracks then be crushed out again as they braided back and forth, new ones coming and going.

Ahead was a long low building, like an old roadside garage. Frayed red tarpaper walls and a rusty galvanized roof. A big hand-lettered sign, MISSALONKEE HARD RIDERS.

The parking lot was spider-webbed with tracks and spotted with oil puddles on the flattened snow. The building was locked, but through the small windows I could see five picnic tables with chairs, a woodstove, a long table in the front, and incongruously an old clawfoot bathtub. On the wall behind the long desk hung a map showing a network of trails, ponds and lakes.

I tried to follow my shooter's trail another half mile but there were now too many identical tracks from similar machines.

Overhead the male eagle was circling over his mate's grave. If only, I thought, he could tell me where this guy went.

Reluctantly I swung around and headed back to Lexie's.

SNOW TIRES for Bucky's 150 were stacked in the barn by the John Deere combine. I put the truck up on blocks and switched tires, then used Bucky's Sawzall to cut out the rusted floor plates and bolted two plywood sheets in their place.

The truck's underbody was an archaeological relic, something that had survived the hundred-year flood and ended up on a sandbank in the Red Sea. But the tie rods and chassis, brakes, brake lines, drive train, tranny, fuel tank and steering column were all okay; this truck was like an old tank that continues to fire although half of it is blasted away.

At Levesque's Salvage on Route 17 I removed the heater core from another 150. Unlike replacing most heater cores, with the 150 you don't have to pull out the dashboard, just the glove box, and you can unbolt it and unhitch it from its two hoses in fifteen minutes. I paid $21 to a guy with earrings and tattoos, installed it in Bucky's and was elated it worked.

With snow tires the 150 was much more cooperative, trundling over snow and ice as if they were barely there. Like the locals I'd also thrown about ten hay bales in the back so she didn't spin out the way a light-loaded pickup will do. Altogether we'd made significant improvements to our lives, and as we headed down to Hallowell to look for Abigail, my feet and ankles warm and toasty, and with a trace of dying sun across the distant peaks, I felt a ray of hope.

IN HALLOWELL I checked out the Water Street bars hoping to run into Abigail, figuring she had to be getting her one-night stands from somewhere. I did find her, but in the most amazing way.

As I slithered along the bumpy brick sidewalk toward Slates I heard a lovely woman's voice slicing through the frozen air. A magical voice, strange words and the soft plaint of a guitar.

There was an open table at the back. I ordered two Tanqueray martinis and listened, stunned, to Abigail.

She sat on a stool on the other side of the room of perhaps twenty tables, in a long green plaid skirt and lacy black blouse, a gut-string guitar on her lap, no mike. She was between songs now, tuning the guitar, her ear to the strings, her long coppery hair hanging down across its neck. "Okay, folks," she said quietly, and everybody stopped to listen, "now I'll play an old poem of a boy gone to war, never again to see his beloved."

It was strange, ancient ballad, the language yearning and complex, her fingering of the guitar simple and sublime. Yet this was the same person I'd met in the Capitol cafeteria; there was a haunting shamanistic appeal to her, a connection to another world. I had that magical rush in my soul we feel in the presence of human-created beauty.

She finished and tuned up again, which, I realized, was a way of keeping in her own world between songs. "Play Danny Boy!" someone called.

"Ay, laddie," she answered in mock Irish, "ye callin out fer a young lady's lament, are ye? And i'tisn't even Irish, that song." Then in her normal voice adding, "It was written by an English lawyer, and the tune's an old English ballad called *Londonderry Air.*"

She clipped a capo two frets up the neck and dropped us all into a timeless elegy, words and melody straight to the heart. A story of love and loss in the Irish Hunger, a young girl singing to her departing lover, knowing she may die of hunger before he returns, if ever he can. And that when he does return and visits her grave she'll know he's there, *and shall sleep in peace until you come to me.*

It was so heartbreaking to realize how often things like that do happen, how often ardent love is quenched by death.

"What does Abigail like to drink?" I asked the waitress.

"That girl will drink anything, long as it's strong. But if you bought her a diaquiri I bet she wouldn't mind."

A lovely idea. "Let's make it a double."

The waitress put the double down by Abigail's guitar case and pointed back at me. Abigail squinted at me through the spotlight and shook her head in what seemed annoyance. But when the set was over she put the guitar on its stand and came to my table.

"You again." She thunked down the remains of her daiquiri and sat.

"I was going to say something stupid like *we can't keep meeting like this.*"

"It's good you didn't."

"Your voice is magical. I was mesmerized. And the guitar…"

She shrugged: *it doesn't matter.*

"You must be Irish?"

"Nuh-uh." Her violet eyes captured me. "Brit, all the way back."

"But you know Gaelic –"

"It was just a passion I grew up with. Other girls were into clothes and boys and I was into tennis and Irish music."

"*Danny Boy* was lovely."

"If that damn song doesn't make you cry nothing will." She raised her glass. "Thanks for this."

"Be careful, it's a double."

"That's what I was thanking you for." She drank a good half and sat back, sighed. "God, I get thirsty up there."

"I don't know how you do it, in front of all these people."

She sniffed. "I forget they're there."

"There's a lesson in Danny Boy."

She nodded. "That few things are what they seem."

THERE WAS NO END of things to talk about.

The music had started in a fifth grade class, then voice and violin, then a guitar from her uncle who'd been in a Sixties garage band. "I could play folk," she said, "the blues, AC/DC, all the great bands, but the Irish melodies were so entrapping I fell into them, fell in love with them, more than anything else."

At Colby she won so many tennis trophies her coach wanted her to try pro. But that meant exclusive dedication to twelve-hour training days and lots of other pain and suffering, and not to playing the tennis she loved. "I don't care so much about winning," she explained, "I just love the game."

Her first taste of politics was in high school junior year as a neighborhood organizer for the Gore presidential campaign. When the Supreme Court Republicans stole Gore's win she vowed to give up politics, as it was useless to fight such overwhelming corruption. But after Colby and grad school she took a job in then-Governor Lemon's office, got quickly disgusted with him and switched to a young Democratic Legislator named Tim Coleman who was going to reform Maine politics. After two terms in the Legislature he was now in his first in the state Senate, and there was no evil he had once fought against, she said, he didn't now embrace.

"He *tell* you all this?"

"He actually boasted about it. One night when he was drunk he told me the four truths he'd learned in politics. *One,* Know everything you can about your enemies – that means everybody. *Two,* There's more than enough fools out there to make you rich. *Three,* A friend's a friend only as long as you can use him. *And four:* People are far stupider than you think."

"Maybe he's right. We keep voting for these bastards..."

"Jefferson said we need a revolution every twenty years, so we're a little overdue." She watched me. "You made it up, this story of our meeting. Why?"

That got me, her change of course. "I've wondered if it was a dream, even."

"Bullshit." She drained her daiquiri. "I don't believe any of that – predestination, synchronicity, black holes." She flashed me a predatory smile. "And I'll soon figure out who you are."

"In the *Old Testament* Abigail was King David's third wife, he who'd killed Goliath, collected hundreds of his enemies' foreskins and waged war all his life."

Her eyes widened. "You looked it up?"

"It means *thy father's joy* in Hebrew."

"Huh." She looked puzzled a moment. "That's spooky. No guy's ever looked up my name." Her lips crimped. "Never had a father."

"That's awful."

She forced a smile. "Can't miss what you never had."

That thought was awful too. I changed the subject. "It's a beautiful name. How the syllables roll off your tongue."

"It's in the family from way back. A great grandmother, others before that."

I didn't mention that though the *Old Testament* says King David's third wife Abigail was intelligent and beautiful, this Abigail was beyond beautiful, she was enchanting. A strong-edged face, sharp brows, a long narrow chin and wicked small mouth. That lovely coiling auburn hair. Deep violet eyes that didn't flinch.

I thought about the guys who'd spent the last two nights with her. And about her husband who'd been dead six weeks.

I wanted her, craved her. But that wasn't why I was here.

She sang one more set and we had a few more drinks as the other tables slowly emptied. In a haze of alcohol and amorous anticipation we shared tales of being kids and learning about the world, about truths and falsehoods, friends and enemies, linking our fingers and staring into each other's eyes.

The way her nose wrinkled when she laughed set me afire with lust and devotion. Her voice was like her songs – deep and contralto like Callas, husky and soft. The candles flamed in her violet eyes and her slim fingers danced across the tabletop as they had across the guitar strings, words rushing through her mind, her body dancing with every thought, her face like an ice wall continually fracturing.

We got delightfully hammered. She let me carry her guitar in its case up the icy steep Hallowell hill to the gracious Victorian, and like the other guys I followed her up a wide winding cherry staircase to an oak-paneled hall then a bedroom with a wide feather bed.

Her long lovely nakedness made me gasp. She settled herself atop me, sighed, biting her lip, "I could do this all night."

"We're about to," I said, feeling immense gratitude to her, the gods, the universe. For this great gift.

It was wonderful. It went on for hours. But lying there in the darkness afterward I wondered if maybe it hadn't been too easy.

GRAY DAWN was seeping through the windows. I raised up on an elbow. "Can I see you tonight?"

"Nuh-uh. I don't do guys more than once."

A dreadful idea. I stretched out beside her, lacing fingers with hers. "Make an exception?"

She Eskimo-kissed me, nose to nose. "In a few minutes you're out of here."

She was lovely to kiss, the lovely angularity of her jaw and cheekbones and avid small mouth, her whole body smelling of sweaty sex, and tired as we were we got into it again. "So," I says a little later, "if I see you downtown some night you won't talk to me?"

She ran a hand up inside my thigh as if checking the goods one last time. "I'll tell you get lost."

"I used to do that, sleep with someone once then not want to see her again. It wasn't just sex, it was something else."

"I love sex. Though in the morning sometimes I can't stand the guy who six hours before was fucking my brains out. But so what, I never have to see him again."

With a strand of her hair I tickled her chin. "That how you feel about me?"

"You're cute. In the next life maybe I'll keep you a while."

"Abigail," I took her hand. "What are you afraid of?"

She gave me the hard stare. "You don't know?"

"Know what?"

"My husband was killed last December. Again the pretend smile. "I'm a recent widow."

"Oh Jesus. I'm sorry."

"I get these moods, sometimes. Get angry, feel like killing someone. So I keep my distance."

"How was he killed?"

She bit me, hard. "You can read about it anywhere. I don't want to talk about it."

"But you're sleeping with all these guys, you said. Like me."

"For a long time he and I didn't have sex. I'm making up for it."

"To get over the pain?"

"There isn't any pain." She sat up, lovely breasts tugging free of the sheets. "I feel sorry for anyone who dies. But my husband? I'd even stopped *liking* him. I'd already filed for divorce."

Wouldn't that make her a suspect, I wondered, in his death? "So why'd you marry him?"

"Back then he was different, fighting to save a piece of the world. He knew the chances are slim but had all this energy... Then it was like a vampire took him over." She stared at me. "Who *are* you? Why am I *telling* you all this?"

I ignored that. "How'd he change?"

She took a deep breath and stared out the icy mullioned panes at the grim dawn. "What's that old saying – If we aren't liberals when we're young we have no heart, and if we're not conservatives when we're older we have no brain?"

"Because he became conservative? You were ditching him for *that?*"

She laughed. "No, it was for the money."

"For the money?" This didn't sound like her.

"He started taking money from bad people – not for himself but his environmental group. Once enviro groups start taking money from the wrong people, pretty soon they're pushing *that* agenda. Like the Sierra Club first taking $26 million from the natural gas industry in return for not challenging fracking, and now it's in the news that they and other enviro groups took another $100 million in Russian oil money to *fight* fracking?"

"It's easy to buy, allegiance."

She swung her feet over the side and stood, a lithe pale silhouette. "What I've learned in six years as a Legislative staffer – working all the way to the top – is how corrupt it is. How big companies make millions off the Legislature, the taxpayer... They get to build a road where nobody wants one or replace a perfectly good bridge, create immoral tax credits –" she laughed softly – "have you seen the new Portland airport?"

"It's huge. Half empty – But your husband wasn't a Legislator –"

"The wind industry buys the big environmental groups, the unions, the NGOs, the media like public radio, the snowmobilers' and hunters' groups – whatever they need to get a bill passed. To get the taxpayers to pay for what *the industry* wants, not what the people need." She went into the bathroom, sat on the can, flushed it and turned on the shower. "How'd you know he wasn't a Legislator?" she called.

I felt caught, shrugged. "Just assumed. Aren't most Legislators older?"

"Older than what?"

"Than you…"

"Some of the Legislators here are the same age he was… How'd you know?"

"I didn't. I was just listening to you."

In a few minutes she came out of the shower looking all slippery and beautiful. I held her, not wanting to let go. "You still didn't tell me about your husband."

She pecked me on the lips. "Get out of here, sweetie. You're history."

Driving back to Lexie's I was frustrated to be no closer to who killed Abigail's husband and why. Even worse, I really liked being with her and she'd just cut me off.

Though in life I've learned:

- *Never lower yourself to "Let's just be friends".*
- *If you want her, never give up till she asks you to.*
- *But once you're sure it won't happen, Stop. You're wasting time you could spend with other women.*

With Abigail I wasn't to *Stop* yet. And whether she wanted to sleep with me again or not, I sensed she could help get Bucky out of jail.

As I was leaving Freedom a big white cruiser pulled out behind me.

Jail Meat

ONLY AN EX-CON can know the fear when a police car locks in behind you.

He's maybe a hundred yards back. You take your eyes off the road to check your speed or look at him in the mirror and you aren't watching the road and begin to wander and now he's going to think you're drunk and pull you over for that.

He nears, slowly, like a shark homing in on blood. You're sweating and shaking and trying not to let the truck wander but now it has a life of its own, *wants* to wander.

He's closer. The tension's so great you ache to find a driveway, anywhere to pull off, hope he'll pass by. You try to keep your speedometer needle a couple of miles over the limit. Pretending you don't see him, just a normal driver enjoying the scenery.

He hits the flashers and in your bones you know you're headed back *Inside*. You don't know why. But you know.

Because that's the way it always happens.

Once you have a sheet you're jail meat.

The same way marketing programs focus on people's weaknesses, sending credit cards to people who can't afford them, or casino coupons to gambling addicts, thus do the cops focus on us folks who've been *Inside*. We're their bread and butter. And it doesn't matter if we're guilty or not.

Even if we're not they think we should be.

So you pull over and roll down the window, a quick check of the cab that nothing's out of place, like you *know* you're guilty – he just has to find it.

"You're not the owner of this truck?" the cop says, peering at Bucky's Maine registration and my Hawaii license, as though I'd been impersonating Bucky and now he'd found me out. Or maybe he thought Oahu was one of those places full of Muslim terrorists when I could have told him no, it's mostly tourists, land developers and crooked politicians.

I note his nameplate, "O. Trask," assuming I'll need it later, and explain him it's Bucky's truck. Being careful not to be too friendly because cops don't like you to be friendly. They want you intimidated.

"Where's this friend, that you have his truck?"

That's a question I don't want to answer. That Bucky's in Maine State Prison isn't going to help a bit.

Trask sits in his cruiser punching in my ID and in a minute he'll have my record. Undeserved as it may be it may someday cost my life.

Cold sweat trickles down my ribs. I remind myself to breathe. My hands are shaking but I can't stop them. I tell myself ten times *Don't worry: there's no weed in this truck.*

He gets out of the cruiser, hitches up his gun belt and saunters back, tosses the registration and license in the window. They fall on the floor. "You're quite a pair, you and Mr. Franklin. Two murderers, he's in prison and you're headed back there the moment we can find anything on you." He thunked his fists down on the open window ledge. "You've got a bum brake light." He hands me a summons. "Fix it in ten days or we bring you in."

He walks off like I was never there.

There was no point to tell him both my sentences were overturned. That I was *never* guilty. Because wherever he's headed next, all he's thinking about is how to get me back *Inside.*

And any hope I had of staying incognito is now gone.

PRECISELY NOON Maine time, 07:00 in Hawaii, Mitchell calls. I had taken Bucky's snowmobile up the trail still trying to track my shooter, and now cut the engine on the ridge above the Missalonkee Hard Riders clubhouse so I could hear him.

"It's a disgrace," he says.

I wondered how he knew I'd been pulled over. "Damn right."

"Did you know about these crooks?"

"Some cops are."

"Cops? I'm talking about these *Legislators!* Man they are *bent.*"

I was confused. "What's new from that?"

"I've been going through some nasty bank records from Maine's public servants. These folks take campaign money from the Wind Mafia, then they take *more* Wind Mafia money under the table, cash into different bank accounts, PACs, their spouses' bank accounts... One guy, a stickler for public probity, this guy is, a leading Democrat, pillar of respectability with four daughters –" Mitchell fumed on.

"That doesn't necessarily make him a crook –"

"Each daughter has over million bucks in a savings account, all foreign banks."

"Jesus Christ I'll marry them." I thought a moment. "So maybe *he's* rich."

"Rich? *Rich?* The bastard was a potato farmer till the potato market went south so he bought himself a seat in the Leg. He wasn't rich then but he sure is now."

"That's American capitalism for you."

"I've been up all night chasing down these crooks –"

"Mitchell you gotta sleep some time."

"This other dame from Portland she sends her Wind Mafia money to the Caymans! Just like some drug dealer! What's a state Representative doing with three accounts in the Caymans?"

I didn't explain you that Mitchell gets really upset with the corporate-political corruption in our country today. As he sees it, he's in a wheelchair for the rest of his life and a lot of our good friends are dead because we tried to protect our country. Thus being reminded of what a festering pit our government has become gets him very pissed off. I'm pissed off too but have lost hope of anything better.

"Mitchell," I says, "all we can do is live honorably ourselves." This is total bullshit but I'm hoping to calm him down.

"No," he says. "That's *not* right. We take *care* of people, Pono. We take *care* of our country."

Over Mitchell's voice I hear a snowmobile coming. "Hold on," I says but Mitchell just keeps expostulating. I slip the .243 from under the tarp and thumb off the safety. The snowmobile comes up the trail on the far side of the clubhouse and pulls up in front. It is dark blue.

The driver is wearing a full gray snow suit and boots. He has a rifle slung over one shoulder. I can't tell what kind, but it's large caliber. Like a .270.

"Mitchell," I break in on his rant and tell him what's happening. "You think it's the guy tried to kill you?" he says.

"It's a dark blue machine."

"On the satpix I never could tell; too late in the day and too cloudy."

"I'm going to slip down the hill, have a little chat with our friend."

"Pono you *can't* kill him. You'll be *Inside* forever –"

"I'm not going to kill him, just discuss things. On second thought," I added as more snowmobiles came into hearing, "maybe I'm not."

The other machines pulled up at the clubhouse and the drivers and passengers all went inside. None of them were carrying rifles.

"Gotta go now," I said.

"Don't do anything I wouldn't do."

"If you were here," I said though the topic was painful, "you and I would go down there and solve this."

"The good old days."

For the thousandth time I felt washed with sorrow that this powerful dynamic guy was now a legless cripple with no sex life. That a guy who could run twenty miles with full gear now has to roll himself to the bathroom.

"Don't worry, Mitchell. We'll catch these guys."

"Your snowmobiler shooter? Maybe." Mitchell was still pissed off. "But these crooked politicians – who's going to catch them?"

THAT NIGHT I went looking for Abigail in all the Hallowell bars and found her at the Liberal Cup. It's a wild place with lots of good beers and it's loud and the food's great. "What a coincidence," I says, "running into you."

She looked straight through me. Like I was a pane of glass or maybe an ice sheet on her next free climb. "Abigail," I says.

"You heard what I said."

"What you said about *what?*" I said, quoting from *The Idiot's Guide to Never Getting Laid*.

"I don't do guys twice." She sucked down beer, gave me a mock smile. "*You* included."

"So don't *do* me. Talk to me."

She checked out the room. "What you have to talk about?"

"I want to know you."

"I don't want to know *you*."

"We had so much fun – you did too... I love just listening to you."

Her lip curled. "I don't care *what* you love."

"Please let me in, Abigail? Please?"

Her face turned glacial. The light went out of her eyes. I had a sudden stab of fear, of what she could do.

"Have it your way." She tossed back her beer, checked the room one last time, dropped a ten on the bar. "Let's go."

AFTERWARDS, leaning on one elbow looking at her naked made me joyous with how lovely she was. Her skin had a golden glow in the dim streetlamp through the frosted window, her hair a lustrous velvety sheen, her body slim and lithe, and she had nice feet and didn't paint her toenails. No lipstick, mascara, nothing. Just her face, her real face, with its passing storms of fear and happiness.

"So what," she yawned, "makes you think you care about me?"

There had to be a way not to lie. "At first I just wanted to fuck you. Now I really care about you. Want to be with you."

She dabbed at sweat in her belly button. "Wasting your time."

I kissed her belly button, down between her lovely thighs, loving the taste of her. She pulled me up, kissed me deeply and we got going again.

A while later she checks her watch on the nightstand. "It's eleven damn thirty. I have to be up at six to prepare for a committee meeting."

I nestled against her, half asleep. She was warm and sweaty and smelled deliciously of sex. I tucked the blankets up around us. "I'll make you breakfast."

She snuggled closer, slim fingers up my ribs. "I can't believe I'm sleeping with you again. Has to be a bad sign…"

"It's wonderful," I mumbled. "Delightful." As often, I was an unwilling double agent. Being with Abigail was beyond joyous, but I was really there to find out who shot her husband. And why.

Which she clearly didn't want me to know.

Or did *she* even know?

Go Deep

DESPITE WHAT I'd told Mitchell his revelations saddened me. I'd had a lingering faith that Maine Legislators were honest people trying to do their best for the people. In fact some of them were so homely I just automatically trusted them. And, as Sylvia's Professor Donnelly had said, Maine people have a tradition of trusting each other. And of fulfilling that trust.

But money corrupts, and most elected officials have their price. In Maine, I was learning, that price is often very low.

Would the wind companies bribing the most legislators also be the most willing to kill? Not do the killing themselves, surely, but just make it happen? Killing isn't hard to do, and can get rid of lots of problems literally overnight.

ERICA WAS SEVENTEEN and I fourteen the summer I left Hawaii for Stroudwater to work on Uncle Jack's farm. She was already an expert at the dance of love and gave me a master's degree before I even went to college. There are few things more fun than an afternoon of sex in the warm grass beside a cool stream in the shade of a benevolent oak, when the magnificence of a young woman's body is new to you and the mysteries of sex just starting to be revealed.

Not that she was a patient teacher. She simply removed my brain, what there was of it, and abraded my private parts while she blissfully explored her own private nirvana.

But between times she was nice to me. Showed me what to do and when, and that the finest thing in life is indescribable bliss.

Apparently in France, those masters of bliss, teenage girls often have relationships with more experienced men – no inarticulate fumbling or putting things in the wrong place, just lovely lessons in orgasmic joy – while teenage boys are taken under tutelage of more experienced women and learn what it's all about and how to bring fun and joy to a woman and himself.

So although Stroudwater is three thousand miles from France and Erica was my elder by only three years, I got a bit of a French education.

Feeling slightly fourteen again, I called her up.

"Bradley, Cohen and Tillson," a sonorous woman's voice.

"Erica Tillson please." I tried to sound lawyerly.

"Who is calling?"

"Sam Hawkins."

"Will she know what this is in reference to?"

It's in reference to ancient fucking, I wanted to say but wisely held my tongue. "An old friendship. From Stroudwater."

Seconds later the sonorous lady was back. "She's in conference all day. I shall leave her your message."

This didn't sound auspicious, but I gave her my Hawaii cell. "Please tell her I'm in Maine. And that it's important."

Sure it was important, but not to Erica. One thing I remembered from fifteen years ago: to Erica nothing was important except what *she* wanted.

So I was dreaming if I thought she'd give a damn about Bucky. Or about the death of Maine.

PORTLAND'S A STRANGE TOWN. It draws you in while revealing nothing about itself but tourist talk. Once the second-largest seaport on the East Coast, sending magnificent sailing ships with Maine crews and captains all over the world, Portland is now a remnant of brick buildings and wooden colonials on a long narrow headland jutting into Casco Bay.

The site must have been beautiful – a granitic pine-clad promontory of rivers, streams and bays of pure green water, the deep cold salty tang of the sea. But that was hundreds of years ago and today's downtown Portland is a jumble of concrete, plate glass, steel, and crumbling highways, its innards gutted in the 1960s by federal "urban renewal" projects that tore down most of its ancient buildings and replaced them with overpasses, freeway exits and glass office towers.

Congress Street, once a magnificent downtown of classy department stores, restaurants, offices, libraries, bookstores and bars, was then killed by the suburban maul – sorry, "mall" – built on what had once been part of the Hawkins family farm, not far from where superbrain Erica had taken me by canoe for those amorous episodes. Of course now Congress Street is a dirty windblown tunnel of empty storefronts, junkies, dumpster divers and broken sidewalks.

It all went round in my head too many times. I'm sure you have the same feeling.

Speaking of dumpster divers, or the folks who stand in the wind and snow and rain on street corners with their cardboard signs asking for food or money – they're dirty and unshaven in tattered clothes, and they go off to the side every once in a while to suck on a cigarette. They remind me of one of my Special Forces HALO jumps (High Altitude Low Opening) – which means you jump out of a plane at about 38,000 feet but you don't get to open your parachute till about 900 feet AGL (Above Ground Level, wherever in Hell that happens to be). As in every jump I went through the usual, falling in my Extended Cold Weather Gear through 50 below at two hundred miles an hour then yanking my chute at 900 AGL.

Well, this time my chute didn't open. I was 900 feet above ground, falling at two hundred feet a second, so I had four seconds to live. And no matter what I did the damn chute wouldn't open.

That's what happened to those folks.

But unlike me, they didn't have a spare chute.

"YOU LEFT A MESSAGE." Erica said, as if this were a criminal offense. But at least she'd called back.

"Yeah," I mumbled, feeling fourteen again. "I'm in Maine and I thought…"

"You told my secretary it was important –"

"Yeah it is. But how are you? It's been a long…"

"Look, I've got a very busy day."

"Do you remember me?"

"You were just a kid."

I risked it: "Not when you were done with me."

Was that a suppressed snicker? "I've got to go. What can I do for you?"

"It's a legal matter of supreme importance but I'll be damned if I'll discuss it over the phone. When can I meet you?"

"I'm not taking new clients."

"I'm not a new client, I'm an old one." I was getting pissed off now. "How soon can I see you?"

"Sam, I don't have time…"

"*Make* time." I scrambled for ideas. "What are you doing tonight?"

"Going home to take a hot shower."

"I'll take one with you."

"We're going to end this conversation."

I was at my wit's end. "Erica, you've had a wonderful impact on my life." Sometimes, I reasoned, you can get more with flattery than requests. "I've appreciated you all these years – don't ruin it now."

She reflected a moment. "You know Three-Dollar Dewey's?"

"I can find it."

"Seven-thirty. I'll give you fifteen minutes."

We can make love twice in that time, I was going to say but again was wise enough not to. "When you hear what I have to say you'll forget about the time."

"I never forget about time."

AT STROUDWATER GRAVEYARD I stopped to give the ancestors a brief update. Climbed the path to the knoll of headstones under the pines. As usual it was so damn cold I had to force myself to perch on the frozen pine root while I brought them up to speed.

"Still haven't found Bucky an alibi," I admitted. "Turns out he had a girlfriend – and then when I went up Eagle Mountain to look for his gun, guess what? Some asshole shoots at me..."

Not a word in shock or protest.

"But I've met this fantastic woman from Hallowell – her ancestors must've lived there same time as Uncle Elias... and tonight I'm seeing Erica – remember when she and I canoed up the River? And by the way, Maine's just as crooked as Hawaii, so don't start acting holier than thou..."

No response.

"So what do you think I should *do?*" I asks, pissed off at their silence.

I sat there thinking for some reason of college football, when as a wide receiver I'd always loved running deep routes. Then realized that's what they were telling me:

Go deep.

THREE-DOLLAR DEWEY'S is a wonderful bar and eatery on the Portland waterfront in one of those ancient brick buildings that has so far escaped attempts by developers and urban renewal experts to make Portland look like Las Vegas. There's sawdust on the old pine floors and thick pine tables and lots of pretty women and big screens on the wall where guys in football helmets keep running into each other at high speed.

She came in at exactly 19:30 in a long black camel-hair coat and a black dress that hinted at the body beneath it. She gave a little hand flutter and crossed to my table. I stood and got a quick peck on the cheek. She tossed her coat across the other chair and looked at me. "You're not what I remember."

"I'm not what *I* remember either."

Despite herself she cracked a grin that quickly died. "So what's this about?"

I was getting mad. "Sit down."

She glared at me, grabbed a chair from another table and sat. It was as if she owned the place, but then she'd always been that way, had owned me entirely for most of a summer. "You look wonderfully like the you I remember," I hazarded.

She gave a sharp grimace. I checked her left hand: no rings. "You were such a kid then," she said.

Her brief smile was like a flash of sunlight on a dark day. The kind that melts a judge's heart and disarms the opposition. So she can get what she wants.

I explained her about Bucky. About the wind turbines, what they did to Bucky and Lexie and all their neighbors, what they were doing to Maine, to America. To the world.

"I don't get caught up in politics," she said.

I leaned forward. "This isn't politics! Your family," I remembered, "has been in Maine since the sixteen hundreds. Don't you *care* about what's happening to Maine?"

"Look, Sam," she looked at me almost kindly, "I'm a

litigator, not a criminal attorney. And I'm certainly not a *pro bono* environmental lawyer. Find one of those enviro groups to take up the fight."

"They're all getting money from the wind industry."

She shrugged: *so what else is new?* "There's nothing I can do to help your friend."

"He's not my friend. I can't stand him. Plus he took away a woman I loved –"

"Yes, but you were going to do twenty years? What woman was going to wait around for that? And why care what happens to him if you don't even like the guy?"

I explained her the whole Special Forces thing, you help a buddy in danger no matter what. Strangely, this seemed to move her. "My first husband was in Iraq," she said.

"Your first?"

"Things fell apart when he got back."

I recoiled. "He volunteered," she added. "I thought the war was a crime, and GW Bush a war criminal –"

"Nearly anyone who served there, saw combat, will tell you that."

"So I said to my husband, you go into this atrocious war and I'll divorce you." She gave her fleeting smile. "We were on the way out, anyway."

"Why?" I risked.

She seemed glad of the question, sliding her Allagash Lager in wet circles on the table. "I fall in love for sex, maybe..." She seemed suddenly vulnerable, alone.

"We all do," I said.

"So with the second husband I tried intellectual companionship instead...he's a professor at Bowdoin...that didn't work either..."

"Why?"

She flashed that magnificent smile again. "You know me..."

"I've never forgotten you…I can remember whole afternoons…"

She slapped my hand. "Enough of that."

"Erica, there's *never* enough of *that*. It's the lovely glue that holds us together, it's warm, it's profound…the secret of life, the gift of progeny and the gift of the soul –"

She snickered. "You've become a poet, I see."

"You're in a relationship now?"

"I don't have time for men. I work twelve hours a day, six and a half days a week. I make six hundred thousand a year, have a beachfront condo in St. Thomas I never use, buy tickets to Europe but never go." She reached out, surprisingly, and squeezed my hand. "Would love to have kids but don't have time."

"How do you do it?"

Her eyes widened. "How do I do what?"

"You win all your cases. I looked you up: you're famous."

"I imagine winning. In my planning I start with the victory and then work back from there."

"From there?"

"I go back each step. What caused that one to succeed. Then the previous one." She looked away, back at me, gathered up her purse. "I think we're done."

I stood. "Yeah, sure." I was furious, distressed, sad, and wanted her. I dropped a twenty on the table and we went out. She walked a half block beside me, took out keys and pushed a button. Ahead of us a titanium 911 flashed its lights. I had an inspiration. "Lock that car," I said.

She looked at me, puzzled. I took her arm. "I'm going to show you something unforgettable."

Perhaps the two Allagashes had relaxed her, or the memories of teenage lust? With Erica you never knew. When I opened the squeaky passenger door of Bucky's 150 it almost fell off. She stepped back to look the truck over. "This *yours?*"

"It's Bucky's. The guy you're going to defend."

"No I'm not." But she got in the passenger seat, squealing the broken coils. "This better be quick."

"I promise you it will be. And fun." I negotiated the 150 into first, swung round and headed up Commercial Street toward Munjoy Hill, the Eastern Promenade and Fort Allen Park, where fifteen years ago we'd made love in her father's Cadillac SUV one rainy night, but when we wanted to leave its tires kept slipping on the steep wet grass, couldn't climb the hill, so regrettably I drove it further down the grass to get up some speed, but then couldn't get back even to where I'd been, till we were on the edge of the cliff above the ocean and had to call a tow truck that itself got caught by running over its own tow bar, so we had to call a second truck to tow out the first – all of which enraged the older generation and brought a sharp, painful end to our relationship.

I turned into Fort Allen Park down the same hill and pulled over. We sat bathed in luscious darkness, Casco Bay's thousand islands spread out before us like a diamond quilt. "I don't get enough of this," she said.

I glanced out at the lovely dark bay and lustrous islands, the magic of it all. "This?"

She reached for me. "Sex."

Widow's Web

B UT ERICA STILL WOULDN'T represent Bucky. "I contacted Matt Rusko," she said when I called her for the third time next morning. "He's a good criminal attorney, said he'd be willing to talk."

"How much?"

"You'd have to discuss with him, but I believe it's about three-fifty."

"Three-fifty?"

"An hour."

It took a while to realize she meant three hundred and fifty *dollars*. "This has to be *pro bono,* Erica. And Bucky needs *you.*" I felt that somehow in the details was the proof Bucky was innocent, and that somehow she'd find it.

"*Me?* You must be nuts. That's like going to an obstetrician for a brain injury. The law is very specialized, Sam. It's not my discipline, defending people who kill people."

"Bucky didn't kill that guy."

"Like I said last night, Sam, how do you *know?*" She paused, exasperated. "The law is precise, it wants facts, not opinions."

We'd been down this road already. "Erica, you know that half the time the law's *wrong,* that lots of cases are judged wrong, that's there's lots of people in jail who shouldn't be and a lot more who aren't in jail but should be. Don't give me that Justice weighing the scales crap."

"It's all we've got, Sam." Someone spoke behind her, she turned from the phone, came back. "Look, I've got to go –"

"When can I see you?"

"I'm leaving in half an hour for Tulsa for a deposition, be back day after tomorrow."

"Let's have dinner, the night you're back..."

"I get in late."

"I hate to eat early."

"Gotta go," she said. "See you."

"I NEVER SEE YOU anymore," Lexie said jokingly, which meant she wasn't joking. Our affair five years ago had been very intense and I have a sharp memory of how her mind works.

"This is getting so complex." I sagged wearily into the kitchen chair where barely a week ago she'd told me her woes, and when I'd promised myself to help her. "It's not just getting Bucky off, impossible as that may seem, it's this whole Maine wind tragedy that's somehow connected with it... And I can't see a way to get one without the other."

She leaned toward me, elbow on the table, chin in her hand. "How's that?"

"Well," I delayed, trying to think it out. "If it was a setup, and somebody killed Ronnie to blame it on Bucky..." I couldn't figure what came next. "Then it's got to be wind industry-related, so if we reveal it we'll blow the whole thing wide."

"What whole thing?" she said.

"The Maine wind scam, the foreign companies, the lies, the investment banks, the politicos..." I looked at her, exasperated. "Maine's going to lose it all. Like Bucky."

"Shifting Baselines Syndrome," she said after a moment. "You can see it right here in my biology classes. People are used to what they have, think that's the baseline, the way things have always been. Fisheries biology researchers realized a few years ago that annual population counts don't take into consideration the original baseline – a sea full of fish – so today's depleted oceans are assumed to be the way things always were. We've lost ninety-five percent of nature, but we think the five percent that's left is all there ever was."

"Like my ancestor Elias talking about the Kennebec River solid with fish. Now if one salmon shows up everyone gets ecstatic."

"My students, they want to understand life, its processes, but the environment around them is getting so degraded we can't get back to baseline. Shifting Baselines," she repeated in that semi-prophetic way she had. When she hadn't had any sex for a while. Which reminded me of how wonderful it would be to do it. Which meant it was time to leave.

"Going over see Uncle Silas," I said, knowing she wanted me to stay.

"Yeah?" She acted surprised, then, "You should."

"Sometimes he just loses it, I have to sit there, wait for him to come back." I didn't want to tell her about Bucky's girlfriend. Not wanting to add to her sorrows. Also knowing the minute I told her, after she got done being pissed off, she'd drop her clothes and come after me. Which was such a lovely temptation that if I'd been a medieval monk I'd have retired to my stone cell with its bed of thorns and whipped myself till the lust was burned out of my bones, i.e., till long after I was dead.

Instead I went out to the bunkhouse for Bucky's coat and boots. It was snowing hard, 18 below, a typical Maine day. The blizzard and accompanying ice particles were horizontal on the howling wind. I unplugged Bucky's truck from the battery warmer and scraped new ice off the windshield. The engine wouldn't catch so I popped the hood and sprayed WD-40 into the Holley 2-barrel carb, and like an old mare tricked by a handful of oats she caught on the first turn, spouting more than her share of CO2 and particulates, and as we rode off into the wintry evening I had the suspicion Bucky's Ford 150 like Don Quixote's Rocinante had its own views on how to pursue my war against the windmills.

Jostling along in Bucky's truck made me think of him: a tough, incredibly haunted soul, of how all our lives had so insanely intertwined. And of Lexie alone in that Maine farmhouse on the forest and steppes, on old caribou tundra not long ago covered by two miles of ice, land the Penobscots and Micmacs had loved every inch of.

And now Lexie'd ended up here because of me – if we hadn't met that night in Honolulu at WipeOut, hadn't had our wild affair, she wouldn't have come four thousand miles from Hawaii for my trial. Where of course she'd met Bucky who'd come to testify against me. And who after I got twenty years talked Lexie into moving with him to his family's farm in Maine, far from anything she'd ever known or been, or wanted.

Maybe women *are* as stupid as men.

A HANDLE OF BLACKBERRY BRANDY was $14.95 at Cumberland Farms and I wasn't driving all the way to Hannaford to save a dollar.

As before, Silas was sitting under that ratty afghan in front of the fire. He nodded in gratitude when I gave him the bottle. "There's two tens in the sugar bowl. On the kitchen shelf."

I got two glasses, put three ice cubes in each, filled them with blackberry brandy and sat across from him. "Snowing like crazy out there."

"Mmmm," he smiled. "Lovely."

"Not if you're driving in it."

"On snowy nights like this we used to hitch the horses to the sled and drive for miles, the runners squeaking under the new snow, the horses' warm breath, the girl next to you under the rug…"

"Speaking of girls," I says, "reminds me of Bucky's girl-friend. Like you said, sometimes after a day or so you re-member things…"

"Yes I do, young man. That's true." He leaned forward on his stick. "Did you get the two tens?"

"You keep your money." After a moment I added, "I have a hard time imagining Bucky having an affair," to bring the subject back up.

"If it does the pipes could freeze."

"If what does?"

"Like I said, if it gets any colder."

"A night like this, yes they could. You want me to run a trickle in the faucet?"

"Already have. You going out tonight?"

"I'm going back to Bucky's."

His eyes glinted. "You too?"

"Me too what?"

"You in the sack with Lexie while Bucky's away?"

I laughed. "No, I'm not," happy to say the truth. "Not like Bucky with… what was her name?"

"Name?" He picked at the afghan. "Yes. Unusual name…" He clacked his teeth. "One of the old ones, you know. Biblical… Damned if I haven't forgotten it again."

I bit back my impatience. "You should write things down. That's what I do."

He sat there, eyes far away, gumming his teeth. "Imag-ine yourself writing it down," I said. "What it would look like written down."

"Absalom, Absalom," he muttered, and I wondered what deity he was praying to now.

"That's it!" He leaped forward in his chair. "Abigail!"

"Abigail?"

"That's the name Bucky said once, let it slip. His girl-friend's name is Abigail."

Oh shit. I was such a fool. I'd been duped again.

There couldn't be two Abigails. Or could there?

I felt like a fly in a black widow's web.

"I'M SCREWING your girlfriend," I says next day to Bucky through the bulletproof glass.

He stares back. "She's not my girlfriend."

"What is she then?"

"You didn't listen, my little story about Waziristan?"

That was the one about the source we had in the Paki-Afghani mountains, we never knew if he was doubling us till the Taliban killed him. Then we knew, too late, he'd been for real. "I can't get the connection."

"She wasn't my girlfriend, she was a way to reach somebody."

"Who?"

"Who do you think?"

I didn't know if he was putting me on or just trying to derail me. "I haven't the faintest fucking idea."

He waved his finger. "Didn't you see the sign? No profanity in here."

The whole place was profane. Bucky was profane. I was sick of it all.

"Through her I was in getting in touch with her husband," Bucky added. "He was coming around. You know what he'd been hustling..."

"Industrial wind?"

"He was seeing through it, for the first time. Was going to come out against it."

"No way, the wind companies own him, all the enviro groups –"

Bucky chuckled. "So who did it?"

"She was going to divorce him anyway. She's certainly not grieving..."

117

"Not true." Bucky shook his head. "Not true."

"So you weren't sleeping with her?"

"I've never touched another woman since Lexie." He watched me a moment. "Thanks to you."

"To me?"

"That I met her."

"Yeah, when you came to testify against me."

He shook his head. "When I came to tell the truth."

"What you said wasn't true. And it got me twenty years."

"You were out in months."

"Not due to you." I was getting furious. "You like this?" I waved at the prison walls, other inmates in their orange suits, the bars, handcuffs and bulletproof glass. "So *you* do the time. I'm finished trying to help you."

He smiled. "You fucking Lexie?"

"Hell no." I wanted to add but didn't, *though I'd love to.*

I walked out angry and disillusioned. Looking back at the grim walls I was reminded of Thomaston, the even grimmer Maine State Prison Stephen King fictionalized in his novella that became *The Shawshank Redemption.* As often, it amazed me that our culture is so dysfunctional that millions of us are behind bars.

In four weeks I was supposed to be in Tahiti. I wanted very much to be there. But with all this going on I'd begun to fear I wouldn't make it. *Don't give it up,* I told myself. *No matter what.*

In three hours I was meeting Abigail at Slates. How to get her to explain the real deal? She didn't even know I knew Bucky. Or that I knew quite a bit about her husband. Though not why he died.

To her I was some guy she'd met in the Capitol cafeteria who she liked to go to bed with.

I liked that part too.

Totally Screwed

S HE WAS at the same table near the back where three nights ago I'd sat entranced by her songs. And where the two of us had talked like old friends.

Her smile when I leaned down to kiss her should have warned me. But I still couldn't decide what to do. Would she give more away if she thought I didn't know?

"So tell me about Bucky," I said.

Her eyes barely widened. For a few moments she seemed to be calculating. "How much you know?"

"Most of it. Just need you to clarify a few things."

"So *you* tell *me*."

"That's bullshit. What's up, Abigail? I want it all."

She looked into my eyes, almost amused. "When I told you my husband and I didn't sleep together any more, that didn't mean I had no sex."

"That's what you implied."

"Nuh-uh." She shook her head. "I had Bucky."

This was crazy. Bucky had just told me they'd had no sex. "You were fucking him?"

"Absolutely." She gave me that penetrating smile. "Jealous?"

"Hardly." However it did strike me that Bucky and I kept ending up in bed with the same women. And getting put *Inside*.

She tugged a lock of hair under her chin. "I bet."

"You and I are both sleeping with other people, no big deal. It's fun."

She widened her eyes. "You fucking Lexie?"

"Bucky just asked me that. The answer, sadly, is no." I sat back, watching her face like a mask that kept shattering. "How'd you meet Bucky?"

"He was testifying against one of these horrible wind projects. I was representing Senator Coleman, who's been paid to vote for them."

Coleman was the Legislator who had wanted to change Maine politics till he became a Senator and one of the state's big-time Democrats employed under the table by the wind industry. I shook my head in frustration. "Doesn't he care about Maine?"

She rubbed a thumb and forefinger together. "Follow the money."

Crazily I thought of that country ballad *The Long Black Veil*, where the guy hangs for a murder he didn't commit because he won't admit he was with his best friend's wife. "Why don't you tell the cops you were with Bucky the night your husband was killed?"

"You idiot." She bit her lip, appraising me. "You don't understand *why* I couldn't?" She looked away a moment, calculating again, abruptly stood, tugged on her coat and walked out.

I sat stunned, knowing I should go after her but so pissed off I didn't. By the time I'd paid and went outside she'd vanished.

This was nuts. Tomorrow I was going back to Hawaii, to hell with them all.

I stood on Water Street's uneven brick sidewalk, breath freezing to my face. No matter what I'd done to piss Abigail off I needed to talk to her. To know why she wouldn't tell the cops Bucky'd been with her that night. And why Bucky wouldn't implicate her, even to avoid life in jail.

It made no sense. Life rarely does. I called her.

Her phone went to voicemail. I drove up the hill. Her lights were off.

I knocked on her front door. No answer. Went around to the back and called up to her bedroom. No answer. Looked through the barn window: the white Saab wasn't there.

A window lit up next door, a woman's round pink face peering out at me, brown curlers and a plaited pink bathrobe.

I sat in the truck trying to figure it out. Called her every five minutes. No answer.

She had walked out of Slates about 19:30. It was now 20:40.

The likely thing was she'd met some guy, gone to his place, had shut off her phone and was having fun. Or saw it was my number and didn't answer.

If I went to the cops she'd think I was jealous.

I felt weird and alone, hadn't realized how much I enjoyed being with her. How much I liked her sharp savage mind. And needed her to fill in the picture of her and Bucky, her husband and whoever killed him.

When I got back to the farm Lexie's lights were out and the bunkhouse was frigid. I lay there waiting for the bed to get warm, strangely missing Abigail, sick and tired of it all.

AT 06:17 I parked the truck down the street from Abigail's, hoping she'd come home. The Saab was still gone. Her phone still didn't answer. By 09:00 she still hadn't appeared.

I was freezing. I phoned her again. "The number you are calling," a nice lady said, "is no longer in operation."

I was starting to get weird fears, seeing her lovely chiseled face, hearing her exciting hushed voice, feeling her lovely litheness and silken flesh in my arms. The taste of her breath.

I'd done something wrong but didn't know what.

ABIGAIL'S ALWAYS ON TIME," a lady named Mildred in the Senator's office said. "Even in flu season she never misses work."

"But she hasn't come in this morning?"

"That's what I said."

"Can you check her calendar, see if she noted something, yesterday or today?"

"You're her friend, you say?" She was distant, reserved. "Excuse me, I have another call –"

"I'm worried about her! She's vanished!"

She came back on the line. "Tell me your name again?"

"Hawkins. She and I were at Slates last night; she stepped out for a minute and never came back."

"Pono Hawkins? Her calendar says she was meeting you at Slates last night. Seven o'clock."

"What's she supposed to be doing today?"

A clicking of pen on teeth while she scanned the calendar. "Meeting with the Senator 9:10, the Energy Committee 10:30 – all day meetings and things to do. She's amazing, Abigail, what she gets done in a day."

"YOU GOT QUITE A SHEET," the paunchy moon-faced Augusta cop said. It was 11:35 and I'd finally gone to the cop shop and this guy was at the desk, "C. Hart" on his nameplate. Of course the first thing when I'm telling him about Abigail he pulls up my record, see who he's dealing with. Cops can smell prison meat a mile away.

"All my sentences got vacated," I says. "I was cleared."

A sarcastic nod. "Good lawyer? A nice envelope of cash somewhere?" He reached out as if to grab my lapel, caught

122

himself. "In Maine we don't do that, mister. Once we get you–" he gave me that mealy-mouthed smile, "we keep you."

"The charges were wrong," I tried to explain. "I didn't do nothing."

"Yeah, you guys never do. I don't know why we bust our asses, risk our lives, chasing you assholes down, and then you get off on some technicality. Me, I'd like to shoot all the lawyers. Shoot you all." He looked at me steadily. "A dead man don't commit another crime."

"She's been missing since last night. We were at Slates and she went outside for a moment, never came back. Never went home, isn't at the office today."

"What, you have a fight?"

"No we didn't have a fight."

"Maybe she's sick?"

"I'm asking you to check her house, see what you can find."

He rubbed his bristles. "We'll get there."

"When?"

"When we can."

I glanced around the cop shop. Two cops on computers, two others drinking coffee and looking out the window. "What," I said, "it's too cold for you guys out there?"

He looked at me grimly. "You're a wiseass are you? See where it gets you."

I went outside and called Abigail's office. She still hadn't come in, Mildred said. "Can you have the Senator call the cops," I said, "see if he can get them to do something?"

"We'll try," Mildred said.

Not knowing what else to do I drove back and parked in front of Abigail's house, begging her to come home.

NOON IN MAINE was 07:00 in Hawaii, and Mitchell was drinking coffee with Stolichnaya and destroying Islamic websites when I called. "Can you take a break?" I said.

"It's already 78 degrees, sun gleaming on the blue ocean. Thank God you're not here."

I told him about Abigail. "People don't usually drop routines like that," he said. "You check the hospitals?"

"Nobody's seen her."

"She liked to fuck new guys, you said."

"Loved it. How I got near her."

"Lucky you."

"I'm really getting worried, Mitchell. Cops don't give a shit. Her phone says it's no longer in service. Can you check it, see who she's been calling?"

"Yeah, and I can tell you within a yard of where she is."

I felt suddenly hopeful. "That would be fantastic."

"Call you back," he said, and was gone.

I imagined him in his basement "IT Palace" rolling his wheelchair silently across the carpet from screen to screen, checking, watching, figuring how our enemies think and work. And how to stop them.

A police cruiser turned the corner and stopped at Abigail's house. A chubby cop got out and knocked on the front door. After a while he went around back, checking windows, peered into the garage. I could have told him her white Saab wasn't there.

He sat in the cruiser talking on the radio. As he drove past he gave me a hard look. *Highway to Hell* rang on my phone so I grabbed it.

"Her phone's not working," Mitchell said.

"What do you mean *not working?*"

"Somebody took the battery out, disconnected everything or ran over it with a semi."

"What about her calls?"

"Last one was from you, yesterday, 15:47."

"That's when I asked her to meet up at Slates. I wanted to hear what she was going to say about Bucky."

"Bucky's a prick but I can't see him banging other women."

"Everybody fucks everybody these days; the uptight ones just pretend they don't."

"Anyway, been no calls in or out on her phone since then."

"I left her tons of messages! Is there a history on the GPS? So you can tell where she's been?"

"I can't find it. Somehow it got smashed up too."

I hung up, found a gear the truck was willing to use, and rattled down the Hallowell hill and upriver to the Augusta cop shop.

"So maybe she shut her phone off." It was the same cop, C. Hart, lethargic and hostile as before. "People do that, case you didn't know."

"I told you, her phone's been destroyed."

"How you know?"

"I got a buddy works for Verizon, he checked it out."

The cop took out a pencil. "What's his name and number?"

"Can't tell you. He's afraid to lose his job."

"You can't tell me where you're getting this story and you want me to believe it?"

"Look, she works for Senator Coleman, never misses a day, never late."

"We looked her up," he says expansively. "Her husband got himself killed, few weeks ago –"

"I know."

He eyed me carefully. "So where were you last December 29?"

I let out an exasperated sigh. "Home in Hawaii."

"That so?" He made a show of stacking papers. "And we've learned she has quite a night life, your Abigail."

"That's her business."

"Yeah? Well, it makes us think she's just shacked up somewhere," he smiled, "screwing some new guy."

"She wouldn't miss work. *Nobody's* seen her! You guys need to get off your ass and find her."

He gave me that cop stare: *I can mess you over any time I want and there's nothing you can do about it.*

I shouldn't have said what I said next. "If something happens to her and you could have stopped it, I'm coming after you."

He gave me the smile prison guards give you when five of them come into your cell to beat you up. "You know where to find us," he said. "And don't worry," he added as I reached the door, "we'll know where to find you."

I CALLED ERICA about tonight and got her in Atlanta on her way home. "Can't," she said, "working on a brief."

"No you're not. I'm coming down to see you."

"No you're not."

"You won't believe the trouble I'm in."

"Nothing new about that. Sam, I gotta go…"

"Abigail's gone missing."

"Oh shit." Erica sighed, listened while I told her. "Okay."

"Where?"

"DiMillo's? Six-thirty?" Nothing more, then, "I'm going to kill you, Sam."

"After we've made love ten thousand times, you can kill me then."

"Okay," she laughed, "I'll kill you then."

It was the first time since I'd come back to Maine I'd heard her laugh.

HIGHWAY TO HELL on my phone. I grabbed it expecting Pa. But my heart plunged when I saw the display: Mildred Pierce, Senator Coleman's PA. Abigail's boss.

"Still no word," Mildred said. "We're getting a little worried."

"What about Senator Coleman, can't he get the cops to do something?" I said.

"He's too busy but we're keeping him updated."

"Good for him."

"Pono?"

"Yes?"

"You were close to Abigail..."

"She might not say so."

"We should talk."

This stunned me. "But she – " I started to say and stopped.

"Why not meet in the Capitol cafeteria," Mildred said. "Do you know it?"

I started to say *that's where I met Abigail* but didn't. "I know it."

"Seven tomorrow morning then?" When I didn't answer right away, she added, "I think you'll be happy you did."

DIMILLO'S IS A MAGICAL place, fabulous food in a gleaming restaurant on a ship moored at the downtown waterfront, surrounded by fishing boats, yachts and the blue waters of the port. In summer it's lovely to sit on the top deck in the sun and chatter of seagulls and chug of tugs and ferries and the salty cool tang of the sea, with marvelous food and wine, and suddenly all the world makes sense.

Though sitting outside in January is unwise, the inside restaurant has a luxurious air of softness, privacy and quiet, the smells from other tables delectable, with just a nod sometimes from the waves, subtle and seductive.

Erica was certainly seductive though hardly subtle. "You have to stop messing with my life," were her first words when she arrived twenty minutes late, tossing her black camel-hair coat over the other chair. "I'm too busy."

I got up and kissed her. Her lips were cold, her hands too. "What are you doing all this for, Erica?"

She smirked. "Having dinner with you? God knows."

"No, why are you working so hard, by yourself? What are you trying to get from it?"

She gave me a severe look, brushing her hair back over her collar. "You ask me again I'm leaving."

The waitress saved me. When she'd left I said, "I'm beginning to fear Abigail's been kidnapped or something."

Erica gripped my fingers and I curled hers into my palms, warming them. "If something's happened to her," she looked at me, hard, "you are totally screwed."

"That's how it seems."

"You have no alibi. According to witnesses you're the last person she was with. She left angrily. You've shown excessive interest in her absence. Despite frigid weather you spent hours in that horrible truck watching for her. You set up a meeting with her under false premises in the Capitol cafeteria. You were seen in public together at The Liberal Cup and Slates, you have a known history of violence toward women –"

"You know that's a lie –"

"That's how the prosecutor will twist what you did in Afghanistan."

I sat back despairingly. Maybe I should just disappear. Right now, while I could, before the Maine cops got me. But do what? Go where?

She gave me a fierce look. "You're a sitting duck. And if something happens to her they'll take you down."

"That has two meanings."

"I know." She picked up the menu. "What are you having?"

I finished my second martini, glanced through the window at the port, the tilted pilings and busy tugs, the cranes and ice-flecked water, and it seemed the universe was like that water, frozen and deadly. I'd been hungry but wasn't now, ordered mechanically hoping I might want it when it came.

"So it's either accidental," Erica said, "or perpetrated."

"What is?"

"Abigail's disappearance." Erica looked at me gently. "Either way we have to find you an alibi."

How strange that days ago I'd been seeking an alibi for Bucky, and now I needed one. And Bucky was in jail. Would I soon be too? "If it's perpetrated?"

"Then they've got you, unless serious evidence says otherwise. They won't look any further... And since *you* didn't do it, someone *else* did. So here's the easy part –"

"What is?"

"To save your ass, all you have to do is find who *did* do it. And prove it." She killed her Allagash, licked her lips. "And somehow stay out of jail till you do."

North Wind

I FOLLOWED ERICA'S 911 to her mansion on the Eastern Promenade. Bucky's 150 looked definitely out of place in front of this two-mile string of sedate, elegant residences overlooking wide lawns, tall trees and island-studded Casco Bay.

Erica owned a two-story stone and clapboard place from the 1870s, tall and stately in gray paint and white trim, a widow's walk atop its gabled, slated roof.

She lived upstairs and rented out downstairs. Her floor was all stone fireplaces, oak floors, Orientals, leather couches and wide windows on Casco Bay. There were two bedrooms, a big one with a king-size bed that got me imagining all the things she'd done on it, and making me want to go there right away, but I held my tongue.

"This is a lovely place," I said mindfully as I could.

She sat on a couch arm, knees crossed under her long batik dress. "I've been thinking – since I got so mad at you for challenging me – that this place too is like the condo in St. Thomas and the tickets to Europe. Stuff I never allow myself to enjoy."

"That's a shame." I stood beside her brushing hair from her eyes. "Why work so hard?" I stopped. "Oh Jesus I said it again. You gonna throw me out?"

"But maybe if I don't work this hard," she rubbed her cheek against the back of my hand, "there'll be nothing. Can you imagine…"

I kissed the top of her head inhaling all the lovely odors of her hair. "There will always be you. And you're magnificent. Without even working at all."

She nuzzled me. "Maybe if I'm not working *I'm* nothing. Or everything's going to cave in… I'll lose it all."

"In twenty-five days, no matter what, I'm leaving for Tahiti."

She leaned back to look up at me. Ta*hiti?*"

"The Tsunami, an international surfing competition. Why don't you come?"

"Oh God," she sighed. "I've got a court calendar nine months long. Not even a free day."

"Fuck all that." I raised her up in my arms, kissed down her neck and around her ear, slid her dress above her waist and kissed down between her slender thighs. "Let's make a plan… you're going to dedicate more time to sex, and less to law. And to start with, I'm going to take away your briefs."

AT 05:00 I slid into my icy clothes. Erica nuzzled me good bye. "To find the perp," she said fuzzily, "all you have to do is swim upstream."

"What the hell does that mean?" I was a little cranky and needed coffee, and was facing a 60-mile subzero drive to meet with Mildred at the Capitol cafeteria in Augusta.

"From the act to its source. Determine what they were trying to get by what they did. Then you'll know who they are."

"Right," I said exasperatedly, closing the door softly when I left.

Since she and I had basically been up all night I started dozing at the wheel, the 150 wandering a bit, so I pulled off 295 and washed my face in snow. Falling asleep at the wheel is a horrible way to die.

I STOPPED AT ABIGAIL'S on the way to the Capitol. No one there. She's having a hot time with someone, I told myself, she's too smart to get in trouble. Telling myself *who would hurt her?*

First thing I'd looked for was her white Saab. It was nowhere to be seen in the area. And had not appeared, according to Mitchell, in any database since its last oil change three months ago. Looking at her Carfax service record it was clear how organized and conscientious this wild woman was.

Her cellphone was still dead.

Mail was piling up inside her door.

According to Mitchell she'd had 217 emails in the last week but she had sent nothing since the last one to me, before we'd met at Slates.

So I'd been the last email she'd ever sent.

The cops knew this too.

And they'd pored through all the public camera records, including all the gas stations, banks and other videoed locations. Neither Abigail nor the white Saab was on any of them. But I was still free as a bird. In a cage.

Three times I'd walked every street in Hallowell and twice in Augusta, checking every driveway and trying to peer into every garage, looking for her angelic face in every department store and fast food joint, seeking the Saab in gas stations and parking lots, never seeing it, as if it'd never existed, nor she.

I'd begun to fear she was dead.

Therefore it was only a matter of time before they pulled me in.

Horrendous as that was, I cared much more about what had happened to her than what was coming at me.

MILDRED PIERCE was a bit like I'd envisioned, gray-haired and rotund, soft-voiced and grandmotherly with oval glasses, a small gold crucifix between ample breasts, a thin wedding ring and tiny diamond on a pudgy finger, freckles on the backs of her hands, sharp blue eyes and a careful smile.

06:55 and the Capitol cafeteria was mobbed, people buying coffee and pastries to go, cups of yogurt, shiny apples and all the other accoutrements of modern gastronomy. We took a table to one side but with all the clatter of trays and voices it was hard to hear.

"Still no news?" she said.

I was still shivering from the drive from Erica's in Portland and the time at Abigail's. "None."

"I've decided to talk to you," she leaned forward, "because there's more to this than just Abigail. But I have concerns."

"Like?"

"My husband works for the State Highway Department. If you reveal what I tell you, he loses his job."

I squeezed her hand. "Understood."

"Good." She squeezed me back. "Abigail's disappearance is tied to other issues."

"Like?"

"I've worked in Maine government ever since I graduated Westbrook College way back in '72. Started as a secretary for Representative Rosenthal, a wonderful man who cared deeply about Maine. When he retired I worked for several different senators and reps..." she looked at me intently "... and every single one of them worked their hearts out for Maine."

"What's this got to do with Abigail?"

"The Legislature's not like that now. It's all out-of-state money, bribery, cash under the table..." She flattened her hands on the tabletop. "It's unbelievable how Big Wind has taken over Maine."

"They took over Hawaii too, till the people fought back. But as long as there's federal subsidies the Wind Mafia will never give up."

"Here in Maine they're almost untouchable. They've bought both US Senators, the State Demo leadership, most Dem Legislators and even some Republicans."

"I grew up in a moderately lefty household, so I assumed Dems were more moral about taking bribes than Republicans. But in reality *they all are crooks.*"

"They *have* to be. Or they wouldn't get the corporate money that gets them elected. And then tells them exactly what to do." She wiped her glasses with a napkin and put them back on.

"You'd be shocked," she said, "to see how the top Democratic Senators dominate the Committee chairs. They come into Committee meetings and tell everyone how to vote. New Legislators are told if they don't vote pro-wind, the leadership will run someone in the next primary against them, make sure they're defeated.

"One new Legislator came on the Energy Committee and I had hopes for him," she went on, "because he hadn't been part of the bunch that created the Wind Law. And he was asking smart questions, poking holes in the wind lobby. So the top Dems took him aside and straightened him out. After that a lobbyist from one of the wind contractors came into the chambers for every vote and stood staring at him, making sure he'd vote the right way."

"I don't need to hear this." Not anymore.

"Once someone asked a Dem Legislator from Portland how she was going to vote on a wind-related bill, and she said, *Just a minute, I have to call my wind lobbyist.* This was the same woman who said on TV that wind turbines in

Maine would cut coal-fired greenhouse gas emissions in the Midwest. But that's ridiculous because there's no connective grid between Maine and the Midwest. So wind projects in Maine could never have any effect on the Midwest. Even worse, Maine wind projects sell carbon credits to Midwest coal-fired utilities so they *can* pollute more..."

"I haven't yet found the recipe for honest government."

She patted my hand, a teacher with a moderately good student. "This breaks my heart, that they'd do this to Maine. And to know when you die that you were instrumental in destroying one of the most beautiful places on earth? To take that to your grave?"

I couldn't speak. About the earth's annihilation and how humans lie about it. It had wrenched my heart so long I couldn't stand it anymore. "So what's this got to do with Abigail?"

She leaned forward, chubby forearms trembling the table. "Pono, have you listened to a *single* thing I've said?"

I thought about it. "The wind industry has paid millions to buy Maine, they're going to make billions, and they're not going to let anyone get in their way?"

She clasped her hands. "And?"

"How did Abigail get in the way?" It froze my heart to think it. "Yeah," I said sadly. "I can answer that."

"I'm afraid," Mildred said, "*she* knew who killed her husband."

"And that would be reason," I made myself say, "for them to kill her too?"

"Look at it this way," she said. "Central Maine Power is actually owned by Iberdrola, the Spanish wind developer that helped bankrupt Spain with windmills. Iberdrola is the largest corporate welfare recipient of US taxpayer subsidies – over two billion dollars. Its *largest* investor is a group of oil sheiks in Qatar, that desert dictatorship whose two main exports are oil and the funding of Islamic terrorism. So every time Central Maine Power raises rates, some of those millions out of our pockets end up in Qatar, and maybe even help shoot down a passenger plane or blow up a school bus – who's to know?"

Sell Your Body Parts Here

I WAS EVEN MORE WORRIED about Abigail after talking with Mildred. One moment I'd reassure myself she was fine, just shacked up somewhere, then I'd realize how wrong this was, that she wouldn't naturally go missing like this.

If something *had* happened to her, why? The question made me so sick I wanted to run down to the cop shop again, but that would just piss them off.

So what could I do?

If something had happened to her she was either dead or kidnapped. She was tough, no one could easily take her down. If she was dead and buried somewhere?

Mitchell could not trace her phone. She'd not showed at work or home. The Saab had vanished. I called Mildred at the Senator's office three times that afternoon but there was never a trace of Abigail.

I kept coming back to the question if she's dead? After I got over the horror of imagining it I tried to figure why someone would do it. What was she hiding? What did she know?

Was it because she was meeting me, and that I knew about her and Bucky? About her husband's change of heart? Was that it?

Had I caused her death? If she *was* dead?

If she was dead. I will not think like this, I told myself. But what if it's true? Or what if I could be saving her, if I only could figure out how?

Who'd hurt someone like Abigail?

The same ones who killed her husband?

In twenty-six days I was leaving for Tahiti.

How could I when Abigail was missing?

"THIS STINKS," Mitchell said.

"You nut." I checked my phone, always a perilous process when driving the 150. "What the fuck time is it out there?"

"03:22. Your fault, you bastard. I can't sleep."

"*What* stinks?"

"I'm still digging into Legislators' private accounts. It's not a pretty story. I'll tell you when I get it figured out."

"In the meantime, you learn anything from my snowmobiler list?"

"You got fifty-one names. Most are couples. Thirty-one are vets – twenty-eight guys and three women. Only five, all guys, would seem to meet your shooter's profile, assuming it was a he, and in shape, somebody hard core."

"Yeah?"

"Anyway I sent the whole list to Lexie. Most have bios and pix. You and her can figure it out."

I explained him what I'd learned from Mildred Pierce.

"That's fucking nauseating," he said. "Like in India, all over the third world. You've got two kidneys, so a body parts broker will buy one for a few hundred bucks, sell it for thousands in London or New York. You get get paid enough to survive for another year or two in whatever overpopulated impoverished autocracy you inhabit, and the broker gets rich."

"Just what the Wind Mafia's doing, selling off Maine's body parts. And making billions on it."

"Gets you in the guts, don't it?"

WHEN I FINALLY get to Lexie's after the night with Erica and the morning at Abigail's empty house and the meeting with Mildred and my chat with Mitchell on the way home, Officer Trask is sitting in the driveway in his battle wagon with the engine running. It was maybe 15 below but Lexie hadn't invited him in. He slid down the driver window as I walked past. "Where," he sniffles, "were you last night?"

"In Portland. Why?" I suddenly feared the worst, they'd found Abigail's body.

"Over at Paradise Lakes somebody shot out four turbines."

"Fantastic!" I raised a clenched fist.

"We think it was you."

"I was in bed all night with a beautiful woman. But I didn't get much sleep, so if you'll excuse me –"

"Not so fast. You have corboration?"

I wasn't sure if he'd said *carburation* or *corporation*. "That truck has carburation," I pointed to Bucky's 150, "it's much better than the fuel injection in this pig of yours." I knew I shouldn't taunt him but kept going, "and no, I'm not a corporation."

He smiled. His teeth weren't great. "You got somebody to corborate your story, is what I said."

I pulled out my phone and hit Erica's cell. It went to voice mail. I hit it again.

"Think fast," Trask said.

Motion on my perimeter caught my eye. It was Max, methodically going from one tire of Trask's battle wagon to the next giving each a good spray.

Trying not to grin I punched in Erica's office number. "Ms. Tillson is in conference," the sonorous lady said.

"Please, I have to talk to her, it's personal. *Essential.* Just for a moment…"

"It's a very important conference."

"This's even *more* important."

Moments later Erica came on, at about two thousand volts. "I'll kill you!"

"Officer Trask of the Freedom Police needs to know where I was last night. Apparently people've been shooting out more turbines."

"Put him on!"

She must have been somewhere private because when he took the phone you could hear her voice ten feet away. "Mr. Hawkins was with me," she said. "He fucked me all night so I'm sure he was there."

When he handed me back my phone he was blushing. Or maybe it was just the north wind.

As he backed down the drive I knelt to to scratch Max under the chin. And I swear he smiled.

"What'd Trask want?" Lexie said when I got in the door, as if he were an inferior form of ferret. And she had that fierce look she gets every time I spend a night with another woman. So I explained her about the Paradise Lakes turbines.

"Good," she says. "Maybe soon they'll all be gone."

"Interesting to know if they can find a bullet."

Her eyebrows raised. "And match it?"

IT'S A 20-MILE DRIVE from Lexie's farm to Paradise Lakes. All the way, through farm fields and forest, all you can see are rows and rows of ugly turbines like satanic three-bladed crucifixes blocking off the sky. And once again it amazed me at the scurviness of American politics, that a governor can set up a multi-billion scam while in office, then make millions on it when he leaves, then use that to buy himself a US Senate seat. Oh, and see to it that his son gets a big job in the wind business.

It must be nice to own the government.

Today was an average wind day so none of the turbines were turning. I took the access road to the top of the first ridge, and from there looked across thousands of acres of turbines, clearcuts, roads, blasted rock and mud where just three years ago had been limitless forest and its myriad creatures. And atop it now these diabolical towers as if they have taken over our world.

I followed the ridge between the rows of towers to the blasted and bulldozed far end looking out over the lakes, and lo, there were trucks and hard hats and a police SUV and all sorts of activity going on.

"Who are you?" a guy in a yellow hard hat says when I pull up.

"I heard there was an accident or something? Some turbines down?"

"What's that matter to you?"

"I'm looking for work, wondered if maybe –"

"No jobs here. Beat it."

Just then the door at the bottom of one tower opens and three guys come out, one with an attaché case. "You get one?" somebody calls.

"Got two. But they're no good," attaché case says.

"How come?" I ask, innocently, as if I belong there.

"All smashed up," attaché case says. "Can't use them."

Yellow hard hat looks me over. "Outta here."

"I can run a chainsaw, a backhoe, you name it. You sure there ain't work?"

"You local guys should know by now, it's all out-of-state workers on wind projects."

SOME OF THE SNOW had blown off the road when we drove to Warren for visitors' hour. I waited in a glass and wire room looking at a tattered *Car and Driver* while Lexie argued with someone in the warden's office.

She came out with a fierce look. "Let's go!"

"What the Hell? We came to see Bucky!"

She turned on me tartly. "He's not seeing visitors."

Rage flamed through me. "The Hell he's not!"

She tugged my arm. "They can't *make* him. He has the right to refuse."

My fingers itched to reach through concrete walls and steel bars and strangle him. "I'll *kill* him."

She gave me a worried glance. "Don't say that in here."

We walked out into the cold. *Fuck you, Bucky,* I said silently. *I'm crossing you off my list.*

BACK AT LEXIE'S I called Lobo into the den and made her sniff Bucky's guns. She wagged her tail and looked at me curiously – *Why are we doing this? I already know what they smell like.*

"This's what we're looking for," I explained her.

Her ears peaked, eyes bright. We went outside. The thermometer said minus 17 but the sun felt good. Lobo dashed ahead doing pirouettes in the snow, barking and running back to me – *Come on, you're so slow!*

There was a good wind but the turbines weren't turning. The male eagle was circling high above the turbine that had killed his mate, his white head gleaming in afternoon sun.

We hiked up the ridge then along it, Lobo sniffing the snow and galloping back, till we got closer to the turbines Bucky'd shot out, and as before Lobo sat in the snow and would go no further.

I crossed the top and down the other side and called her. After a minute she showed, ears back, tail between his legs. "The turbines aren't running," I said. "You'll be okay."

We went down to where Bucky'd hid the .308 and spent the whole afternoon doing wider and wider sweeps, but Lobo never found the scent of Bucky's gun. It had probably been a waste of time but I'd had to make sure. One by one to knock off options, narrow down the search. And options didn't always turn up positive.

WHEN SOMEONE TRIES TO KILL YOU, you can run away and hope they won't find you. Or you can circle back on them and make sure it doesn't happen again.

So there's really no choice.

After midnight I gave up trying to sleep, got dressed, grabbed Bucky's .243 and drove from Lexie's to the snowmobile trail beyond Jane's.

The trail's crust was hard packed and crunchy underfoot. The night air stung my nostrils. The ghoulish flickering strobes of the turbine towers bloodied the snow.

A quick hour's trek took me to the ridge above the Missalonkee Hard Riders clubhouse. I crouched in a spruce thicket and watched it a while then dropped down to the clubhouse, popped open a back window and squeezed through.

Inside was cold as outside and stank of cigarettes and old beer. Moving forward I banged my knee on something that hurt like hell. I flicked on my headlamp. It was the damn bathtub. It was full of empty beer cans and empty five-pound plastic ice bags.

Now I understood. During meetings they'd fill the tub with Coors Lite. Not a tantalizing thought.

Trying not to bang into anything else and keeping the headlamp hooded I checked out the place. A long desk down the front of the room with metal folding chairs behind it. A bunch of plastic picnic tables with four metal chairs each. Two pool tables in one corner, a rack of cues on the wall. A trails map on the opposite wall above a wide riverstone fireplace that smelled of dead ashes and beer, and down which a frigid wind descended from the open chimney. There was a white industrial sink at one end with a shut-off cold water faucet, two ancient Admiral refrigerators beside it with their doors hanging open.

A fat-bellied woodstove crouched like a toad against the back wall, a *2015 Maine Heating Oil* calendar with a photo of a large-breasted woman pinned to the pine slab wall behind it. Circled in red was February 18, *6 pm till ???* was *Feb Members Mtg.* I tried to remember today's date; yes, the meeting was tomorrow night.

And in a drawer under the long desk a members' list. And next to each name an address, phone, and the license number of their machine.

I trekked back to Lexie's in a better mood. Dawn was beginning to tint the distant treetops; coyotes called hungrily from a far valley. *Thank you* I said back to them, to the one who'd called and saved my life. It might have just been accidental, but I've known enough animals to think it may have been intended.

Coyotes often understand people better than people do. Which may explain why people shoot, trap and poison them.

By the time I crawled into my bunk at Lexie's I was half-frozen and dizzy with exhaustion, and gray day was upon us.

That's when the cops called.

Welcome to Vacationland

OFFICER HART, the same paunchy sarcastic Augusta cop on my phone. "It's now been three days she's gone, or whatever she's done. We want you down here, make a statement."

"Statement?" I pried open one eye. Then the other. "What the hell for?"

"Once it's this long we have to investigate. Even if we don't think there's nothing to it."

"I can't do it right now."

"Be here by ten or we come get you."

I sleep till nine, shave and brush my teeth with soap, find something half-clean to wear and bolt down Lexie's coffee and doughnuts. Rocinante doesn't want to start, perhaps nervous about what lies ahead. Leaving a bilious wake of smog and particulates we finally wander, slip and slide our way to the Augusta cop shop, where they invite me to a back room with a dirty floor, faded walls, speckled casement windows, metal chairs and a metal table. The paunchy cop, C. Hart, and a tall skinny one with a Hemingway moustache whose badge said "F. Dilfer", plus a video recorder and another camera high up on the wall. I'm afraid for a moment and wonder should I say nothing without a lawyer? Don't be silly, I tell myself, we're trying to find Abigail. You're not a suspect.

So I tell them about seeing her at the Capitol cafeteria, that I'd thought I'd met her somewhere.

"What day was this?"

I tried to remember; yes, it had been a Sunday night when she'd come home with the maroon Subaru , so Monday morning when I followed her to the Capitol and set up our little meeting. "Last Monday."

"What were you doin there?" the skinny tall cop with the Hemingway moustache said.

What could I say? I wasn't going to bring up Bucky, or Abigail's husband's death, or tell them why I was really here. "I was wandering around the Capitol, doing the tourist thing."

"In fucking February?"

I remembered there was a library across the parking lot, a museum. "I went to the museum, lady at the desk said there's a cafeteria at the Capitol… I was having a doughnut and coffee when Abigail came in."

"That's a nice museum," C. Hart says.

"Yeah."

He leaned toward me, belly against the table. "What'd you see there?"

"Don't remember much, just took a glance around."

"Really? That morning? Monday, February 9?"

Sweat was running down my ribs. "Yeah."

"Funny," he sat back. "Museum's closed on Mondays."

"So maybe it was Tuesday! This is *bull*shit – I ask for help finding this woman and you start implicating me?"

"You're a perp. Perps often start the search for someone they've done in."

I laughed. "You saying I killed Abigail?"

He gave a sardonic sigh. "Heavens no."

"I wouldn't hurt anybody. I like her. I'm afraid for her."

"You wouldn't hurt nobody?" C. Hart said. "You shot that woman –"

"She was dying. Burned alive. Begged me to do it."

"Yeah. Right." He clasped his hands, elbows on the metal table. "So you met Abigail at the Capitol cafeteria?"

"Yeah."

"What then?"

"I ran into her next night at Slates. She was singing Irish songs. Playing the guitar." *It was very beautiful,* I wanted to say but no way he'd understand. *She* was very beautiful. She *was*...

"So you talked to her?"

"Yeah. After she was done."

"Where was this?"

"At my table."

"She sees you, comes over?"

"I sent her a drink. She came over."

"What next?"

"We spent a long time talking."

"Then what?"

"Went to her place."

"So you were screwing this dame? Who's now disappeared?"

"That's her business. And mine."

"And he was the last one to see her," Hart says to Hemingway.

"When was that?" Hemingway says.

"Night she disappeared," Hart answers. "They had a fight at Slates, she left in an angry hurry and he followed her out. Nobody seen her since."

Hemingway leans back, hands clasped behind his head. "No shit."

"We got three witnesses at Slates, two waiters and the guy at the cash register."

"Jealousy?" Hemingway turns to me. "Found out she was screwing other guys, got upset? That's what's usually going on when guys kill women."

I stood up. "What are you insinuating?"

He smiled at me. "Nothing. For the moment."

"What are you doing to find Abigail?"

"We're checking," Hart said.

"Checking what, for Chrissake?"

"Where the fuck she is."

I wanted to hit them both. "*Please* try to find her."

"One thing we *have* found," Hemingway said, "is a paper napkin with your name and number. In her office."

"I gave that to her."

"Really?" He raised his eyebrows.

"One way or the other we'll find her," Hart adds. "But in the meantime, till she shows up, you're a person of interest in her disappearance."

"Fuck you. I'll get a lawyer."

"You go right ahead," Hemingway said. "But we don't want you leaving Maine."

"Right," Hart said. "Welcome to Vacationland."

That's when Pa called.

PA WAS A SEAL in Vietnam, where he learned as I did later in Iraq that defending freedom ain't always what it seems. This also explains why I love the Seals though when I was younger I often got in fights with them. They were the people I grew up around, quiet guys with that far look in their eyes. And when you punched them it hurt your fist not them.

Later I'll explain you some of what happened in Nam, and how Pa and millions of other people paid for it. By the time he got home in '73, when for the U.S. it was all over but for the last screams of the wounded, he'd had his brains removed and replaced with the most horrifying video game you can imagine.

It took him nine years to find Ma, a person I remember deeply though she was killed by a drunk driver when I was seven. As I got older he'd had plenty of women but never lived with one. So in my youth I was coddled and loved by many different smart and interesting women, most of whom it appears found Pa too hot to handle, but who were all lovely and caring to me. From which maybe comes my love of women. Or it's just DNA.

He spent the next thirty years as a professional diver, not the kind who takes you out on a reef tour, but the kind who gets called when a plane goes down in five hundred feet of ocean and somebody has to go to that depth. Or for a problem on a drill rig in Indonesia or the North Sea, or to check out a damaged hull in Singapore. After those thirty years he retired to a hut on posts in the verdant upper reaches of Waipio Valley, one of the loveliest places on earth.

And now I'm standing outside the cop shop in a bitter wind, that 808 area code lighting up like a beacon from home. 11:12 in Maine is 06:12 in Waipio – before sunrise, a little early for Pa.

"Hey," he says, "how is it back there?"

I explain him a bit about Bucky. "This the guy what nailed you?" Pa says.

"He thought he was doing the right thing."

"And this was the girl you was with before he nailed you? The one I met?"

"Lexie? Yeah, till I got the twenty years..."

"Your own damn fault you got that."

"What was I going to do, Pa, with that Afghani girl writhing in agony? She was dying anyway –"

"Yeah but then to shoot her dumbfuck husband?"

"He's the one who lit her on fire!"

"So what? Nearly every Muslim believes this whacked-out shit about women! You gonna shoot them all?"

"Pa, what the fuck you call about?"

"Call about? Oh yeah, I forgot. Went to the doctor yesterday. Can you believe that? How many years since I been–"

"Yeah?"

"So I realized I should call you."

Oh shit. "Yeah?"

"Have to go into Hilo, do some tests."

"What *kinda* tests?"

"They're gonna to look down a tube in my stomach, some other stuff."

"Pa, what do they think it is?"

"Hell, they don't know. Most everybody in Nam got exposed to Agent Orange. Just matters can you survive it. You know the VA."

Overworked, underfunded and understaffed, the VA moves slowly. "How soon?"

"They're having me do it right away."

Sitting Duck

GOING CRAZY about Abigail I kept looking. Wrapped in a horse blanket in Bucky's 150 I drove the streets of so many Maine towns but never saw her white Saab. Like a penitent pilgrim I wandered every shop and café, every Dollar Store, Hannaford, mini-mall and hippie market.

No Abigail.

Sometimes it hit so bad I hate to admit but I choked up, holding it in and trying to look normal, saying to myself I will not get emotional. But when you really care for someone in danger you'll do anything to help them. No matter the cost.

Not that I knew what that would be. Not yet.

"YOU *NEED* A LAWYER." Lexie came back from the reefer with two glasses of ice and Tanqueray, shoved one across the table at me and raised hers. "To the old days."

"To the old days," I said, unconvinced. We'd had dinner and I'd washed the dishes while she planned tomorrow's biology class but it was far too early to sleep. I'd shown her the list of names I'd taken from the Missalonkee Hard Riders clubhouse, and she'd known fifteen out of fifty-one. "I'll narrow it down," she said, looking mean.

I loved it when she looked that way but I was too worried about Pa – now the cops were restricting me to Maine, what if the tests turned out bad and he needed me?

She downed her gin in a long languorous swallow, slapped the glass on the table and leaned forward smiling into my eyes. "Remember how we *were?*"

That made my privates tingle. "I remember."

"So get over it already." She took my hand. "You and I, we're going to get Bucky out. Then we're going to ride off into the sunset together." She slid her fingers between mine. "And when we do I'm going to be riding on your lap."

This was one of the infinite things I'd loved about Lexie, that she liked to be on top. "Why do I need a lawyer?" I said defensively.

"Why?" She looked at me the way she used to sometimes, as if I'd proven once again I had no brain at all. Her voice went up an octave, *"Why?"*

"Yeah. *Why* already."

"*Why?* Because the cops don't care who did what or who's guilty. If they cared about guilt they'd arrest all the lobbyists and half the Legislators in Augusta. If Abigail turns up dead they want a suspect so they look good on TV. You're a recidivist – if Abigail stays missing, of *course* you did it." She refilled her glass to the brim. "Here," she shoved the bottle at me. "Get some sense."

"*Why?*" I repeated.

"*Why?*" She went up another octave. "Because they *want* you. Just like they *wanted* you last time! When they didn't give a damn *why* you had to kill that dying woman in Afghanistan! They didn't give a *damn,* the Army and the Pentagon and DOD and Colin Powell and Donald Rumsfeld and Cheney and that smarmy little turd Bush – they didn't give a *damn!* They wanted *you* as a poster child showing we punish war crimes – that we're going to crucify you while we perpetrate *real* war crimes elsewhere." She dropped her head a moment, long hair on the table, then raised up and looked into my eyes. "I won't go through it again."

I bit my lip. "Nobody's asking you to."

Tears flooded her eyes. "I'm not losing you again."

I felt miserable, hemmed in, afraid. I didn't want more jail time and didn't want to be monogamous either. If I ever got *out* of jail.

Twice I'd learned how the law can kidnap you from your life into its soul-annihilating horrors. So I had lots of fear knowing it can grab you just because it wants to. Particularly if you satisfy some political or financial goal.

"The Pussy Riot girls are in trouble again," I said.

"Putin wants to look tough on Ukraine."

"I love those girls," I added, with a certain longing. In my mind they were all lovely, naked and irate, a wonderful combination.

She refilled her glass, looked at me through it. "If all the pussies on the planet rioted there'd be no more war."

"True."

"Speaking of Pussy Riot," she caressed my fingers, "Abigail had this thing about doing guys only one night, you said?"

"Yeah but she did it again with me."

"If she *was* doing guys only once, then she's not somewhere with a guy. Unless they're really into tantra."

"Even then…"

Lexie grinned, a little high. "How *was* she?"

"Fantastic. The all-night kind of thing."

"You and I had lots of those."

"Stop taunting me. We're not going to do it."

"That's why it's safe to taunt you." She took a reflective sip, running the gin round her tongue, enjoying the taste. "And if Abigail turns up safe you're no longer at risk."

The thought was overwhelming but cut like a knife. I wasn't just fearing for Abigail, I missed her, wanted her. "And then all we'll have to do is get Bucky out."

Lexie leaned toward me, elbows on the table. "Hey, what if *he* knows?"

"Who?"

"Bucky." Lexie slapped the table. "That bitch -- what if *he* knows where she is?"

This made me wonder did she know Bucky and Abigail were lovers? If they were? I played dumb: "How would Bucky know?"

"He talked to her a few times, met her at a hearing." She shrugged. "He might have an idea –"

I stood. The room stayed relatively stable. "Let's go see him." I headed for the door, pulled it open a crack to check how hard the blizzard was howling.

"We can't go now!" Lexie called. "It's almost midnight!"

"Just taking a leak." I slid sideways through the door and yanked it shut, crossed the barnyard's squeaky new snow and pissed against a post, the wind snatching it away.

The problem of Bucky literally weighted down my shoulders with fear, exhaustion and defeat. Like the dangers facing Maine from its implacable enemies. Like my own dangers. I stood there taking deep breaths of frigid wind that tasted deliciously of snow and frozen forests. Even in the worst of situations, I reminded myself, there's sometimes a way to win. The idea seemed true and irreversible as the wind.

The turbines weren't turning but the strobes fluttered across the snowy wastes with a ghoulish glow.

After the icy night the kitchen was hot and stuffy. "We'll go see Bucky in the morning," I said. "Put your coat on, come outside."

We stood side by side inhaling the north wind, arms round each other's backs like veterans returned from the wars, this woman I'd loved so much and now couldn't have, not by my rules or hers, till we got Bucky out. It seemed a perverse version of some medieval romance, a knight sworn to save the husband of the woman he loves.

Which made me think again of Abigail. Maybe Bucky *did* have an answer. And I'd been too stupid to ask him. I gave Lexie's ribs a little squeeze of thanks; she squeezed me back. Lexie and Abigail – right there was enough reason to avoid monogamy at all costs. Impossible to love just one woman. And there was Erica, too.

But right now what I cared about was Abigail.

"DON'T YOU *DARE* come visit me," Pa said when I called.

"Cops won't let me leave Maine."

"Jesus why are you always in trouble?"

"I'm not always in trouble. Just sometimes. Anyway in a few days this'll all be cleared up and I'll be there."

"I don't want you to come. I been ducking death a long time, now it's my turn. I don't mind. This pain, so goddamn bad you don't want to live."

That broke my heart.

Shooter

I WENT BY ABIGAIL'S next morning hoping something had changed. But no, the house looked closed-up, forsaken, as if after someone's death. I stood on the granite doorstep and peered through the leaded glass door panel. Inside seemed uninhabited, the hardwood gleaming, the Persian carpets lustrous reds and blues in early sun.

On the floor inside the door was a pile of mail. Why hadn't the cops picked it up? Gone through it?

On top a handwritten envelope. Twisting my head back and forth I could barely see it through the rainbow glass. READ THIS NOW in red magic marker, above her name and address. No return address.

I backed away, returned to the truck. Couldn't decide whether to ask the cops to check that mail, or wait till night and do it myself.

AT STATE PRISON Bucky still wouldn't see me. I would've paid good money to strangle him. I drove back to Lexie's feeling displaced, annoyed and weirdly nervous for my life.

Lexie met me at the kitchen door brandishing the Missalonkee snowmobilers list. "I've compared it with Mitchell's. Only three of them might've shot at you."

I slumped into a kitchen chair, weary from thinking about what I'd learned from Mildred, what Mitchell had said, even more from Abigail's aching absence. The spider web around me, and around Maine, was growing deeper, multidimensional, and for the first time I feared it would devour me, and Maine too. I glanced at her short list. "How come these three?"

She pulled up a chair, list in one hand, yellow pad and red pen in the other. One by one she explained why the other ones – people she knew – didn't do it. Some were too old or didn't snowmobile much anymore or were away in Florida right now. Or didn't have hunting licenses and probably couldn't shoot this well.

The three she picked out were all veterans. One was a forty-seven year old retired cop from Bangor, another drove the local tow truck, and the third, Titus McKee, was a semi truck mechanic and ex-Ranger. "In one of the photos Mitchell sent he was still in uniform." She turned her screen so I could see. "On it are three Sharpshooter medals."

He was a big brawny guy with a hard jaw and harder eyes. In the other two pix he was older, bearded, even more wide-shouldered and truculent. "You know anything about him?" I said.

"I'll call Don and Viv. Haven't talked to them in two years."

"Why's that?"

"They were the first to sell out to WindPower. And now it's so bad they have to leave. Serves them right." She found a tattered phone book, peering into it.

"Lexie, you need reading glasses."

"Do not." She dialed a number. "'Lo, Don? It's Lexie. Yeah, me. Sorry to hear you have to leave... Yeah, we hope Bucky's getting out soon – it's ridiculous, what they're saying. Hey, someone was askin about Titus McKee. Ain't he your neighbor?"

They talked a minute more and she shut down. "Titus McKee is a local tough guy, repairs big trucks. Don says he can hit a duck on the wing with an iron sight 30-30."

I thought of all the shooter's near misses snapping past my head. This was my shooter. I *knew* it.

And I was going to get him.

Maybe tonight.

ABOUT 30 SNOWMOBILES were parked in front of the Missalonkee Hard Riders club for the February members' meeting. In the quarter moonlight they all looked dark.

It was 19:21. Lexie'd dropped me off beyond Jane's on the snowmobile trail, and I'd walked the hard crust all the way to the clubhouse in less than an hour. When I reached the ridge above the clubhouse I'd made myself a nice snow hole and crawled inside to watch the fun.

I could see directly into the main room, the picnic tables, metal chairs and the long desk at the front. The sweet smells of oak smoke and baked beans and the melody of "Penny Lane" drifted uphill on the wind. Inside, people in snowmobile boots moved back and forth carrying paper plates and beer cans, finding seats around the picnic tables, talking and laughing.

The bathtub was full of beer cans and ice. There were about twenty liquor bottles on the long desk, piles of plastic glasses and paper plates. "Penny Lane" finished and "All You Need Is Love" started with a trumpet blare.

After a while I slid out of my hole and circled west around the clubhouse to the snowmobiles in front. Watching the door I began to check out their registration stickers with my penlight. About halfway through I found Titus McKee's. It was a deep cherry color, almost black.

I stifled the urge to sabotage it. First of all, he might not be the shooter. And second, why warn him somebody doesn't like him?

Crossing round the back I eased toward the small window behind the woodstove. Sparks and cinders were dropping from the top of the flue onto the snow.

At the table nearest the window, with a plate of beans and hot dogs and two cans of Miller Lite, sat Titus McKee.

"You can't even come out to piss!" said a voice behind me, "but you run into some peeping tom."

Three big guys, open-fisted, smelling of beer. With the Beatles so loud I hadn't heard them. Caught in a corner of the building, pinned between them. "I was thinking of joining," I said. "Came up to have a look before I went inside."

"You was thinking of joining," the middle one said cheerfully. "Who asked you, fuckface, to *join* us?"

The one on the right had something long and heavy in his right hand, a baseball bat. Even punching the other two in the gut I couldn't break past him.

I leaped at the guy with the bat knocking him down and sprinted for the woods dragging the middle guy on my back till I elbowed him off, the third guy coming after me, one of them yelling for the people inside as I plunged and scrambled downhill through deep snow, my pursuer and the rumble of snowmobiles behind me.

Death Sentence

I COULDN'T OUTRUN them. And with their headlights they'd easily pick up my thigh-deep trail and run
me down. I scrambled left through blowdown maples
and ash, a maze of crisscrossed trunks no snowmobile could
get through, ran down to the stream and raced up its icy
slippery moss-frozen bed to a bridge as the last of the machines snarled downhill on my trail.

Three snowmobiles still sat in front of the clubhouse.
The lights were bright inside, people moving, a guy with a
phone to his ear. I ducked along the front of the clubhouse,
picked the oldest snowmobile as most likely to have a stan-
dard ignition I could wire.

The clubhouse door swung open and I dove back in the
hemlocks. It was a woman in a stocking hat. She stood still,
listening. "They're still chasing him," she called, and went
back inside.

But she was wrong: some of the snowmobiles were coming back up the mountain.

I cut the wires, twisted them back and forth with cold-
deadened fingers till finally it caught in a blare of burnt oil.
Not switching on the headlights I gassed out of the parking
lot and fast downhill toward Route 220, two guys running
down the snowmobile track after me.

The track was crowned, high and icy, and I kept hitting the cutbank of ice and rock and spinning nearly off the track on the other side, trying to glance back and judge the distance of the headlights racing after me.

This machine's tread was ragged too, didn't cut into the ice. I pushed it harder, testing the edge of how fast it'd go with jumping the track and smashing into the trees. The noise was enormous, filled the night and added to the terror and the knowledge of my mistake.

The headlights were coming up fast behind me – they were more powerful machines than mine – funny how you think these thoughts in instants while your brain is trying to figure what to do – and I cut left off the snowmobile trail into dark timber.

It was thick spruce and hemlock with low nasty boughs ripping my face as I hunted a way through them, hearing now the roars of my pursuers, their lights flitting across the trunks.

I drove into a deep hemlock thicket, boughs and sapling snapping, needles in my face, out the other side and skittered downslope and across a deep brook, engine choking as we climbed the other bank through brambles and willows across Route 220 and on the far shoulder to the Wilson Corner stoplight, stowed the bike behind the Irving station and waited at the crosswalk.

Snowmobile headlights were racing along the shoulder toward me. The light was green, cars and trucks flashing through. The headlights got nearer; three snowmobiles followed my tracks into the Irving station. The three guys dismounted and followed my machine's track around back.

If I ran across the highway into the woods they'd quickly run me down.

The light turned red, bloodying the frozen road. A logging truck down-geared to a shuddering stop beside me, brakes hissing and valves rattling. I walked back alongside the truck to its rear, jumped up on a slippery frozen log and scrambled forward to a niche between a huge pile of young logs.

The light turned green. The trucker ground into low first and chug-chugged down the road working up the gears, and as we curved away I saw the three guys get on their machines and head back the way they'd come.

Now my problem was how to get off this truck. Often a logging truck will go a hundred miles before it stops again, particularly at night with few folks on the road, and if the mill is far away.

But these skinny frozen logs, when I felt and smelled and saw them, were all hardwoods so probably headed for the firewood market, to a local wood seller who would cut and split the logs and either sell them green or store them till next fall and call them dry.

It'd been minus eighteen when Lexie'd dropped me off, so now with the wind chill from the truck doing sixty down Route 220 , it had to be minus fifty in my niche. But I couldn't move, fearing the trucker had a rear camera focused on his load, would see any motion.

The wind wailed past, digging into my ribs, my frozen cheeks, hands, elbows and feet. My phone rang like a messenger from another world, then again and again, but I let it go, too cold to move, not daring to open my coat. Strips of torn bark writhed along the dead trunks and lashed my face, the truck trailer groaned and the tires rumbled under the tons of trees, the trunks cracked and shifted around me. But despite all that had just happened it was sad to lie among these young lives sacrificed to heat human homes and thicken the atmosphere with CO_2 and soot.

I began to wonder if I might have got away from the snowmobilers only to freeze to death on this truck. But that wouldn't happen – I could always crawl forward till he saw me, or could bang on the cab roof.

So I lay there in the howling darkness realizing how lucky I was.

I WAS EVEN LUCKIER ten minutes later when he pulls up at a bar called *The Ro..dway* in big red slanted letters on the roof and the *"a"* missing. A parking lot of pickups and trailer trucks, a few Subarus, Saabs and Volvos from the other side of the social divide, country music blaring out the door and it felt like heaven inside in the heat and smells and sounds of life.

The clock said ten-thirty and the place was full, lots of tough-looking logger types and cute mean-looking women. Lots of tattoos. So I felt right at home standing by the heat vent with my triple Tanqueray martini in a beer glass.

Two cops come in while I'm calling Lexie. I head for the back while the cops talk to the bartenders and as they turn to scan the crowd I duck into the men's room.

But they would check this too, I realized, so knocked on the women's. No answer. I went in and locked the door hoping they were less likely to look here.

A minute later they did open the men's room door and go in. Then their voices trickled away and I cautiously stepped outside. No one.

My phone beeped. Lexie. "What happened?" she said. "We got cut off."

"Yeah we did," I said, aching to be *there,* in that warm kitchen, with an old friend. Aching to be safe.

SHE PICKED ME UP in half an hour. Despite all my peregrinations I was only eighteen miles from her place, having gone first south to the snowmobilers then north on the logging truck. I sat by her woodstove basking in its heat, trying to figure what to do next.

"Your face's all tore up," she said.

"From driving through those hemlocks." I shivered; it didn't seem possible I'd escaped. "But what would they've done," I wondered, "if they'd caught me? What's the penalty for looking in a window? When I could've said I was lost and hoping to get warm?"

"With the cops already wanting you? You crazy?"

"I'm no closer to having a chat with Titus McKee."

"You should ask Mitchell to run a check on him."

My phone rang again. Oh yeah, I remembered. It had rung many times during my trip with the logs. "This may be him," I said.

It was Pa.

"CANCER," he says. "I got a few weeks. A month, maybe."

Oh Jesus Christ. What can I do to make this not happen? "Oh fucking Jesus, Pa."

"Agent Orange, just like all the other guys. Gets you sooner or later."

"What kind of cancer?"

"Pancreas. I didn't wanna tell you. But figured you'd be pissed I didn't."

"I'll be there tomorrow night, Pa."

"Screw that. You take care of your friend, there, that guy in prison."

"He's impossible. I've given up on him."

"Don't."

"I'll tell you about it when I get there."

"Funny, me and the other guys who made it through the war, years later we all get killed by our own weapons... Like stepping on an old Claymore."

"Tomorrow by sunset," I said. "Just leave the light on."

LEXIE GOT ME a 06:45 Delta flight from Portland to Atlanta and another arriving Kona at 17:42. I'd leave Bucky's truck in long term parking at PWM and didn't give a damn what C. Hart had said about staying in Maine.

So Lexie and I sat there at the kitchen table not saying much. Remembering our history of unhappy separations.

When we'd been together five years ago, before my second Afghanistan tour and then my first stretch, we went one week to Waipio to see Pa. He was instantly delighted by this smart, amazingly hot woman, and she fell for his scratchy voice and rough, ironic strength. We had a wonderful time with his weed and cane liquor and eating fresh *opakapaka* off the rocks, doused in Pa's fresh lime, with fresh lettuce, leeks and tomatoes from his garden and papayas, passion fruit and mangoes from his trees, talking and talking, going back in the past, trying to share and understand life.

Lying later that night beside Lexie in the camp bed on Pa's thatched veranda I wondered what Pa dreamed of, alone in that back bedroom under the eaves, why he'd never married again. With Lexie all warm and silky-skinned against me I couldn't imagine living alone, wondered about the life Pa and Ma had had till she died.

For the first time that night he'd talked about a woman in Nam, long before Ma. He and the guys had been in the boonies "wasting gooks" (that's what Seals did, and that's what it was called back then), and he was crazy from losing friends and killing so many people.

On weekend R&R in Hué he met a young Vietnamese teacher. They made love the whole weekend, almost without stopping. She was as crazy from the war as he was. For the next three months he wangled R&R whenever he could, took dangerous missions and stayed on point and on LPs just so he could get back to her sooner.

And when Tet hit he spent a week fighting and killing and watching hundreds of young Americans – and many thousands of Vietnamese – die for a absolutely no reason at all. And realized the human race is simply insane and he wanted to marry her and go back to Hawaii and try to forget everything. But when he got to her place the whole neighborhood had been leveled by our thousand-pounders, and yes, a survivor said, her blood and gristle was somewhere out there under the rubble.

"So," I said after a while, "you and Ma?"

"Listen," he leans forward, that way of his. "There's more than one magnificent woman out there, there's millions of them –"

"So why you ain't married again?"

"Fuck that, Sam. I never wanted anyone else. Not after your Ma."

"So there ain't millions of em out there."

"Jesus Christ." He gives me his low look. "Will you stop bein a lawyer?"

"All I want to know, Pa, is how to live."

"That," he grins at Lexie, "you gotta find out for yourself."

I thought a moment. "What was her name, this woman who died?"

He said nothing a while, then, "Germaine."

"If you'd married her I never'd been born."

"Yeah," he'd grinned, back to his old self, "there is that."

Now I glanced across the table at Lexie in this wintry Maine kitchen with its rustling woodstove, the pitiless night outside the snow-glazed windows, seeing her as she'd been that tropical night in Pa's Waipio bungalow, her still-girlish earnest charm, her young sexual fire blazing like a steel mill, her slender fingers and kindly face, and I wanted so bad for all three of us to be back there, before Pa had cancer, before my last Afghanistan tour and the trial and jail and getting free and another trial and more jail, back before Bucky sent me to prison then talked Lexie into Maine, and the best reason to save Bucky now was to show him that other people aren't like him.

"I'm really going to miss you," she said, our fingers twined. "Jesus Christ I am."

"And God I you too." The fear of ending back *Inside* made me crave her even more. If I didn't go to the bunkhouse now we were going to make love, out of the sorrow of what was happening, to heal a cleft far too deep. "I'll tell Pa your latest."

"Jesus," she sniffed, "don't do that."

I stood, stiff from the night's horrible chase and my travels on the logging truck, my head spinning with pain and weariness. Pa was dying. That was *all* that mattered. One way or the other I was going to get there.

"Maybe you *should* let the cops know. That your Dad's dying and you need to get there."

"They won't let me leave, Lexie –"

"We'll get a court order."

"By that time Pa'll be dead."

"But what if they've already put out a bulletin on you – like to TSA?"

"Then I'm fucked."

"Yeah, you are. So maybe they didn't put out a bulletin–"

"We'll know tomorrow, won't we?"

Painkillers

NOBODY ARRESTED me at the vast and empty Portland airport. Two hours later we were in Atlanta, having traversed an unending spectacle of housing developments, industrial zones and highways, all under a blanket of snow and ice. Soon, it seemed, there'd be nowhere left in North America for humans or animals to escape to.

Atlanta was another planet. Corridors of people, shops and food. Ships passing in the night, we humans, looking down or ahead, each on our private voyage toward death.

These were the kind of thoughts I was having sitting in my mini-seat on the Airbus 330 to Hawaii, contracting my knees so as not to bump the seat in front of me, keeping my elbow to my side of the narrow elbow rest, watching out the window at the unending undulating heartlands of America. They seemed good, honest, and full of hard-working, caring people, giving me the feeling we all have about our country: *We have something good here, something true, let's cherish and protect it.*

Over the West the same human occupation, roads and ski resorts and cities eating into battered forests, then the empty Utah and Nevada deserts crisscrossed by ATV trails, the over-logged California hills and a far hazy view of San

Francisco, then hours of bright blue sea spotted with white clouds and their gray-green shadows. The sea seemingly empty of man, if you didn't know better.

Then whacked by the perfumed tropic damp air of Hawaii, watching the sun set through the oily volcanic fog, standing in line at Budget Rentals in Kona scratching my whiskers, over-dressed in the heat, renting an Altima for the long ride to Pa.

It was a good half hour north on Highway 19 past miles of concrete hotels shadowing beaches that when I was a kid were miles of empty sun-bright sand. Then up the volcano to Waimea, where once was a country road you could wait hours on for a ride and is now a four-lane trashy highway.

Shifting Baselines Syndrome, Lexie had called it. We think what we grew up with as the baseline, not realizing that most of what had been there was already lost. Soon we'll lose the rest and barely notice.

Like my being used to Pa's being here, and now he'll be gone. And how bad that is for him. To know that soon you will not exist.

Same as us all. Just sooner.

I bought Chinese takeout in Waimea and drove down the volcano's north slope to Honoka'a then west to the Waipio Valley overlook. For those who don't know it, Waipio is a deep tropical valley of 2,000 foot cliffs, verdant jungles, rivers and a few taro patches. A mile across and five deep, it shaped like a huge W with twin waterfalls at the back and a black sand beach facing the sea. A road snakes down the near cliff, in case you want to risk your vehicle, but rental cars aren't permitted to venture down it.

One of Hawaii's most sacred places, Waipio was the boyhood home of King Kamehameha. Before the great extinction, when over 90% of Hawaiians died after the Europeans arrived, thousands of people lived in Waipio, but now it's just a few loners like Pa.

I left the Altima at the top, grabbed my backpack and hiked down to the valley floor two thousand feet below. Rather than follow the jeep trail I short-cutted past the heiau – the sacrificial pyramid – across the first and second rivers onto the Kamehameha trail. It's a narrow path over volcanic rocks through forests of huge monkeypod trees. The Hawaiians call it the King's Path, for Kamehameha, who vanquished his enemies and united the islands only to see them slide into white men's hands.

AT THE END of the King's Path the trail hunches up through banana trees to a grassy clearing and tin-roofed bungalow with a screened porch in front and a chicken coop and fenced garden behind, a light in the kitchen making my heart leap to be seeing Pa, and an even sharper pain from soon losing him forever.

He sat on the front porch in one of his old canvas chairs. Craggy and thin-faced, not like he'd been last time I'd come two months ago. He gave me a huge smile and pushing himself up wrapped me in his long arms. "Just like you said, you got here by sunset."

Hugging his strangely skinny shoulders I saw behind him the sea ablaze with billowing crimson clouds, the sparkling blue-green froth, the magnificent porcelain sky. "Just barely."

He sat roughly back down, the chair tilting. I dropped my backpack in the corner and sat beside him. "I brought egg rolls and grilled chicken. What you got to drink?"

"You left that bottle of gin, last time you were here."

"Christ, Pa, you didn't drink it?"

"Hell no you know I like my own stuff."

"Your stuff would kill an elephant. No wonder you're sick."

"Sick? When I think about this goddamn Agent Orange, what it's doing to me, what it's done to my friends, I wonder how has anyone survived over there in Indochina – not just Nam but Laos and Cambodia – we drowned them in that stuff."

I put a hand on his arm. It felt thin and cold. Chicken skin, the Hawaiians say. "So tell me how things are…"

"Sometimes the pain's real bad, sometimes not. They want to start me on morphine – that's the beginning of the end, turns you into a vegetable…But the pain's getting worse. Every day. They want me in the hospital but that's no place to die."

"There's no chance?"

He looked at me humorously. "Of beating it? No chance. It spreads like wildfire, pancreatic cancer. Even now," he pointed to the middle of his body, "feels like the whole place is on fire."

"Oh Jesus I'm sorry, Pa."

He nodded, said nothing. "Like what we did when we poisoned those three countries with Agent Orange then set them on fire." He looked at me. "There is a connection, you know. Between what you do and what happens to you."

I shook my head, didn't want to think about this.

"Yes there *is*. I'm getting punished. For what I did."

This was a black cave with no exit. "You guys, you didn't know what you were getting into. What you were going to be asked to do. If you'd known you never would've gone in."

He smiled. "Not unless you were a psychopath."

"In Afghanistan, me too, there were times… Iraq too. You pull down on some guy, and his whole life flashes before you, his wife and kids, his hut, his goats, that how he was brought up is why he's here now and you take him down but he stays inside you."

"Some guys don't even count them. They don't even wake up at night."

"Good for them."

Pa chuckled and I knew we were off the subject of guilt, at least for the moment. "Get yourself some of that gin," he said. "And bring me my cane liquor. There's a joint on the counter by the stove."

"It's okay you drinking?"

"I don't give a fuck."

The kitchen was small and dark because Pa hadn't switched the battery on. I filled two tall glasses with ice, poured one full of gin and the other half full of cane liquor, topped it with tonic water and squeezed in a slice of lime.

"One thing about dying," Pa said as I handed him his drink – "Ah this looks lovely, thank you – one thing about dying is I live so deeply now, every moment counts." He chuckled again, as if everything were becoming a joke. "Maybe time is elastic, and we all get the same, just stretched or contracted." He flinched, hardened a moment. "Why don't you light that joint –"

I lit it and passed it to him. "How bad?"

"Spasms are real bad. Like that one. Goes away." He tensed again.

"What are you doing for it?"

"Besides the cane liquor and weed? Nothing. But I'm gonna have to."

I wanted to tell him I'd be here, for him, as long as he lived. But even that I couldn't say. The cops wanted me in Maine, could use my absence to put me away. And Abigail was still missing.

"There's a whole bunch of painkillers," he went on. "I don't want none of them. Makes me remember those tons of opium we flew out of Nam and Laos, all headed for US markets, where of course we spent more billions trying to interdict them."

"Same in Afghanistan, half the guys we put in to run the place are tied to drugs."

"So you and me," he looked at me curiously, "why were we *protecting* that?"

The ancient unanswerable question. "We did the right thing in 2001," I said. "Hitting the Taliban. But then Bush let everything slide, said we're not doing any nation building when that's exactly what the place was ripe for – we could have modernized that country, shut down the madrassas and got the women out of their goddamn burkhas – "

"Bush didn't didn't give a shit about Afghanistan. He wanted Iraq, all that oil. Wanted to pretend he was a man. And by letting Bin Laden go free at Tora Bora he cost hundreds of thousands of more lives, some of them ours."

"So as usual our talks boil down to the problem with being a warrior is you're putting not only your life but your freedom and morals in somebody else's hands."

"Yeah," Pa said. "That's the fuckin problem."

TROPICAL NIGHT had fallen. The coconut fronds were blackly outlined against the gleaming stars thick as milk.

A cool wind was coming downriver, rustling the leaves. Farther up the valley a rooster was calling, another answered. The mynahs in the mango tree began to cease their chattering and chortling and settle into sleep. A Black Witch moth battered against the screen, red eyes glittering. Pa snickered. "A bit early for him to show up."

"It don't mean shit, Pa." Like I mentioned before, the Black Witch is a huge moth who visits when there will be a death in the family. But as Pa said, this wasn't the season.

When I looked around the comfortable cabin it seemed impossible that this place where Pa had lived so long would soon be empty, the rusty Datsun pickup without a driver, the chickens in a new home. We create an exoskeleton where we live, I realized, that slowly collapses when we die.

"You know, Pa, I can't stay –"

"Stay? Of course not. Damn good you came."

"I have problems in Maine, a friend who's missing and I'm afraid she's dead."

"Listen, Sam, I ain't going to stay around for my death either."

I laughed, loving him so much. "Where you planning to go?"

"Gonna to sail one of my old canoes out to sea, with some food and booze. Go far as I can go."

"Jesus, Pa."

"Jesus my ass."

"I said that because it's a lovely idea. But I'm scared of it."

"This guy in Martinique once, old friend of mine, French Intelligence. You never met him... For his eightieth birthday he windsurfed halfway down the island to a dinner his family'd organized, but part way there, out in the middle of the damn ocean, his mast breaks."

"Oh shit."

"So he's sitting on his board in the high seas and it's getting dark and there's a great white circling that then bites off the back of his board. But somehow he manages to splint the mast and at midnight arrives at his party when everybody's afraid he's dead. When he come in they thought he was a ghost."

I tried to imagine splinting a windsurfer mast in high waves at night, a shark circling. "Unfucking believable."

"I've always wanted to just sail out to sea. And now I will." He tossed off his drink. "So that means I have to leave before I get so weak I can't go."

I refilled our drinks and brought out the egg rolls. "How'd you know," Pa said. "Damn only thing I care for anymore is Chinese food."

"From the Jade Palace."

"In Waimea? Thanks."

"I always bring you this stuff, Pa."

"I know, I know. But thank you anyway."

He'd eaten one bite and put it down. "You ready for your chicken, Pa?"

He looked at me gently. "In a while."

I ate mine slowly, hungry as I was. Thinking of how tough Pa had always been, always hungry for food and life, and the pain I felt for his loss was even worse than mine for losing him.

Highway to Hell on my phone. "Sorry, Pa." I reached to shut it off and saw the number. "It's Lexie."

"You tell her hi for me –"

"Hey it's not even six a.m. where you are," I says to her. "What's up?"

"Yeah yeah so what." Her voice rough, as if she'd been smoking. "The cops have been around. Keep asking where you are. Just called again."

"What you tell them?"

"You have some new girlfriend somewhere, I don't know where and I don't give a damn."

"They ain't been calling my phone."

"They're probably tracking you?"

"I disabled that."

"How's your Dad?"

"They say why they want me?"

"Not a word. He ain't good, huh?"

"Yeah."

"I'm sorry, Honey. So sorry. But you better tell your Dad goodbye and get your ass back here."

"Not this soon, Lexie. I can't…"

"They're going to put out an all-points on you. You'll get grabbed at HNL and sent back here in chains."

Upriver

PA WATCHED me reflectively. "You gonna tell me, this Maine thing?"

I explained best I could, how wanting to help Bucky I'd tracked down Abigail, the widow of the man he'd supposedly killed. But then when she went missing all the attention turned on me. So I was not only terrified for her but also the major suspect in her disappearance.

"It's after midnight," Pa said. "But tomorrow you can take a night flight to the mainland then another to Portland – get you there, what are we Monday – get you there Wednesday afternoon."

My spirit railed against this. I didn't want to leave my dying father. Going to sail out to sea, he said. I wanted to be there, on the beach, watching till he disappeared over the horizon. I wanted to go with him.

I did not want him to die alone. I did not want him to die.

"Funny thing is," he said, "I'm going to be dead long before you get this sorted out, so I'll never know what happens. Christ if you end up back in jail again…"

"I won't, Pa, don't worry." I was lying, just to say this.

"That last time, Halawa Prison."

"You never missed a visit. You kept me sane." This choked me up. "Even in Leavenworth, you came much as you could…"

"That fuckin motel there they never turn on the heat. And food? Kansas has the only eggs in the world even the yolks are white."

Upriver a pueo hooted, echoing off the cliffs. The sacred owl of Hawaii, soon to be extinct. The divine protector of the human spirit. I shivered; no matter how hard I tried to fight, everything seemed doomed.

Pa had hardly touched his food. "Even the weed," I said, "don't make you hungry?"

"Those days are gone..." He snickered. "They were fun, though."

I put the leftovers in the reefer and rolled another joint. We sat on the porch hearing the frogs, the wind in the palms, the distant rumble of the ocean and all the other night sounds of the Hawaiian jungle, watching the vast progression of the stars across the night, till a scimitar moon rose above the cliffs and glowed into the room.

"I wish I could figure out how to help you," Pa said.

"I'm fine." Again I feared the lie would turn against me.

"If I was you, you got two choices: one, disappear –"

"That won't work –"

"Shut up. Listen. Have Smyrna make you a new life so you got it you need it."

Smyrna was my cousin Sally's longtime lover who had been in the Agency as a disguise technician. Last year she'd made me a false face that saved my life. "I don't need one. I'm good."

"Or the other choice is more difficult – if this girl comes back dead."

"Please, I've been through that a thousand times..."

"Somehow you gotta prove your innocence, that you went back there because your friend, this Bucky guy –"

"He ain't my friend."

"– whatever you call him then, because he was falsely

arrested and that means the real killer's out there still. And this poor girl –"

"Abigail."

"God knows where she ends up in this mess."

"God knows."

"Well if there is an afterlife I'll be there watching over you. I'll do what I can."

"I know that."

"Trouble is," he snickered, "I don't think there is one."

"It's so evil, death. Imagine, we live and learn and grow and then it ends. Pointless. Death is a crime. Death is murder."

"Point is have as much fun as you can. Along the way. The Devil hates fun. Our happiness drives him crazy."

I thought about this. "So when anyone tries to preach against having fun, you know who they're working for."

"Even if *they* don't."

I laughed. "The road to Hell is paved with good deceptions?"

"You said it," he coughed. "I didn't."

"Fuck it, Pa, I got to leave in the morning and I could sit here on this porch with you for weeks, months, just talking – who's got the right to take that away?"

"Son, son, you're getting too worked up. It'll get in the way of your saving yourself. Like in a firefight, focus on who's shooting at you and from where, and take them out."

"Depends how much ammo you have."

"Stop feeling sorry for yourself."

This gave me a good belly laugh. "You're absolutely right."

He put his cold hand on mine. "And that, my son, is why you're going to win."

HIGHWAY TO HELL again. Again I go to switch it off but it's Mitchell.

"I'll call you back," I says. "Tomorrow."

"Where the fuck are you?"

"With Pa. I'll call you –"

"Did you know every Maine Legislator can take up to a million a year under the table, and doesn't have to declare it to the Legislature, just to the IRS, which keeps it secret? You *know* this?"

"No."

"These pro-wind Legislators, they've been taking so much wind money they could buy the New York Yankees."

"Okay, okay... I'm heading back to Maine tomorrow. I'll call you on the way to Kona."

"I'm chasing them down. Seeing what they do with their payoffs."

"Some payoffs aren't in cash, Mitchell."

"There's always money underneath. Root of all evil."

"THAT WAS MITCHELL," I say to Pa.

"Even though I never met him I feel I know him."

"It's like his entire life now is protecting others. So they can have what he can't."

"A good life."

"To have a good life, he says, you gotta do as much good as you can."

Pa shifted uncomfortably. "Let's have another hit and one more drink. There's a story I got to tell you."

It began to rain, tinkling on the tin roof and pattering through the palms. A softness to the air, a redolence of jungle and earth. I got the drinks and rolled another one and sat back down. "You ain't gonna eat anything, Pa?"

"How many times," he looked at me, "you go into combat? When a fight was coming and you knew it?"

I tried to count them. Didn't want to. "What you getting at?"

"Remember how your gut burns? You catch yourself not breathing? You notice the skin on the back of your hand and wonder if soon you'll never see it or think again, that hand will never move again – you know all that shit –"

"So?"

"I never told you the night that changed my life. Now I'm gonna die so I'm gonna tell you." He grimaced from the pain, trying to hide it. "Phoenix."

"I always figured you did that. You never said."

"It's not what anybody wants to talk about. Not then, not now."

If you don't know about the Phoenix Program just Google it. Patterned on Nazi tactics used against French Resistance networks in WWII, Phoenix was run by the CIA, Seals, and Special Forces. The idea was to use torture and widespread murder to intimidate villages from backing the Viet Cong. In the Phoenix program over fifty thousand people, mostly civilians, were tortured to death or otherwise killed between '65 and '72, many shot discriminately, and another thirty thousand beaten, jailed and broken.

It was revelation of their participation in this program that later caused several presidential candidates such as Nebraska's Bob Kerrey to drop out of contention.

"We went up the Mekong into Cambodia one night," Pa said. "Of course we weren't supposed to be there. So we had rubber sandals, dark plain clothes, AKs, no dog tags, nothing that could be American... A local guy was going to lead us to the hut of a Viet Cong major, some liaison with the Cambodians. The idea was cut his throat, a few others, get out silently – sowing terror – the whole Phoenix deal.

"We took Swifts then transferred to two dugouts with electric motors. The local guy's name was Rith, I remember. Means *strong* in Cambodian, something like that. He spoke Vietnamese too, so I translated for us. After two hours the river narrowed and there were islands in the middle. *Bao dai dai*, Rith whispered. *Go slow.*

"We pulled ashore and Rith led us up the bank along a trail beside a little paddy that was black and glittering with stars... I remember thinking how lovely it was. The village appeared out of the darkness, a dozen huts with tall thatched roofs, the smell of smoke, shit and rotten fruit, you know the deal. And here and there a glimmer of coals through an open door...

"Rith grabbed my shoulder, pointed to the huts, ticking them off, *mai, quon, sey*. Third one from the left. Two of our guys split right and left to provide cover for anything outside the third hut. My buddy Mack and I took a path across the paddy toward the huts.

"We reached the third hut and knelt on either side of the open door. You could smell inside, the green boughs laid on coals to keep away mosquitoes. I pulled out my KA-BAR – it sounded so loud, sliding from the sheath. I went into the hut and Mack slipped in behind me.

"In the light of the coals I saw the glisten of a rifle alongside this slender guy... Rith had said he was small and slender, the VC major. It took me like five minutes, you know, to reach him, on all fours, knife in my teeth.

"When I reached him I grabbed the knife and yanked up his chin, cupping his mouth like we were supposed to, you know, to get a clean cut, and his eyes opened and I realized his hair was long and silky..."

"Jesus, Pa –"

Out beyond the taro fields a donkey was braying, and Pa listened for a moment, as if it were decipherable, some universal truth. "It was a teenage girl. I guess she must've been crippled, or something – what I'd thought was a rifle was a crutch. I looked around in there – there wasn't any VC major, just this girl, an old mama-san, a couple kids, an ancient white-haired man..."

A mosquito landed on his forearm and Pa waved it away. "Maybe it was forever, that I stared into her eyes and she into mine. You could say anything about her look – pleading, terrified, startled... but at the end she knew, as I did, there was no choice. I'd made a mistake; *we'd* made a mistake. But if I let her live she could wake the village and we'd never get out. I was responsible for the rest of the team..."

"Jesus."

He nodded, facing the darkness, swallowed, then, "That was when my head went upside down. Even more than Tet."

By that he meant the woman he'd loved who'd been blown to bits by thousand-pounders. "It was good I got wounded soon after Tet," he added, "or I'd have gone mad."

The wound was a bullet that smashed his femur and got him choppered out of a forward LP before it was overrun, and had put him three months in the hospital and left him with a limp and pain he never spoke about. And that instant I realized that one of the reasons I'd ended up in Special Forces was to avenge his wound, to make him whole again.

"I was the only one of us survived that war," Pa said. "Mack got it the same firefight I was wounded in. The other two went upriver one night and never came back."

He turned on me. "And this is why I never married again after your Mom died. Why I would never again fall for anyone. I'd learned that every woman I loved would die to fill the soul of that crippled girl."

I felt sickened, went outside, came back in. "The Koran says that all the good we do is from God, not from us. And all the evil we do comes from us."

"God can't have it both ways."

There was nothing I could do to shrive Pa of his sins. We are all, I realized, stuck with our sins. We can atone for them but can never be absolved. Nor should we.

"I'd love to go with you, Pa. Sail out in another canoe, keep you company all the way." Saying it I realized how shamefully foolish it was – what was I going to do when he fell out of the canoe, drag him back in? Pull him up when for the last time he went under?

Fight off the sharks?

PA's face had grown more haggard and pale; it was not just the awfulness of the memories and the progress of pain and death, even more it seemed a recognition of humanity's fate, the earth's, all life's.

"An incomprehensible mystery, life," he said. "When I was younger I expected to understand it better when I got old. But I don't... In some ways I understood it better then."

He leaned forward, punched his palm. "When you're young you have sex, life, danger, exaltation, nature, the ocean – maybe *that's* understanding life."

"It doesn't seem fair," I said, "to live through all this and not understand, that it's a dream –"

"– and in the end," Pa chuckled, "it kills us."

Rascal the cat leaped up on the table and flopped down beside Pa, one foreleg over Pa's wrist. "We've been together fourteen years." Pa rubbed the big cat behind the ears. "He knows I'm going. Knew it before I did."

"I wish I could take him –"

"Old Ambrosio wants him." Ambrosio was a Filipino taro farmer and fisherman, Pa's upstream neighbor. "He's got mice." He scratched under Rascal's chin. "We don't have mice here, do we, Rascal?"

For an instant I imagined this house after Pa and Rascal were gone, the mice, centipedes and scorpions taking over, the place falling apart, eaten by jungle.

"The tragedy of getting old," Pa added, "Winston Churchill said, is not that you're old, but that you're still young."

LOVE AND WAR. I sat out on Pa's front patio in the sifting darkness of the palm trees, the high buttresses of the valley walls cutting off the lower sky. Westward, above the rims, gleamed Venus, below her the bloody glint of Mars.

Love and War, our two choices. And we keep choosing both.

NEXT DAY when I hiked back down the King's Path two black dogs were playing on the beach where the river meets the sea. They ran in circles spattering sand, in and out of the foam. They were playing with some kind of a cork buoy, little bigger than a tennis ball. I had a fleeting sense of their joy – joy is what God loves most – and I wondered can we maximize the world's joy and minimize its pain – or is all our joy built on others' pain – the lamb at the feast, the mouse in the cat's jaws?

WIA

H E HAD NO ARMS beyond the elbow, stainless steel struts below the knees. No chin, just a mouth that ended with the upper jaw. He was taking his Big Mac from the paper bag when I saw him at the Atlanta departure gate for Portland, using his cut-off elbows to hold it, remove the paper, and bring it to his mouth.

Everyone seemed to be avoiding him so I went over and sat. He glanced at me, nodded, went back to eating. Outside was a glaring cold day, snowy clouds scurrying across the tarmac. On the TV screens clamped to every location and angle in the room was an advertisement for hair spray then for huge pickup trucks, another for cash loans, then an emergency weather report that it might rain in Iowa or, very importantly, there could be a storm in the ocean somewhere off Bangladesh.

Then comes a special report on terrorism and who is being quoted, his mousy little moustache quivering with self-importance, but Maine's own Artie Lemon, a recently minted member of the US Senate Intelligence Committee, and he's giving us the lowdown on ISIS.

From which I deduced that "Senate Intelligence", like we used to say in SF about "military intelligence", is definitely an oxymoron.

When the armless, legless vet was done with his Big Mac he balled up the wrapper and bag and took them to the paper recycling bin. With his steel legs set in shiny new Adidas he had a jaunty bowlegged walk.

The TVs shifted to a another show called "The Talk". This consisted of a number of heavily made-up women, half of them extremely obese, one who'd had so many plastic surgeries she looked like a Martian, all in a half-circle round a table talking endlessly with great TV energy about absolutely nothing.

The vet rearranged his backpack, took out a boarding pass and went to the counter. He had the high squeaky voice of someone whose voice box has been shattered and whose lower jaw is gone. He asked the clerk if he could get a window seat. When the clerk said they were all gone, he nodded okay and came back.

"Here's mine." I handed him my boarding pass.

"Nah," he said. "I'm good."

"I don't like the window anyway. Afraid of heights."

He looked at me with untroubled brown eyes. A small guy, maybe five-eight. The kind the Marines and Special Forces love because they're so gritty and strong. "Headed home?" I said.

"Gonna stay with my sister in Rumford for a while."

This meant that after being brought back from shattering death and then two years of agonized days and nights, repeated surgeries, battles with infections, hopelessness, insanely mindfucking drugs, sorrow and all the aftermaths of IED annihilation, the numb painkillers, the memories of dead buddies, the knowledge that the rest of his life would be this lonely painful path with no lovers and no children, they had now set him out to try to make it on his own, in the bosom of whatever family he could find.

"Iraq?" I said.

He tried to grin. "Mosul."

"I did a tour there, and two in Afghanistan."

He nodded. "I did Afghanistan first."

"You had all your fun early."

We laughed slightly, in that strange mode you get in with other vets where you try to make light of dangers and losses. Usually it doesn't work but you try.

"At least," I said, "we don't have GW any more being landed on that aircraft carrier proclaiming victory."

"We get sent down the wrong path, " he said, to himself more than me. "It's only afterwards we understand. When it's too late."

"That's what my Pa said about being a Seal. You were in the middle of it before you knew what atrocious things you were going to have to do."

People were boarding. He stood, slung on his backpack. "Thanks for the seat."

We walked down the ramp. "If I'd been in the next seat in that Humvee," he said, "I wouldn't even be here now."

It occurred to me sadly that for most of life he was not and could not be here now. I wondered at his courage, and doubted I could match it.

Courage, I got thinking as the endless sprawl of half-despoiled America unrolled below us, courage is not just bravery under fire – although that horrifying event often brings out incomprehensible valor in young men. But the truest, more profound courage is in the shattered semi-survivors of IEDs, grenades, RPGs and all the other engines of human diabolicism, engines which did not even rival the horrifying destructiveness of the weapons used by our own side.

These young men, some without arms and legs, with half a face, no genitals, no future, and no hope – these were the most courageous – to go forward every day, see other healthy young men with young women, others building lives that these guys could never have, and keep the will to survive despite all this – these were our greatest heroes. To be cut off from every promise and act of life, but to be alive to realize you would never have even a shred of it, like the quadriplegic survivor of an IED doomed to lie on a bed the rest of his life, all because GW Bush, Cheney, Rumsfeld, Hillary Clinton, Biden and a lot of other folks who had never seen war wanted to prove how brave they were.

As if sending young men out to be eviscerated, to cause the deaths of a over a million people, all for no reason, were an act of courage rather than a cowardly and criminal lie.

ON THE WAY TO LEXIE'S I again checked Abigail's house. It looked even more abandoned than before – snow-drifts across the driveway, icicles on the gutters, old foot-prints frozen in the snow. The pile of mail inside the door had grown, but I could still see the corner of the envelope that said READ THIS NOW in red magic marker.

It still made no sense the cops hadn't looked through the mail. They seemed totally disinterested in her disappearance.

It was almost as if they knew where she was. Or what had happened to her.

I walked back down the slippery sidewalk and scanned the house for the best way in. Lots of big windows, old glass that's easy to tape and break.

Tonight.

FIVE MINUTES after I got to Lexie's her land line rings. "Yeah?" she answers, hand on her hip. "He's here." She gives me the phone, blocking the receiver with her palm. "Viv Woodridge, lives down the road."

"Mr. Hawkins," the woman says, formal-like. "I'm sure Lexie's told you about me and Don? We're the ones leaving town, next week –"

"I've heard. I'm sorry."

"You're the one who helped stop the wind project in Hawaii, Jane says."

"Maybe."

"There's something we'd like to talk to you about, before we leave."

"Go ahead –"

"No, no, I mean in person. Can you come over tonight? It's rather important."

"I just got back, let me check with Lexie if I have to be someplace." I wanted to break into Abigail's tonight and gave Lexie a pleading look: *Please think of something!*

But she must have been pissed at me for some reason because she said clear and loud," No, Sam, you're free all evening!"

"Come for dinner, then," Viv said. "Six o'clock? And tell Lexie come too, she wants."

"No way I'm going over there," Lexie says when I hang up.

"Why's that?"

"They were the ones who first took WindPower money. Sold out, and now they can't live there because of the noise, and they can't sell."

"How much they get paid?"

"Everyone who takes money from WindPower has to sign a gag order. But from what I hear it's about eight thousand."

"Eight thousand?" It was astounding to lose your home for so little. "What happens if they do talk?"

"Jail time plus they get sued in civil court and lose whatever they've got left."

My head pounded with intercontinental fatigue and the grind of the turbines up on the ridge. "I don't know why I said yes, really don't want to..." I slid into a chair thinking of the similar scam that had almost destroyed Molokai, Hawaii's most beautiful island, before a bunch of brave people stopped it. And of what was now happening to Maine. And because of the Maine Wind Law no one could stop it. Straight out of the Supreme Soviet, 1932.

In the former Soviet Union the commissars in Moscow would decide to build a dam somewhere, payback for some other crooked favor done elsewhere. So five thousand miles from Moscow some magnificent region of verdant valleys, rushing streams, flowered hills and ancient homes would be flooded to fill a concrete monstrosity, allegedly to send electricity to Moscow.

And by the time that power got there it wouldn't fry an egg.

But think of all the money made along the way. It made you sick: *What we humans are versus what we could be.*

THE NIGHT WAS CLEAR AND SHARP when I left Lexie's in Bucky's 150 headed for Don and Viv's. They were in their sixties, Lexie'd said. Viv had been a public health service nurse in one of those backwoods Maine towns where everybody takes good care of everybody because there's nine months of winter and nobody has any money. And because as kids they used to take refuge in each other's homes when their own folks were upset just because they'd set an empty shack on fire or painted the back of somebody's garage purple or something else innocent as that.

And while Viv was taking care of people who worked ten tough hours a day and had nasty injuries and no health care, Don was working in the woods at thirty-five below in winter, ducking the widow-makers and tumbling logs, watching Maine's forest disappear.

Except for the gnashing wail of windmills on the ridge above it, theirs was a lovely home – the woodstove throwing off its beneficent heat, hooked rugs on the broad spruce floors, a friendly kitchen with a white porcelain sink, chuckling refrigerator and a pine table and chairs. And with a glass of home brew and three bowls of venison stew in my stomach, seeing the two of them with their calm kindly recognition of each other that masked a connection so deep you could hang your clothes on it, it reminded me of Pa and Ma before we lost her to a drunken driver in the wrong lane on a Sunday night.

And it got me thinking how we're dropped into this universe that goes on forever and we don't know where we come from or really what we are, if we're here just for the transit or if something comes after. And being with Viv and Don it came to me like sudden lightning: *All we have is love.* And that maybe if there is a God then our love for each other feeds God and makes God stronger, and our multilateral hatreds tear God apart.

And at that moment, with the plaid plastic placemats on the pine table, the needlepoints of woodpeckers, beavers, whitetails and chickadees hung on the pine walls, the crackling woodstove, the pictures of their three kids on the mantle and Don's work boots sitting lopsided on the threshold – I understood, briefly, the meaning of life.

And that the first rule is: *We do not hurt each other.*

When the kids were young he and she'd built this home on the lake shore with Eagle Mountain tall, rocky and tree-clad across the lake, and now just like Lexie's and Bucky's, like Jane's and everyone else in the area, their house was worthless. The endless howl and grind of windmills – "like a vacuum cleaner," Don said, "that never shuts off." He glanced at the woodstove as if seeking an answer there, in conflagration, turned back to me. "We took that money... we were stupid... Had no idea."

"I don't blame you." And I didn't. How could anyone?

"At first we tried to sue them," he continued. "But we didn't have money for lawyers. So they offered us the seven thousand to drop our complaint... I'm not excusing us but we didn't have a choice."

"You know what it's like?" Viv said, "to suddenly have seven thousand dollars? But we had so many debts... It didn't last."

"They said they'd buy our place if we wanted," Don said, "for what it was worth before the windmills."

"It was in the contract," Viv said. "But then they had some other paragraph that made this one untrue."

"What's the worst is at night," Don said. "The flashing strobes. Like a cop car outside your window all night, his flashers flashing."

I looked at the beautiful living room, the rough-sawn one-by-twelve pine panels and the pine battens atop them, the spruce two-by-twelve staircase, the pine trim. It had the rough beauty of real wood – when you run your hand down it the grain tickles your palm. And it smells so good, that wood. Of pitch. For years it smells good.

"Why can't you move this place?" I said.

"Costs nine thousand six hundred," Don said.

"We checked it," Viv added. "With three different house movers."

"You can't get a loan?

"Us?" Don said.

"What about your retirement?"

"After I retired the mill got sold to a New York investment fund that borrowed the money to buy it. Then they emptied our retirement fund to pay off the loan and now we have no retirement fund. That's happened to most folks round here."

It was nine-twenty-two on the wood clock with the blue jay beak and tail showing the hours and minutes. With the time change from Hawaii I felt I'd been traveling between solar systems.

"In the basement," Don said as if sensing my fatigue, "we have all the signed papers. Under the gag agreement we can't show anyone. Well, Viv and me, we've decided if you can use them we'll give 'em to you. To Hell with consequences." He pulled himself up straight and I got a sense of what a big tough guy he'd been, and how work in the woods wears you down and kills you young but barely pays you enough to live on.

"So what's in them?" I said.

"If we agreed to vote for the turbines they promised us the seven thousand. That was a fortune to us, with Viv's diabetes and my injuries and the leaky roof and all the other stuff that needed fixing."

"So they paid you that?"

"Not till the turbines were built. Then we got it, but only five hundred dollars every three months." He looked down, shook his head." Can you believe that?"

"But they promised you seven thousand –"

"It was in something else they had us sign. They called it an addendum. On how they could pay us."

"The same one that took away their promise to buy the house," Viv put in.

"What else?"

"Lots else. We'll show you in the morning."

As I headed back toward Hallowell to break into Abigail's house I worried about Don and Viv's gag agreement. I'd caused enough trouble for myself; I didn't want to screw up anybody else.

A WHITE CRUISER picked me up out of Liberty. I was the only game in town, maybe, so he pulls me over, lights flashing so bright you could've seen them from the International Space Station. I roll down the window and sit there nervous. It's 21:48, a little late in Maine to be out visiting.

Then I start to get out of the truck and he bullhorns me, "Get back in the vehicle!" which of course I do, not wanting to get shot.

Up saunters O. Trask, the guy who'd stopped me before in Freedom, one hand on the butt of his forty-five. He shines one of those foot-long cop flashlights in my eyes so I can barely see. "You was ordered to fix that brake light."

"I did."

"It still don't work."

"Damn. Must be a short somewhere."

"License and registration," he says. As if he hadn't seen them before.

I handed him my Hawaii license and start to reach for the glove box to get the registration and he says real fast "Keep your hands on the steering wheel!" which of course I do, still not wanting to get shot.

As I mentioned, Don and Viv had recently cooked up some very fine home brew that if you wanted to get to Mars in a hurry it was what you would put in your rockets. And not wanting to hurt their feelings I'd drunk more than my share, plus like most loggers Don had some home-grown in the greenhouse out behind the garage and though I hardly ever break the law he'd induced me to smoke more than a bit. Thus I was easy money for a back-country cop with cold balls and nothing to do on a winter night.

He goes back to his warship and radios me in. They have a long chat, him and the cop shop, then he comes halfway back, hand on his gun. "Get out of the vehicle," he calls, which of course is the opposite of what he told me before.

I get out, and lo and behold the bottle of home brew Don had pressed into my hand as I was leaving tumbles out and smashes on the icy road. My first thought was what a sad waste and my second thought was *I am fucked.*

By the time it takes to sing what I can remember of *The Star Spangled Banner* he has me in cuffs in the back of the warship, Bucky's 150 sitting all lonely on the side of the road, and we take a trip to the station house where they read my rap sheet on the computer with enormous excitement and I get to puff into a breathalyzer, and the disappointment on their faces was tragic when I come up with 0.05, well under the limit.

In seething frustration they throw me out to walk the two miles back to Bucky's truck in the bracing ten below, boots squeaking happily in new snow, a soaring joy in my heart at being free, reminding myself to replace the brake light bulb again and check the wire for a short, imagining what the waves are like right now on Oahu's north shore, because even if it's 22:30 in Maine it's not yet sunset in Hawaii and there's time for a few more marvelous rides.

Though I was truly beginning to fear I wouldn't make it to Tahiti in time for the Tsunami. *No,* I kept reminding myself. *Don't give that up.*

But now it was too late to drive to Hallowell and check Abigail's mail so I turned round and headed back to Lexie's.

On my right Titus McKee's driveway crossed the roadside brook on a bridge made of an old railroad flatbed car without its wheels. In the glare of the headlights you could see a *For Sale* sign beside the driveway, which wound uphill through a dark pasture to a log home on a knoll. Behind it the conifered crests of Eagle Mountain rose up to the blasted, broken ridge and its carnival of flashing strobes. Why, I wondered, isn't *he* complaining about the infrasound, the strobes, the constant fifty decibels?

A few hours later I'm tucked in at Lexie's when a whole troop of headlights comes up the road. There's a metallic banging on the bunkhouse door and when I open it there's cops spread out with automatic weapons ludicrously pointed in my direction.

It's O. Trask, beaming with joy. "You're coming to stay with us a while," he says.

I scratch my balls, being sleepy and all. "What the fuck for?"

"Don and Viv Woodridge's house burned down tonight," he says cheerily. "Unfortunately they didn't get out. We think you did it."

And my first thoughts are the horror and sorrow of it, then what Don had said just a few hours ago, "When they want, the Wind Nazis will get you. Any way they can."

By going to see Don and Viv, I realized, I'd sealed their fates.

And mine.

If I'd just stayed home and made love with Lexie like any sensible person none of this would've happened.

Going through Hell

WITH DRAWN GUNS three of them watched me dress. It was not a pleasant experience. As in most situations like this however I was quite calm. There was no way I could change things, just had to see what happened next.

What happened next is Lexie comes out the kitchen door with a baseball bat, followed by a snarling Lobo. "What the fuck *you* doing here?" she yells at Trask.

He's clearly taken aback by this blonde vixen holding her short bathrobe shut with one hand and swinging a Louisville Slugger with the other. "Lady keep your distance!" he calls.

"You know who I am, Orville Trask! You let him go right now!"

"We're taking him in on suspicion."

"*Suspicion!*" she screams. "Of what?"

"Murder and arson."

"*Murder!* What the Hell! Who?"

"Don and Viv Woodridge. We think he burned their house down. While they were sleeping."

"Oh my God!" She halted, stunned. "They're dead?"

"Crispy."

She dropped the bat. "This is awful!" She turned on him, tears in her eyes. "Don't you *see* what's happening?"

"Happening?"

"Who do you think *did* do it?" She shoved past Trask to me. "I won't let them take you!" She swung on him. "You're crazy! *Crazy!* If you think he did it."

Trask regained his composure, grabbed my arm. "Stay out of this," he says to her, "or you'll be arrested too."

"You know what this creep does?" she yelled at the others. "He pulls over women for no reason and says he'll let them go for a quickie or a blow job!" She turned on him. "You tried that with me, didn't you, you scaly little serpent!"

Trask ducked his head and shoved me toward a waiting police Expedition like the oil tanker I'd rented two weeks ago. But the back seat was a cage and I was in it, in more ways than one.

"Call Erica in the morning," I yelled to Lexie. "Tell her what's happened."

Trask dropped into Drive and we headed out Lexie's road in the macabre glow of the wind turbines. "Who's Erica?" he wanted to know.

"She's a TV producer," I said. "You're about to be on Good Morning America."

An unnerved silence fell over our Expedition. The dashboard digital said 03:17. A little past my usual bedtime. And far earlier than my normal arising.

"That true?" the other cop asked Trask. "You tried to get her to fuck?"

"Nah it's a lie."

"Did she do it?"

"Don't believe none of it."

"Too bad. She's a hot piece."

"We got *this* guy," Trask thumbed back at me. *"That's* what matters."

I breathed steady and deep, not too fast. Whatever this was, I could deal with it. Whatever it was.

I GOT A CELL to myself in Augusta, the jail equivalent of four stars. But only because, Trask said, I might kill another prisoner. Which was hilarious except he seemed to believe it.

Room service breakfast was at 06:15. Perhaps grogginess lessened my appreciation but it seemed tasteless and unnourishing.

Lexie was there at seven, in a fury. I could hear her through concrete walls. "He's got nothing to do with this!" she yelled. "You're *not* going to keep him!"

It wasn't long after Lexie left to teach her first class that Erica showed up. From what I could tell she was not happy either. I sat there on the concrete bed in the metal and concrete cell, back *Inside* where I never wanted to be. But like many diseases jail gets easier to catch each time you get it, and pretty soon you realize you're going to spend the rest of your life with it.

In which case I'd never get to see Pa one more time before he died.

Nor find Abigail.

THEY BROUGHT ME UPSTAIRS to confer with Erica. She was fierce-looking and very pissed off. I wasn't sure if it was at the cops or at me for dragging her all the way from Portland.

"I don't even *like* criminal work," she snapped.

"I'm not a criminal."

"I had a hearing scheduled this morning. The judge was not pleased I cancelled at the last moment."

She looked lovely and distracted and full of furious determination. "Thank you for coming," I said.

"Even when you were fourteen you were trouble. So tell me everything."

I explained her as best I could, from when I left Lexie's and drove to Don and Viv's, about the secret papers they were going to give me. Then I'd left, Trask pulled me over for the brake light and brought me in when the bottle Don had given me fell out and broke. I'd been under the alcohol limit so they'd had to let me go, I'd gone to the bunkhouse only to be woken up four hours later.

"You tell them anything?" she said.

"There's nothing to tell."

"That's not an answer." She questioned me more on the details, talked with the cops about what happened, came back into the room. "You sign away your rights?"

"Rights?" I thought a moment. "They never read them to me."

"What? They *forgot?*"

"Holy shit." I was astounded to realize. "They forgot."

She nodded. "Arraignment's at three-thirty. See you then."

She was gone, and the world felt empty. It was very hard not to be depressed.

"Oh my God," I begged, "what can I do?"

"Be nothing," came the answer.

ARRAIGNMENT was in the judge's chambers. He was a tall stooping bald man with thick eyebrows the color of his black robes.

Erica wasted no time in tearing into Trask and his buddies. "This man," she pointed at me, "has been the subject of continued persecution by the police. It was clear that the bottle which fell out of his truck had not been opened, yet Officer Trask arrested him for it. When he was cleared by the breathalyzer they made him walk several miles to his truck at ten degrees below zero. His previous imprisonments were both reversed: he has no criminal record, yet they treat him like a recidivist. He's a friend to the people of Eagle Valley and would have never harmed the Woodridges. By wasting time harassing him the Police are failing in their duty to find the real perpetrators of this crime. And," she turned sweetly on Trask, "this officer is so deficient in his training that in his frenzy to implicate my client," she paused for effect, "he never read him his rights."

You could hear the shocked intakes of breath. The judge raised his eyebrows at Trask, who bent his head, shook it side to side. "Sorry, Your Honor," he said softly. "It was a dangerous situation –"

"Dangerous?" the judge said. "For Mr. Hawkins perhaps. From what I understand he's defended our nation through three tours in two of the most dangerous places on the planet." He turned cool eyes on me. "Is that right, Mr. Hawkins?"

"Yes, sir," I said with proper military humility.

"Are you a veteran, Officer Trask?" the judge asked mildly.

"Yes, your Honor."

"What branch, if I may ask?"

"Army, sir." After a moment he added, "That is, National Guard."

"Ah, yes. And you were in combat?"

"No, your Honor."

55 MINUTES LATER I was clutching the passenger seat of Erica's 911 as the snowy Maine landscape flashed past. Compared to Bucky's pickup it was like riding in an F-18 instead of a wheelbarrow. Seeing Erica behind the wheel smiling as she upshifted and downshifted through the curves back to Lexie's, I felt like a kid whose big sister has just saved him from a losing fistfight.

And as always when leaving jail unexpectedly you have a stunned elation, a fierce joy to be back in the world. But the sorrow of Don's and Viv's deaths, though I barely knew them, near-destroyed it. And there was no way to make that go away.

"A scam," she snapped. "Somebody behind it."

"What – arresting me?"

"No way it would've stuck. So you ask yourself why'd they do it?"

This was a revelation for me. And shows the value of good counsel. "I never thought of it that way."

"Of course you didn't. It was clearly intimidation and attempted coercion. I could go after them just for that..."

I felt suddenly humbled and protected by this lovely, brilliant woman, had again the surging sense of deep life I'd felt walking out of the jail. "What I don't get," I said after a moment, "is who and why."

"I'd love to have some one-on-one with Orville Trask and find who's told the cops to put the pressure on you."

I couldn't imagine her and Trask one on one. "Oh I don't mean it that way," she said as if reading my mind. "I want him under oath, see where it goes."

A STOP sign flashed past, snow-covered. "Don't you ever slow down?" I queried.

She hit second putting my eyeballs in the back of my head. "So you love me?" she said.

"Ever since I was fourteen."

"God you were fun."

"Remember the first time? You wore a red dress and we were in the grass under the apple tree –"

"Then you bumped that wasp nest."

"How could I know it was there?" I grabbed my seat belt as we howled through several significant changes in the road's direction.

"So you love me?" she repeated, hitting eighty-five in second and dropping nonchalantly into third. "But you're not going to stop fucking other women?"

"Of course I'm not going to stop fucking other women. And you shouldn't stop fucking other guys."

She hit fourth, reached over and grabbed my privates. "We've got a deal."

She double-shifted down to third, engine screaming happily as we took the cutoff for Lexie's farm. "Don't you ever get tickets?" I added, hoping this might slow her down.

"Nah," she grinned, and in her lovely grin I saw again the seventeen-year-old girl with the barnyard freckles who'd seduced me on her way to Harvard. "I just buy them off."

"How's that?" I says, curious, as this is a subject of much prison talk.

"Every cop has his price." She put a hand on my thigh. "Though most of them don't know it."

I thought of her naked on the bed a few nights ago. With enough time, I reflected, she could probably swing the Supreme Court, at least the men. I pointed at a logging road that cut left into heavy timber. "Go there."

"What?" she geared down, "I don't have snows!"

"Just a few feet."

She pulled in, killed the engine. "You *nut!*"

"Jail makes me so horny." I couldn't stop kissing her. "And you know I can't have sex with Lexie," I nipped her ear, "so I'm stuck with you."

"We can't do it in this car, it's too small."

I leaned closer, dizzied by her smell. "Like we learned in Special Forces: *Never say it can't be done.*"

LEXIE AND ERICA WERE NOT PLEASED to meet each other. But Lexie made coffee and we sat round the kitchen table eating Country Kitchen doughnuts and drinking the coffee with fresh cream and I got used to being a badminton cock unmercifully shuttled back and forth between them.

"They key is Abigail," Erica said finally. "She shows up dead is one thing. She returns to the living is another."

At this point any chance of her returning to the living seemed gone.

To avoid being confronted by Lexie after Erica left, I went out to split wood, trying once more to figure who would kill Abigail, and for what reason? I didn't put it to myself that way, but that's what I meant.

You don't take the risk of killing someone unless they represent danger. For whom was Abigail a danger? How could I know, when I didn't know what she knew?

1. If she knew who killed her husband, she'd be at risk from them.
2. If she admitted she was with Bucky the night her husband was killed, that would also put her at risk from the killers.
3. If she was about to blow the whistle on some huge Legislative scam, she'd be at risk from whoever was behind it.
4. A funny thought just hit me: What if *she* killed her husband?

It was one of those off-the-cuff cerebral perambulations that often turns on lights in the rest of the brain. Which in my case is always a good idea. But made no sense at all.

Except she'd said she didn't love him, was preparing for divorce, that they didn't make love, which is the primary force, the gravity, that holds a relationship together.

Then I remembered how she was – fiery, ruthless, smart, and despite herself very caring, not a person who hurts anyone. Not even her husband, twit as he may have been.

Abigail, I begged, *please come home.*

THAT'S WHEN Mitchell called. "Ought to be some way," he says, "to do a flyover –"

"A flyover?"

"Concentric circles out from where this girl disappeared. Like in the Panjshir, we had tons of sat data but nothing beat a close-up look from a thousand AGL."

"All it did was get guys shot down –"

"You worried about that in Maine?"

What he was saying was true, that low overflights, like a thousand feet about ground level, might show things satellites didn't, particularly side angle stuff. Not that we had real time sat data for Maine. Nor did we have to worry, hopefully, about a plane getting shot down. Though any plane was at risk from wind turbine towers, some of them over half that height.

"So I checked," Mitchell goes on, always one step ahead, "see if any of our guys was up there..."

"Yes, Mitchell." I yawned.

"Remember Clarence True?"

I rubbed my scalp, hoping to encourage my brain. "Yeah maybe."

"Air Force Intel –"

"Oh them." There was a deep rivalry between SF and AF Intel. Not that we didn't work together and protect each other, but... I stopped rubbing my scalp to slow the blizzard of dandruff into my eyes. When Air Force Intel guys were with us they got to paint the targets for our planes to hit. When they weren't, we painted the targets, but they thought they did it better.

"So I checked addresses," Mitchell says. "This Clarence True, first loot, lives someplace called Gorham, works for FAA."

"That's near Portland. Near the airport."

"Got a pen?" Mitchell took another swallow. "His cell number's 333-7429." He drained his glass and slapped it on the table.

"What you drinking?"

"You ever try Reyka? Icelandic vodka? Goes down like water."

"I remember a stopover there, before we pulled out in 2006. Naval Air Station Keflavik."

"The women," Mitchell said. "Tall, blonde and beautiful..."

It twisted my heart he could reminisce about women after losing his legs and privates saving me from that RPG in Afghanistan. But Mitchell was not a man to feel sorry for himself, or make others grieve for him. "I remember you dead drunk in bed with two of them," I said. "All I could see was your olive drab socks sticking out from under the covers."

"I can't believe you can remember anything from then."

"Yeah, maybe even memory's a fiction."

"So call Clarence. Maybe you and he might see something."

Something might be just what I didn't want to see. Abigail's car, abandoned. A body at the edge of a field, half covered in snow.

"OF COURSE I remember you," Clarence chuckled. "Are you still a wiseass?"

"Probably."

"You got that nasty rap pinned on you..." He was referring to when I shot the Afghani woman to put her out of her agony, like I already explained you.

"An Army lawyer, West Point grad, she got me out." I didn't bother to tell Clarence I'd been back *Inside* thereafter, for saving Mitchell's ass. "You got a little time, I could come down, see you?"

"Of course." You could hear the broad heavy smile in his voice. "You Special Forces guys, we always got time to help you out."

"Tonight?"

"Whoa, you in a hurry? Okay then, how 'bout seven-thirty?"

ON THE WAY DOWN I stopped at the Stroudwater grave-yard. Nothing had changed except the snow level had gone up a foot or two. When I reached the pines on the knoll a doe dashed over the side and across the frozen river, and somehow it seemed a bad omen.

Nothing had changed with them while everything had with me. "The woman I told you about from Hallowell," I said, "she's missing. She may be dead. The cops seem to think I did it. And they think I shot out the four turbines at Paradise Lakes... The whole thing sucks..."

Wind blew snow crystals back and forth between the graves. The ancient pines creaked overhead. "Pa's sick. He's dying... And now Don and Viv got killed and the cops are looking at me for that too..."

They popped right into my head, Winston Churchill's words. *When you're going through Hell, keep going.*

GORHAM WAS ONE of those places that had been a village when I'd spent my teenage summer in Maine, and was now a huge suburb of Portland, as everyone was moving north from congested southern New England and congesting Maine in the process. Clarence was an older version of who I remembered, with gray now in his black curls, a little heavier round the middle, but still not a guy you'd want to mess with.

"So what's it like, the FAA?" I says. Portland Airport was where the Saudi 9/11 terrorists had entered the US on their way to fly our airliners into the World Trade towers, but that was long before Clarence got there.

"We're playin catchup right now." He pinched his lower lip between thumb and forefinger, figuring how much he could tell me. "This ISIS shit, man, they're determined to take down our civil flights... new bomb techniques, new materials we can't identify." He looked out across a back yard of bare maples and half-melted snow toward the distant airport and the huge shopping center beside it.

"My family," I said, "once owned all that land."

"You'd be a rich boy now. 'Stead a showing up in that old pickup."

I had explained him what I wanted. He'd nodded at once. "Sure thing. Though chances are we won't see much except clearcuts... Man they are tearing up this place."

"Maine?"

"Even in the five years since we come here." He nodded toward the kitchen where his wife was checking homework for their twin seven-year old daughters. "You want another Guinness?"

I shook my head, back to thinking of Abigail. "I know it's a long shot."

"Never know what we might see."

I stood. "Thanks, man. See you tomorrow."

"Seven hundred. Augusta airport."

"Can't thank you enough."

"What you did back then, for everybody, that's thanks enough."

HEADED NORTH in Bucky's truck I reflected on the powerful link among those of us who have put our lives on the line for our country, that we need to make no other judgment than that about each other. Even Bucky, who'd helped put me *Inside,* to whom I was nevertheless bound by ancient ties because he'd once saved my life, and now I was determined to save his. They were both comforting and perilous, these ancient links, but I couldn't imagine any other way to live.

Whores, Cutthroats & Priests

IT WAS A NASTY morning, dusting snow at 06:45 when I parked Bucky's truck by the old Huey on display outside Augusta airport. Clarence was already there, his prop turning slowly to keep the engine oil moving in the minus twenty cold.

"How was it, coming up?" I said.

"Windy." He hunched his shoulders in his airman's leather jacket with its furry collar. "You getting in, or standing outside to chat?"

I climbed aboard and belted in. "You know how to fly this thing?"

"Not really. But us black folks is fast learners." He placed his hand on my knee briefly as we accelerated down the runway, the Cessna hopping all over the place in the side gusts. "Don't you fall out now."

"You crash this thing you'll really piss me off."

We started concentric circles over Abigail's house in Hallowell, Clarence trying to keep us tilted so I could look down on the snow-clad rooftops, the chimneys trailing smoke, snow-tufted cars and pickups in driveways, a few crows agitated by our passage over their heads, scattered trees then the wide slopes of my ancestor's cow pasture, the empty Maine Turnpike in its cocoon of ice, dirty downtown Augusta and its frozen river, the two malls and acres of empty asphalt blasted out of the granite hills, then abbreviated meadows and cut-down forests, the slow throb of the Cessna's engine and the propeller whack, the jiggle of belts and buckles, and spreading to the horizons all around us the vast landscape of Maine.

"Musta been Ungodly beautiful," Clarence said, watching his instruments and the sky around us, chewing on his lower lip. "Longfellow's forest primeval. The murmuring pines and the hemlocks..."

From this height the tragedy of Maine grew clearer, the few islands of older forest in a sea of clearcuts and denuded saplings, the crisscross of logging roads, the mounds of logging slash, the trailer homes tacked to back roads like rowboats haphazardly moored in stormy waters. It was early Saturday morning but already the logging trucks were flitting to and fro like busy ants bearing their newly dead forest to the firewood sellers and pulp mills. "What they gonna do," Clarence said, "when all the trees are gone?"

"Burn camel shit," I snickered, "like our friends in Afghanistan?"

"Yo, what's that?" he said, tilting us on one wing so the horizon was suddenly at ninety degrees.

It was a white car, half snow-covered under pines at the end of a logging road. "Go lower," I said.

"I'm on the deck now." He circled again, just over the treetops. There was so much snow on the car I couldn't be sure but it looked like a Saab.

"That could be it," I said, a catch in my throat. "Climb higher so I can locate this."

Clarence took it back to thousand AGL till I could see the logging road tailing away from the black line of the Augusta-Belgrade road. "I've got it," I said, a bleak calm settling over my heart and making it hard to breathe.

Clarence swung back toward Augusta. "You want me call it in?"

I thought a moment, suppressing the fear and pain. "Let me check first."

We landed in a flurry of new snow, Clarence dismissing me quickly. "I need to get back before this snow gets meaner."

"Thank you, Bro." I slapped his shoulder. "I owe you."

He gave me a quick hug. "No you don't."

IT TOOK AN HOUR to get there. The logging road was too deep in snow for Bucky's truck so I parked and trudged through knee-deep drifts for maybe a mile till the stand of pines appeared. There'd been no recent car tracks, so the car Clarence and I had seen had been there long enough to tie in with Abigail's absence.

Not that I wanted it to.

The stand of pines had somehow escaped the loggers, standing tall and windy in the driving snowstorm like a memory of the past, not that I gave a damn about that now.

There it was under its blanket of snow, the white car.

An old Audi down on its rims, similar enough when covered with snow to a Saab, with a bullet-cracked side window, and needles and leaves on the passenger seat where squirrels had made a winter home.

"Dear Abigail," I said into the teeth of the snowstorm, "if you're out there please come home."

ON THE WAY BACK I drove through the growing blizzard to Don's and Viv's place, not wanting to be there but hoping the signed agreements they'd wanted to give me might somehow have survived the fire.

After Erica's attack yesterday on the cops they'd backed off and now said it was a kerosene fire. Like how some folks have a kerosene stove in the living room to supplement the wood heat in the basement when it gets real cold, and sometimes the pilot goes out and the kerosene vapor keeps seeping into the room and pretty soon while you're sleeping you die and don't even know it.

Don's and Viv's once-beautiful log home was a shambles of charred spars, burnt drywall, twisted plumbing and blackened trash. The snow was picking up again, soft large flakes that made your skin feel cold when they stuck to it.

I wandered the carbonized kitchen knee-high in scorched appliances and heat-shattered dishes. Some things seemed hardly touched: a toaster handle, a butter dish, a carving knife with *Vivian and Don* engraved in the handle.

The basement stairs had burned so I had to climb in a lower window. The room was waist deep in half-burnt joists that had collapsed from the floor about. In one corner were the carbonized remains of what had been two metal file cabinets. With nothing inside but ashes.

I had squeezed halfway out the window when I hear a crunch of boots. "Get out of there!" a woman yelled.

She was early fifties, tall and very thin with a jutting jaw, angular face, fierce eyes and dyed black hair, in a sheepskin vest, narrow jeans and lambskin boots. Her head arched forward on her skinny neck like Cruella de Vil's in *101 Dalmatians*. I wiped my hands on the snow and stood. "Who the hell are you?"

"I am an attorney and my client owns this place. And I want you out of here. Unfortunately the police released you when there was evidence you caused this. Even if this case goes nowhere in criminal court we intend to pursue you for civil damages."

"Civil damages?"

"This house was my client's property. We think you destroyed it. That's arson, and it's property damage and loss."

"Who's your client?"

"WindPower LLC."

"You people," I could barely speak, "are just plain evil."

"Once you're jailed," she called as I walked toward the 150, "I'm going to attend every parole hearing you ever have. And make sure you never get out."

Heading back to Lexie's I had five more things to think about:

1. Who would risk killing two people just to destroy evidence?
2. What difference did it make who owned the property when it burned?
3. But since WindPower owned it now they could restrict access, inhibit investigation, and steal evidence?
4. What had been in those signed agreements that was so dangerous for them?
5. Or had it just been a sorrowful accident?

That's when Mitchell calls to say he's been able to pick up tons of police conversations, and that I'm a frequent subject. "The word is to get you," he says amiably. "Any way they can."

"So who's putting heat on the police?"

"Look, I'm just your IT consultant, sweetheart. Take those questions to your lawyer."

"Can you zero in on the police and fire and rescue radio traffic, night before last?"

"Does the Pope pray?"

Wasn't twenty minutes later he calls back. "Get me something serious to do."

"What you mean?"

"The fire hit 911 at 23:51. Called in by a neighbor."

"So it started before midnight."

"Yeah. While your dead friends still owned the house."

LEXIE WAS IN A FOUL MOOD when I got back to her place. I felt heartbroken and defeated by Don's and Viv's deaths. But I did the usual, made martinis and sat her down at the kitchen table.

"Weird fucking world," she says.

I said nothing, unable to disagree.

"I wasn't going to tell you, but the Legislative hearing today was so awful, so fraudulent..." She shook her head that quick way she has, one of the billion reasons I love her. "You got your plate full already."

"I'm doing fine," I said, as if that could make it true.

"The Legislators just sat there, clearly bored by us citizens who'd come from all over the state, driven many hours on icy roads, taken time off work, just to ask for a little protection from this industrial nightmare happening to Maine."

"Which Legislators?"

"The Energy and Utilities Committee. Taking testimony on two bills that could protect just a little bit of Maine – a state and national park – from wind development, and they were just going through the motions, were going to vote NO no matter how many people were begging them to pass it, no matter how disastrous it is –"

I'd promised myself not to care about this anymore. "Follow the money."

"They even admit they passed the Wind Bill without *any* of them even reading it... *None* of them knows anything about electricity generation or the outdoors, none of them gives a damn." She was getting next to tears which meant then she'd get even madder and at that point it would be good for me to get out of the way. "They're so corrupt they don't even *try*," she added, "they don't even *try* to look democratic anymore."

It made my heart hurt, this devastation of Maine, and I hated all the quislings who were hustling it. "Everyone knows the Maine Legislature's crooked. What we didn't know is *how* crooked they are." I poured us both a tidbit more. "So the question is, given the shortness of life and the multiplicity of its joys and dangers, what to *do* about this?"

"One of Committee members sat there checking her phone the whole time, not even noticing the people testifying, never took a note, paid no attention at all. Then she takes out a box of Kentucky Fried Chicken and starts munching, even though the rules are no food in Committee chambers... She's the one who when asked how she was going to vote on a wind-related bill said, 'Wait, I have to call my wind lobbyist to find out...'"

"So," I repeated, "you've got a crooked Legislature and fake enviro groups hustling money from the wind industry that's hustling billions from the taxpayer. And you can't get the news out because public radio and most other media's bought and paid for by the wind industry, who are making so much taxpayer money they can throw it at everyone, buy the entire state government if need be... and most of the state's newspapers are owned by a politician who takes major donations from the wind industry..."

Dry oak crackled comfortably in the woodstove and threw tongues of orange light across the scarred linoleum. The air tasted of oak smoke, steaks and fries on the stove, the hint of lime at the bottom of a glass, the memory of everyone who'd lived here. The life of someone who visited once for an hour back in 1782 and sat in this kitchen with his beaver hat on his knees. The loves, transgressions, sorrows and joys of nearly two hundred and fifty years. This kitchen now full of warm peace, two people who care about each other talking over the immutability of fate, the ancient human war with evil.

"Whores," Lexie says. "Whores, cutthroats and priests. When you look at history, they're who always run things.

And the tragedy's how many beautiful places, people and other creatures they destroy."

"I take exception to blaming whores," I said equably.

"Yeah, there's nothing wrong with being a whore. What politicians do wrong is pretending they're not. And while a whore actually gives you something for your money, a politician takes your money and screws you in a different way."

"So on every level," I add, "we should free ourselves from their control."

"They'll keep screwing us. Strip mines, wind *farms*, toxic spills, wars, corporate-funded elections, pesticides, recessions, clearcuts, bailouts, trade agreements, you name it. They have all the money and power and we can't stop them." She cocked her head. "So what then?"

"I've been thinking maybe the dark side of the moon."

She reached her glass across for more gin. "It's either that or revolution."

Drowning in Mysteries

THE RED-LETTERED ENVELOPE in the mail inside Abigail's door was driving me nuts. So just after midnight I drove to Hallowell and parked three blocks from her house.

A few dim streetlights shuddered in the icy wind. Bare-limbed tree shadows danced over the glassy streets. My boots crunched in the crust that blew away in chunks. There were upstairs lights in a couple windows; everywhere near Abigail's was dark.

Her façade of tall windows and pale siding towered over Larch Street like a haunted house, tethered to the corner between a wider street of rambling ancient homes and a narrower steep street coming up from the River that was probably in 1830 the path my ancestor took leading the cow to pasture on the ridge.

One option was to go up to the front door, smash a corner of the leaded stained glass window, reach inside to turn the handle, grab the mail and leave. Sure I'd be more visible, but who'd be looking at this time of the frigid night? But I was damned if I was going to break that beautiful glass.

Instead I wandered up the steep side street past Abigail's driveway and barn, just like any Hallowell resident on a normal one a.m. stroll at twenty below plus wind chill.

Beyond Abigail's driveway and barn a twelve-foot spruce hedge separated her place from the uphill neighbor. I slid through it along the back of the barn to the rear of her house. There was a small lawn deep in snow, then four steps up to the back door landing.

The top half of the back door had small panes. Regular glass.

Behind me and to my right was the back of the big square house where the woman with the round pink face, curlers and plaited pink bathrobe had seen me one of the first nights I was checking Abigail's. But no lights were on there so I figured she was asleep.

I crouched in the lee of the hedge and waited twenty minutes to ensure no one had seen me and called the police. A cruiser would have been here in ten minutes, so if by twenty they hadn't rolled by, chances were they didn't know. And it was a lot easier to get away when you still outside, or to explain loitering rather than breaking and entering.

I crossed the back lawn, crackling the hardened snow and frozen grass, almost slipped on the steps, and with a gloved fist popped the bottom right-hand pane, shards tinkling on the floor inside.

Reaching through the broken pane I opened the door from inside and waited in the living room watching another twenty minutes to see if the cops arrived. If they did I still had time to get out the back and into the hedge and hopefully away.

I couldn't just grab the mail and run, because then the cops would notice the next time they checked, that someone had been there. But since the mail hadn't been touched, were they even checking the place?

With a shielded penlight I flipped through the mail. Mostly utility bills, bank and credit card statements, free newspapers, shopping coupons and ads – a diagnosis of America. Two handwritten letters.

But no big envelope with red magic marker saying READ THIS NOW.

Couldn't be. I'd seen it.

Three times I checked that pile of mail. It wasn't there.

I could have cried. I could have choked. I was going crazy.

Despondently I left and drove back to Lexie's farm and rolled into the bunk at 02:20, exhausted and wondering at my sanity.

So of course Mitchell called.

SHE'S TOTALLY BENT," Mitchell yells as if we're talking into tin cans with six thousand miles of string between us, "that Representative you asked about – Deborah Johnson?"

"You know what time it is?" I grumped.

"You were awake."

"It's only, what..." I tried to subtract five hours from 02:30, "like ten-thirty at night your time?"

"Nine-thirty-two, sweetheart. Do your math."

"Mitchell, I'll call you at four am Hawaii time, wake *you* up for a change."

"She's the one you said calls her wind lobbyist to find out how to vote? The one who was a checkout clerk at Walmart before she became a Legislator? Well, right away I hit pay dirt. It was easy – these Legislators are security slobs. She and her husband – he runs a Burger King franchise, they have three bank accounts. Twenty-four grand in savings, a $10K money market and a checking account that that's nineteen thousand in the red, almost maxed out on cash advances."

"Sounds like the all-American family," I yawned, trying to wake up.

"Her election committee, however..." He said nothing, drawing it out. "They have seven accounts with varying balances, total about a half million, more than enough to get her reelected. But I wandered around inside one of these accounts and found it transfers twenty-five grand a month in "loan payments" from the campaign to a bank in Cleveland that takes a two hundred dollar hit and sends it to a bank in Miami. But that bank isn't really in Miami, it's in the Turks and Caicos. And from there things start to really go downhill..."

"Meaning?"

"Maybe it's the Caribbean weather, it's too warm..."

"Huh?"

"Has to be some reason there's so much corruption in the Caribbean..."

"Mitchell –"

"So anyway the Turks and Caicos bank doesn't really exist, it just forwards wires. So this twenty-five grand is off to Luxembourg and from there I hit a wall. But I've hit the same wall before, when we were tracking wires out of Saudi and guess where they were going?"

"Pakistan?" This was based on my previous experiences with al Qaeda and the wind industry.

"No, you idiot. First Prudential Investment Bank of Boston."

"But you can't track it –"

"So what I'm doing next is having a look at First Prudential. And see if anyone or anything else looks familiar. It's the whole Demo leadership... looks like there are payoffs from the wind developers to over half the Legislature–"

"It's the endless question, Mitchell: what do we do about all this?"

"We do like Afghanistan: We take them down. One at a time."

I was so tired I didn't want to take anybody down. "Have a look at Maine Audubon's website. It's supposedly an organization of thousands of Maine bird lovers, but half its top contributors are wind industry. It testifies in legislative hearings and public meetings that wind projects don't really hurt birds, when ornithologists everywhere are saying wind projects will drive more bird species to extinction than climate change."

"Maybe more money's changing hands than shows up on some of these organizations' books. I'll look at the finances of top directors and board members, see what connections we find."

I had a sudden burst of almost hope. That we might get to the bottom of this. And save Maine.

Or would it would be like Jane once said, "If you love Maine, in five years don't come back. What it's going to look like then will make you sick."

But all this was totally out of my element. If I hadn't had Mitchell to help me in Hawaii with the Wind Mafia I'd be in prison now. Which meant I wouldn't have come to Maine, and wouldn't now be getting framed for whatever has happened to Abigail.

"When I think about it," I says, "If Abigail does show up alive I wouldn't put it past these cops to kill her and pin it on me."

"Wow," Mitchell said. "That's how bad they want you?"

"Yeah. That's how bad."

"A fucking mystery, all this."

I WAS DROWNING in mysteries. Next morning sitting in the creaky wooden rocker by the bunkhouse woodstove I tried to get them straight in my head. As in any military scenario it helps to separate unknowns into categories then seek links between them:

1. Abigail
   - Can I still save her?

- If she's dead – I could *barely* think this – who did it?
- What was in that letter with red magic marker? Who took it?
- Why did she vanish when I asked her about testifying for Bucky?
- Her affair with Bucky – he says there was no sex, she says there was?
- What did she really feel about her husband Ronnie Dalt's death?
- Did *she* know who killed him?
- This made no sense but I had to add it: *Did she kill him?*

2. Ronnie Dalt's murder
   - Who killed him? Why?
   - Had he really stopped selling out to the Wind Mafia?
   - Who set Bucky up for the murder?
   - Why has Bucky stopped talking to me?

3. The shot-out turbines
   - Who took Bucky's .308 that he hid after shooting out the first three?
   - Who shot at me when I was up on the ridge looking for it? Titus McKee?
   - Who shot out the latest four?
   - Do any of those bullets match the ones I dug out of the tree?

4. Mitchell's discoveries
   - Why be surprised? Hasn't everyone seen *House of Cards?*
   - It is however destroying Maine. How can we stop it?

5. The cops are targeting me. Who told them to?

6. Don and Viv's tragedy

- Who would risk killing people just to get rid of the signed agreements?
- What was in those agreements that made them so important?
- Or, a scary thought: did they do this just to implicate me?
- Why – what danger was I to them?
- Why did WindPower LLC's lawyer Cruella want me off the site?

7. Me
- Am I totally crazy to be helping the guy who jailed me then stole my woman, just because he once saved my life?
- Why am I in trouble in frozen Maine instead of surfing in Hawaii?
- I want to see Pa one last time. What will happen if I leave Maine?
- If, tragically, Abigail is dead, how can I avoid a murder rap?
- How can I get to Tahiti in eighteen days?

Other than these I had few questions. I'd have liked to know the origin of the universe and what it was like to be a tyrannosaur. But I was so damn worn out I hardly cared.

I'm good in combat because instinct takes over. Instinct and thousands of hours of training. But figuring my way out of this spider's web wasn't instinct. I had to pick it apart skein at a time. And for this I had no training.

Plus I'm not unduly bright. And lazy too. Not a good combination.

MEANWHILE THE FIRE'S crackling contentedly in the woodstove, Lobo's snoring on my bed (the turbines aren't running), and I am suddenly overcome with that primal joy of being warm and safe in the middle of a blizzard. How lovely to stretch out under the rough blankets smelling of horse sweat, dog and woodsmoke. Once you don't give a damn how dirty things are, I realized happily, how easy life becomes. Then of course I remembered how fleeting this was, that I was safe in the moment only.

Wood warms you three times, they say: when you cut it down, when you split it and when you burn it. But sadly now in Maine wind projects are driving the price of electricity so high that everyone's burning wood to stay warm, and the roads are clogged with logging trucks while the forests are bared and of course the CO_2 goes through the roof.

I was trying not to dwell on Don and Viv. They'd been wholehearted, warm people, still in love after all these years. People who loved their country and their neighbors and tried to do good by both.

I've seen so much death, in Afghanistan, Iraq and elsewhere, but I never can steel myself against it. The extinction of a human life – or an elephant, wolf or chickadee for that matter – is such a sorrowful loss, that in a sense I realize all my battles have been against death.

Not that we can win, of course. But even when we're getting beat up we have to fight back.

And now I was caught up in Don's and Viv's deaths. And directly in Abigail's disappearance. And the cops wanted me for both.

"WE WANT TO SEE YOU." It was C. Hart, the paunchy Augusta cop, on the phone. "Nine a.m. tomorrow."

"You have news of Abigail?"

"We'll tell you. Just be here."

"Tell me now!" I yelled, but he'd shut down.

So I called Erica and actually got her on her cell. "I can't be there," she says. "I've got meetings all morning."

"You've always got meetings. You don't have a life."

"You're always in trouble. You don't have a life either."

I didn't tell her about breaking into Abigail's. "So what should I do?"

"Say nothing."

Sitting there in the woodstove's all-embracing warmth, thinking of Erica, the cops, Abigail and her dead husband, I suddenly understood how it all might have happened.

Abigail's husband Ronnie had supposedly been killed because he was turning against the wind industry. Abigail worked for Senator Coleman, one of the Legislature's most powerful Dems, who had a big investments in industrial wind and received lots of tasty under-the-table handouts, legal contributions and other dreck.

Had Abigail finally convinced Ronnie how corrupt the whole wind scam was – is that why he turned against it, if he did indeed turn against it? Had she shown him proof – bank records, under-the-table contributions, sealed agreements, other political-corporate deals? If so, either the wind company or the Senator or some wind construction company would have wanted him silenced. Wanted them both silenced.

Had them both silenced.

Mildred might know.

THIS TIME WE MET at a coffee shop near the Capitol. She was on her way home and kept looking out the window at the new-falling snow. I told her what I'd been thinking, that maybe the political side killed Abigail's husband, not the industrial wind side. "But only," I said, "if he had something on them."

"Abigail could've given him that, whatever it was. If it was proof."

"Would he have changed sides? Did you ever meet him?"

"Several times. WindPower throws big parties every time they get another victory – when some town's beaten down, forced to take the turbines, when WindPower kills some proposed regulation in the Legislature, or buys their way out of court… I've seen him there, also at the Senator's Christmas party, he showed up with her."

"What was he like?"

"Tall, gangly, big Adams apple, skinny head, balding slightly, kind of a geeky slope-shouldered stance. Never shaved close enough. Wore wide-lapelled suits from J.C. Penney but used to tear out the labels."

I looked at her amazed. "You should be a novelist, Mildred."

"And," she laid chubby hands one atop the other on the table, "he had bad breath."

"God why'd she marry him?"

"Abigail's half crazy," she said, and instantly came into my head that Leonard Cohen song about *you know that she's half crazy and that's why you want to be there.* "Or maybe we're all crazy," Mildred added, "and Abigail was the sane one."

I tried not to think about the *was* Mildred had just used. "Maybe she was giving Ronnie the truth about Big Wind so they both had to die."

"Abigail was a whistleblower. She cared about what was fair for Maine people and wasn't afraid to stand up for it." Mildred nodded, seeing Abigail in her memory. "She had courage, that girl. Lots of courage."

This made me feel no better. In war the most courageous are usually the first to die.

"What could she have given her husband that was so dangerous?"

"Dangerous? The book."

"The book."

"The little green book where the Senator kept a list of all his real funding. It went missing a few days before Ronnie Dalt was killed. We didn't even know it existed till the Senator started interrogating us about it."

"Real funding?" I was getting excited now.

"The under-the-table, one-million-max, per year. Money he has to pay back with pro-wind legislation, like Senator Alfond did. He has to get certain bills through and strangle others or the wind money shuts down."

"What's in this book?"

"You should've asked Abigail. I think she's the one who took it."

Little Green Book

S O I HAD TO BREAK INTO Abigail's again in hopes of finding this little green book. In my imagination it had lined accounting pages where each sellout was listed, each exchange of cash for a piece of Maine. Where would she have put it? Or did she still have it, wherever she was?

Or had somebody destroyed it?

At 02:17 I parked the same three blocks above her house and hiked down the slippery chiaroscuro of frozen streets. The temperature had risen to ten below, with a keen north wind, the stars like shattered crystal between the tumbling clouds. I slipped into the spruce hedge behind her barn and waited twenty minutes to see if the cops showed. When they didn't I crossed the snow-crinkly yard and tried to reach through the small window pane I'd broken last night and my hand clunked into new glass.

I jumped back rubbing my knuckles, glanced up at the house grim, austere and empty as before. Yet someone had fixed the glass.

This meant I should get out of here, squeeze back through the hedge, up to the truck and never return. But I wasn't going to.

I didn't want to break the glass again. I tried the handle. It opened.

That made me want to leave, fast.

WANTING TO RUN, I stepped inside.

A great *wham* made me dive for the floor smashing my ribs into a chair. I rolled to a crouch ready to fight but it was just the furnace coming on – I'd let in a blast of cold air and set it off.

I stood massaging my ribs and swearing silently. Why was the back door unlocked?

Who fixed the broken pane?

I reached in my pocket for my penlight and it came out in pieces. Broken when I hit the chair.

I crouched low, trying not to breathe, listening, waiting for the rib pain to subside, the words *Leave right now* thundering in my brain. *Leave this instant.*

Instead I crossed the kitchen into a hallway then the dining room, oriental carpets soft and silent underfoot, the white damask on the mahogany table and the twelve mahogany chairs with their pale needlepoint cushions starkly visible in starlight through the ice-clad windows.

Living room dim, couches, coffee tables, armchairs, bookcases, potted plants, more Orientals, a sense of abandonment. I headed up the stairs I'd climbed several times with Abigail barely two weeks ago, keeping to the silent edge of the oriental runner, halting to hold my breath and listen every few steps, tasting her absence.

Only the sound of this ancient wooden home creaking in winter wind, the moaning trees, once a distant diesel pickup warbling its way along Water Street far below.

Where would Abigail have put the green book? Most likely in her bedroom or her office beside it. Everything about Abigail was order and efficiency. Even when she made love. Where like all good deal-makers she extracted all she could get.

God love her.

Why was the back door unlocked?
Who fixed the window?
Why am I even trying this without a light?

HER BEDROOM gave me a stab of sorrow, the bed where we'd had so much fun, the memory of her getting dressed in pale dawn, a winter nymph. A half-open oak dresser with underwear still fragrant of her, two bedside tables piled with books, too dark to read the titles. A dark-covered notebook.

I took it to the window to see better. A green cover. But inside only music and lyrics.

In her office I scrabbled in the desk drawers hoping for a flashlight. Found an old cell phone but it was dead. Pencils, pens, scissors, scotch tape, stapler, paper clips, markers – all exuding a faint memory of her. But no flashlight.

Maybe in the bathroom there'd be a night light.

No. Abigail seemed unafraid of everything, certainly didn't fear the dark.

Damn. I was going to have to turn on a light.

No curtains on the windows. Abigail didn't give a damn who saw her. "It was the first thing I did after Ronnie died," she'd said. "Took down those hideous mauve curtains."

Who would see if I turned on a light? At 02:00? What about the next-door neighbor with the round pink face, curlers and plaited pink bathrobe? Would I wake her?

Would she call 911?

If she did would I have time to get out?

This was crazy. Angrily I flipped on the bedroom light, did a quick recon of her books and papers finding nothing, inhaling the lusty scents of see-through nightgowns in her closet as I reached past them but there was no hiding place behind, looked under the bed, in the bathroom with its see-through shower we'd made love in one night.

Everything was reminiscent of her but she was nowhere. I flicked off the bedroom light, checked through the window that no cops had arrived, and went into her office and turned on the light.

Three walls of bookcases full of books. An old cherry double-sided desk, three computers, lots more books, three tennis rackets leaning against one corner, their handles taped and polished by wear, and two guitars on three-legged stands in another. The ancient desk was the kind they used to make in Maine, with a wide top and a set of drawers on each side, for two people to work on it facing each other. *If I could look at Abigail right now.* Please, to see the flickering moods shadow her face, her small sharp mouth, tall incised cheeks and violet eyes, the tumble of tawny hair over her lovely brow, biting her lips as she concentrates on something – even making love she does that and it makes you want her even more.

No green book in any of the drawers. I quickly feel behind the books in the bookcase. Nothing there but an old Margaux bottle, empty. Then behind another shelf a Mason jar of weed. Nothing unusual about that – most Maine homes have a stash somewhere.

Unfortunately just then a gray Taurus with no roof lights pulls up out front. I hustle downstairs but already two cops are coming in the back and another at the front so I head back upstairs past the still-lit office up to the third floor and a creaky corridor of empty stale rooms, my footsteps hollow on old floorboards. In one naked room a square trapdoor in the ceiling just low enough that I can reach it leaping up one-handed. I pull myself up into a cold attic and reset the trapdoor just as a cop jangles up the stairway and starts checking the second floor rooms.

My heart's hammering so hard I can't hear. I know I'm done. Finished. I wonder if they'll shoot me and stick a drop gun in my hand, imagining one of them rolling the cartridges across my dead fingers, to show it was me loaded the gun.

"Clear up here!" he calls. A voice answers below and he clunks down the stairs.

I wait a half hour. No sound but this frozen old building creaking and moaning. The attic so achingly cold I can't stop shivering. The joists and rafters lined with foil-backed fiberglass insulation glittering faintly in the light through the gable windows. I lift the trapdoor silently and slide through it, awkwardly trying to pull it down after me and it clatters loudly into place.

I crouch there unmoving for ten minutes; no one comes. I slide along the corridor wall to the stairs. The light I turned on in the office below is off.

Staying to the side of the stairs to avoid squeaking them I go down to the second floor. Somewhere outside a motor rumbles. I look out the window; the gray Taurus is gone and snow is falling in great thick flakes.

Could they all be gone? Or are one or two still here, waiting?

If they're going to shoot you this is where it will be.

If they're here, where are they?

THE OLD HOUSE shivered and creaked. Wind gnashed at the gable ends, rattled the windows and wailed away. It came to my mind unbidden, *silence is the enemy,* but I couldn't figure why or how.

If the cops were still here I just had to wait them out. The fact that I was cornered made it worse but I couldn't change that. And if they were staking out the place how could I leave to get to the cop shop by nine?

04:17. Sitting on the fourth step from the top I tugged Bucky's coat tighter but it didn't warm me. Beyond the windows the streetlit night was pale with flailing snow, the trees and houses gone, only this rabid wind circling this house like a demon trying to tear its way in.

A creak on the stair one flight below. Another one two stairs closer. Somebody coming up fast.

If I moved he'd hear me.

Another creak below. Two of them.

They'd stopped. Wind battered the windows; the house shook.

For a long time they made no sound.

04:48. Two hours to first light.

I've known a lot of cops but none of them would be this good, to wait silently in a rattling old house for two chilled hours in the hopes of catching a malfeaser upstairs, when all you had to do is yank out your Glock, turn on the lights and nail him.

No way I could now risk turning on a light. But earlier, who'd seen the office light and called the cops? The curlers lady lived on the other side, she could have only seen the window's dim glow on the snow. Which implied an unusually high degree of watchfulness on a winter night.

Or was it one of the two saltbox colonials across the street under huge old oaks? No, they were lower because of the down-sloping street, could have barely seen the lit window through the snowstorm.

Maybe the unmarked Taurus just happened by on a routine patrol – but why? Crime doesn't exist in Hallowell – except of course Ronnie's murder and Abigail's disappearance. And except for all the crimes perpetrated in the town's fine restaurants by Maine's cabal of legislators, lobbyists, lawyers, sham enviros, PR experts and all their other accomplices. But it's always been like this, as Aesop says, *we jail the petty crooks and elect the big crooks to high office...*

05:53. Snow completely blankets the windows, giving one a false sense of haven. On the streets outside the snowplows were grumbling like old bears, pushing everything aside, their chains clunking like great claws.

It was too cold to sit any longer. Not a sound from below. I got up and walked downstairs like I lived there. Nobody. I told myself it had just been the Afghanistan memories that keep me up most nights. That's all.

So my choices now are do I try to get out while it's still dark and the blizzard is hiding everything? Or wait for first light to search the rest of the house for this allegorical green book? My lizard brain said *Let's stay* while my body wanted to run.

So we stayed.

Keeping an eye out windows for errant cop cars – not that I could see them through this hurricane of snow – I went down to the kitchen, found some Starbucks Italian Roast but couldn't locate a grinder (did she take it with her?) so with a small cast iron frying pan I mashed the beans on the granite countertop, boiled water and dumped them in it, stirred it a bit and drank this delectable nectar slowly, letting it overwhelm my taste buds and warm my body all the way down to the toes.

In the freezer were blueberry pancakes I put in the toaster and in the reefer maple syrup from a farm in Winthrop. I made lots more coffee and ate all the pancakes. They were whole wheat with wild blueberries and I was sure she'd made them. Then I chugged more syrup and licked the leftover off the plate, washed everything and put it away, licked then washed the syrup off my face and began searching the house.

Nowhere in the kitchen, pantry, dining room cabinets or living room was a little green book. I even opened heat vents and checked ceilings for crawl spaces and behind the closets for false walls.

This pissed me off. I feared for Abigail so badly that I found myself angry at her for disappearing, for not telling me the whole story so I could've helped her.

For maybe being murdered.

Again I searched the bedroom and office and the vacant third floor where I'd scrambled up the ceiling trapdoor to hide from the cop, but never was there anything hidden except two dead mice and a child's pewter spoon which I left in situ, but no little green book.

Was Mildred selling me a line?

Why would she do that?

INTO ABIGAIL'S CELLAR I go, flick on the ancient black wire lights at the top of the stairs, go down the cobwebbed wide old pine steps to a dirt-floored musty jumble of low-beamed rooms, one with an ancient pile of coal in a corner, another dominated by a black cast iron furnace and fuel tank, several pine-planked cubicles of broken furniture, old lumber, a rusty push mower, boxes of canning goods and other stuff, and mysteriously a venerable Old Town canvas canoe, and how they got it down those narrow crooked stairs I cannot imagine.

But no green book. With the exception of the furnace nothing down here had been disturbed in years.

It felt spooky in the cellar so I go up to her bedroom for one last search, thinking when she and I had so much fun there, and her absent proximity near drove me crazy as I tried to figure what to do next.

It was 07:52 and I had to get out soon to be at the cop shop by nine. And if they knew I'd been here maybe they were just waiting to arrest me.

Then I thought of the barn.

The blizzard was slowing down. You could make out dim outlines of the two saltbox colonials across the street, and from the kitchen window see the pink-faced curler lady's window. So I was going to have to cross the back courtyard in some visibility to get to the barn.

Nonetheless I chanced it, having checked the house one last time that I'd left no trace except fewer pancakes in the freezer, shut the door behind me, unlocked as before, and stepped through a side door into the barn's frigid tall dimness, its hand-hewed beams and tracks of early sky through broken siding where the wind hissed in.

At the far end three beautiful old cars making my heart pound. A Hudson, maybe '52, a lovely sleek Packard about '48, an immaculate blue Studebaker Avanti with a blue leather interior. I wanted to touch them, caress their sleek fenders, raise their hoods and stare lovingly at the engines, open their doors and sit inside them.

I checked the garage all over, finding nothing, and returned to the house for a last look at the mail. The red-marked letter still wasn't there. I bent down to leave the mail as I'd found it. And as I stood saw the little red pinhole over the door.

I was on candid camera.

And in twenty minutes I had to be at the cop shop.

Corruption Rate of Return

A T THE AUGUSTA COP SHOP they didn't seem glad to see me. I wasn't happy either, having spent most of the night hiding from them, and the remainder expecting them to grab me any instant. And there'd been the worry of the drop gun. A lousy way to die.

And now they had me on candid camera.

Hemingway was at the desk. No, he said, Officer Hart wasn't in yet.

I sat there wondering if it was better to tell them I'd been at Abigail's rather than them seeing it on the camera shots the alarm company would have forwarded to them by now. I could say I was there because I'd seen the red-marked mail, but already Hemingway was chewing his moustache and checking furtively that I wasn't armed, then with his foot set off a bell that rang elsewhere, and another cop sauntered in, this one in a flak jacket, and they were looking at me the way two cats look at a sparrow.

Luckily, as one might put it, C. Hart arrived and nodded me into a back room with Hemingway. "You're like a piece of shit I can't dig out of my shoe," Hart says amicably. "You keep showing up when I don't want you."

I shouldn't have said it but I did, "Maybe you should stop walking in shit. Or does that turn you on?"

He gave me an amused look, said nothing.

"This is crazy," I snapped. "You guys aren't even *trying* to find her."

"Her?"

"Abigail, for Chrissake."

"Tell us again," Hart says, "what you was doing the night she disappeared."

So I explained him all over again. He shook his head despondently, looked out the window. "You're more trouble than a rabid skunk. And I ain't even allowed to shoot you." He tipped back in his chair, thumbs in his belt, Caterpillar hat down over his forehead, looking me over.

"I'm surprised you didn't," I ventured, not really wanting to discuss it.

"That's against the law." He cleared his throat, leaned forward. "Even if we want to we're not supposed to."

This didn't give me the reassurance he perhaps had in mind. And I was getting pissed at their overall disinterest and perhaps pushed too far. "How come you're not checking her mail? What about that envelope with the red letters? Who took it?"

He eyed me patiently like the hangman waiting for his victim to finish praying. "I don't know what you're talking about. We didn't take anything."

"Have you been checking her mail?"

"That's for us to worry about."

"Goddamit did *you* take that letter?" I realized I was yelling but couldn't stop. "*What* does it say?"

He rubbed his face, an exasperated whiskery sound. "Dilfer," he said to Hemingway, "you think we should bring him in?"

Hemingway took out his chewing gum, looked at it and dropped it in his shirt pocket. "Prob'ly we should. But Jesus Christ he'll get that woman lawyer from Portland get him out again. And each time it looks more like harassment."

"Every time we catch a fucking criminal," Hart said, "it's harassment."

SO I'D DUCKED JAIL one more time. But maybe the last. It was clear I needed a backup life. With that in mind I called Smyrna, as Pa had suggested. She has a beauty salon on the rich end of Waikiki, but before that she was a disguise tech for the Agency. And she's my cousin Sally's longtime lover, so we're family too. As I explained you, she once made me a false face so thin and real you couldn't find the edge between it and your skin.

After all the usual preambles she says, "*Why* the hell are you in *Maine?* The weather's *lovely* here."

I explain her a bit about Bucky and all. "Pono," she says, "what's going on?"

"What do you mean what's going on?"

"What do you *mean* what do I *mean?* It's obvious. You're in trouble again, Pono. I can smell it."

"Look, Smyrna, don't you have some poor lady waiting for you to douse her head with chemicals? I'll call you some other–"

"Don't you *dare* shut me off!"

"Alright already. I need a passport, DL, couple live cc's, whatever else, all in the same name, all valid."

"I'm not doing this for you. Not unless you tell me what for."

"You're out of the game, remember?"

"No I'm not."

So I explained her about Abigail missing, Don and Viv's dying in their burning house, my repeated arrests, the whole deal. And that I wanted to see Pa again before he died.

"If you're on a local hold," she says, "it's all over the cop net. They'll grab you at an airport, bus station, lots of places. It's what they're waiting for – so they can put you *Inside*."

"I know, I know. So can you do this?"

"Sweetie of course I can do this. I'm just not sure I *should*, that's the problem."

"Problem?"

"Yeah, for your sake."

"Smyrna, if Abigail turns up dead I am totally fucked, and I'll never get to see Pa one last time."

"You always been close, you two. Even when you were a little kid on his shoulders. How happy you were, the two of you."

"Always have been." The words caught in my throat but I pretended they didn't.

"You know how hard this is? To make stuff that works?"

"That's why I called you."

"You called me because you don't have anyone else."

"You know that's not true."

"Yeah but what good are they?"

"Smyrna, don't be jealous. So if this were possible, how soon would it be?"

"A few days. I'll let you know. And Pono?"

"Yeah?"

"When you get the passport and cards, use them fast. They got a short shelf life."

"Like lots of us."

"Even shorter. At least I hope so."

TITUS MCKEE was next. I had figured out the links between WindPower LLC and the Demo leadership in the Legislature, and Mitchell was on his way to finding where the money went. But I hadn't forgotten that someone had shot at me barely two weeks ago, and if I hadn't been very lucky and very fast I would have died on that snowy bare-treed ridge and long since buried somewhere.

If you've ever been shot at you know what it's like. The snap of the bullet past your head, the echoing muzzle blast, your mind racing to figure where it's coming from and can you find cover before the next one hits you. It happens in instants though it seems very slow, and the most horrible feeling on earth is being exposed to fire with no way to hide.

So needless to say it had pissed me off. Fury, a determination to get even, which of course is how wars start small and grow big – the more people harmed the more wanting to get even, and from there it's a geometric progression.

None of this concerned me right now. I'd let Titus slide because I'd had to visit Pa in Hawaii, illegally of course since the Maine cops had a restraint on me, and then Don and Viv had died and Abigail was still gone, and I was running out of hope for her, for Maine and myself.

Titus worked for Stearing Motors, the regional trucking garage. For this I envied him, as few things are more peaceful and rewarding than working on an engine, long as you have the time, you're not cold or wet, and you know what you're doing.

Mitchell's recon of Titus' phone had brought little. They'd put the house up for sale but their realtor said no one was interested. Not surprising, with that howling wall of turbines on the mountain above them.

Titus's wife Doris's father in Machias was ill so she called him daily and also her two sisters. She also called constantly other residents near Eagle Mountain, sharing tactics for reducing the noise, to keep the kids from bouncing off the walls, that kind of thing.

Titus had a few buddies that he talked with briefly, mostly about going ice fishing or working on motorcycles, but he was pretty much a homebody.

The rest of the household was even less rewarding. Their three daughters emitted an avalanche of emails, FBs, twits, tweets and other foolishness. Though they'd done well in school before, this year was a disaster, and everyone was having trouble sleeping.

Titus never sent emails nor responded to the random ones sent his way. Doris had a full email life but all of it in-nocent. Most significantly, the McKees had never received anything from the industrial wind developers or their law-yers or political accomplices.

But I didn't really care about all this because I'd already decided he was my shooter and I was going to get even.

How I had not yet figured out.

First was a little night recon on the McKee estate. That it would be minus thirty-eight plus a wind factor of twenty really didn't matter. Even though I hated cold weather, in SF I'd learned to live with it, and live well. And there was plen-ty of Bucky's yellowed long underwear to get me through.

About 20:00 I was on the slope above Titus's house, shiv-ering in a little ice hole I'd made in accordance with the latest SF instructions. If I'd had any brains at all I would have been in bed with Erotica (add "ot" in the middle of "Erica" and that's what you get). Or with Lexie for that matter. I'd want-ed to bring earphones and my collection of every recording AC/DC ever made, but feared someone sneaking up behind me through the frozen night. Like happens in Afghanistan.

But this wasn't Afghanistan. By 21:30 all the McKee lights were out. The turbines howled dismally on the ridge, the red strobes flitted across the snowy hills like dervishes, wind hissed through the pines and the birches cracked with cold.

03:21. *HIGHWAY TO HELL* on my phone. "Look," I says, attempting to be polite, "I'm trying to get some sleep here."

"I broke in," Mitchell says.

"Nice," I says, trying to end the conversation so I can go back to my semi-frozen sleep.

"What are you," Mitchell says, "in bed with some chick? Lemme talk to her."

I look out at the snow plumes spinning in the bone-eating wind. "She's right here," holding the phone so he could hear the wind.

"I broke in," he repeats. "Got inside WindPower LLC."

Even my blood began to throb. "How?"

"They set up all these barricades. After last time..."

Last time was when Mitchell got into their system and discovered everything they did from kiddie porn to murder to buying governors and legislators and killing the necessary journalist or two.

"...but they forgot the safeguards." Mitchell sounded like a proud father, and this, sadly, was the closest he was ever going to get. "So I go through this guy in Estonia, he has a key, and I'm inside."

"Cool," I says, still trying to stop shivering and wake up, not giving a damn about who in Estonia might have a path into their system, or why.

"Bastards have a program," Mitchell says. "Pretty sophisticated. In each state, how much they have to give to each politician for how much in return. Same for the enviro groups. How to buy them all at the lowest possible price."

"Which bastards?"

"Not just WindPower LLC, a whole bunch of wind developers. They share this data on Legislators, how much to give each one."

"And?"

"*And* my ass, baby. I'll send you the file." With a click he was gone.

For a moment I feared I'd hurt him somehow, realized I hadn't. Just the hurt of knowing what life is like, for other folks.

At 06:58 the sun pretends to cross the horizon but it's a chimera, a mirage. At 07:24 it actually lifts itself portentously off the tips of the distant conifers and floods us with its miraculous warmth, bringing us way up to twenty below. Face flushed with its radiance I cross the ridge and hustle my way down to the logging road and along it, boots crunching, breath freezing to my face, the last 2.5 miles back to Lexie's.

I smell bacon before I get in the door. "It's not bacon," she says. "It's fatback." I take my coat off and stand shivering by the woodstove, its heat not reaching me, for the night had gone into my bones. Bucky's thick wool trousers wouldn't warm so I stripped them off and stood in Bucky's long underwear beside the hot iron stove.

She dumps scrambled eggs and bacon on my plate. "So what'd you see?"

"Not a damn thing." Even the hot coffee cup wouldn't warm my fingers. "Got a call from Mitchell."

"Oh?" Her eyebrows raise. She'd know him when she and I had our hot days and nights together in Honolulu before my last tour in Afghanistan. As much as Lexie loved me I always thought she loved Mitchell even more. Which was fine with me – he'd saved my life. But sadly she was never going to have him, or he her. You can read all about it in *The Sun Also Rises*.

And believe me I'd give any woman up if it'd make Mitchell whole again. Or give almost anything else up, too.

Lexie went out to the bunkhouse and brought back my Toshiba, finds the email from Mitchell –

"Hello dears,

Hope the Maine winter is treating you well. Following is a copy of a WindPower LLC internal document which initially came from another wind company, and has been forwarded by WindPower to several more, as well as to 5 DC and Portland lobbying firms and a Portland law group which turns out to be more hustlers from the wind developers.

FROM: Byron Spaeth, President and CEO, WindPower, LLC

TO: WindPower LLC Board of Directors and Vice Presidents

RE: CONTRIBUTIONS RATE OF RETURN

DATE: January 7, 2015

Because wind power makes no sense economically, electrically or environmentally, wind companies must purchase politicians if they are to succeed. But it is always difficult to determine how much to pay individual politicians. Many things influence this choice: how well the politicians follow instructions, their willingness to undercut opposition, their reelection potential, and their relative cost.

Needless to say, the more regional or national a politician the more they cost; however in Maine some Legislators with the power to make or break us can be bought quite cheaply compared to states like Massachusetts or New York.

The attached formula will make such decisions easier and more profitable. Please review it carefully and get back to me with any questions or comments.

1. CALCULATING YOUR CRR – CONTRIBUTIONS RATE OF RETURN:

It is not only possible but essential to rate expenditures on politicians versus the resulting profits. In general: PE = < 1.4% RP.

Thus PE (Political Expenditures), such as direct & indirect lobbying, cash under the table, plane rides, dinners, vacations, hookers, etc. should never exceed 1.4% of the RP (Real Profits) that will result from them. To put it another way, Real Profits should always be more than 70 times the Political Expenditures necessary to obtain them.

Real Profits, of course, is how much we actually make on a project, not what we show the IRS. And remember, the losses we show the IRS means we make even more money avoiding taxes.

So for a given politician if PE is $5 million (say you max out on contributions, be sure all your employees, subsidiaries, wives, boyfriends and girlfriends max out also, host banquets, campaign flights, plenty of hookers of all shapes and persuasions, lots of under-the-table money, certain drugs as appropriate, trips to Honduras, Paris and Goa, a private table weekend in Vegas – all the usual), it should lead to a minimum of $350 million in RP – direct after-tax real profits for the corporate entity or industry which has purchased all or part of this politician.

As a stunning example, our wind industry paid Obama $71 million for his first campaign and got $62 billion in taxpayer subsidies in return. Real Profits were only about 1/3 of that, say $20 billion. Still, that $20 billion is nearly 300 times the cost to obtain it – not bad for a no-risk operation. And remember, that's national, and Maine politicians are far cheaper.

2.   HOW DO I DECIDE HOW MUCH OF A POLITICIAN TO BUY?

There is an equation for this, too: $\dfrac{RP-PE}{PE} \times PV = CRR$

Or put another way: $\dfrac{RP}{PE-1} \times PV = CRR$

Put simply, Real Profit (RP) less Political Expenditure (PE) divided by PE times the politician's Proportional Value (PV) equals CRR, the Contributions Rate of Return. In essence, how much money we make divided by how much we invest times the politician's proportional value will tell you not only their CRR, but also what percentage of them you need to buy.

Assessing a politician's PV can be complicated. A lot of them will work for us then their voters find out and dump them, and we have to start all over again with whoever gets elected to replace them. It's frustrating, but keep your eye on the ball: We can make many more billions here in Maine.

By the way, politicians will always say things like "You'll have to do better than that; the other side just offered me a quarter million." With this formula you can rate easily if more expenditure is necessary, and in the meantime learn how to trim their egos, put them back in their place.

Reading this I realized the corporate contributor looks down on the politician the way an intelligence agent looks down on someone he's bribed into betraying their country.

Not that the contributors wouldn't troll for the same money if they were politicians.

But as the old saying goes, even crooks don't like crooks.

Strobes

THE TURBINES WERE BAD so Lexie'd gone to the Wilderness Motel in South China. Exhausted from my frozen night with Titus, I hunched in my bunk with hands over my ears, mad at myself for not going with Lexie, turbine shock waves rattling the windows and throbbing my bones. Lobo was gone, Max too. I went into the house for some TP to spit on, wad up and stick in my ears but that didn't help either.

The sound was maddening, made you want to run, throw up. It was like a very slow explosion, the unending 747 touchdown, a howl of tortured steel and sky. The blinking red strobes made you dizzy and sick; they bounced off the snow and shot a steady flicker through the windows. Like Don and Viv had said, it was like a cop car outside your house with its flashers on all night.

Finally I sat in the kitchen with a glass of gin in the hopes that might make me sleepy. It didn't. I went outside to call Lobo, no response, the red lights going round like a mad carousel.

That's when I got the crazy idea of visiting Titus again.

AN HOUR'S HIKE up the mountain brought me to the wasteland of red-flashing howling turbines then another hour down to Titus's, where I dig my snow hole again and settle in for a long winter's night.

There was no question of sleeping. With nothing to do but shiver and watch Titus's motionless house, till at 20:23 something dark stepped out Titus's back door, crossed the back lawn and started climbing through knee-deep snow toward me.

Titus McKee. With a rifle in his hand.

I was unarmed; he could kill me and no one'd ever know.

No point to run; he'd shoot me in two seconds. That shiver of awareness down the back, what a bullet will feel like. I hunched silently in my hole, waiting to leap on him if he gave me time.

He reached a little gully below me and swung to his right, climbing through sparse junipers and bare-stemmed willows till he passed on my left, rifle slung over his right shoulder, his frozen breaths rising cloudlike in the semi-lunar night.

The shock of expecting to die then not dying nearly knocked me out. Forcing myself to breathe deep and steady I sat on the edge of the snowhole and tried to figure what next. Then I followed Titus up the mountain, keeping about fifty yards to his left and below him, ducking from bare trunk to bare trunk as he barged his way uphill through deepening snow never bothering to look back.

It was insane to follow an armed man who wanted to kill me when I had no weapon. But something kept me going despite the fear, despite the anger at my own stupidity. That maybe I'd be able to take him down and leave him up there.

Titus broke out on the ridgetop to a line of nine turbines that were still turning.

What he did next blew my mind.

He approached the first turbine till maybe seventy yards away and knelt down next to a pile of shattered trees. Holding the rifle barrel against a thick near-horizontal root he aimed at the turbine housing fifty-five stories above, using the upended root as a brace.

The gun's barrel flamed, its blast racked the night. On the turbine high above came a bright flash. *Holy shit*, he was using incendiary rounds, a high-powered rifle with a fast, flat trajectory that would drive the bullet deep into the turbine mechanism.

There was a *clik-click* as he opened the breech, then *click-clik* as he chambered the next round. Silhouetted against the snow, he was visible enough to see him pocket the ejected empty cartridge.

Another great *wham* as he fired again, the round blazing off the turbine nacelle. He fired again, dead on, straight into the gear box, then three times more, all incendiaries. From another pocket he took more bullets and reloaded and emptied the magazine into the generator in the back of the turbine.

After the last round he bent over, feeling the ground and snow around him. For a moment I couldn't figure what he was doing then realized he'd lost an ejected cartridge. He got down on one knee and really began to search. Finally he stood, slung the rifle and jogged along the blasted ridgetop road toward the next tower. He fired two magazines into the second turbine then turned back down the mountain toward home.

I waited fifteen minutes then crossed to where he'd shot at the first turbine. There was a wide swath where he'd dug in the snow looking for the missing cartridge. As I hadn't seen him pocket it I hoped it might still be there. Using my phone light I scanned the area seeing nothing but churned-up snow and sodden leaves. Like Titus I knelt and felt around in the snow but still found nothing.

Standing I glanced at the tree roots. It was a big pine that had been cut then the roots had been dynamited. I turned the phone light on the root mass and there in the midst of dirt and rootlets was a glimmer.

I wiped my gloves clean and pulled out the cartridge. A 30-06, not from Bucky's lost gun.

And not a .308 ASYM like Bucky's or a .270 Fiocchi like the guy who shot at me.

I found a good boot print and shot a pix with my phone. A few small flames were licking up the side of the further turbine. The closer, maybe a hundred yards from me, was leaking a waterfall of oil that the wind flayed into a wide stain on the snow.

As I headed back to Lexie's the forest grew silent and I realized all nine turbines had stopped, though their strobes were flashing madly.

If Titus shot at me why was he also shooting out turbines? Actually, shooting out the turbines made sense: now he and his family could sleep.

Had he shot the four other turbines the cops tried to blame on me?

But why shoot at me?

Was someone paying him to kill me?

Or was my shooter maybe not on the Missalonkee Hard Riders list at all? Maybe my shooter was, as the Mainers say, *from away?* From one of these Texas energy combines trying to build thousands of turbines in Maine?

Titus must know if they caught him for shooting out the turbines he'd probably do time. Same as Bucky, but then Bucky had the murder rap too. I realized I was feeling responsible for Bucky and told myself not to. For Lexie too, and Abigail bless her heart and even Mildred Pierce, and for all the people in Maine who were losing their lovely mountains.

Felt responsible for the whole human race. *That* was my damn problem.

In fifteen days the Tahiti Tsunami. I wasn't going to make it.

SIRENS WERE WAILING in the distance. From Lexie's front window I watched two fire engines pass, then a cop car then two more cops, all flashing madly. I went out on the front porch.

Up on the mountain the second of the turbines Titus had shot was blazing merrily; the other emitting a volcano of black smoke. But with all the snow on the access roads there was no way those fire engines would make the climb.

The cops and firemen were standing in the field between Lexie's place and Jane's watching the turbines burn. The cops backed two snowmobiles off a trailer and with a fireman on the back of each headed up the mountain.

Meanwhile I checked the pix I'd taken of Titus McKee's boot print to compare it with the Red Wing boot print left by the guy who'd shot at me. No match. The boots Titus was wearing were worn, the sole markings nearly illegible. Two sizes bigger.

If Titus had been my shooter he'd been wearing different boots and scrimping his toes.

That's when Mitchell calls. "You won't believe," I says, "what Titus did last night."

"I'm very sorry, man, to tell you. I think I found Abigail."

Setting Bail

"IS SHE *OKAY?*" I almost begged him.

He was speaking slowly as he always does, driving me crazy. "Don't know. You need to check."

"Where? Where *is* she?"

"I started thinking this through," Mitchell answered steadily, "if Abigail's missing, what are the options? And one of the options was she'd had an accident somewhere, or she'd parked the car where no one could see it –"

"The cops've looked everywhere. Accidents get reported."

"So I was thinking could there be an accident they didn't see? Like under a bridge or something, or could the car be parked at the end of an old logging road, under a snow-covered tarp somewhere?"

"We already checked that, Clarence and me." I sat back, waiting for the truth. "Tell me."

"There's a vehicle upside down under a bridge not too far from Augusta, got it off real time. Probably impossible to see from the bridge. On the satpix it's hard to tell, but may be a Saab. From the angle and distance I can't make out the plate or if anybody's inside it. Need you go check."

"Tell me where."

IT WAS A WHITE SAAB upside down in the water at the bottom of a gully where the back road from Augusta to Belgrade cuts over Hawkins Brook. Not ten miles from where Clarence and I had seen the white Audi. A place I knew well as it had once belonged to my Maine ancestors, as a lot of Maine acres had once belonged to them.

Hawkins Brook is a steep hundred-foot canyon of white flashing rapids, bare trees, ice and frozen granite. The Saab was almost under the bridge, impossible to see from the highway. From the snow on the chassis it looked like it had been there several days.

Oh Jesus Abigail, I prayed aloud as I tumbled and slithered down the near-vertical canyon. *Please don't be you.*

Frosted windows with smears of black blood inside. Scratching at the icy glass I could make out a dark-haired head hanging down above the steering wheel, still in the safety belt.

Looking up you could see where it had gone off the road's shoulder just before the bridge rail began, had spun over when it hit a tree, landed in the brook on its nose, and fell back on its roof.

I wanted so badly to yank open the door, hold her, warm her. But I'd seen enough bodies to know she was dead, this lovely woman I'd made such happy love with, and now if I left one fingerprint or DNA or messed up even one clue the cops would get me. For tampering with evidence. For pretending to find my own victim.

I'd have to call in an anonymous tip. Then I'd no longer be a suspect in her death. Or would I, I wondered, glancing up the canyon to where the Saab had run off the road. What if she was already dead inside it?

Anyway they'd still suspect me of killing Don and Viv, and whatever else they could find.

With a pine bough I brushed where I'd wiped the glass.

Swearing, half-crying, I climbed out of the canyon and stumbled back Hawkins Brook Road to Bucky's 150, only remembering later the State Police cruiser that passed, and the flash of his camera.

DON'T KNOW HOW I made it back to Lexie's. All I was seeing was Abigail's lovely face, hearing her deep contralto, her tangle of brilliant thoughts and ironic empathetic mind.

What I do remember is when I came round the last curve before Lexie's farm both turbines were blazing and Lexie's pasture was full of fire trucks, cop cars, news vans and assorted gawkers.

There to greet me was C. Hart, all bundled up in a flak jacket and parka, a fur cap whose earflaps hung down like a disheartened rabbit's. "We been looking for you," he smiled, pulling open my door.

Still stunned by Abigail's crushed Saab and the body inside I thought that's what he meant – that they knew she was dead and I was no longer a suspect. "I was going to call it in," I mumbled, getting out.

"You were, were you?" Hemingway said, coming up beside Hart. "So who was your fellow perp?"

"Nobody," I said dumbly, not understanding.

"We've got you now." He pointed to the flaming turbines.

I stared up at them, blazing against the pure blue sky. "What the hell..."

"You come nicely," Hemingway said, "and we won't cuff you."

"Come where?" Now I was really dumbfounded.

"You think we don't know?"

"Know *what*, for Chrissake?"

"You're just like your buddy Franklin, shooting out these turbines. After you do time for arson you're going to be working the rest of your life to pay WindPower back. Millions of bucks, buddy."

Now I was pissed. "I didn't shoot out those damn things."

"So who did, sweetheart?"

I wasn't going to say it. If Titus had shot them out he'd had to have a reason. And apparently unlike me he'd covered his tracks. So he was also probably not the guy who'd shot at me, and in any case I wasn't going to turn him in. I stared Hemingway down. "You try to pin this on me you're nuts."

"Pin it on you? No way. We're not pinning, we're arresting you. We *know* you did it."

"How?"

"We tracked you back here." He glanced down at Bucky's boots on my feet. "And you're still wearing the evidence."

I WAS SOON BACK in the same Augusta jail cell. It was no worse for wear but I was. This time I might never get out.

And this time they didn't forget to read me my rights.

Not that I really had any. Being between a rock and a hard place, because the only way I could get out was by fingering Titus, and no way I was doing that. And no way I could claim to the cops I wasn't there when the turbines got shot out.

My one call, to Erica, did nothing to improve my day, and I won't mention the language she used when I told her where I was. Though I must say that given my sorrow over Abigail's death I didn't much care what anybody said.

My mind stumbled over whether to tell the cops I'd found Abigail. There were several problems with that, the major one being *how did I know?* I couldn't tell them about Mitchell given his position with Naval Intelligence, and I couldn't imagine a way of explaining how I found her otherwise.

Arraignment was for nine next morning so I was in for the night. My adjacent companions included two drunk drivers, a kid with a nose ring who was high on crystal meth and kept pacing and yelling, a slob who'd hit his wife (may he rot in here forever), and a guy in a button-down shirt and blazer who'd accumulated too many parking tickets.

"So you shot out those damn turbines?" one of the drunks called.

"No," I yelled back.

"Well you shoulda," he grunted, which was scarce consolation.

"Damn things," button-down said. "They're going to ruin Maine."

"Oh yeah?" the other drunk said. "They already have."

I couldn't stand another night *Inside* so I made a decision which however could further complicate my life. C. Hart was about to go off shift when I yelled for him.

"No," he snickered. "You don't get another phone call."

"I don't need one," I snapped. "I found Abigail."

His eyes widened. "Bullshit."

"She's dead."

I got around how I found her by saying I'd driven over the bridge and saw the old tire marks that had swerved off the edge, and stopped to look over the rail. He left in a hurry, talking into his shoulder mike, and suddenly the world got very quiet, as if a soft snow were falling, and all life had died.

ERICA WAS IN A PREDICTABLY fiery mood next morning for the arraignment. "Look," she whispered, "this is the last goddamn time I'm driving up here to save your ass."

"I didn't do it," I said. "Shoot out those turbines."

"Don't you understand *that* doesn't matter? What do you think the law is, some fairness process? You are going to be blamed for every crime in Maine so if I can get you out of this one you're going to get your ass the hell back to Hawaii and never return." She eyed me ferociously. "Do you *understand?*"

Getting the hell out of Maine seemed like a very good idea but I was damned if I was leaving Bucky and Lexie in the lurch and not making sure Abigail hadn't been murdered when her car when over the bridge. I took a deep, sad breath. "I won't ever bother you again."

Shockingly she took my hand, squeezed it gently. "I'm sorry about Abigail."

It made tears sting my eyes. All I could do was nod. I guess I'd been too many years away from combat and I'd lost the hardness you gain from seeing your friends die.

"I DIDN'T DO IT," I told the same tall balding skinny judge. The only other folks in court this early were Erica, C. Hart, Hemingway, and Cruella, the nasty attorney from WindPower LLC.

The judge stared out at me from under his thick black eyebrows. "What is it with you? Are you *paid* to get in trouble?"

"No sir," I added earnestly. "If I done it I'd be the first to say so. I don't believe in lying. But I didn't do it."

He scowled as if the whole process gave him indigestion. "Look, I can't let you walk out of here... I owe these guys," he nodded at the cops, "the chance to make their case. I can't release you on your own recognizance as your counsel has requested," he eyed Erica darkly, "so I'm setting bail at fifty thousand dollars dollars –"

"That's not enough," snapped Cruella. "He's a terrorist and you need to keep him in custody. My clients can't afford another fire."

I turned to her. "I didn't do it."

"Shut up," Erica said.

It was a crushing amount of money, as I had maybe a hundred seventy-five dollars left in my checking account, and only one outstanding payment of five hundred due from *Surfer News*. I glanced randomly at Cruella the WindPower virago, then at C. Hart, who smirked happily.

"We're posting bail immediately," Erica said.

I stared at her. "With what?"

"Shut up."

I swear the judge smiled.

"Your Honor," Cruella snapped, "he is still a suspect in the fire that killed Mr. and Mrs. Woodridge and also destroyed my client's property."

The judge scratched his bald pate. "I thought that was accidental?"

"We're not sure, your Honor," C. Hart said. "We're ordering more tests."

"Well, until you do…"

"And," Hemingway said, "he's still a suspect in the Abigail Dalt disappearance."

"But she's dead!" I interjected, nearly choking on it.

"The accused," C. Hart nodded at me, "identified her as dead from a car he supposedly found under the Hawkins Brook Bridge –"

"I saw where tire tracks had gone off the road," I added hastily.

"But it wasn't her. It's some woman from South Portland. Been missing since February nineteen."

"It's not Abigail?" I almost fell to me knees in relief and joy. *"Why didn't you tell me?"* I turned to the judge. "Abigail was my friend. She is my friend –"

"She's still missing, your Honor," Hart said crankily. "And we think this guy knows where she is… Or what he may have done with her."

The Bird Cemetery

THAT ABIGAIL HADN'T DIED in that Saab under the Hawkins Brook Bridge seemed an impossible gift. I felt rapturous yet terrified: there was no guarantee she wasn't dead, just that she hadn't yet been found.

And it was sickening to feel grateful that the poor woman from South Portland had died and not Abigail. I followed Erica out of the Kennebec County courthouse. "I don't have fifty thousand dollars."

"I do."

Now I was angry. "I'm not taking your money."

She pinched my chin. "It's only bail, honey. I just guarantee it."

"You're incredible," I added, a wave of gratitude and guilt washing over me.

"Just show up at the hearing."

"You told me I should leave and never come back."

"Yeah, when this is water over the dam."

"I have to go see Titus McKee."

"Who's that?"

I explained her about following Titus up the mountain and how he'd shot out the two turbines. "Damn it, why didn't you tell me!" she seethed, turning on her heel toward the parking lot not waiting for an answer.

"I'm not turning him in!" I said.

"Of course not!" she yelled back. "Just put yourself in jail forever!"

"Would you?" I asked.

She turned on me. "For shooting out a turbine? No, I wouldn't." She paused. "But how are we going to prove you didn't? When it's your boot tracks in the snow?"

"DAMN TURBINES DRIVE my family crazy," Titus McKee said, sitting at his kitchen table with his massive forearms cradling his little daughter. "Rosie here, sometimes she cries all night." He grimaced. "So like Bucky I took them out."

"I would have too. But I didn't, and now I'm getting blamed for it." I'd decided direct confrontation was the best approach, so had driven up his driveway, knocked on his door, and told him I'd seen him do it.

"What the fuck were you doing up there?" he'd said.

"I was following you."

He'd glowered at me. "Why?"

"I thought you'd shot at me, the other night."

He cocked his head frowning, a *this guy is crazy* look. "I don't shoot at people. Not lately."

So we'd got into Afghanistan, all that. Turns out we'd both been in Kunar Province at the same time, he with the Rangers and I with SF, in that nasty nest of ruthless mountains and homicidal Islamic tribesmen that we called *N2KL* and "Enemy Central" where so many of our friends died for absolutely nothing. I didn't tell him about shooting the burning girl and if he'd heard of it said nothing. "So what makes you think *I* shot at you?" he said.

I explained him how I'd tracked the shooter's snowmobile back to Missalonkee Hard Riders, not adding that I'd broken in and taken the membership list. "Lots of people use that trail," he'd said. "Why me?"

I didn't want to mention Mitchell or that Lexie had helped pick him out. "Don and Viv, they suggested it might be you."

"Those crazy fuckers. I feel bad for them though they brought it on themselves."

This interested me, since I was a still a suspect. "How?"

"Tearing the community apart, taking money from the wind power crooks."

"You ever hear of Abigail Dalt?"

He thought, shook his head. He had the kind of direct answers that made you trust him, a truculent self-awareness that forbid deceit. It made me like him despite his innate hostility.

"I'm out on fifty grand bail," I said. "I won't finger you, but how we going to get me out of this?"

He chuckled, rubbed his mouth with a massive grease-stained hand. "Let's pin it on Griver." He laughed, shook his head. "Hey Dor," he called to his wife in the living room where she was knitting. "Suppose we can say Dawson Griver shot out the turbines?"

She came into the kitchen, tousled his hair. "Don't you even dream of going there."

He chuckled again. "Just joking."

His wife reached down for Rosie who shook her head and held onto Titus like he was a life raft in a storm. "C'mon honey, time for jammies."

Titus smiled down at her. "You go with Momma now."

"Who's Griver?" I said.

Doris folded Rosie in her arms. "Dawson Griver? Our local nut case, got out of the crazy bin when they cut the funding…" She buried her face in Rosie's neck and blew, making Rosie giggle.

"So how we going to solve this?" I repeated, having a personal interest in finding a solution.

"Let's blame it on the enviro hippies," Titus said.

"But they're the ones who *want* the damn turbines," Doris put in.

"Fuck it," Titus snickered. "Blame them anyway."

This made me think of Abigail's dead husband. "Too bad we couldn't blame it on Ronnie Dalt."

"Who's that?" Titus said, giving his wife's thigh an affectionate squeeze as she left the room.

"An enviro guy, used to be in favor of turbines, supposedly changed sides."

"Blame it on him anyway."

"He's dead."

Titus raised his brows. "Too bad. Shit, we could've used him."

I took a deep breath. This wasn't getting anywhere. Titus saw me, nodded. "Before they nail you, I'll admit it."

I liked him too much for this, shook my head. "We'll find a way."

"Maybe another wind company did it – they're all at each other's throats. Maybe Green Dividends – Mafia scumbags that own the garbage business in Boston, they're building windmills all over Maine... Hell, there's American Renewables out of Texas, they've come up here and bought all the legislators in three counties... They all want to kill each other..."

Rosie slippered into the kitchen to him and raised her arms. "Up!"

He took her in his beefy arms, kissed the top of her head, glanced at me. "You stay put, I gotta read Rosie a story, be right back."

When he was gone I scanned the kitchen, small and homey, the tiled counters and hand-crafted cabinets, the linoleum floor and old maple table where I sat with the bottle of Shipyard that Titus had given me, the propane cookstove, the chipped porcelain sink and softly humming refrigerator, and it all seemed shelter in a storm, something Titus and

Doris had built with their own hands, as he had mentioned, and now were being driven from it by tax-dodging multi-millionaires and their political servants, for whom this little island of a family had no significance whatsoever.

Doris came in holding her knitting to her chest and sat in Titus' chair. "How old is Rosie?" I said.

"Two. Going on eighteen."

"So I noticed. You have other kids?" I asked, knowing they did.

"Three older girls, they're with their grandfolks, getting away from the turbines." She said nothing, then, "We had another one last year... I was pregnant... He didn't make it."

I felt cold and empty inside. "I'm sorry." Feeling stupid for saying it.

"The turbine infrasound makes cows abort. So maybe people too..."

"Bastards." What else could I say?

"We have to leave. But now the house is worthless..."

Same old story. I nodded uphill. "Maybe they'll stop."

She shook her head. "They won't ever stop. Not till they've chased us all out."

I wanted to console her somehow. "There's more and more people fighting this."

"That won't matter. What people want doesn't matter any more."

WHEN I GOT back to Lexie's the turbine fires were out, the two wind towers spiring into the sky like dead skyscrapers with blackened tops, the fire engines and cop cars gone.

"How'd they put them out?" I asked her.

She looked up from a biology lesson plan. "Choppers came and sprayed something."

"So our world is silent for a while."

"There's still all those others along the rest of the ridge," she snapped, as if I were being irrationally positive. "What'd Titus say?"

I started to tell her, stopped. If she didn't know she couldn't be charged with withholding evidence. "He doesn't have any idea."

"He the one shot at you?"

"Doesn't seem so."

She scowled at me, aware I was keeping something from her. I imagined her suddenly as if she and I were old, long-married, with all the deep love and casual irritations that can bring, and again my heart ached for what we'd lost and now could never have.

She went into the hall, came back with a FedEx envelope. "This came for you."

A false return address. Smyrna. I opened it and a Belgian driver's license, a Visa and Amex cards fell out, all in the name of Pierre Van Brughe. "The new me."

She looked doubtful. "Hope they work."

I stood. "Going for a walk."

"You do that."

Lobo got up from her bed by the woodstove, shook herself, wagged her tail. "Okay, love," I said, "let's do it."

Lobo running ahead down the snowbound lane gave me a moment's intimation of bliss, that magnificent joy animals evoke when given a chance at freedom, an ecstasy we poor humans long ago lost. And so we keep at our subterranean ways while slaughtering wild animals – wolves, geese, elephants, whales and thousands of others – who live at a far deeper emotional and spiritual level than we.

The knife-cold wind cut my nostrils, Lobo's breath a dancing cloud round her head, my own breath freezing on my cheeks, the air a razor blade down my lungs – it was time to confess: *this is how to live.*

I wondered what that meant then understood: when you're deep in life you're in touch with all that matters.

I challenge any guy in bed with an exciting woman to disagree that *that's* bliss, or for her to disagree, for sex is lovely. Or a bear atop a rocky crag pensively watching a sunset, a porpoise soaring bright-eyed through green golden waves, a young eagle reaching high as she can fly...

So when I see it in other creatures I'm reminded it's often lacking in me. That magic moment when everything makes sense, and the entire universe is in concert with what you want... Epiphany.

And no matter how much I worried I *was* deep in life, despite Abigail's perilous absence and the cops wanting me for Murder One, despite Pa dying in Waipio while I couldn't leave Maine to be with him, despite trying to free Bucky and help the Lexie and Titus and the thousands of other Mainers whose lives and homelands are being wrecked by industrial wind, while trying to get deep inside every interesting woman I meet and loving every day of snow and sun, and trying to live like Lobo, in the *now*.

But it can be a pain in the ass, living in the *now*.

Atop the mountain a huge Hyundai excavator crouched over a pit surrounded by tall mounds of dirt. Strange, it hadn't been there before. At the edge I looked down.

Thousands of birds, many thousands, in a pit maybe twenty feet wide and twenty deep, mutilated bloody corpses and chunks of feathers and bones. Bats, too, with tiny outspread wings. You couldn't tell, really, what most of them were, here and there a Canada goose, two golden eagles side by side, lots of crows and blue jays, cardinals, a few loons lower down, tons of fluffy chickadees, bats, wrens, sparrows and other little ones.

The fir tree shadows lay long across Lexie's snow-packed road when Lobo and I returned, stunned and silent.

"Oh yeah," Lexie said. "They bury them in case people come to count the dead birds. Every month they dig a new pit and hide them all."

THE WORLD'S OLDEST BIRD, Lexie said, is the loon. So perfectly evolved that in sixty million years it's barely changed, this mellifluent singer of the wild Maine nights whose language Thoreau calls a dialect of our own. Each fall the loons say goodbye to their mates, leave their lakes and fly many thousands of miles to Greenland or Honduras or down the Patagonian coast even to Antarctica to spend the winter, and return next spring to their lake and mate. To raise their young who then in fall depart on the same magical, mystical and perilous adventure.

But of course most of the loons that once filled the Maine nights with nature's greatest symphony have been killed off, by pesticides, motor boats, fishing lures, lead shot, arsenic and sewage. And what few are left, ornithologists fear, will soon be exterminated by the wind industry.

Not to worry, says Lexie, maybe in sixty million more years God will create another loon.

I COULDN'T SLEEP, feeling a presentiment of great evil. An even greater evil than WindPower's bird cemetery.

23:50 in Maine was 18:50 in Hawaii. Time for my daily call to Pa.

Every day he pretended to be okay. But not today. It was in his voice. Weak, for the first time. Hesitant, as if words failed him. "How's the pain?" I said.

"Pain? There's not too much pain." He cleared his throat. "They got me on... what's the name of that shit... Morphine! Makes your brain real foggy."

"Who the hell's injecting you with that?"

"Nobody, nobody for Christ's sake. It's pills." He coughed raggedly. "I gotta go."

"Where you going?"

"Sit on the porch and smoke."

"Good idea, Pa."

"I've got the damn canoe ready... Maybe tomorrow."

I decided suddenly: "I'll be there fast as I can."

"Don't you dare," he was saying as I cut off.

With Abigail still missing, and me now on bail for the turbines Titus had shot out, plus my still being a suspect in the possible homicide of Don and Viv, there was no way I could leave Maine without proving my guilt. And leaving Erica on the hook for fifty grand.

Even if I was under "voluntary restraint" in Maine it wasn't voluntary. My FBI file had been flagged so any time I crossed a border, or did an out-of-Maine transaction, got picked up by a camera, or worse by a cop, I was done.

But Pa was going fast and I wanted to see him before he launched that canoe into the unknown. The thought of him paddling alone into the Pacific to die was a sorrow I could barely deal with. But if that's what he wanted I'd make damn sure I was with him when he did it.

Taking Over Maine

FIRST I had to call Erica, though the very thought was scary.

It didn't turn out that bad. "You don't forfeit bail by leaving Maine," she said hurriedly, as if I should know. "You just have to be here for your court appearance – in two weeks."

"I'll be back before then."

"However you're under statewide restraint as a person of interest in Abigail's disappearance, and also for allegedly setting that fire in – what was their name's house?"

"Don and Viv Woodridge."

"Yeah, them. So if you get caught outside Maine you'll probably be jailed when they bring you back. As your attorney I can't recommend you do this."

"What if I tell them my father's dying?"

"They couldn't give a shit. Get this through your head, Pono: they *want* you."

"But why?"

"Somebody's put the heat on. You figure it out."

WITH MY NEW PASSPORT, driver's license and credit cards from Smyrna and wearing Bucky's red wool jacket I took off for Hawaii. Lexie drove me up Highway 27 to three miles from the Canadian border at Coburn Gore. This is where a well-connected Maine engineering company with lots of hirelings in the Legislature wants to blast a cross-Maine superhighway out of the North Woods – but get this, it will be a private toll road, not be for Mainers but for Canadian trucks only, of course paid for by Maine taxpayers. One more coup de grace for what's left of the loveliest place in eastern America. Not to worry, though, they'll have to pay a lot to buy all those lawmakers, and won't that money trickle down, somehow?

It was late afternoon, the air crisp, razor-cold. The lines of distant fir tops across the lonely lakes were as sharp and serrated as if they'd been cut out and pasted there.

Near Coburn Gore I kissed Lexie goodbye and walked down a frozen logging road toward the border. The air cutting into my lungs, the nearby boughs and branches snapping from cold in the deepening dark, the hiss and twinkle of the crust under my feet, all gave a sense of peace, hopefulness, loneliness and danger.

The border was a two-hundred-foot wide swath of herbicided clearcuts that snaked across the hills with a chain link barbed wired topped fence down the middle. I hiked for a mile or so through the woods alongside it. The night was clear and I expected there'd be cameras all along the fence line, and somebody watching on close circuit somewhere, even maybe a chopper ready to swoop down on any miscreant stupid enough as to try to cross.

Finally I just said fuck it and walked into the clearcut, threw Bucky's red wool jacket over the barbed wire top, climbed over, unhooked the jacket from the barbed wire and sauntered into Canada.

Already it felt different, less uptight maybe. Try it yourself – cross the border into Canada and note how different you feel.

I walked all night by the stars till I reached another logging road and then headed toward Sherbrooke and the highway to Montreal.

Dawn broke with icy clarity above the treetops. It had to be close to forty below so walking fast continued to be the best option. But I was happy to be free in the moment, in the beauty of the forest, accompanied by the nattering chickadees flitting from tree to tree along my path, seemingly immune to the cold.

After sunup I got a ride with a logger in a pickup all the way to Sherbrooke. His roaring heater quickly put me to sleep amid our desultory communications via his Québecois and my surfer French. By noon I was in Montreal Airport and at 13:20 my alter ego, Pierre Van Brughe, took off without incident on Air Canada to Vancouver, changing to another flight arriving in Honolulu at 21:40. Along the way Pierre had numerous Tanqueray martinis, avoided conversation with his neighbors, and slept, waking occasionally surprised to find himself in midair where the temperature outside was even colder than in his previous night's wanderings.

It was too late to catch a flight from Honolulu to the Big Island so I called Pa to say I'd be there in the morning. He seemed dazed and listless. "You gonna make it till I get there?" I said, hoping to shock him into a last bit of life.

"Yeah," he said, then nothing, then, "I'm glad you're coming." Which damn near killed me.

In Vancouver I'd called Mitchell, who was a twenty-minute taxi ride from Honolulu airport, and it again wrecked my heart to see him when I got there, wheeling himself gallantly from room to room, happy I was there, but all I could remember was how agile he once had been, how full of towering life, before that RPG.

We sat in his computer den with his usual bottle of vodka – now the Icelandic Reyka he'd mentioned, while his many computers hummed softly, discussing things among themselves and planning their world takeover, and I brought him up to speed on Maine, on Lexie and Bucky and Abigail and all the trouble I was in.

"That's what happens," he said tangentially, "when you're not surfing."

"I got the Tahiti thing in two weeks."

He snickered. "From what you say, not likely." He paused, scanning his screens, came back to me. "Terrible about your Dad."

"You think I should do it, help him paddle out to die?"

"It's what he wants? There's your answer."

"I'll never be able to visit his grave... He won't have one."

"Sure he will." Mitchell nodded over his shoulder toward the ocean hiding beyond the tourist traps of Honolulu. "The Great Blue."

"The Great Blue," I mused, thinking at once of what I'd thought two days before, walking in the Maine winter night with Lobo – epiphany. There seemed a connection but tired and sorrowed as I was I couldn't find it.

And anyway, why was I worrying about visiting my father's grave when it was likely I be spending my life in prison?

"Here," Mitchell swung a screen toward me, "here's the latest email from your wind energy friends in Maine..."

My eyes were gritty after nearly fourteen hours flying but it came in all too clear:

FROM: Byron Spaeth, President and CEO, WindPower, LLC

TO: WindPower LLC Team

RE: TAKING OVER MAINE

DATE: January 23, 2015

We have a serious problem with Governor LePage. Despite our intense efforts to defeat him, he beat our Democratic candidate, and he's opposed to wind power. As well, we lost the Democratic majority in the Maine Senate so we don't have a rubber stamp there any longer. So we must HUSTLE every contract we can get before the Governor can stop us. As usual, no need to worry about wind speeds, local opposition, scenic beauty, tourism, birds or bats or other crap – none of it matters. We still have the Dems tied up so tight that if we hustle we can build TEN THOUSAND TURBINES in Maine in ten years! And make a HUNDRED BILLION DOLLARS!

So PLS read the following carefully (if you don't I'll fire you!)

Your Best Boss and Best Friend (until I'm not).
WINDPOWER, LLC
MO for Maine

1. We're stuck with this Governor. He's fought us on higher electric rates, floating turbines, new transmission lines, generally been a stick in our wheels. His appointees are even trying to make us do environmental studies, and it's going to get worse.

2. We must keep the Legislature sweet. The Dems still control the House, and they've been our lapdog for years, let's keep them there. Any incumbent on our side who raises his rate we pay him or her, no questions asked. As long as they're not going down in the next election.

3. But also check out new candidates. We're grooming a few now – the enviro look, patriotism, hard work, you know the image (the button-down plaid shirt, jeans and work boots is always a winner). But if you see a new candidate who might play for our team let me know ASAP.

4. Keep working the enviros. We're getting them at slave wages. They send out millions of emails and go to hearings and

knock on doors and do half our work for us. Overall we've paid less than a million to all the Maine enviros during the whole of last year – you can't beat that for ROI.

5. Run enough ads in the papers to keep them on our side. A newspaper rarely bites the hand that feeds it. Particularly when it's starving. And people believe the damn ads. Go figure.

6. Plus we own the big southern Maine papers. So check them every day and make sure they keep singing our song.

7. And we own Maine Public Radio, they run our ads and pro-wind talk. But we're increasing their funding too, just to be sure. And we'll be running more on private stations too, they're so cheap.

8. And we own the birders. They support turbines that kill millions of birds. Go figure.

9. Keep up the pressure nationally. As long as Obama's in the White House we can stick taxpayers for billions in turbines as fast as we can build them.

10. Don't be afraid to spend money to get us into the end zone. Each turbine built is a gold mine for our company. We'll make billions, so share generously with our friends, and anyone you can impress. It would be a shame to lose the whole deal because we didn't spend a few million more (it's not even our money, remember?).

The saddest thing, I realized, turning from that screen, was that it didn't surprise me.

"Don't let it get to you," Mitchell said. "Some day we'll reveal all this."

"It'll be too late."

"Yeah," he grimaced. "Seems for Maine it's maybe already too late."

AT 11:00 NEXT MORNING I reached Waipio Valley, all the way wondering is Pa still alive, will he know me, should I help him paddle out to sea?

Along the King's Path I couldn't help but remember how I'd felt the last time being there, still hoping he could beat death, what he'd told me of the woman he'd loved in Hué and how she'd died under American bombs, of the crippled girl whose throat he'd cut and how once that happened he could never go back to who he'd been, never expect a woman he loved to live.

And it occurred to me that the girl I'd shot in Afghanistan was the same thing, even though she'd been burned alive and begged to die, even so I was marked for life and never could be with a woman I loved – like what had happened with Lexie... Like my brief interlude with Abigail, and now she was absent and probably dead.

Things you don't want to think about. But if you want epiphany, I realized, they're the other side of the coin.

When I got to Pa's place he wasn't there.

The Great Blue

I RAN DOWN the path till it burst open onto the wide black beach, and there he was sitting under a coconut palm, his canoe on the sand beside him.

"Hey," he tried to give me a big smile. "You came."

I sat beside him, out of breath. "Said I would."

"It's time."

I felt all hollow inside, as if anything I said or wanted would be wrong. "How the fuck you get this canoe down here?"

"Ambrosio." His neighbor Ambrosio was the kind of guy you could depend on when you needed to die. For a while Pa said nothing more, his dim eyes on the surf, the seabirds pecking at the foam, the black beach in which the tumbling white cumulus and blue sky were perfectly reflected. "You're not," he said finally, "going out with me."

"Just a couple miles, Pa. I'll borrow a canoe from Ambrosio."

"Nope." He coughed. "Don't make me talk."

We sat for a while, my brain and heart in torment, he watching the surf. "You have to push me out... too high."

By this he meant the breakers were too tall for him to get the canoe through, they'd swamp him. I tried to imagine what it would be like, out on the ocean in its usual eight-foot swell, him in that little canoe.

"Fuckin sharks," he said, as if reading my mind.

"You should die on land, Pa." It hurt so bad to even say it. "Let us bury you."

"I'm a fuckin Seal," he coughed. "Seals die in the water."

"Not if they have a choice."

"Shut the fuck up. Don't argue me."

I smiled and squeezed his forearm, shocked anew how skinny and weak it felt.

For a while we didn't speak. The waves rolled steadily in and toppled on the sand, throwing up foam and mist, sliding up the beach and hissing back, steady as a beating heart.

"Come all the way from Japan," he said. "Those waves."

"Which way would you go?"

He snickered. "Go west, young man."

"You should go back, die in your own home." How hard it is, I thought again, to talk of death to someone who's dying.

But Pa wasn't one to mince words, or kid himself. "I got maybe a day," he said. "Maybe two."

"Shit, Pa," I joked, "you're gonna live forever."

He smiled spit-flecked lips, his haggard face already half a skull. "I love you, son. I've always loved you with all my heart." He took a breath. "For who you are, not just because you're my son." He laid a spindly hand on my arm. "Time to go."

He pushed himself to his feet, rocking there on feeble legs, bent over his canoe. "Help me. Drag this."

Stored inside the canoe were ten bottles of water, four bottles of cane liquor, a plastic baggie with morphine pills, six joints and waterproof matches, two cans of salted peanuts, a plastic yogurt container for bailing, two jars of peanut butter, two cans of Spam and two of baked beans, four papayas, a handful of passion fruit, a rain poncho and a fishing pole. "Where the fuck you going, Pa?" I said. "Alaska?"

He pushed weakly at the canoe. "Too cold up there." The canoe slid a few inches. "For Chrissake help me."

With my heart screaming I pulled his canoe down the soft wet sand to the water's edge. He climbed inside and grabbed the paddle. "Give me a push."

I leaned down to hug him. "I love you Pa."

"I know you do for Chrissake. Push me out."

I stripped and waded into the surf, tugged the canoe free and swam it ahead of me out through the roaring waves. It took a little water but broke through, riding triumphantly over the crests, his paddle flashing as it rose and fell against the swell.

When he was maybe fifty yards out he turned and waved, a last skeletal glance against the midday sun, and slowly, slowly the canoe drifted away, the paddle flashing, into the western ocean from which our Hawaiian ancestors a thousand years ago had come.

I swam ashore and sat on the beach too numb to think, almost not breathing, my heart empty of everything but sorrow. He turned into a spot and vanished, and I watched after him long after he'd disappeared.

Night had fallen. I rose, my body sore and cold, dressed and walked back up the King's Path to the empty house and sat on the porch trying to understand. Kept seeing him out there under the endless blanket of the stars, the night waves rushing past, alone and free.

I didn't give a damn about myself or what might happen to me in Maine. I wanted to be out there with Pa.

98 HOURS after leaving Lexie's I was back, having landed in Montreal at 21:00. It was too cold and dark to travel, so Pierre Van Brughe stayed at the Best Western for $85 US, then by bus and hitchhiking reached Coburn Gore, took a quick hop across the border and a few bus rides and hitches

and now I was sitting in Lexie's warm kitchen with Lobo's muzzle on my knee and it seemed I'd never left. Except that Pa was out on the Pacific somewhere, or dead, and that was a hole that could never be filled.

"Things have been busy while you were gone," Lexie said, turning from the counter where she was mixing oatmeal chocolate chip cookies to take tomorrow to her students. "The Maine Supreme Court approved WindPower's destruction of Passadumkeag Mountain over the lawsuits of all the folks who live near it –"

"I don't want to hear." Passadumkeag is one of eastern America's most magnificent mountains, a long soaring backbone of trees and granite, and it was impossible that anyone would harm it. But it was true, I realized, what Doris McKee had told me before I left: *What people want doesn't matter any more.*

"Hilarious that Maine Audubon is supporting WindPower even though Passadumkeag is a major flyway… they got more money from WindPower – shows right up on their website…"

It occurred to me that soon they'd be selling little plastic birds, made of course in China, that you could put out on your bird feeder since all the real birds were being shredded by the wind turbines, and they'd still be taking money from industrial wind.

It was hard not to think of all the magnificent people who have loved and protected Maine – Thoreau, Teddy Roosevelt, Margaret Chase Smith, Longfellow, Edna St. Vincent Millay, Eleanor Roosevelt, Franklin Roosevelt, Sarah Orne Jewett whose *Country of the Pointed Firs* is one of America's 19th Century masterpieces, Harriet Beecher Stowe who helped deliver America from slavery, E.B. White, Stephen King, Kenneth Roberts, Nelson Rockefeller, who gave so much of his inheritance to Maine, Joshua Chamberlain, the man who saved the Union at Gettysburg…

What would *they* say, what would they feel, when they saw the wind turbines everywhere desecrating their sacred Maine for no reason except making millions for these execrable investment banks, their hired politicos, lawyers, contractors and other thieves – what would *they* say?

Percival Baxter, that unruly old man who gave Maine its greatest treasure, Katahdin and all the lands around this magnificent mountain, the first place the sun hits the United States. Gave it to the people of Maine *To be forever wild*. What would he say, to the hundreds of howling turbines being built around Maine's most sacred mountain?

Nathaniel Hawthorne, Mary Ellen Chase, Rockwell Kent, Robert Coffin, Mary McCarthy, Erskine Caldwell, Henry Beston, Booth Tarkington, May Sarton... the list goes on and on... what would they say to this desecration of Maine?

"How's Bucky?" I said to change the subject.

"Saw him yesterday... He's losing hope." She sat at the table, mixing bowl on her knees. "So am I."

"Yeah, me too."

"Sometimes it seems we just can't beat them. On any level."

I told her about what Mitchell had found in the Wind-Power emails, the one from their CEO telling his "team" they could build ten thousand turbines in Maine and make billions if they could only get Governor LePage out of the way.

There was no point in martinis or further talk. We ate a silent dinner and I went to bed early, thinking of Pa out on the endless sea – or was he dead already?

Lobo climbed on my bed, snuffling her wet snout against my neck and wriggling tighter into the covers. Then came a thunderous thump at the door; not daring to ignore it I opened and in stalked Max, who sniffed my boots and leaped onto the bed, turned around three times and settled down by my pillow. And soon it seemed the world could not be totally hopeless when you had a dog and cat to share life with.

HIGHWAY TO HELL was screaming in my ear. I glanced around; the room was dawn-gray. I found my phone. "Damn it," I muttered, half-asleep. "Can't you wait till tomorrow?"

"Tomorrow?" Erica, not pleased. "If that's how you feel–"

"I thought it was Mitchell." I rubbed my face trying to wake up. "Lovely to hear your voice."

She sounded sleepy too. "I set my phone to message me every time Abigail shows up on a police wire."

"Oh Jesus." *May she not be dead.*

"Police have her. In Ellsworth."

"She's *okay?*"

"I wouldn't say she's okay. They holding her on Murder One."

The Fix is In

"**M**URDER ONE?" I half-yelled at Erica, trying to wake up. "What the Hell? Why?'

"For killing Ronnie Dalt."

Abigail was alive! I felt a soaring joy, a crazy need to see her. "Killed her husband? That's nuts."

"I don't make the rules, sweetie," Erica said. "Just circumvent them."

Could Abigail have killed her husband? No, she wouldn't murder anyone. Or would she? Then I had the sudden realization that if she was alive I could no longer be charged with killing her.

"I'm going back to sleep," Erica said. "Just wanted you to know."

"Thank you, thank you so much," I added, but she was gone.

Abigail was alive! I had to see her, couldn't sleep, got up and stumbled around the bunkhouse stubbing my toe on the woodstove while Lobo watched me with that curiosity dogs exhibit about people: *what you're doing is stupid, but then again you're only human.*

But I was still the only suspect in Don's and Viv's sad end. And for shooting out Titus's turbines. Each meant serious time. And Cruella from WindPower LLC still wanted to sue me. Go ahead, I told her. You'll get an ancient Karmann Ghia, a few surfboards and trophies, and a couple of well-used wetsuits.

And Pa was still out there on the ocean maybe. Or worse.

Abigail had said she didn't like her husband, but she was far too smart and empathetic in her own sarcastic way to ever hurt anyone.

Or so it seemed.

Now Bucky would be free. The cops couldn't accuse two people of the same crime.

Not unless, I realized, they'd done it together.

"AMAZING," was all Mitchell could say. "All this time, when you were begging them to do something, they were already looking for her. For murder."

"I don't believe it."

"Anyway I've been thinking this out in a wider dimension... All these communities getting hit with wind projects are suing, trying to stop them. So if they succeed, guess what?"

"The fucking towers don't go up."

"Which can become precedent – ask your friend Erica– and put the whole scam at risk." He waited. "So in goes the fix."

"Fix?"

"The Maine Supreme Court. The fix is in. Came down from the White House: Crush these anti wind appeals and lawsuits. This is a national security issue. Wind power is an essential segment of our new energy matrix, and its opponents are funded by the Koch Brothers and other far-right oil groups. Throw out or deny all anti-wind suits."

"Nah, can't be. These judges are sworn to be independent."

"I have it."

"Have what?"

"A call from Shannon O'Lear on the White House staff to Judge Drury on the Maine Supreme Court. The whole conversation. She called every judge the same afternoon."

Perhaps it should have made me happy to realize that here was another crooked level we could reveal, but all I felt was sorrow.

BY 11:30 Abigail's in Augusta jail and I'm on the other side of the glass.

"What the fuck," I say, "is this all about?"

She looks at me hard. "I didn't like him any more but I would never have hurt him in any way."

I had the same rush of awareness I'd had with Bucky when he'd told me the same thing barely a month ago in Warren State Prison. "I believe you."

She nodded as if she expected this. It made me feel closer, trust her even more. I went back to my earlier thought process. "Who wants to pin it on you?"

She shrugged. "Whoever did it?"

"Or whoever wanted to stop you before you blew the whistle –"

"Maybe," she nodded. "Yeah, maybe."

"So that would be our perps –"

"WindPower LLC..." She gave me a half-smile. "I can kill their projects. I can invalidate *them*. And half the Demo leadership." She glanced up at the ceiling looking for the pickup. "I shouldn't be saying all this."

"Everyone at your office is delighted... We were all afraid you were dead."

She looked down, nodded. "I'm sorry. I didn't know... what to do."

"Mildred cried when I called her. But they can't understand the murder rap."

"I can."

"I talked to a lawyer in Portland. She's seeing if she can get you out."

"On what?"

"She's pushing personal recognizance but thinks they'll want two hundred grand."

"I can do that." She leaned forward. "The insurance. From Ronnie's death."

It took me a minute to digest this. "Okay. I'll tell her."

"I want to get out." She looked into my eyes. "I want to be with you."

"What the fuck were you doing in Ellsworth?"

"You don't know? You don't *know?*"

"Obviously I don't."

"Running away. I knew the cops were ready to arrest me. And you were pushing me to testify for Bucky. That he was with me when my husband was killed. To exonerate him. Which I couldn't do."

"Why not?"

"I was with somebody else."

My head spun. I was out of brains entirely. Used up.

"And now," she gave me the look, "I'm done with all that. I want to be with you."

I went out into the cold morning sparkling with light, unable to think, to reason, grasping at straws. Now Bucky would go free. When he came home to Lexie I wanted to be far away. To go where, since I still was on local custody?

Though Pa was burning a hole in my mind there was nothing I could do for him. He was out there in the Pacific somewhere, or drifting dead, or sunk, and as so many times since Afghanistan I tried to understand *death,* make peace with it, could not.

Why raise us up, only to put us down?

What mattered now was to free Abigail. She'd been framed, but how? By whom? It was just one more level of mystery and despair.

LEXIE WAS IN a strange mood when she got back from teaching. "So if Abigail's in jail for killing her husband," I said, "then Bucky should go free."

She went right where I'd gone in my head. "Unless they killed him together."

"Why would they do that."

"He was banging her, wasn't he?" She sat across the table from me, chin in her propped hand.

Her eyes were red, I realized. Nervously she yanked at a tangle of long silky hair, as if it were an enemy. "Look, Lexie…" I stalled.

"He *was,* wasn't he? He was fucking Abigail."

"I asked him, in prison. He said no."

"I asked Uncle Silas. He said yes."

"Uncle Silas couldn't find his dick in a rainstorm. Nor remember anything."

She clenched her fists on the table. "I know Bucky was screwing her. I know. Soon as he gets out I'm dumping him."

I wasn't going to tell Lexie that Abigail had said they were doing it, though Bucky'd denied it when I'd asked him in prison.

She brought her fists to her mouth as if stifling something. "He can have this house and the windmills and this poisoned farm and I'm going back to Hawaii."

I reached for her fists and pulled them into my hands as if they were little creatures and I could warm them. "Even if he was, what difference does it make?"

"What difference?" Her voice went up a few octaves, Lexie-style. "What *difference* if my husband's fucking some *slut?* Are you *nuts?*"

"So have you been such a loving wife?" I thought of what she'd said about her and Bucky, how their marriage had devolved from fun into duty. "Or just put in the time?"

A tear ran down her cheek. She grasped my wrists. "Oh God Sam, it's been so hard."

I nodded. "And it's going to keep on being hard... Driving up here today I realized it was like Pa, the pain will never go away."

Her grasp tightened on my wrists. "Oh God don't *say* that."

"We can love more than one person at a time, Lexie. You know that." I stood and kissed the top of her head, smelling the dusky essence of her. "I'm asking Erica to push for Bucky's release, and Abigail's too. Once Bucky's out I'm leaving here."

"You can still stay here... the bunkhouse's fine – you should *stay* – Bucky'd want you to!"

I was crushed by tears in her eyes. "Bucky can't stand me, nor I him."

"You're moving in with Abigail. Aren't you?"

I shrugged. "She isn't out yet. And she hasn't asked me."

"So what's Lobo gonna do, if you leave?"

"She's your and Bucky's dog, not mine. Or rather, you and Bucky are her people, not me."

She laughed, then a wide smile. "God I love you Sam."

I sat down again. "And I love you. We'll always have that."

She shook her head, biting her lip again. "That is such bullshit."

What's Right

WHAT WERE YOU DOING," I asked Abigail, "in Ellsworth?"

"Staying with Samantha, a friend from grad school, and her husband."

"They know why you were there?"

"I told them I had to get away, after Ronnie's death. They have a big farm in Surry, lots of room." It was as if otherwise they wouldn't have wanted her, a window to something hurting in her soul.

"So what are we going to do," I said, "to prove your innocence?"

"Like I said, find the real perps."

"How?" The impossibility of it overwhelmed me.

Erica had whittled Abigail's bail down to $100K, a sum which Abigail promptly furnished from a money market account she'd set up with Kennebec Savings from her husband's insurance settlement. Abigail and I drove in Bucky's 150 to Surry to get her Saab out of her friends' barn, and now we were sitting in her kitchen, where ten days ago I'd made myself blueberry pancakes in the early dawn while hoping the cops had given up trying to find me.

"So where's the little green book?" I said.

She looked at me, shock in her violet eyes. "You know about it?"

"Mildred told me. I broke in and looked everywhere for it."

She glanced up toward the second floor. "It's in my desk, the top drawer."

"No it isn't."

She leaped from her chair and dashed upstairs with me behind her, and yanked the drawer open. "It was *here!* Right *here!*"

It was the same drawer I'd checked during the night I'd searched her house. She sat down, hands covering her face. "Oh shit."

"Is there any other place it could be?"

She shook her head. "They took it."

"Who?"

"Whoever wants to pin this all on me."

"The cops were here."

"No! When?"

I explained her all about the cops looking for me the night I'd broken in, and about the letter with the red magic marker note that had disappeared also.

"Whoever took the green book," she said, rummaging in the desk again, "maybe they took that letter too."

"It'd be on the camera." I pointed to the pinhole camera above the doorway. "The one the cops put in."

She shook her head. "Ronnie had that installed."

I recoiled, confused. "Why?"

"He was starting to get worried about people breaking in. Kind of how he unraveled, you know."

"Maybe he was right."

"So now it's just my word against theirs –"

"Without the book? Mildred'll back you."

"Not without the book. It was proof. Now they'll just say we're disgruntled employees, fire us."

"Let's check the camera monitor, see who's been here."

She shook her head. "It's a twenty-four hour loop. Doesn't store anything."

"Oh shit."

"Yeah, oh shit."

I changed the subject. "Were you sleeping with Bucky?"

"I told you I was. Already."

"Were you?"

She shrugged. "There was a while there, I'd sleep with anybody."

"Were you?"

She half-shrugged. "He wouldn't have wanted to anyway."

"Why'd you lie?"

"Lie?"

"To me?"

"Who the fuck were you to be asking? I hardly knew you, remember?"

"But why say yes? It don't make sense, Abigail."

She pulled off her sweater, unbuttoned her blouse, slid out of her levis and came into my arms. "This is what makes sense."

BUT AFTERWARDS I was still confused.

"I told you I was sleeping with Bucky," she said, her lips against my shoulder, "because if you thought I was sleeping with lots of guys then you wouldn't love me."

"I knew you were sleeping with lots of guys. I didn't care."

"You knew? How?"

I wasn't going to tell her I'd been doing night recon on her. "You told me."

She nuzzled against me. "I don't remember. There's so much lately I don't remember. Don't want to…"

"Why didn't you want me to love you?"

"I didn't want anyone to love me. Not even Ronnie."

There was a crater inside her, an absence. It made me think of Afghanistan, where if there's a crater it's because something explosive had impacted there, an IED or bomb or shell. But what had impacted on Abigail? And when?

"You wouldn't let Ronnie love you?" I said tentatively.

"No it's not that..."

"What is it?"

"Go to sleep. I love you."

I pulled the blanket up around her shoulders, my arm cradling her lovely gracile back. I had to say it. "I love you too."

But who did I love?

MAKING LOVE IS VIOLENCE also, I lay there think-ing, the penetration, the Grail's lance and sacred chalice in which life is created and nurtured to birth. And which we degrade with pornography, advertising, religion and shame.

Her arms in the streetlight were pale and long, her hair had lost its color and seemed brown now; she was sleeping alone in her world. It seemed unconscionable that in the morning she'd dress and leave for her office as if she'd never been missing, and I'd leave, each of us folding further into our own worlds till one day we died, and this marvelous mo-ment we'd had together would long ago have ceased to exist.

She stirred and spoke in her sleep, her voice deep like humming wires, soft like moss and warm like rain, and I knew that yes I loved her but didn't understand why it brought me such despair.

"WHO IS DAWSON GRIVER?" I asked Lexie.

"Oh Christ, him," she answered.

"Could he have shot at me?"

"How the hell do I know?"

I shrugged, a little hurt by her snappiness, but told myself it was because I'd spent the night with Abigail. It was confusing but inevitable that even though Lexie couldn't have me any longer, it still pissed her off when I was with someone else. Even Erica, who had twice got me out of jail, had nonetheless been subject to Lexie's wrath. "It's in my genes," Lexie'd once said.

"You do look hot in jeans," I'd answered, earning a brief scowl.

I'd come to Lexie's to clear out my stuff to move in with Abigail, and this entitled me to a heightened level of antagonism. "I'm picking up Bucky in the morning," she said.

"They're letting him out?"

"He's still a suspect but now they're giving him Own Recognizance, seeing how he's got a farm and family and all that. They don't realize the farm's worthless –"

"Tell him I fixed his damn truck."

"So now I don't need you any more."

"C'mon Lexie, don't be nasty."

She sat down hard, fists gripped before her face. "I can't do it any longer."

"Do what?"

She looked out the window where fat flakes of new snow were falling. "I don't want to *be* with him."

"I asked Abigail. They weren't fucking."

She shook her head as if none of that mattered. "Not being with him all these weeks, I've learned I prefer it… Don't even want to see him."

"Cut the shit, Lexie, he's your husband. You chose him over me."

"I did not!" She slapped the table. "You were down for twenty years! We've been *through* this –"

"A million times." I didn't want to get into it but couldn't help myself. "But why the fuck you end up with *him?*"

She tugged at her hair ruthlessly, as if it were her enemy. "I told you goddamit. It was the closest I could get to being with you."

I got up, couldn't take it any more. "It's your bed," I said bitterly. "Sleep in it." I walked out, threw my stuff in the trunk of Abigail's Saab, bent down for a last lick from Lobo, and drove miserably away, as if for the last time, from Eagle Mountain Farm.

"I'M DOING A PRESS CONFERENCE," Abigail said. "Tomorrow morning."

I looked at her across the table where we'd just finished our steaks, fried potatoes and salad. "Where?"

"In the Capitol rotunda. I'm going to reveal the whole damn thing, the wind company payoffs and the Legislators who take them, the bribed enviro groups, the media... everything."

"To whom?"

"The papers, TV, everybody."

"You think they're going to believe you?"

"It's a start."

"You're going to lose your job."

"Screw it. I've got another hundred grand of Ronnie's insurance. I can sell the house." She slapped her hands on her thighs. "I'm done."

"What about Mildred? Will she back you?"

She gave me a complicated look. "Mildred's two years from retirement."

"I see." I poured the last of our bottle of Côtes du Rhône. Not great, but in Maine you take what you can get. "You've contacted all this media?"

She nodded. "I called the major papers and TV and radio stations."

"They're all in bed with the Wind Mafia..."

She grabbed my wrist and shook it. "It's the *truth*, Pono! Don't they *care* about the truth?"

I thought of my two jail sentences. "One person's truth is another's prison. You know that."

She gripped me tighter. "It's all we have." She shrugged, took a breath. "What else do we have?"

I thought of what Mitchell had found via the internet, all the WindPower internal memos, the descriptions of how easy it was to bribe Maine elected officials, the tracking of wind company bribes from Legislators' private accounts to banks nobody'd ever heard of. All of it useless in court because illegally obtained. "You're still charged with killing Ronnie," I said at last. "How's this going to affect that?"

She shook me harder. "We've got to stop worrying about consequences, Pono! We just have to do what's right."

This didn't impress me. Many times, it seemed, doing what was right just got you into deeper shit. Sometimes with no way out.

SHE WAS IN THE SHOWER at 07:10 when the cops arrived. "Imagine finding *you* here," C. Hart grinned.

I blocked the door. "What you want?"

"We're taking your lady friend down to the station for a little chat. There's some new evidence we want to discuss."

"She's got a meeting this morning."

He stuck his foot in the door. "We're not asking her, Mr. Haskins. We're taking her."

Say Nothing

"I WISH I'D NEVER MET YOU," Erica said when I
called her.

"Who else do I have?"

"How's that my fault?"

"What should I tell Abigail?"

"Say nothing."

"Say nothing," I told Abigail as she dressed, her hair
still wet from the shower.

"Screw them," she snapped. "I'm doing my press conference."

"Erica says you have to go with the cops, be cooperative. Just don't say anything."

"What have I got to tell them?" She looked at me furiously. "Somebody set this up to ruin the conference. How
will it look when I'm not there?"

"I'll go. Explain things."

"Yeah," she scowled, as if at the police, the world. "You
do that."

AT 08:50 I arrived at the Capitol rotunda. People were
walking in and out of the building but no reporters or TV
were there. I stayed a half hour then went back to Abigail's.
She arrived soon after, threw her purse on the sofa. "They

asked me about my relationship with Bucky. I said I already told you about that, they said tell us again."

"So then what?"

"I told them we'd become friends because of his involvement in the anti-wind struggle, that he'd met my husband but I didn't think he'd had anything to do with his death. They said were you with Bucky when your husband was killed..." She shrugged. "I said no."

"That means either of you could have done it."

"You could say that."

"Where were you?"

"When?" she temporized.

"When Ronnie got killed."

"Here. With an afghan on my knees, watching *House of Cards.*"

I thought of Officer Trask asking me after the four turbines got shot out, *you got corboration?* "You got any proof?"

"Proof I was here? You kidding?"

"You told me you were, with somebody else –"

"I was."

"So why won't he say?"

"He's married. Two kids. A state senator. He'd lose everything."

"The alternative for you may be life in prison."

"Where would I get a gun?"

"From Bucky. The .308, that's what the prosecution's gonna say."

She laughed, said nothing, then, "I wouldn't know how to shoot anyone."

"Did Ronnie know," I persevered, "that you were fucking somebody else?"

"He could have cared less." She sat on the couch, hands on knees. "What happened at the Rotunda?"

"Nobody came."

"Shit!" She snatched her cell phone from her purse, hit a number. "Hi Jim," she said. "You weren't at the Rotunda this morning –" She waited, listening. "But Jim... I see. No, I didn't cancel, a friend of mine was there... Who told you it was canceled? No, I didn't ...Okay, thanks."

She killed the phone, looked at me. "Somebody called him, left a message the press conference was canceled."

"Who?"

"It was just a message, no callback number."

Every move we make, I realized, they already know. "What'd you do with your phone, in New Hampshire?"

"I shut it off, took out the battery and killed the GPS."

"When'd you turn it back on?"

"When they arrested me."

"Turn it off again. And the GPS."

She killed the phone and dropped it on the table. "There's nothing they won't do."

"Yeah," I nodded. "Nothing." I thought a moment, picked up the phone. "and that's how we're going to get them."

She looked at me comically. "You've lost your mind."

"I often do. But not this time. I want you to turn on this phone and call me."

"Call you? You're right here."

"And tell me you've got the copy you made of the little green book, and what do I think we should do with it."

AT NOON I called Mitchell in Honolulu. "Time you were up," I said.

"Up? I been up two hours."

"Wanted to get you before you started work."

Ice cubes clinked. "Yeah okay."

"That the usual?" I was referring to his daily breakfast of three raw eggs and two shots of vodka in a tall glass of fresh-squeezed orange juice.

"What else?"

"If somebody's got a bug on a cell phone, can you trace them?"

He grumped. "Not easy."

"I didn't ask if it was easy."

"Lemme try."

"One more thing?"

"Fuck you."

"Go back to last December 29, the day Ronnie Dalt was killed. Can you get the calls of all the top WindPower guys, find who they called, get the live stuff?"

"Jesus you asshole, anything else you want?"

"Through the next day too. I want to hear what they're talking about."

"They're all ex-Enron guys, they're talking about scams. About screwing people."

"I want it. Word for word."

"Anything else you'd like, your Highness?"

"Tell me the cure for existential angst."

"It's right here, sweetie." He rattled the glass. "That and a little of the good green."

"Mitchell, you're going to get yourself piss-tested."

"Navy doesn't give a shit. Long as I produce."

"Speaking of that, what's the latest? That you can tell me?"

"You lost your clearance. I can't tell you shit."

"C'mon, I need to sell it to somebody –"

He chuckled. "Fucking Iranians've almost finished their bomb, ISIS is ready to take over Baghdad, the Muslims are planning more attacks in Europe, Libya's going over to ISIS and starting raids into Tunisia and Egypt, the Saudis and Qataris are sending ISIS another five hundred million bucks, Al Shebaab and Boko Haram are terrorizing Africa, al Qaeda and the Taliban are taking over Afghanistan, our President is assuring us that Islam is a religion of peace and these terrorists aren't really Muslims, and most Americans are worried about who's on the next episode of *American Idol.*"

"We're ripe for the plucking."

"C'mon, buddy, don't lose your faith."

"Faith seems to be all we have right now."

"I'll get back to you," he said, and was gone.

UNDETERRED, Abigail started calling journalists one on one and in late afternoon I went to see Bucky. He, Lexie and I sat at the kitchen table where she and I had disinterred our love, examined the corpse and buried it again. If he knew he didn't say.

He put his hand on my wrist, a very unlike-Bucky gesture. "I can't tell you what it means, that you came back for me."

"You came back for me, don't forget," I answered, embarrassed, remembering when Bucky had crossed a field of flailing bullets to grab me. There was such appreciation in his face it shamed me in a way I didn't understand. Perhaps, I wondered, he knows Lexie and I didn't fuck, that we honored him?

"Lexie and me been talking," he said. "That maybe we should part."

"None of my business," I looked at her, "but I don't think you should."

He smiled slightly, toying with the coffee cup that seemed tiny in his hand. "Why not?"

"Because you love each other. You've been through Hell – the windmills, losing the farm, prison –"

"The windmills... We were fine till then. Farm was running great. We were even making money," he tried to laugh, "which is almost against the law in Maine."

"A lot of people are trying to find lawyers," I said, "to sue the wind companies for driving them from their homes and wrecking their property values."

"Lawyers," he rubbed his thumb and forefinger together, "want money. The one thing those of us hit by the windmills don't have."

I thought of WindPower's nasty woman lawyer Cruella, that she would probably sell her mother to win a case. "This ain't the country we fought for."

Bucky nodded, drained his coffee. I stood up, wanting to go. "You need a better alibi," I said, "for the night Ronnie Dalt was killed."

"I went to see Abigail." He glanced at Lexie and her fingers tightened round her cup as if she might throw it at him. "She wasn't there."

I had to say it. "She says she was. On the sofa watching House of Cards with her married state senator boyfriend."

He sat back chewing on his lower lip. "That ain't true."

"And after you found she wasn't there you came home?"

"Yeah." Bucky looked at Lexie. "Right."

I looked at her. "Right?"

She nodded. "Right."

"Then why the fuck wouldn't you see me, when I came to prison?"

"I knew what you were going to ask me and I didn't want to implicate her more."

"You think she did it?"

He turned away, shook his head. I sighed, disgusted, weary of it all.

"All those weeks in jail," he said, "I kept thinking I'd helped to send you to prison, after Afghanistan."

This was a subject I didn't want to touch. "Forget it."

"I can't. Never will." He stood clumsily, this hulking muscular guy who seemed such a weird mix of determination and gentleness, came across and hugged me awkwardly. "I can never make it up to you." He stared into my eyes. "But it changed me. I don't think principles are worth a shit. All that counts is love."

I felt embarrassed by his emotionality and unshaven nearness, repulsed by his smell of coffee and prison. "Don't let it get you, man." I went out and sat on the snow with Lobo, looking for early stars between the towers' flashing strobes. The turbines were silent, the twilight cold and deep. "Tell me," I said to Lobo, "what the hell is going on?"

She reached out a snow-wet paw and patted my cheek, one of the most loving gestures I've ever received.

"Okay, you win," I laughed, and went back inside. Bucky and Lexie were sitting at the table, his hand on hers. "Me and Lobo, "I said, "we're going up the mountain."

She smiled but there was venom in it. "Don't get shot."

Eagle Killers

A BRIEF THAW had crusted the snow that Lobo trotted over while I broke through noisily. This made for slow going so it was dusk when I reached the top.

I cleared a soft place in the snow and sat thinking of Pa. He was dead now and I'd never know where. Feeding the fish, he'd said. They feed us all our lives so when we go, we should return the favor.

Why was I up here? I could say it was to give Lobo a run, but she had the run of the place anyway, and like her wolf ancestors would travel miles every day, seeing what was new, hanging out with friends, avoiding the turbines and enjoying the beauty of life in the Maine woods and mountains.

I'd been here enough times before: first with Lexie looking for where Bucky'd hid the gun he'd used to shoot out the first three turbines, then when I'd returned and been shot at by someone I later assumed was Titus McKee, then tracking the shooter's snowmobile, then chased from the Missalonkee Hard Riders clubhouse, then following Titus to the top to be astonished when he shot out two more turbines. It seemed my life was going in circles with no progress, while my enemies wove a web tighter and tighter around me. My enemies? I didn't even know who they were.

Ronnie Dalt had been killed with a single bullet in the chest while he was standing or walking across the Maine Environmental Resources parking lot in Augusta. Someone had fired from a line of trees uphill on the edge of a little park, and the bullet had hit the wallet in Dalt's chest pocket, mushroomed and smashed its way through his rib cage. Because the bullet had allegedly matched those from the three turbines Bucky'd shot out, he was the obvious suspect. And the shooter had been careful to pick a firing spot where the bullet would be found, thus implicating Bucky.

Abigail had told the police, and later me, that she didn't worry when Ronnie didn't come home because he often slept on the couch in his office when working late. And the back story, of course, that she didn't tell the police, was that she had company at home, and didn't particularly want to see Ronnie anyway.

Or he her, perhaps. It was, unfortunately, too late to ask him.

Bucky'd said Abigail wasn't at her house so he'd gone home. She said she had been there, with her state senator boyfriend. One of them was lying.

Or maybe both.

Maybe there was no state senator boyfriend and she and Bucky shot Ronnie?

I called Lobo and we started back downhill. In five days was the Tahiti Tsunami. *You'll be there,* I told myself, but didn't believe it.

That's when I found the male eagle. He lay headless on the bloody snow, shattered wings spread ten feet apart. I knelt beside him but of course there was nothing I could do... turbine blades spinning at two hundred miles an hour had cloven him in half and thrown him all the way here.

I held his frozen, clenched claw, as if somehow I could transmit that I would fight for him, for him and his mate whom he'd grieved for all those months of lonely tall circles above the turbine that had killed her.

Sickened and empty-hearted I trudged back to Lexie's. Couldn't not tell her. She sat on with elbows on the table and face in her hands, nodding her head. The way you acknowledge the death camps, other extinctions, all human evil.

She went to the sink and washed the tears from her eyes. "Obama's thirty-year eagle kill permit racks up another score."

How sad that after Rachel Carson helped bring America's eagles back from near extinction, that we should lose them now to the illusory politico corporate scam of wind "farms".

All we were doing, really, was killing the symbol of America. Our icon, our metaphor. Who we are.

"YOUR STATE SENATOR BOYFRIEND," I said to Abigail. "It's time to drag him out of the closet."

She turned her face up from my shoulder and scanned me irritatedly. "No way."

"You'd rather go to jail for murder?"

"Oh I'll get free," she said offhandedly, snuggled against me.

"By letting Bucky take the fall?"

She shook her head, her hair tickling my face. "He'll be okay."

"Look, Abigail –" I wanted to wake her from this weird complacency "– your husband was murdered. So somebody did it. Somebody's going to be blamed and hopefully go to jail."

"The Wind Mafia. Has to be them."

"Unless it's Bucky?"

She half-hid her face under the covers. "No, it isn't him."

"How do you know?"

"Bucky wouldn't do that."

I knew this was true but pressed her anyway. "You know him that well?"

"I told you, we had a thing –"

"You said you'd told me you were sleeping with him so I wouldn't love you."

"He was afraid of his wife."

I thought of Lexie's simmering ferocity. "She says he was with his Uncle Silas when Ronnie got killed."

"That *bitch?* You going to believe *that bitch?*"

This stunned me. "You hardly know her."

"He told me a mouthful."

"About her?"

She rolled over, her naked back to me. "He couldn't stand her."

My head spun. Was everyone lying to me? All I could see was a twenty-foot wave, green-gold in the dawn off Oahu's North Shore, a huge warm and frothy tunnel I could ride to nowhere anyone had ever been. Why was I here?

I'D BEEN ASLEEP an hour when Mitchell called. "I'm going to kill you," I said.

"No you won't," he chuckled. "Not when you hear."

"Who's that?" Abigail mumbled.

The floor was freezing under my naked feet. I wrapped a coat around my bare shoulders and ducked into her office, stubbing my sore toe on her computer table and sending her laptop crashing to the floor. "Fuck!" I yelled at Mitchell. "Fuck!"

"You shouldn't use such words."

I bent to pick up her laptop and the table fell on my toe. Now I was really mad. "What is it?" I seethed.

"Maybe I should call you back," he teased. "When you're in a better mood?"

I sat on the floor gripping my ruined toe. "Mitchell, what *is* it?"

"You asked me to check on Ronnie Dalt's phone the day he was murdered?"

"Yes! For Chrissake *what is it?*"

"Well, I only found one interesting call."

My toe was clearly broken, sending out throbs of pain with every heartbeat. Biting my lip in fury I waited.

"Well..." Mitchell said.

I waited, damned if I was going to give him the pleasure of begging.

You could hear his mouse clicking. "What time is it, Mitchell?" I finally said.

"Here? Oh, about 21:00."

"That's two a.m. in Maine. Do you *know* that?"

"Ah, here it is... Ronnie got a call at 22:50 the night of his murder, from guess who?"

"Mitchell I'm really going to kill you."

"Dannon Ziller."

"Who the fuck is Dannon Ziller?"

"VP of WindPower LLC. He called Ronnie at almost eleven pm, cell to cell. And a few minutes later Ronnie was dead."

"Maybe I won't kill you after all," I muttered. "At least not right away."

"I'm not worried. We're all going to die some day."

"Who was that?" Abigail murmured when I came back to bed.

"I knocked over your computer," I said, "but it seems okay."

She reached a soft hand against my chest. "Who was calling you at this hour?"

"You ever hear of Dannon Ziller?"

"He's an exec at WindPower, was an Enron crook. A total schmuck. Why?"

"Did Ronnie know him?"

"They worked together on turning Legislators. Dannon supplied the money and Ronnie supplied the foot soldiers."

"Foot soldiers?"

"The enviros who would go out and knock on doors, begging people to vote for the Legislators who backed the Wind Mafia. And they wrote letters to the editor, all that crazy stuff. So what about Ziller?"

"Nothing. Mitchell just mentioned him, that's all."

She folded herself tighter against me, already half asleep. "He should learn to call in daytime."

I lay there, my brain afire. There were too many questions, one of them being why I hadn't wanted to tell Abigail the truth.

WHY HAD ZILLER at WindPower telephoned Ronnie Dalt just before he was killed? That was the million-dollar question, but I couldn't figure out how to ask it, or whom to ask. Did he want to know where Ronnie was, so he could tell the shooter? Or was he verifying that Ronnie'd changed sides, was no longer going to provide the Wind Mafia with his environmental foot soldiers, and thus it was time to kill him? Or was *he* the shooter?

"What more can you tell me about him?" I asked Abigail over breakfast.

She looked up from her four fried eggs and half a pound of bacon. "I *told* you, he's a jerk."

"That doesn't tell me anything. All wind power people are jerks."

She dipped her toast in a yolk and bit it off, crunched on more bacon. "He's one of the ones that goes to towns promising 'community benefits'." She took another long slab of bacon, dipped it into her eggs and ate it with a big slug of black coffee. "Paying off all the locals who can be bought.

Buying town governments new fire trucks and other stuff. Bribing folks who dreadfully need the money."

I told her about Don and Viv Woodridge, how they'd had to take the WindPower money and then sell their house for nothing to WindPower and then died in the fire that no one seemed to be investigating. "Even if it was just that the pilot flame died," I said, "why did it die?"

"They really trying to charge you with that?" she said through her toast and coffee.

"Seems so."

"I had a chat with Barbara Lloyd yesterday. She's a reporter for the *Portland Times,* didn't want to come to the press conference..." *The Portland Times,* also called the *Pravda of Wind,* is one of the Maine papers owned by Congresswoman Maude Muldower and her husband, derivatives billionaire Irvin Goffman. In fact they own nearly all the print media in Maine, and use it to push their own brand of industrial wind politics and enrich their friends.

"So this reporter, Barbara Lloyd," Abigail said, "she finally told me why she didn't attend press conferences about the wind scams. Said she'd lose her job if she wrote an anti-wind story. And blacklisted. She'd never get another job in journalism." It had been made clear by the owners – Congresswoman Maude and her billionaire husband – that no anti-wind reporting was allowed. The line to follow was that any anti-wind opposition was funded by the Koch brothers and the folks who don't believe in climate change."

"But Congresswoman Maude," I countered, "is the fifth-richest person in Congress – why does she need money from the Wind Mafia?"

Abigail spread half a jar of Rose's lime marmalade on her toast. "Funny about the very rich... they always want more money."

I couldn't help smiling at Abigail as she devoured her breakfast like a starving mountain lion. It's been my experience that women with big appetites are wonderful in bed, and conversely, those who eat like mice are less so. "And Congresswoman Maude wants to be Senator Maude?"

"For that you need powerful friends, and lots of dollars in your Super Pac to buy other pols and helpful cronies..."

"When I think of all my friends who died in Afghanistan and Iraq – to protect this?"

She chewed down her toast and refilled our cups, slid a hand up my thigh. "Welcome to the new America."

IT WAS TIME to call Professor Donnelly at Bates, the former teacher of the reporter in Hawaii, Sylvia Gordan, who'd been murdered by the Wind Mafia. I gave him a rundown of what I'd learned, briefly mentioning my own multiple legal jeopardies.

"I warned you, young man, what you were getting into."

"Do you know anything about this billionaire financier Irvin Goffman and his Maine newspaper monopoly?"

"Pono," he said gravely, "why do you want to mess with that?"

"It may relate to what I'm doing."

"The only relevance it will have is to get you in more misery. Don't you want to go back to Hawaii?"

Suddenly I didn't feel comfortable on the phone. "I know you're busy – but can I come see you?"

He sighed, and I sensed he was evaluating something I didn't understand. "Where are you now?"

"Hallowell."

"Come right on down. It will give me a chance to talk you out of this."

Tarred and Feathered

"YOU SHOULD DROP this investigation of Irvin Goffman," Professor Donnelly leaned back in his squeaky leather chair, appraising me across steepled fingers.

I set my coffee cup on the table between us and sat back too. "Why's that?"

"As you said, you're already a suspect in two crimes you haven't committed – this seems to be a habit of yours, getting blamed for other peoples' sins..."

"When I was trying to find Sylvia's killers I got to know an extraordinary guy, the head of one of the Hawaiian crime syndicates, and he gave me some great advice –"

"That was, pray tell?"

"Do no harm. Don't even hurt your enemies, he said, and soon you won't have any enemies..." Saying this I remembered I'd been willing to hurt Titus McKee when I thought he was the one who'd shot at me.

"But you do seem to have lots of enemies –" He sipped his coffee reflectively. "And that's why you need to leave Irvin Goffman and his hideous wife alone."

"The trouble is they seem connected to the situation I'm in. So if I don't get to the bottom of it I'll never get out."

"You've seen *House of Cards?*"

"I've heard of it."

"It's the story of a Congressman who becomes Speaker of the House, then Vice President, then President. At each step he has anyone in his way eliminated, usually by political connivance, bribes or murder. He throws a young woman journalist under a train, gases a loyal ally to death and makes it look like suicide. It gives you a ringside seat into how corrupt our political situation actually is."

He sat back, fingers clasped across his belly. "Irvin Goffman is already the subject of investigations into his funding of the owner of one of Maine's most destructive wind companies... He uses his newspapers to lobby for industrial wind while his Congresswoman wife pushes it on the political side."

My head swam. This was far above it. "I've heard that journalists on his papers can get fired if they write an anti-wind story."

"No doubt. It's a total media blackout on anything negative about wind projects."

"But how is that different from what Governor Lemon did, helped pass the Expedited Wind Act then made millions in the ..?"

"It's all timing. Governor Lemon got into the wind business *after* he'd helped write the laws. That's legal in our venal political regulations. Like all these Senators and Congressmen who go into lobbying after they quit Congress – that's how they make their multiple millions."

He watched me. "Back to what I said earlier, young man, do you know the meaning of 'sacrifice'?"

I thought of all my friends who had died in Afghanistan and Iraq. "Sure, to give yourself to something greater."

"Not originally. From the Latin, it means 'to make sacred' – *sacer*, 'holy', plus *facere*, 'to make'. In the *Old Testament*, first-born children were sacrificed – burnt alive – by their fathers to please God, to bring good harvests... Abraham was going to sacrifice Isaac to please God, remember?

But God had finally had all the dead children He needed, so he let Isaac live."

"I don't get the connection."

"The Wind Mafia and all their associated hooligans are going to make sure you are 'sacrificed' to make sacred the takeover of Maine by the wind industry. Like they wanted to do with your friend Bucky – is that his name?"

"Yeah."

"But now they're blaming this young woman, the dead man's wife, it appears –"

"Abigail."

"And so your friend's off the hook, though they still have him for shooting out turbines, apparently. And she's anti-wind, so she's just as good a scapegoat as this Bucky was – even better, for apparently she was going to blow the whistle on them."

"So if Goffman owns all the media, how do we get out the truth?"

He waved that annoying finger at me again. "We don't, young man. One of the frustrations of journalism is knowing far more than can ever be revealed."

This was too easy. "I'll find a way."

He stood; the meeting was over. "They're going to use you to sanctify the evil they do."

I limped on my broken toe into the cold clear noon. A few students straggled between classes; snow lay deep across the lawns and high up the sides of the elegant stone and brick buildings. I got in Abigail's Saab and drove back Route 202 toward Augusta, empty of hope and solutions.

It could have been Halloween: all these Tammany hobgoblins handing out the poisoned candy of industrial wind media hustle and "community benefits" to their readers and constituents, who stuffed them in their mouths with the credulous innocence of children.

HERE'S ALL I could figure out, so far:

1. Ronnie Dalt's murder: WindPower LLC seemed responsible. I just had to figure out how. That meant learning more about Dannon Ziller.

2. Abigail: My joy that she'd come back from the dead was beyond description. Yet now she was charged with her husband's death, and still as much a danger to WindPower and their political allies as Ronnie had been, because she could blow the whistle on them. And if they hadn't been able to pin his murder on her they would have probably killed her too. So she was still at risk.

3. Bucky: he'd been a perfect target because he'd admitted he shot out the three turbines. But he was probably going to do time for that and was thus less of a problem for them, so they didn't need to keep pinning Ronnie's death on him.

4. Titus McKee: he hadn't shot at me, and would've said so if he had. He'd got two more turbines (for which I was still blamed). Had he shot out the other four turbines at Paradise Lakes for which no shooter had been found?

5. Irvin Goffman the derivatives billionaire and his wife Congresswoman Maude: they were typically nefarious but like all super-rich "movers and shakers" had extensive PR and law firms and kept any dirty work far beyond arm's length. The best solution for them was to reveal their links with WindPower LLC and hope that might help to bring them down, or at least paint them with the dreck they had partially induced.

6. The cops: who had arranged for them to ruin Abigail's press conference, to continue to harass me? What was the link between them and the Wind Mafia?

7. Lexie: God knows I loved her but one can love more than one person at a time and no way I was going to interfere now that she and Bucky were together. They were totally screwed by the wind turbines above their now-valueless farm but there was nothing I could do about it.

8. Who had stolen Abigail's little green book of Legislative dirty deals, and the letter that had said in red magic marker READ THIS NOW?

9. Me: All I wanted was to get back to the South Pacific and surf; I'd had enough of trying to save the world and had done two prison stretches to show for it. So I had to find the true perps for Don and Viv's fire and duck the charge for Titus's shooting out the two turbines without implicating Titus. And because I love Maine I had to help find a way to bring WindPower LLC to justice. And because I loved Abigail I had to get her free and safe too.

Holy shit, was that all?

MARK TWAIN describes in *Huckleberry Finn* how snake oil salesmen were treated back in the day. When they came to a community to sell their worthless remedies they were tarred and feathered and run out of town. Things have gotten very PC since then, but when wind scammers come to Maine with their sweet-talking money and deadly towers it's time to throw them out.

Personally I prefer tar and feathers but sadly that seems no longer an option.

Pay Dirt

15:00 IN MAINE was of course 10:00 in Hawaii so I knew Frank Hamata would be up and busy. Before he retired Frank was Vice President of a Hawaiian utility but quit when they fell under the spell (and cash) of WindPower's plans to cover the Islands with 550-foot turbines.

I got to know him when he called one day about surfing lessons. "For years," he said, "I've been looking out the glass wall of my office at the surfers in Kewalo Basin, and I've finally realized I'd rather be with them than up here."

"I don't blame you," I said. So next day we started surfing. Within weeks he was competent and in a few months good. And was, he told me, far happier than he'd ever been "in that office". We became friends, and he was the first to explain me the evils of wind power back when Sylvia Gordon was killed for investigating a wind power deal and I'd been determined to find her killers and also hunted by them, and the lead suspect in her death.

"So Pono where are you?" Frank said.

When I explained him where I was he was genuinely sorry. "It's seventy-eight here," he said. "What's it like there?"

I glanced at the thermometer outside Abigail's kitchen window. "It's up to eleven below."

"Pono you should come home."

"I can't." He understood. Because of my SF background he always assumes I'm on some mission or another. So I asked him about Dannon Ziller and Enron.

"I remember hearing of Dannon Ziller," Frank said. "He was one of the many Enron crooks who escaped jail time by having expensive lawyers and friends in D.C. For those who don't remember Enron it's a story worth telling." And without transposing our entire conversation, here's what he said:

At the start of the Falklands War in 1982, Maggie Thatcher soon learned that the UK could not fly troops from Britain all the way to that embattled, frigid little island not far from Antarctica without midair refueling. But Britain had neither sufficient air tankers nor the bases to fly them from, so she called her good friend Ronnie who happened to be running the US at the moment. Now Ronnie was already semi-Alzheimers but his advisors were not; we can refuel you, they said, and in return why don't you let a good friend of ours named Ken Lay, the CEO of Enron, break into the UK electricity market?

The UK electricity market was publicly owned and both cost-effective and efficient, but Enron promised to lower power prices if it could build a little power plant of its own. So it was allowed to build Teesside, the world's largest gas-fired power plant (1,875 Megawatts), which sucked up a lot of Britain's North Sea gas in just a few years before it was ignominiously shut down, made billions for Enron and shattered the UK's public electricity market. Under the banner of deregulation, American energy companies went on to devour the UK's twelve regional utilities, firing thousands of people and miraculously raising electricity rates while simultaneously cutting services. And Enron became a giant electricity broker in the US, creating its own house of cards built on lies, false finances, and illusory generation sources.

But Enron had friends in high places: GW Bush and Cheney tried to have Ken Lay appointed Secretary of Energy. However by then Enron was collapsing under the weight of its own transgressions, causing multiple brownouts across the US, dragging down the stock market, stealing nearly one hundred billion from its investors, robbing its employees of their dividends and retirement funds, and causing, among many other cataclysms, the destruction of one of America's "Big Five" accounting firms, Arthur Anderson, which had been assiduously covering up Enron's crooked books for years.

In the ensuing investigations (there is nothing our elected officials like better than biting the hand that fed them the moment it comes under public scrutiny), Enron was publicly tarred and feathered, and the very lawmakers who had given it carte blanche became its most superficially hostile opponents.

A few top Enron execs did a little time in country club jails (they were white businessmen, after all), the regular Americans who had been fooled into buying Enron stock said goodbye to their savings, Ken Lay supposedly died and was buried, and a lot of top Enron crooks parachuted themselves into the wind industry, which was then becoming a multi-billion-dollar cartel built on taxpayer subsidies, Enron-like false promises, political connections, and rigged results.

Dannon Ziller, former VP of the most illicit of Enron divisions, now held a similar post at WindPower LLC, and had been the last person to talk to Ronnie Dalt before a .308 slug ended the latter's life.

WHEN ABIGAIL came home from her last day at work she sat on my lap kissing me so intensely I could've actually believed I was some kind of hot guy. She has a totally prehensile mouth, our tongues interlacing and playing with each other like two puppies, mine exploring round her lovely sharp teeth and the smooth roof of her mouth, her nipping mine slightly, pushing into my mouth then withdrawing fast like a reluctant virgin's, each tasting the other's essence, our lips so in touch it felt like our whole bodies were one, which of course led me to kissing down her lovely breasts while she bit the back of my neck and my hands slid up her dress and pulled down her panties which caused all kinds of further disrobing and you can guess what happened next.

A long while afterwards we lay together sweaty and exhausted on her living room sofa, my chest against hers, our hearts thudding against each other with the same beat, in the same tempo, making me think of the *little death*, as the French call the orgasm, and how frail and temporal is our human heartbeat, and how sacred the short time we have while it lasts.

And that we must not waste it.

IT WAS 23:00 when I left Abigail's for the parking lot in Augusta where her husband had died. The same hour, the same place, what did I hope to find?

From the front door of his office building I walked diagonally across the parking lot toward where his car had been, a Rav4 she had subsequently sold. "I didn't want to look at it, think of what'd happened."

The wind as usual cut down my neck. Without success I tried to find under the ice, sand, and salt the remnant of blood where his life had bled out. What had he been thinking, those last seconds before the bullet hit? About the wind takeover of Maine and what he'd done to make it happen? How he might yet stop it? About his failing marriage?

What had it been like for him to wake up every morning beside this insatiable sexual goddess? How had he, of all people, ended up with her to begin with?

Was there something I didn't understand about their marriage? Was Abigail being straight with me about it? About anything?

It was spooky to look uphill toward the line of hemlocks at the edge of the park where the shooter had hidden. Under the parking lot's halide lights Ronnie would've made an easy target from the trees barely forty yards away. I scuffed at the asphalt but couldn't find where the bullet had buried itself after traversing Ronnie's chest; I'd seen so many bullet wounds in those horrible years in Afghanistan and Iraq and yet sadly they're all the same: the bullet when it hits flesh takes on a life of its own, spinning, ripping, changing direction, splattering and shredding bone, hemorrhaging blood vessels like a demonic spirit burning with hatred for life... It made me wonder as I stood in the ravaging cold with my collar wrapped tight round my neck how could any human being create such a hideous thing as a bullet? Yet I too had used them, thousands of them, had killed, nearly been killed, and seen my friends killed by them – and as so many times before I couldn't understand why.

From the line of trees it was such an easy shot; you lean through the feathery boughs and put your illuminated crosshairs on a man's chest... the simplest is to set it up ahead of him then let him walk into it; the muzzle velocity of a .308 depending on the cartridge is about 2,900 feet per second, meaning it would cover the distance from these trees to Ronnie's chest in about 1/23 of a second, faster than the mind can think or the eye can see.

From the shooter's stand in the trees it was a quick trot to the corner where he could have jumped in a parked car and been long gone before the police, even if they had been called, could get there.

"PAY DIRT!" Mitchell exclaimed. As usual it was after midnight my time and as I slipped carefully out of bed, favoring my toe, I wondered what had him so excited.

"We've got Ziller!"

This seemed unlikely, as no doubt Ziller was sleeping the comfortable sleep of the unjust in his Portland mansion. "Huh?"

"I got into his phone."

This woke me up. "And?"

This time Mitchell didn't beat around the bush. "Thirty seconds after he hung up with Ronnie Dalt he called a dude named Jesús Truman."

"Who?"

"He's a Boston thug, a wet work guy, a Cuban originally from Miami. He's stupid too, because he'd left his phone's GPS on, and a half hour after Ziller called him he was a hundred and ten yards from Ronnie Dalt's office."

Kill Zone

I COULD SMELL BLOOD. That this slimebag Boston killer might be my man. And that I was going to take him down.

"I'll send what the Feebies have," Mitchell had said. "He's the enforcer for Mass Hauling, a Boston-based trash business that has a monopoly on much of the state. Done time for vehicle theft, child abuse, stalking, assault and battery..."

"One of those kinda guys." I'd known a lot of them, in my own two stretches.

"Interestingly, Mass Hauling also has what they call a "renewable energy" division called 'Green Dividends' that builds wind projects. It has five in Maine."

Now I really smelled blood. "And?"

"The Boston Feebies figure Jesús for several murders but there's never anything to link him. They say he's fast and leaves no clues, always has a bulletproof alibi. Likes to use a knife. Interpol thinks he was a hired killer for military dictators in Guatemala and El Salvador."

"Our allies..."

"His father did Bay of Pigs, part of that whole Trujillo mafia. Jailed by Castro, released to us in '65. Worked his way up in the Cuban Mafia drugs and prostitution business in Miami. Jesús born '79."

That made Jesús thirty-six. "Where's Jesús now? Can you trace him?"

"From recent credit card transactions and his GPS locate he seems to be at home on Beacon Hill in Boston. 127a Acorn Street."

"Guy's stupid, to leave on his phone."

"Check the surveillance videos: he's very in shape, that lethal way of moving, you know it, the inner toughness. Fast on his feet, shaved head, gold earring in his left ear. Drives a new black Camaro with black wheel rims and tinted windows, Florida plate UXO 995. Oh, and he has a tattoo up the inside of his left bicep that says *"La vida es sueño"*... which means –"

"Life is a dream."

"Yeah. Something like that."

"How'd he get Bucky's .308?"

"How do I know? Ask him."

"I will."

TWO MINUTES LATER Mitchell sent the videos, pix and other stuff. In one photo Jesús was smiling into the camera, a movie star look, white teeth, dark eyes and tan. A video of him playing soccer for a local club. Fast, in perfect shape, quick changes of direction that left other players flatfooted.

Maybe I should have gone to the cops. But the evidence of the cellphone calls wasn't enough. Circumstantial: Jesús Truman could have come to Augusta for many reasons. Same as why Dannon Ziller called Ronnie. Any defense attorney would be all over it.

And I wanted to nail them.

I slipped back into bed, suddenly aware of the cold. "What was it, honey?" Abigail kissed my shoulder, half-asleep, warm under the eiderdown.

322

Her calling me "honey" made my heart leap. To be loved, if only for a moment, is a glorious thing. To be included in what another person cares about.

Particularly if you feel the same way about them.

Even more so if your life's at risk.

"Gonna be gone a while," I said.

She pulled closer. "Don't. *Please* don't."

I snuggled against her. I never had a teddy bear but she was one now: not just a sexual savage but a warm, cuddly, all-forgiving friend.

Or did she know of some danger I didn't?

KNOWLEDGE IS DANGER. The more you know the more you're at risk. So everything I shared with Abigail only increased her peril. Yet I needed her to know enough to reveal if I didn't come back.

For breakfast we'd made ten scrambled eggs, a pound of bacon, lots of toast and Country Kitchen doughnuts. Mugs of Italian espresso, the elixir that drives one harder into the core of life. "So if something happens," I says, smiling to show the impossibility of it, "you and Mitchell have to get this all out there."

"But like you said, it's circumstantial..."

"If I go missing, *that* won't be." This was Marine Corps logic, I realized: send a bunch of grunts to wander around out there till they get shot at, then use your airplanes and artillery to pound the shit out of the shooters, chopper out your dead Marines and send the survivors back to wander some more.

"They'll just assume you jumped bail. They'll be trying to arrest you and won't give a damn you're dead." She gripped my forearms. "Let's find a way, a way to do this – you not going down there."

"We've been over this." I stood, on the verge of giving in, of staying with her and letting fate take its course.

"That's a betrayal of who you are," I told myself, and went upstairs to pack a few things – another pair of Kinvaras, a couple of shirts and sweats, the KA-BAR.

Lips tight, Abigail drove me to the Hertz counter at Augusta Airport where Pierre Van Brughe rented a silver Impala with Pennsylvania plates.

I rubbed noses with Abigail. "I love you, girl."

"I love you too, you bastard." Tears flashed in her eyes. "Just come back."

IT'LL BORE YOU TO DEATH, the drive to Boston. The first part, Augusta to Portland on 295 is fine, lots of trees but few elevation changes. But south of Portland it's all chewed-up forest and too many exits, overpasses and big-box stores. With more and more "civilization" all the way and then you're weaving your way insanely through Boston traffic, a literal paradise for anyone who wants to break the law.

Maine was part of Massachusetts till 1820, when it finally seceded, chiefly because the more affluent and mercenary Massachusetts was bleeding it dry with land speculation, and pro-British Massachusetts merchants had refused to defend it during the War of 1812, when the British occupied parts of Maine. I felt similarly out of touch in Boston – a Hawaiian bumpkin adrift in this rushing metropolis of glinting towers and smoggy streets, this mob of humans and vehicles, the roar, the stench, the flashy windows, concrete, asphalt, *concrete.*

Though there were pretty women everywhere.

Jesús Truman lived conveniently nearby, the upper flat of a two-story brick square on Acorn Street in Beacon Hill. I checked it out for an hour but there was no action so I headed downtown to the HQ of Green Dividends, the "renewable" energy subsidiary of Mass Hauling, the Boston garbage monopoly that Jesús Truman "worked" for.

Green Dividends lived in one of those glass towers that adorn so many once beautiful places on our planet. A kill zone for life. You stand in its frigid shadow trying to find the sun above this glass canyon, and it's hard to see the forest that was so recently here, the beautiful balsam-shaded brooks headed out to the sea, the needle-cushioned earth, all the creatures who'd lived here. You could say that now lots of people lived here, but it seems wherever we go we push out everything else.

Green Dividends was on the 17th floor. I wandered, a tourist, into their vast lobby with its teak floors, Danish furniture and a petite desk at the back with a petite black girl at the helm. After all the usual "May I help you" we established that I was a journalist from Hawaii doing a survey of renewable energy on the mainland. And could I talk to someone.

Someone wasn't available right now but tomorrow at 14:00 I could see the press VP, so I wandered back through the lobby past charming pictures of Maine's magnificent mountains, lakes, streams, rivers and ridges. And guess what? Not a turbine in sight.

When I got in the elevator who was there already but WindPower's evil attorney Cruella all touted out in a brown pantsuit. "What are you doing here?" she grunted. "You should be in jail."

"You're a succubus," I said. "A vampire. You drain the life and beauty out of everything."

"If you're stalking my clients I'll have you for that."

"How does it feel, living on welfare?" I pushed G, stepped out and walked the 17 stories down to the ground.

But now they knew I was scouting them.

Finding Jesús

JESÚS STILL wasn't home. Nor was his black Camaro parked on any nearby street. Something felt wrong.

I called Mitchell. "Can you find Jesús?"

"Not right now. Tied up, something else."

"Let me know when you can."

He called back twenty minutes later. "You're on a wild goose chase. He's at or near the Senator Hotel in Augusta."

"Oh shit."

"How fast can you get up there?"

"In late afternoon traffic? Five hours…"

"Catch a plane."

If Jesús was at the Senator he was four miles from Abigail.

STUCK IN BOSTON TRAFFIC I checked Travelocity for flights to Portland but by the time I would get to Logan, turn in the car, grab a flight, rent another car in Portland and drive to Hallowell it would take longer than by road.

I called her. "Where are you?"

"Where are you?"

"Abigail stop fucking around. Where are you?"

"Home. Looking up…"

"Get in the car, go somewhere. No, wait." My brain

raced. If she went somewhere busy like Walmart he could kill her there easily and get away. If she was driving he could catch her with the black Camaro and blow her away on the highway. She couldn't stay home... "I want you to go to the cop shop, Augusta. Tell them you want to stay till I get there."

"Pono are you crazy? I'm having fun. I've got a bowl of peanuts, a Stella Artois and a joint and I'm looking up neat places we can go when this all blows over. And in an hour I have to be at Slates to sing. So I'm not going to see Officer Hart or *any* of them... Ever been to the Azores?"

I was so exasperated I wasn't watching the car in front and had to jam on my brakes and *wham* the car behind me hit me.

We were in the middle of three lanes. I finally pulled over by a Burger King and he wheeled in behind me and leaped out. A huge guy, very black. "What you stoppin so fast for?" he yells, coming at me.

"Cool down, man. Nobody's hurt."

He leaned into my face. "You gonna pay to fix my car?"

A waste of time to explain that he was at fault. I stepped back and kicked him very hard in the nuts and he went down like a redwood tree, moaning and yelling and holding his crotch.

My car's rear bumper was shoved halfway in the trunk. The front bumper of his shabby Monarch was split and driven into the grille. Both cars still drivable.

I took the keys from his ignition and threw them across six lanes of traffic.

I didn't need to have the stupid bastard chasing me.

"WHERE YOU AT?" I says soon as I get Abigail back on the phone, keeping an eye on traffic.

"Where I was five minutes ago. What happened?"

"I got rear-ended."

"You okay?"

"Fine, look…"

"I'll be at Slates." She crunched peanuts. "Drive safe…"

I called her back but of course got voicemail. "Damn you Abigail!" I stared furiously at the hazy line of vehicles ahead of me crawling like a great centipede toward the jaded dusk.

TRAFFIC EASED up after Portsmouth. "Where is he now?" I asked Mitchell.

Mitchell's keyboard rattled and clicked. "Where are you?"

"Kittery."

"Son of a bitch!"

"What? *What?*"

"Jesús is in Hallowell."

MY MIND RACED for some innocent reason he'd be in Hallowell. There was none.

Green Dividends' wind "farms" were all further north. No one from the company lived anywhere near Hallowell.

"Hey, don't worry about Abigail," Mitchell had said as he cut off. "Jesús wants *you.*"

I wanted to speed but if I got caught I'd be arrested. Then Abigail'd be on her own. I imagined her walking back up the hill after Slates… An easy kill.

At 21:17 I pulled up on Second Street three blocks from Slates. But when I tried to open the trunk for my KA-BAR it had been jammed shut by the crash. I left without my knife and circled down toward Slates looking for a black Camaro.

If Jesús was hunting her he'd know she would be walking home… he didn't have to hit her in Slates, in fact that would be a bad and complicated idea.

He'd either be here or already waiting at her house.

I killed my phone and slipped down the alley behind Slates. Over the roar of the kitchen fan I could hear her lovely voice. I went in. She was sitting on a wooden chair, a capo and a tall glass of booze on a chair beside her, the Washburn sideways on her lap, and she was leaning forward to listen to someone in the audience.

All the tables full – young couples, older matronly ladies and skinny men with hearing aids, two families with kids, three brawny bearded guys. No one looked like Jesús.

Then I saw him. At a front table by himself, asking her a question. She was smiling, head tilted, as she listened. One of his hands was on the table, the other under it. Over the other voices and squealing of chairs I couldn't hear what they were saying.

He was maybe about to kill her and I needed to stop him. Or he was just trying to set up later and I had time to take him down.

She leaned back and began to strum. Unexpectedly Jesús got up and headed for the door. I turned my back facing the announcements on the bulletin board, and didn't think he saw me as he darted out the door.

After five seconds I followed him. He'd crossed Water Street and was trotting down a dirt path between two buildings toward the River. I sprinted across and looked round the corner of one building. He'd vanished, the night very dark, underfoot a steep eroded bank down to the dirt road along the River.

He had a gun and a knife and I had nothing. But I had to take him down.

Behind the row of old brick buildings a dirt road ran next to the River. Black outlines of a few parked cars and trees, blocky buildings and slumping back porches. The River rushed and rumbled, tearing at its ice. The snow crusty, blowing away in crystals at every step. On the wind a spicy tang of antiperspirant.

He's here. My heart was hammering; I tried to slow down my breath. *You can get him.*

Knives

A N ENGINE CAUGHT, growled. Halogen head-lights flicked on. A dark car, parked further up the dirt road, hidden by a building. I ducked down the riverbank as its headlights flashed over me. It turned and accelerated up to Water Street. A shiny black Camaro.

I sprinted up to Water Street and uphill to Second Street to my rental Impala and drove in rectangles above downtown but the Camaro wasn't there.

I still didn't think he'd seen me, either in Slates or following him. Nor would he recognize the Impala.

I drove past Abigail's and further uphill and checked a few streets before I found the black Camaro three blocks from her house. Florida UXO 995. The car empty, the hood still hot.

Wrapping my scarf round my face I strolled toward her house, just a normal Hallowell evening stroller at ten below. No one else outside, the houses silent behind bright windows and the blue glint of televisions, oak smoke heavy on the air, the icy sidewalk crunching underfoot.

A car came uphill clanking its chains. Somewhere a door opened, a snatch of song. Further downhill someone was whistling and calling, "Louie! Lou*ie!*"

Hands in pockets I ambled past Abigail's, the windows dark, the yard snow-hard and empty, no fresh tracks.

Through the garage door windows the pale outline of the Saab.

A shape crossed a living room window against the streetlights through the front door. Just a flash of motion. But enough.

It was time to call the cops. But what would they get Jesús for, if he let himself be caught? Breaking and entering? He'd say he'd come back to see Abigail, she'd told him to, the door was open... Which is why he'd spoken to her, at Slates.

And if the cops did come he'd know he was burned and disappear, and we'd have someone new hunting us down. Someone we didn't know.

Abigail would be home in 45 minutes. Whatever I did, it had to be fast.

I slipped along the spruce hedge to the back corner of the barn. Hoping he was still in the front of the house I crossed to the back door. It opened.

He was more skilled than I, had picked the lock.

I slid into the kitchen and eased the door shut behind me.

THE KNIFE DRAWER was under the counter beyond the sink. It squealed if not opened slowly. Suddenly the kitchen exploded with light as a window across the way flashed on – the old bag with the curlers – blinding me, silhouetting me. I ducked behind the chopping block table and waited. No sound from Jesús so maybe he hadn't seen me.

The light flicked off. My pulse thundered, my breath, the hiss of floor tiles under my fingertips, the wind against the windows.

The knife drawer slid open silently. Like all good cooks Abigail had very sharp knives. By feel I picked a twelve inch stainless, thicker and stronger than carbon steel. Like an Italian dagger, long, slim and very pointed. The handle perfect in my palm.

BUT SADLY I COULDN'T KILL HIM. Though he'd killed Ronnie Dalt and no doubt others. Had probably tried to kill me, was about to kill Abigail and me, unless I stopped him.

But killing him would put me in far worse trouble, and we'd never learn all the fine things he could tell us. Like who hired him to kill Ronnie, maybe to kill me, and whatever other crimes he'd committed for Green Dividends and its trashy owners.

So I had to take him down, have a chat, *then* deliver him to C. Hart and Company.

Though it was crazy to pursue him like this. He surely had a gun and probably a knife and flashlight. And could turn the house lights on any time and shoot me before I could get to him. Or wait and knife me in the dark. But I was furious, wanted payback, and intended to take him down. And he didn't know I didn't have a gun.

But maybe he'd gone out the front when I came in the back. Was outside waiting for me. Easier to get away from there, after he'd shot me.

I stepped into the dining room, knife underhand, blade up, imagined blood on the Orientals, how his knife would feel in my gut. Wondered what he was thinking.

Maybe he still didn't know I was here?

Or was I walking right into where he wanted me?

The dining room so dark you couldn't see who might be beyond the table and chairs. Or beyond the door into the front parlor with its frozen view of Larch Street.

Silhouette. That's how you find somebody. A break in normal outlines, an unexpected curve or blocky shadow. Not easy when a mistake can get you killed.

Car coming uphill. Abigail?

It slithered past.

I crouched to glance under the table. Hard to see but maybe no one. All shadowed from the frosted streetlight through the tall panes, the darkness. I held my breath but heard no sound of breathing, motion.

Why would he be here anyway? Better to come up behind me while I'm kneeling here.

I circled the table. No one behind the chairs or by the china buffet or against the walls. No one under the table. No one in the front parlor nor at the front door where the red letter had once lain.

Beyond the front door the living room was bathed in silvery darkness. No one behind the three silk couches or two ottomans and armchairs. Nothing else but tall windows and taller bookshelves. I switched the knife to my left hand and from the fireplace took a steel poker.

No one in the little study beyond: just a Shaker desk on dainty legs, a cassocked chair, more bookshelves, a cacophony of book covers in the dim light.

If Jesús was here he wasn't on this floor.

Except I'd forgot the laundry room.

Off the kitchen a walk-in pantry and laundry room, and beyond that the cellar stairs. I'd forgotten them.

If he had been there he could now be anywhere behind me.

It was like an infantry sweep. If the enemy gets in behind you, you have to do it all over again. At even greater risk.

If I turned on a light he'd shoot me. The silencer's little pop and I'd bleed out on one of these rugs.

It's amazing in these situations how incredibly tight you get, how every irrelevant stimulus is wiped out. You're there, soles on the carpet, knife in your hand, listening for every tiny sound – air disturbed by a moving hand, an intake of breath through nostrils, the shift of weight on a floorboard – and every instant can bring you death.

I unlocked the front door and ran round the building to the back door but it was locked.

He must have just locked it. Or before? Was he still downstairs?

I sprinted back through the front door into the dining room behind the table holding my breath.

A click from the kitchen, a low hum. The freezer switching on.

He liked knife work, the Feebies said. So maybe he'd try that, not use a gun.

It was all I had to hope for.

A creak overhead. Her bedroom. Or the wind.

I waited for my heart to slow then inched into the kitchen. No one. The pantry had no door, no one inside. The laundry room door was closed. Had it been?

I tried to remember the kitchen when I'd first entered. On my left in darkness had been the laundry, the pantry to its right, beyond them the door to the cellar.

Yes, the laundry door had been open.

He wouldn't have shut himself inside. I yanked it open and whipped the poker into where he should be.

Nothing.

I slid the cellar door bolts shut. If he was down there now he'd have to break the door to get out.

In the darkest corner of the kitchen I texted Abigail: *Don't come home.*

Then slid back into the dining room, to the darkness behind the table.

His move.

His Move

WIND CREAKED the shingles and wailed across
the ancient glass. It hissed snow down the streets
and tore at the trees. The house crouched under
it like a beaten dog.

I wanted badly to bring in the cops. But that wouldn't
work. I crossed to the stairs and dashed silently up to the
second floor.

Here I had to make a choice. If I went to the third floor
first he could follow me. But if I was able to clear the third
I'd know he was below me. I sprinted upstairs and there
was no one on the third floor landing.

One by one I checked the rooms. No one.

Somewhere below a floorboard creaked. I had an instant of shock, that he could be so maladroit. Or was it a
trap, and he wasn't there at all?

I thought of Genghis Khan: *Never be where you seem.*

I didn't have that choice. But he did.

What he didn't expect was speed. I dashed to the second
floor and her bedroom, swung the poker into every corner
and under the bed, grabbed the headlamp off her bedside
table and moved into her office where I doubted he was as
there was no place to hide.

Across the corridor the master bath with its white porcelain clawfoot tub and the glass shower where Abigail and I had once made love happily under the pounding hot water. A sink with a shelf over it and a mirror cabinet above.

You never know in the peripheral darkness but it seemed inside the tub was darker. Expecting I had a gun he'd shielded himself in the cast iron tub till he could get a clear shot at me.

Holding the headlamp wide in my left hand, my body protected by the door jamb, I flashed it on. In the clawfoot tub were three pillows, in the shape of a torso with a raised head.

"*Nada màs,*" Jesús said behind me. "Don't move a fucking muscle or I blow your head off."

I said nothing. There was nothing to say.

He flicked on the lights. "Drop them, the knife and that metal thing."

I did, blinking against the sudden brightness.

"Turn round."

I did, still cursing myself for being so stupidly trapped. He was smaller than I'd thought. Wiry, dark, narrow-faced, black ponytail, silver rings on two fingers, gold earring, rolled-up sleeves with bluish tattoos and a silver bracelet on his left, what seemed to be a 9 mm Sig Sauer in the right hand.

"So tell me," he said. "What the *mierda* you here for?"

The question seemed ridiculous, given he was going to kill me. But I had to get him out of here before Abigail arrived.

"I live here. That good enough?"

"*Mierda* you do." He looked at me critically. "You fucking this cunt?"

I shook my head. "Just a renter."

That seemed to satisfy him. I took a breath. Could it be he didn't know who I was?

"I should have shoot you," he said. "On that mountain. Now I got to do it all over again."

I wanted to say *Maybe you're a better shot from ten feet,* but didn't dare.

"So maybe I make you a deal," he said, "instead."

I waited.

"You don' want hear?" He poked his chin at me, cocky as a little rooster. My gut was knotted in fear of death; it felt even worse to be shot by a scumball like this.

"So what you want to know?"

"How you find about me?"

So he was worried about invisibility. Because if I knew about him probably someone else did too. He needed to find out who and kill them also. Anyone who knew.

"I got into Verizon," I said. "Tracked your calls and where you were when Ronnie was killed. Easy, a kid could do it."

"You *mierda* motherfuck you don't know how to do that."

I couldn't keep my eyes off the Sig Sauer. The suppressor on the front made it seem even more deadly When you're about to be shot the greatest terror is the black hole in the muzzle. Waiting for the bullet to smash you down. "I took a class."

"You lying." He nodded at the bathroom. "Get in, that tub."

This was to avoid spreading blood everywhere. My blood. I tried to smile. "I'm not that dirty." My mind racing to tell him something so he wouldn't kill me, how to get him out of the house before Abigail came.

"I got into the Senate phone logs," I said. "Dannon Ziller called them after you killed Ronnie. They told me."

"*Who* tell you?"

"The two Senators I talked to." I looked at him. It was my only chance. "They gave you up, Jesús."

"Bullshit they did." He nodded at the bathroom. "Get in the tub."

"You said we made a deal –"

He smiled. "You tol' me already, how you find me. So we don' need a deal any more." He twitched the Sig. "Get in the tub."

A car was climbing the hill, the familiar muffle rattle of the Saab – a tailpipe clamp was missing and I'd been waiting for warmer weather to replace it.

This was the worst thing that could possibly happen. If she came in, he would get us both. And would make it look like one of us had shot the other. Case closed.

The offended squeal of the barn doors as she shut them behind the Saab. The squeak of her boots across the back yard. *Please Abigail please go.*

Then nothing.

I leaned back against the doorjamb I had so recently used as a shield against his expected bullets. There were ten feet between us. I'd be dead before I reached him.

But Abigail would hear the shot.

And hopefully run.

But that was not like Abigail.

"You bullshit me too much," Jesús said. He raised the gun, stepped forward. "You wanna know when you die? People, they like to know."

He moved a step closer. His finger tightened on the trigger. I couldn't stop watching the black muzzle hole. Waiting for the flash.

A shape behind Jesús coming up the stairs. A wraith out of the darkness that became Abigail. I shook my head, wishing her away: *Leave while you can.*

"What you shake you head for, man? That ain't goin' save you."

He was a sadist, wanted to drag this out. *Go,* I told Abigail silently. *Go away.* "How many people you waste, Jesús?" Appealing to his ego.

He strutted a bit. "I tell you, man, you only the nine person I kill."

"Wow. Does that include Don and Viv?"

"Don and *what?*"

"The folks in the house you burned down."

"Oh that, that was accident, man. I was following you, to shoot you on your drive home, then that *mierda* cop he arrests you... So what could I do? I go back, burn down the house so those signed papers they disappear."

Abigail moved closer, a framed tennis racket in her hand; now I had to distract him, keep him talking. "How'd you know I was up on Eagle Mountain?"

"When I shoot at you? They tell me to. They hear you are coming from Hawaii, so they get worry. Not my fault – I *had* to shoot you."

"They?"

"Same guys, hombre. Get in the fucking tub."

Closer Abigail came, twitching the tennis racket like a whip. "How'd you get Bucky's gun?" I said.

"When he shoot the towers, Mass Hauling send me up there next morning, see if I can find who did it. So I track him over that mountain, find the gun, no problem."

"Then you used it to kill Ronnie Dalt..."

"They tell me, use the same gun. So I do."

"I bet it was you who left the cartridge casing up by the turbines he shot out –"

"I fire that gun, take the casing up top, leave it where he was shooting."

"Then you left one in the bushes where you shot Ronnie..."

"They're easy to fool, the cops."

He started to turn; I feared he'd seen her. "Jesús!" I said. "Guess who else knows about you?"

He rounded on me. "I already can figure that, fuckface."

She smashed the racket into the back of his skull and he dropped with a *thwump*.

Talk about a forehand.

"I TOLD YOU NOT to come." I said.

"Lucky I did." She looked at Jesús on the floor. "Back door was unlocked. You would never leave a door unlocked."

"Never."

She gave me a quick kiss. "It's one of the things I love about you. I feel safe."

My eyes were wet. Must have been what we'd just been through. "And loved."

"Mmmm," she kissed me again, one of those self-surrendering kisses that make you self-surrender right back. "And loved."

In her office I tugged an extension cord from the wall. Her yellow printer light died out.

"Pono *what* are you doing?"

I held it up. "Can you get more more of these?"

Her eyes widened. "What are you planning?"

Ecstasy

"**Y**OU GOT TWO OPTIONS, JESÚS," I told him when he returned to the land of the semiliterate.

He moaned. Blood was trickling down the side of his head. He focused on me, tried to swing a fist, without success as both wrists and ankles were wired with extension cord to the four legs of the tub, and he was inside it. Naked. This was not to my eyes a pretty sight, but maybe Abigail enjoyed it.

It took him a while to integrate all this. "What you want?" he said, a little unclearly.

I explained him.

"I got nothing to do, that guy getting whacked."

"So why are you here?"

"Met her at the bar, wanted to see her, when she got home."

"To kill her?"

"Shit no." He looked around. "Gimme my clothes."

"Who were you killing her for? The same people you killed Ronnie for?"

"You!" he spit, "you're out of your fucking mind."

"Have it your way." I re-gagged him with a hand towel while he swore and bit and twisted. "We'll come see you every so often. So you can lie there and decide how long before you tell us. We're in no rush."

"GOT ANY DRUGS?" I asked her when we'd stepped across the bedroom out of hearing.

"You know where I keep the weed."

"Real drugs. LSD, mushrooms, peyote –"

"Whatever I had's long gone."

"How soon can you get some?"

"Tonight? It's almost midnight –"

I shook her head slightly, hand behind her neck, leaned closer. "It's important!"

She sat on the chair at the top of the stairs. "Let me think–"

I went in and checked on Jesús. Happy as a clam in shit. Nearly.

"I know a guy," she said.

I fished in Jesús' wallet, gave her three hundred bucks. "Whatever it costs, just get some."

"He's a pretty well-stocked guy. What you want?"

"The best would be acid, uppers and ecstasy. If you could get that…"

She was gone, the Saab's tires squeaking on the new snow that had started falling. I sat with Jesús, feeling the need to cheer him up.

He looked at me balefully, shook his head and grunted, from which I discerned he wanted me to take off the the gag. When I did he inhaled fast and opened his mouth to yell so I had regretfully had to pop him one, which put him back out. I'd never hit a restrained person before and it didn't feel good, but he was a heartless killer and I had no pity for him.

I dug snow off the window ledge and dumped it on his face. He grunted, tried to pull with all his might at his extension cords, fists white with effort.

"Ain't gonna work, Jesús," I said.

"What you want?" he said again, his mouth working funny from the whack on the jaw I'd given him.

"I told you."

"My head hurts, I don't remember."

I explained him again. "I don't need to turn you in, Jesús. I just need to know who's paying you. It's them I want. You give me proof who it is and I let you walk. I will however ID you to all my Special Forces buddies, and if anything ever happens to me – even a bad cold – they'll find you and totally destroy you no matter where you hide. So that will be our deal: you leave me alone and I leave you alone..."

This of course was a lie, but now was no time to tell the truth.

WHILE JESÚS was digesting all this I called Mitchell. "So Abigail snuck up and whacked him?" Mitchell said, "I *have* to meet this girl."

"If she hadn't we'd both dead."

"What a silly way to die, Pono. You're losing your edge."

"Question is, should I visit this Dannon Ziller from WindPower? He has to be who ordered the hit on Ronnie Dalt."

"No need. The cops can find the phone logs, same as I did. And Jesús will sing on plea bargain. So let the cops dig into this guy Ziller, not you."

"By the way, I have Jesús' iPhone."

"So plug it into a computer somewhere and I'll download it."

"He needs to get put away. For a long time."

"Looks like he's going to be. Him and WindPower both."

"High time."

Mitchell chuckled. "You might say that."

ABIGAIL CAME BACK with three acid capsules, a small bottle of Adderall and four tinfoil-wrapped tabs of ecstasy.

"Fantastic!" I exclaimed. "What you have to do for it?"

She handed me back Jesús' money. "What you think?"

"Was it fun?"

She grinned. "When isn't it?"

I ground up a tab each of acid, ecstasy and two Adderall and powdered them into the bottom of a Portland Seadogs mug, added a little water, and left it on the bathroom shelf where Jesús could see it.

"I gotta piss," he said.

I looked down at him. "That's why you're in the bathtub."

"Christ," he mumbled, "you people are animals."

As I love animals I didn't take this at all askance. But he'd given me an idea. "Can you go down to the pantry," I asked Abigail, "and bring up those two rodent deterrents on the third shelf up, right hand side?"

"We don't have rats –"

I smiled down at Jesús. "Yes we do."

When she brought them she looked at me strangely, tugging back her hair, so pretty and alive I wanted to make love right then, but Jesús was in the way. "You like rap music?" I asks him.

He grimaced. "What you care?"

I plugged in the two deterrents and they started yowling. The principle, as I remembered, is infrasound – that horrible sub threshold wavelength that wind turbines emit and that tortures people for miles around. And in addition a sharp jagged tweeting and moaning that would drive even the deaf crazy. This combination is sometimes very good for chasing off rats in my experience but less so for mice.

In the Legislature, however, it would work quite well for both.

In a closet Abigail found one of those light show lamps that flash kaleidoscopically jagged colors, so, not wanting him bored, I installed that on a chair beside him.

Jesús didn't seem to appreciate all this concern. It was clear he didn't like rap at all, and wasn't really into light shows. To avoid going deaf Abigail and I stepped out and shut the bathroom door, and I sat down by the keyhole to keep an eye on him, his pretty little Sig Sauer on my knee.

HE WAS FULLY RESTRAINED but to make sure he wouldn't get loose we planned to take turns watching him through the keyhole, with plugs in our ears and her noise-cancelling headphones on top of them.

Having seen much violence I abhor it, and was determined to learn from this guy without physically hurting him. Even though he was a multiple murderer.

As the US, the UK, the French and Israelis have all demonstrated, it's possible to learn a lot from someone without doing physical harm. And afterwards they can return to their prior lives not realizing how much they've told you.

One could argue we were doing him violence this way too, but he was a lethal prick and I wanted him *Inside* forever, before he could kill anyone else. And this was the only way I could learn enough to make sure that happened. Plus I wanted his bosses *Inside* too.

At 01:23 I went in, checked all his restraints, and used the spray attachment to wash his pee down the drain. He kept shaking his head and mumbling, so I ungagged him.

"Christ I'm thirsty."

When like Jesús you're scared and out of your element you tend to hyperventilate, exhale and sweat lots of H2O. Up to a quart an hour, so you get thirsty fast. This was a good tool for encouraging conversation. The other tool being sleeplessness.

Anyway I needed him thirsty for another reason. "I'm not giving you water till I get something real."

"Fuck you." He tried to shrug. "Have it your way."

I wanted to say "I am", but no time is more dangerous than when you think your enemy is down.

Never exult.

Never feel safe. It's too dangerous.

AN HOUR LATER he asked again for water. He'd been yanking his restraints and his wrists were scraped red. "You got to stop doing this," I said after I'd checked each one.

"Gonna give me water?"

"What you got to tell me?"

He clamped his teeth over his lower lip as if to shut himself up. I bent down to re gag him.

"What you want?" he whispered.

"You know what I want. You can tell me now or tell me later, it's up to you." I started to tie the gag across his mouth but he shook his head. "Give me some fuckin water I tell you something."

He was stalling in the hopes backup would arrive. This worried me but there was no way to deflect that except to move him, which was infeasible.

I re-gagged him over his protests. "Water when you talk."

"I FOUND MORE CONNECTIONS," Mitchell said.

"Yeah what?" I was very sleepy from watching Jesús through the keyhole. Abigail was snoring lightly on the bed and I spoke low to not wake her. Though I'd been waking Jesús every time he dozed, and that was exhausting me too.

"The morning after Ronnie was shot?"

I rubbed my eyes. "What?"

Ice cubes rattled on Mitchell's end. "You asked me check all the WindPower exec phone calls?"

I glanced through the keyhole at Jesús. He was doing his silent twist and shout. "Yeah?"

"Morning after Ronnie died there was an absolute blizzard of calls between WindPower, three state Democratic Senators and a Portland law firm called Gleason and Falz."

"That's the bitch been harassing me. Name's Ursula Heap but I call her Cruella."

"Well, back on December 30, she was worried about something."

"Mitchell," I sighed, "you're marvelous. Maybe I will marry you after all."

"You should be so lucky."

"Love to know, what they all talked about."

"That's what discovery's for."

"Think we can get there?"

"Yeah," he took a drink, licked his lips. "Maybe we can."

MOST BRUTAL MEN are not courageous. Like these Muslim scumbags beheading people, raping and selling women and children, torturing and murdering. In my three tours in Islamic countries I learned many times that they're brave when they're many and you're few, when your hands are tied and they have a knife at your throat, or when they have their finger on a detonator and a school bus of children is about to get blown away.

So I didn't anticipate too much courage from Jesús.

"I was working for Mass Hauling," he croaked.

"Tell me something I don't know."

He thought about it. His face was drawn, pasty and dry, lips cracked. I started to feel sorry for him then remembered what he'd done.

"You'll give me water?"

"All you want."

"How do I know?"

I smiled, shook my head. "You don't have a choice."

"Okay." He licked his lips, a leathery sound. "I was supposed to come here, get the copy of some damn book."

"What kind of book?"

"The original was green, medium size, hard cover... Full of numbers. That's all I know."

"You find it?"

"Shit no."

"Who asked you to find it?"

He flinched. "Gimme my water."

I took the Seadogs mug from the mirror shelf and filled it from the tap, so he could see, and sat down in front of him, beyond reach. "You fuckhead," he said.

"Who sent you for the green book?"

He shrugged. "You know it."

"Say it."

"Mass fucking Hauling."

I leaned the mug down. He raised his head sideways and drank till it was empty. He collapsed back. "Tastes like shit."

"Lots of sewage treatment plants upriver."

He drank two more mugs before I cut him off, not wanting him to chuck. He fell back in his bounds. I plugged in his rat rap and psychedelic light and departed.

For the next hour I watched Jesús through the keyhole. He was about to depart for a brand new universe but didn't yet know it.

A universe where your only hope is another human being.

To whom you'll gratefully tell everything.

Nada Màs

NO TWO OCEAN WAVES are ever the same. I've sat for years on my surfboard waiting for the next good one, and never have two been the same. Nothing's ever the same: no two same faces, voices, universes or grains of sand.

And no two interrogations are the same. Plus it's rare to debrief a prisoner who's personally tried to kill you. And a woman you love. And has killed her husband. Lends the discussion a personal intensity that's hard to resist.

By itself, LSD can be fun, and a learning experience. But not knowing he'd taken it, and mixed with the others, it had completely dislocated him from normal "reality": habitual neural pathways are blocked, allowing stimuli that in normal life we disregard to take over our worldview. He didn't see or feel or know his "normal reality"; it had never *existed*. There was only *now*, each instant of pitiless cascading universes, worms in his heart and vampires in his brain, his body afire and freezing as he fell through unknown dimensions and smashed into death after death, tormented by memories that never were, grueling tortures, lost love, the death of every victim from the start of time... Over and over, every instant.

That was the easy part.

Then came the Adderall. In large quantities it drives your heart faster and faster, burns your life at both ends, screams you through exponentially accelerating time, puts you on a motorcycle at three hundred miles an hour and you can't slow down, get off, you're going to die. But that's still the beginning...

Ecstasy is just what it says. I recommend it to everyone, but not combined with either of the others. Ecstasy knocks down emotional walls, creates warm connections between us, elevates everyone to friend and spiritual lover...

And inspires an aching need to confide...

HE WAS PRETTY CRAZY for a while, writhing and moaning. Wide-eyed, terrorized, not understanding who he was or what was happening.

Hell is other people, Sartre said, and this certainly applied to Jesús. The people who must have made his early life Hell, and then the other Hell-soaked victims and victimizers who since then had been his daily bread. Evil's a disease; we pass it to each other and down the generations, the way each war generates the next.

Now every time I got up to leave the bathroom he'd beg me not to.

"WHAT *IS* THIS?" he whined. "What am I?"

"We're cops and good guys."

"What's cops?"

"People you tell the truth to." Knowing that saying this, like a hypnotic prompt, might actually stimulate him to do so.

"Can you stop them? Can you?" he writhed, "can you *please?*"

"Stop *what?*"

"The lizards... oh God the snakes... The fire's so hot, so cold... Please *help* me!"

"We're cops and good guys," I repeated. "I'll be the cop and you're the good guy, and you do the Miranda…"

"Miranda?" He tried to remember. "I don't do Miranda."

"Not you, silly. This guy you're playing…."

"How many times I hear that damn thing. Can say it by heart."

"Let's play you doing the Miranda and I'll help with the snakes."

Jesús did his Miranda. Not that it counted for anything. But I wanted it to seem right to him when Hart & Co asked him to do it. And he eagerly added that really it *was* true, what he was saying. He'd show you his phone logs and travel itineraries to prove it. And he'd taken the first half up front, ten grand straight to Security International Bank in Jakarta.

"You get a deposit receipt?" I said. "Be good to have, prove the money's yours."

"I printed it out and taped it to the underside of a drawer in my bathroom then deleted the file."

"You're a smart guy, Jesús." I wasn't going to explain him that even most four-year-olds could saunter into his computer and restore that file, or that taping stuff to the underside of drawers is to guarantee the cops will find it. Instead I gave him more water.

He'd explained me already how this guy would call when he wanted Jesús to do something, but Jesús never knew who it was because it said *No Caller ID.*

I gave him one more sip.

If you've ever been *Inside* you've known lots of guys like Jesús – paid by cash in a drop envelope, or, like some Legislators by untraceable wires to foreign accounts. But being careful, Jesús also tracked his client back, finally, to Mass Hauling.

"They're in all kinda shit," his voice like a jet's engines powering down at the end of each sentence. "So even when I figure it's them I don't say. Better they *don't* know I know."

"You were telling me about your dream, about what Mass Hauling made you do."

"They're coming back –"

"Who?"

"The salamanders, the snakes…" He twisted and writhed, trying to escape them.

"Dannon told me they only paid you five grand to kill Ronnie Dalt –"

"Ziller? He did?" Jesús spit. "Fuckin liar."

"He told me all your conversations, the price, when to do it."

"Was twenty grand, not five." He couldn't keep still, head flipping back and forth. "Keeps… More bad…" He tightened up, fists clenched, almost sprang out of the tub. "You're supposed to keep them away!"

I let him ride it out. What else could I do?

EVERYTHING HE SAID got recorded on Abigail's iPad on the sink counter where he couldn't see it. But would never be admissible. Plus delivered under duress.

Duress means you have to tell the truth.

Which Jesús finally did. And proud of it. Luxuriating in the warmth of my approval.

"But why," he said, "kill this guy on their own side?"

"They didn't tell you?"

For a second he looked almost rueful. "They never do."

"But they told you what gun to use…"

"It was the Winchester I took from where that guy Bucky hid it."

"What ammo you use?"

"Same as him. There was a box of ammo in the gun case. That ASYM load with a solid copper bullet. I got another box too, just to make sure, from Gun Palace in Waltham."

ASYM was what Bucky had used to shoot at the turbines. High velocity match grade accuracy, and as their specs boast, "fight-stopping terminal performance". Which means it knocks down whoever might be attacking you. With the Barnes Tipped Triple Shock solid copper bullet for deep penetration, and no separation of the copper jacket from the lead core because there is no lead core – the entire bullet is copper. Deadly for turbines, deadly for people.

"Were you already in the trees," I said, "when Dannon Ziller called?"

"Shit no, I was at the Senator. Fucking this Vietnamese hooker when my phone rings."

"Wow, so you had to jump out of bed, get dressed, and race over to Ronnie's office?"

"Shit no. Ziller was just calling to tell me they'd decided."

"Decided?"

"To take this guy out. I had time to finish fucking that chick first."

"How you know her?"

"We keep her on call."

"We?"

"Hell, not me. Green Dividends. For when them Legislators is in session."

"Why couldn't WindPower decide sooner, about killing Ronnie?"

He tried to shrug. "Ask them."

"Did you shoot out the four turbines at Paradise Lakes?"

He thought. "Paradise Lakes, never hear of it."

"Who told you to set Don and Viv's house on fire?"

He looked at me suspiciously. "Don't know no Don and... Who?"

"I told you: the Woodridges. The house you burned."

"Oh that? That was an accident."

"You said you did it, to burn those signed papers."

"Was an accident they died. Dumb fucks, why didn't they go out?"

"They were asleep."

"See, I didn't know this." He tried to lift his hands in protest. "How can I be blame', if I didn't know?"

I looked at him. "How'd you know I was coming?"

"They tol' me."

"Green Dividends? How'd they know?"

"Her phone, they listen to it. They listen to everybody. They didn't like it, you coming here. They say if I can get you up there, dump you somewhere, maybe years before somebody find you. So I rent a snowmobile and go up there."

I stood by the bedroom window awaiting the feeble dawn. Abigail dragged herself awake, hugged me on her way to the other bathroom, went downstairs and came up ten minutes later with two huge cups of Italian Roast and a box of Country Kitchen chocolate powdered doughnuts.

"I DON'T WANT TO KNOW about this," Erica said when I called her.

"Off the record, like, what should I do?"

"It's too late for what should you *do!* You shouldn't have *done* any of this."

"He's nearly through it now. Doesn't remember much."

"How long since he broke in?"

"That was last night about nine and now, it's what, almost seven a.m.?"

"I suppose you can still claim it was later when you hit him –"

"Abigail hit him –"

"Whatever. And then you waited for him to come round, to ask him questions, before you called the cops."

"Something like that."

"And you'd assured yourself his head wound wasn't severe enough to require immediate care..."

"What's the downside?"

"Of *what?*"

"Giving them Jesús?"

"Probably everything." She thought a moment. "I'm coming up. Do *nothing* till I get there."

WHILE WAITING FOR ERICA we wormed Jesús into his clothes and gave him a coffee to spruce him up. He was still half in another world, eyes like a deer in a trap. I'd untied his ankles from the tub and retied them together and then his wrists behind his back and sat him on the floor. He was remarkably accommodating, still under the impression I'd saved him from something, though he wasn't sure what it was and who, if anything, *he* was.

When Erica came in she gave Abigail a hug. "I was worried about you, girl!" She looked down at Jesús on the floor. "So this is it."

"Yeah," I said. "That's it."

Erica put her phone on speaker and called C. Hart. He was not overly friendly.

"My client has been speaking with the man who killed Ronnie Dalt," she said, "and has recorded him saying so."

For a moment Hart said nothing, then, "You what?"

"And who tried to kill Abigail Dalt. *And* my client. He's a hired gun from Boston. It's all recorded and therefore not admissible as is, so you'll have to figure how to make him say it again. That's your problem..."

"So where you got this guy?"

JESÚS WAS STILL HALLUCINATING when Hart & Co arrived, didn't seem to understand who they were and why they were there. But since it was a clear case of B & E –

Breaking and Entering – they cuffed him, read him his rights, which may have given him a flashback of our drug-induced game, and he was off to Augusta jail before he knew it.

After the other cops took Jesús, and Erica raced back to Portland for a meeting, C. Hart sat at Abigail's kitchen table with his hands clasped before him, looking at his thumbs. "This is all pretty incriminating."

"You said it," Abigail said.

"Although most of it's off the table as testimony, our DA, Randy Solomon, will find a way to get it in. And we're going to have a good talk with Jesús."

"So where's the little green book?" Abigail put in.

He pretended like he'd never heard of it, then nodded. "We took it. As an exhibit."

"Of what?"

"Motive. Of why they may have wanted to kill your husband."

"It's also evidence of political fraud," I said.

He shrugged. "That ain't my jurisdiction."

"And that letter," I said, "with the red letters that said *Read This Now?*"

"Yeah, yeah, we took that too. Some mass mailing church advertisement, promising the end of the world."

Holy shit, I thought, what a fool I've been. "You guys fixed the broken pane?"

He looked truly surprised. "What pane?"

"The fucking window in the back door –"

"Oh that," Abigail laughed, "that's my cleaning lady. She sees something broken, she has J&T come fix it right away."

"J&T?" Hart says.

"Jeremy and Todd. My carpenters."

"What made you think Bucky shot Ronnie Dalt?" I asked him.

Again he looked uncomfortable. "That woman."

I looked around. "What woman?"

"The WindPower lawyer –"

"Cruella."

"Huh?"

"Ursula Heap."

"She called the Chief, said she'd heard through contacts in anti-wind groups that Bucky'd shot Ronnie."

"She say why?"

"Because he was in love with you, Maam," Hart nodded at Abigail. "He killed Ronnie to get him out of the way, so he could dump his wife and be with you. That's what Ursula Heap told us."

Abigail looked stunned. "I was just a way for Bucky to reach Ronnie. He and I were both asking Ronnie to speak the truth about wind."

"That's where the little green book came in?" Hart said.

"Ronnie was going to reveal it, the next day," Abigail said.

"How you two talked on the phone about having a copy of that book," he said. "That was smart. So this Jesús guy had to come looking for it."

"We had him anyway. Phone intercepts."

"Yeah but are they admissible?"

I stared into his eyes. "Who told you to put the heat on me?"

He faced down, hesitated. "These same guys. Their political friends."

"What, Green Dividends?"

"Yeah them and that other bunch."

"WindPower LLC."

"You said it. I didn't."

"What political friends?"

He nodded at the ceiling, as if indicating higher-ups. "We get advised by the Agency or FBI when there's a suspected terrorist in Maine..."

This was hilarious, considering that more than once I've risked my life to save one of their agents. "I don't have issues with the CIA or FBI."

"Tell that to our Senator. The one on that Intelligence Committee."

Then I remembered. At Atlanta airport on the way back from Hawaii, when I'd spoken with the armless and legless vet. Artie Lemon had been on all the TVs, a newly minted member of the Senate Intelligence Committee, giving us the lowdown on ISIS.

As if he would know.

"So Artie Lemon had somebody finger me to the Maine police as a potential *terrorist?*" I actually laughed, having taken down a few real terrorists in my life.

"You said it. I didn't."

In the end Hart had been an ally, told me as much as he could.

But that was all I was going to get out of him.

Gone with the Wind

WHEN WE LOVE someone or something of course we'll put ourselves in harm's way to protect them.

The same with our country. The same with Maine.

Because protecting our country, I'd learned, and protecting Maine from these sleazeball wind promoters and all their accomplices, *is exactly the same thing.*

Gone With The Wind is America's second-most popular book after the Bible. Its renown comes from our love of this great land, our history, our tenacious determination, our passion for reason and justice, our smarts and our caring for others. Maine's story is similar, the same emotions, the same beauty, the same power.

The South was destroyed by General Sherman's brutal March to the Sea. Can we still save Maine from being destroyed by the brutal march of wind turbines across our peaks and mountains and far out to sea?

While the wind profiteers talk glowingly of a world covered by turbines, the truth is we're losing everything. All of nature, the wilderness, the outdoors. Losing the magnificent beauty of all these wild species, losing their DNA, losing the human wisdom that comes from being part of the world and not its destroyer.

So let's defend Maine, not hand it over to wind crooks and politicians. Let's keep it what it's meant to be – fairness and equality, openness and strength, and vast natural beauty – mountains, forests and seascapes which nurture a deep moral fiber that teaches other states and nations what path to take.

Everyone who loves Maine can help. And we need our saints, the greatest spirits of American literature and advocacy who have loved Maine – Thoreau, Teddy Roosevelt, John Muir, Margaret Chase Smith, Dave Brower, Henry Wadsworth Longfellow, Edna St. Vincent Millay, Edward Abbey, Sarah Orne Jewett, Harriet Beecher Stowe, E.B. White, Kenneth Roberts, Joshua Chamberlain, Percival Baxter, Nathaniel Hawthorne, Marguerite Yourcenar, Mary Ellen Chase, Rockwell Kent, Robert Coffin, Mary McCarthy, Erskine Caldwell, Henry Beston, Booth Tarkington, May Sarton, our beloved Senators Margaret Chase Smith and Ed Muskie and so many more... please come help save the Maine you've loved. Please, before it's too late.

We all know that when corporations fund elections and pay off environmental groups there can be no democracy, no resource protection or true freedom. So we must rid ourselves of the elected officials and groups who are the propagators and benefactors of this disillusion.

And we all pretty much agree that not only Maine but our entire country needs reform, though the political and money folks try to keep us apart with false rivalries – R vs D, left vs right, that kind of silly thing. We all want a country that's safe, has opportunity, honesty, fairness and good. Hardly a person in the United States doesn't want that.

Why not ditch our toxic politicians so crooked they'd sell their grandmas to a house of ill repute for another ten grand in SuperPacs? Why not kill corporate bribes and scurrilous lobbyists, establish political contribution limits and online referenda, stop funding pro-wind "enviro" groups, and go back to individuals and communities, not PR and sound bites?

Why not kill the turbines and SAVE THE EAGLES? And all the other birds?

Wouldn't that be a GOOD START?

Wouldn't that be FUN?

Let's do it.

Like we learned in Special Forces: *Never say it can't be done.*

THE TAHITI TSUNAMI was in three days. I spent most of the first day at the Augusta cop shop giving them more testimony on WindPower, Dannon Ziller and their crooked governors, legislators and hit men. I also told the media everything, knowing that the papers owned by Congresswoman Muldower's husband probably wouldn't print a thing.

Turns out Maude's husband and co-conspirator Irvin the derivatives billionaire were partners with WindPower's Ziller in another corporate welfare scam, but there seemed no way to prove it hadn't just been "friendship". And they could spend millions in lawyers to prove it.

Jesús was already saying for a reduced charge he'd testify that Ziller had ordered Ronnie Dalt's death. According to Erica, this would probably bring down WindPower LLC and their odious lawyer Cruella, so their claim against Bucky for shooting out their three turbines would probably be vacated. As well as their spurious charge against me in Don and Viv's fire.

And because Jesús worked for Green Dividends it would expose them also to prosecution, possibly for conspiracy to murder, which seemed to be a habit of theirs.

Nonetheless these useless turbine towers all over Maine were going to stand there for years, slowly rusting, still killing birds and bats, the money set aside for their dismantling long gone.

Hart & Co were doing their best to pretend they'd never believed I was guilty of anything. Needless to say, they'd run out of things they hoped to charge me with except the two turbines that Titus McKee had shot out. And as they had taken photos of my (Bucky's) boot soles and matched them up to the pix they had of them in the snow, there was no doubt I'd been there.

I gave them a short adaptation of events. "I'd gone for a walk and saw this guy park by Jane Fowler's place and head up the hill. So I followed him."

"Why? That sounds pretty fucking dangerous."

When you're lying, I remembered, put in as much truth as possible. "Since I'd been shot at up there I wanted to see if he was my shooter."

"Were you armed?"

"I had Bucky's .243. Which fires a different slug from what you've found in those two turbines."

"Both turbines burned. We never got a slug out of them."

"That's not my fault."

"So you're saying if this Jesús guy was your shooter," he said, "maybe he's the one shot out those two turbines?"

I didn't want to pursue this for it might endanger Titus. "You'll no doubt want to discuss that with him."

"Christ we waited hours for his lawyer to show. Some dame from Portland."

"Ursula Heap."

He gave me an odd look. "How'd you know?"

"I know a lot more than you think. Or want me to."

He sat back, gathering papers. "Is that right?"

I didn't push it. I was leaving in forty-six hours for the Tsunami, but didn't want him to know. For fear he'd try to keep me in Maine.

MY LIFE ENDED UP a bit more complicated than expected.

I'd made a brief stop at the Stroudwater cemetery to bring the ancestors up to date, telling them about Pa's trip out into the ocean, not that they'd said a word. I'd then headed for Jefferson to drink a few goodbye blackberry brandies with Uncle Silas. "You tell Bucky," he said, "stop shooting people."

The night before I left Maine for Tahiti, Abigail and I were at her kitchen table while more snow fell outside. It was dinnertime but neither of us could be bothered. We both felt terrible about being separated, but she got out the Tanqueray and green stuff and we worked on that for a while, and felt better.

She reached out and squeezed my arm. "I've decided."

I ran my fingertips between her fingers the way she likes. "What?"

"I'm going to Tahiti with you."

A warm rush filled me. I hadn't wanted to leave her, and it was lovely to think of the time we'd have together in the palm-shaded sunny tropics, the surfing parties and fun.

Five minutes later rings *Highway to Hell,* Erica's number. I went into the living room and sat on a fluffy couch. "You finally convinced me," she said.

"Of what?"

"That I'm working too hard, have to cut back, take a vacation."

"Fantastic, where are you going?"

"Where am I *going?* You *invited* me. If that's the way you are..."

Now I remembered having asked her to go with me to the Tsunami, back when Abigail was telling me to get lost. I glanced at the kitchen, couldn't see Abigail. "Tahiti?"

"I've bought the tickets. Non-refundable, to make sure I don't back out."

I bit the bullet and agreed we'd meet at Portland airport tomorrow at 10:00. I went into the kitchen and sat down across from Abigail.

"We're going to have company," I said.

She flashed that wicked smile. "Might be fun."

LEXIE CALLED next morning as Abigail and I were packing. "Guess where I am?"

I was trying to print boarding passes and not paying attention. "Where's that?"

"Portland Airport."

"Portland Airport?" Terror gripped my heart. "*Why,* Lexie?"

"Bucky and I are done. School has a ten-day break and I'm coming to Tahiti. To be with you."

Who of us is master of his fate? Sure, there'd be some fireworks. But I loved all three of them. What is it you have in tennis? A foursome?

Like we learned in Special Forces: *Never say it can't be done.*

THE END

ABOUT THE AUTHOR: Mike Bond grew up in Maine, graduated from Deering High in Portland, and has been active in Maine environmental issues since working with Dave Brower and writing a book for the Sierra Club on protection of the Allagash River. He has since been involved in preservation of Baxter State Park, the Appalachian Trail and Moosehead Lake, in Maine rivers restoration, the proposed North Woods National Park, and in many other battles to protect Maine. A former Wild and Scenic River master planner, president of several environmental groups, wolf expert and wilderness advocate, he gives frequent testimony and TV and radio interviews worldwide on environmental problems including elephants, wolves, whales, tigers, raptors, rain forests, climate change and ecosystem loss. In addition to working as a war and human rights journalist he is the author of five best-selling critically acclaimed novels, as well as hundreds of essays on wilderness protection, endangered species, and renewable energy. Family resident in Maine since the 1600s.

SAVING PARADISE

The first Pono Hawkins thriller
from Mandevilla Press
the first pages...

*"To tourists Hawaii is an air-conditioned tanning booth
with shopping, booze, bikinis, and lots of smiling low-paid
help. The real Hawaii is something else..."*

When a beautiful journalist drowns mysteriously off
Waikiki, former Special Forces veteran Pono Hawkins, now
a well-known Hawaii surfer and international surfing cor-
respondent, quickly gets embroiled in trying to solve her
death. What he learns soon targets him for murder or life in
prison as a cabal of powerful corporations, foreign killers
and crooked politicians focuses the blame on him.

Haunted by memories of Afghanistan, and determined
to protect the Hawaii he loves from dirty politics tied to
huge destructive energy developments, Pono turns to Special Forces buddies and his own skills to fight his deadly
enemies, trying to both save himself and track down her
killers.

Alive with the sights, sounds and history of Hawaii, *Saving Paradise* is also a rich portrait of what Pono calls "the
seamy side of paradise", and a relentless thriller of politics,
lies, manhunts and remorseless murder.

IT WAS ANOTHER MAGNIFICENT DAWN on Oahu, the sea soft and rumpled and the sun blazing up from the horizon, an offshore breeze scattering plumeria fragrance across the frothy waves. Flying fish darting over the crests, dolphins chasing them, a mother whale and calf spouting as they rolled northwards. A morning when you already know the waves will be good and it will be a day to remember.

I waded out with my surfboard looking for the best entry and she bumped my knee. A woman long and slim in near-transparent red underwear, face down in the surf. Her features sharp and beautiful, her short chestnut hair plastered to her cold skull.

I dropped my board and held her in my arms, stunned by her beauty and death. If I could keep holding her maybe she wouldn't really be dead. I was already caught by her high cheekbones and thin purposeful lips, the subtle arch of her brow, her long slender neck in my hands. And so overwhelmed I would have died to protect her.

When I carried her ashore her long legs dragged in the surf as if the ocean didn't want to let her go, this sylphlike mermaid beauty. Sorrow overwhelmed me – how could I get her back, this lovely person?

Already cars were racing up and down Ala Moana Boulevard. When you're holding a corpse in your arms how bizarre seems the human race – where were all these people hurrying to in this horrible moment with this beautiful young woman dead?

I did the usual. Being known to the Honolulu cops I had to call them. I'd done time and didn't want to do more. Don't believe for a second what anyone tells you – being *Inside* is a *huge* disincentive. Jail tattoos not just your skin; it nails your soul. No matter what you do, no matter what you want, you don't want to go back there. Not ever.

So Benny Olivera shows up with his flashers flashing. If you want a sorry cop Benny will fill your bill. Damn cruiser the size of a humpback whale with lights going on and off all over the place, could've been a nuclear reaction – by the way, why would anyone want a family that's *nuclear*? Life's dangerous enough.

So I explain Benny what happened. He's hapa pilipino – half Filipino – and doesn't completely trust us hapa haoles, part white and part Hawaiian. To a kanaka maoli, a native Hawaiian, or to someone whose ancestors were indentured here like the Japanese or in Benny's case Filipinos, there's still mistrust. Didn't the haoles steal the whole archipelago for a handful of beads? Didn't they bring diseases that cut the Hawaiian population by ninety percent? And then shipped hundreds of the survivors to leprosy colonies on Molokai? While descendants of the original missionaries took over most of the land and became huge corporations that turned the Hawaiians, Filipinos, Japanese and others into serfs? These corporations that now own most of Hawaii, its mainline media, banks and politicians?

I'm holding this lissome young woman cold as a fish in my arms and Benny says lie her down on the hard sidewalk and the ambulance comes – more flashing lights – and she's gone under a yellow tarp and I never saw her again.

Couldn't surf. Went home and brewed a triple espresso and my heart was down in my feet. Sat on the lanai and tried to figure out life and death and what had happened to this beautiful woman. Mojo the dachshund huffed up on the chair beside me, annoyed I hadn't taken him surfing. Puma the cat curled on my lap but I didn't scratch her so she went and sat in the sun.

I'd seen plenty of death but this one got to me. She'd been young, pretty and athletic. Somehow the strong classic lines of her face denoted brains, determination and hard work. How did she end up drowned in Kewalo Basin?

Benny's bosses at the cop shop would no doubt soon provide the answer.

Made in the USA
Middletown, DE
14 September 2015